Joseph Conrad and Popular Culture

Joseph Conrad and Popular Culture

Stephen Donovan
Blekinge Institute of Technology
Karlskrona, Sweden

First published in 2005 by
PALGRAVE MACMILLAN
Houndmills, Basingstoke, Hampshire RG21 6XS and
175 Fifth Avenue, New York, N.Y. 10010
Companies and representatives throughout the world.

PALGRAVE MACMILLAN is the global academic imprint of the Palgrave Macmillan division of St. Martin's Press, LLC and of Palgrave Macmillan Ltd. Macmillan® is a registered trademark in the United States, United Kingdom and other countries. Palgrave is a registered trademark in the European Union and other countries.

ISBN 13: 978–1–4039–0810–0   hardback
ISBN 10: 1–4039–0810–9   hardback

This book is printed on paper suitable for recycling and made from fully managed and sustained forest sources.

A catalogue record for this book is available from the British Library.

Library of Congress Cataloging-in-Publication Data

Donovan, Stephen, 1970–
    Joseph Conrad and popular culture / Stephen Donovan.
        p. cm.
    Includes bibliographical references and index.
    ISBN 1–4039–0810–9 (cloth)
        1. Conrad, Joseph, 1857–1924 – Knowledge – Popular culture.
    2. Popular culture in literature. I. Title.

PR6005.O4Z659 2005
823'.912—dc22   2005047042

10 9 8 7 6 5 4 3 2 1
14 13 12 11 10 09 08 07 06 05

Printed and bound in Great Britain by
Antony Rowe Ltd, Chippenham and Eastbourne

For Jeremy
en av oss

Contents

List of Plates and Figures

Dust Jacket. Joseph Conrad photographed by Alvin Langdon Coburn, 1916. Reproduced with permission of George Eastman House.

Plates

Figures

Acknowledgements

The original idea for this project came to me during a conversation with Åsa Theander four years ago. Since then, her patience has been sorely tested by my long absences, anti-social hours and apparently boundless capacity to hold forth about a certain novelist. For her constant intellectual companionship and irrepressible good humour I am eternally grateful.

At Blekinge Institute of Technology, Danuta Fjellestad has been an exemplary head of department and a true friend, giving me the freedom and, more importantly, the confidence to bring this project to completion.

For their many kindnesses and suggestions I am deeply grateful to the following scholars: Richard Ambrosini (University of Rome III), Keith Carabine (University of Kent at Canterbury), Laurence Davies (Dartmouth College), Linda Dryden (Napier University), Bo Ekelund (Stockholm University), Gail Fincham (University of Cape Town), Robert Hampson (Royal Holloway College, London), Richard Hand (University of Glamorgan), Susan Jones (St Hilda's College, Oxford), Urban Lundberg (Institute for Futures Studies, Stockholm), Gene Moore (University of Amsterdam), Ronald Paul (Gothenburg University), Matthew Rubery (University of Pennsylvania), Allan Simmons (St Mary's College, London), Michael Titlestad (University of the Witwatersrand) and Luisa Villa (University of Genoa).

For commenting on earlier drafts of individual chapters I owe a special debt of thanks to Vreni Hockenjos (Stockholm University) and Tim Youngs (Nottingham Trent University). They are, needless to say, in no way responsible for the final text. Gavin Sprott kindly gave permission for the reproduction of his mother's woodcut 'Rio Grande' and his great-uncle's watercolour portrait of Conrad and Captain David Bone. Günter Krenn (Filmarchiv Austria) generously shared the findings of his research into Austrian film history. Alexandra Lemonidis translated from the German with her customary elegance.

For their encouragement and hospitality, I would like to thank my parents, Paul and Fiona, my brothers, Alan and Jonny, and all my friends, particularly Renata Dwan, Mark Flynn, Carl Hall, Bjørg Hawthorn, Andrew McCallum, Anna Rimington and Karen Shoop.

I have been greatly assisted in my research by the expert staff of the New York Public Library, the British Library, the Bodleian Library and

Blekinge Institute of Technology Library, as well as the following individuals: Rosemary Addison (Napier University), Ronald Bleach (Granville Bantock Society), Vivian Bone (Edinburgh University Press), Carolyn Creal (Spartanburg Regional Museum of History), Grace Eckley, Markus Feigl (Vienna City Library), Vic Gatrell (Gonville and Caius College, Cambridge), Phoebe Harkins (Wellcome Library), Caroline Hudson (Maine Maritime Library), Solveig Julich (Linköping University), Judith Knelman (University of Western Ontario), Christine Lambert (John Johnson Collection, Bodleian Library), Bill Linskey (Brixton Historical Society), Joanne Martell, Alistair McCreely (Napier University), Luke McKernan (British Universities Film & Video Council), Niki Pollock (Glasgow University Library), Carl Rosa (Timexpo Museum), Paul Smith (Thomas Cook Archive) and Richard Underwood (Penningtons).

It has been my good fortune to be able to present material from this project at several scholarly gatherings: the Conrad Society of America Conference, Texas Tech University, August 2000; the South-Western Conference on Popular Culture, Albuquerque, March 2001; the Joseph Conrad Society UK Annual Conference, London, July 2001; the Conrad and Territoriality Conference, University of British Columbia, August 2002; the English Department Research Seminar Group, Blekinge Institute of Technology, October 2002; the Media History Research Seminar, Uppsala University, October 2003; and the SLLS Seminar at the English Department of the University of the Witwatersrand, March 2004. Many thanks to David Attwell (University of the Witwatersrand), Donald Rude (Texas Tech University) and Pelle Snickars (Stockholm University) for inviting me to speak. Earlier incarnations of Chapter 1 and Chapter 3 were published, respectively, as 'Sunshine and Shadows: Conrad and Early Cinema', in *Conradiana* 35/1 (Spring 2004), 237–56, and 'Conrad's World of Advertising: "An Anarchist" (1906) and "The Partner" (1911)', in *The Conradian* 28/2 (Autumn 2003), 72–95. I am grateful to the editors of both journals for permission to reprint.

Lastly, I would like to acknowledge the financial assistance of the Joseph Conrad Society UK, the Swedish Foundation for International Cooperation in Research and Higher Education, the Swedish Research Council, the San Michele Foundation and the Anna Ahrenberg Foundation.

Abbreviations

Works by Joseph Conrad

Except for where indicated below, quotations from Conrad's work in the text are from the Dent Collected Edition, London, 1946–55.

AG   *The Arrow of Gold*
AF   *Almayer's Folly*. Floyd Eugene Eddleman and David Leon Higdon, eds. Cambridge: Cambridge University Press, 1994.
C   *Chance*. Martin Ray, ed. Oxford: World's Classics, 2002.
Inh *The Inheritors: An Extravagant Story*. With Ford Madox Ford. Stroud, Gloucestershire: Allan Sutton Publishing, 1991.
LE   *Last Essays*
LJ   *Lord Jim*
MS   *The Mirror of the Sea*
N   *Nostromo*
NN   *The Nigger of the 'Narcissus'*
NLL *Notes on Life and Letters*. J. H. Stape, ed. Cambridge: Cambridge University Press, 2004.
OI   *An Outcast of the Islands*
PR   *A Personal Record*
Res *The Rescue*
SA   *The Secret Agent*. Bruce Harkness and S. W. Reid, eds. Cambridge: Cambridge University Press, 1990.
SS   *A Set of Six*
SL   *The Shadow-Line*
T   *Typhoon and Other Stories*. Paul Kirschner, ed. Harmondsworth: Penguin, 1992.
TH   *Tales of Hearsay*
TLS *Twixt Land and Sea*
TU   *Tales of Unrest*
UWE *Under Western Eyes*. Jeremy Hawthorn, ed. Oxford: World's Classics, 2003.
V   *Victory*
WT   *Within the Tides*
Y   *Youth, Heart of Darkness, The End of the Tether*

Other frequently cited works

CCH Sherry, Norman, ed. *Conrad: The Critical Heritage*. London: Routledge, 1973.

CL *The Collected Letters of Joseph Conrad*. Frederick R. Karl and Laurence, eds, vols 1–5; Karl, Laurence, and Owen Knowles, eds, vol. 6. Cambridge: Cambridge University Press, 1983–2002.

JCIR Ray, Martin, ed. *Joseph Conrad: Interviews and Recollections*. Iowa City: University of Iowa Press, 1990.

LL Jean-Aubry, G. *Joseph Conrad: Life and Letters*. 2 vols. London: William Heinemann, 1927.

Introduction

I am not a popular author and probably I never shall be.

Conrad to the Baroness Janina de Brunnow,
2 October 1897 (*CL* 1: 390)

When it comes to popularity I stand much nearer the public mind than Stevenson who was super-literary, a conscious virtuoso of style; whereas the average human mind does not care much for virtuosity.

Conrad to Alfred A. Knopf, 20 July 1913
(*CL* 5: 257–8)

The UK National Sound Archive in London contains a recording made in about 1970 of an old sailor singing the sea shanties of his youth.[1] Its mood is curiously poignant, with the auditors of this lone voice singing songs meant for a group seeming to realize that they are hearing the aural memories of a vanished era of seafaring, perhaps for the last time. Midway through the interview, the oral historians ask for the well-known shanty 'Rio Grande'. 'This is an awkward one,' the old chanteyman replies before taking a quick swig on his stout and gamely attempting a rendition. He calls out the chorus with gusto:

> A-way, Rio,
> Heave a-way for Rio,
> Sing fare ye well,
> My bonnie young girl,
> We're bound for the Rio Grande!

In the old days, he explains, sailors deliberately mispronounced the word 'Rio' as 'Rye-oh' because making the word into 'more of a mouthful'

1

Figure 1   Freda Bone, 'Rio Grande', woodcut illustration to David W. Bone, *Capstan Bars* (1931). Reproduced with kind permission of Mr Gavin Sprott.

better suited the rhythmic movements of men working at a capstan (Figure 1). The song was for the same reason always sung slowly, unlike the stage versions of 'Rio Grande' that he has heard since retiring from the sea. To illustrate this, he sings a few lines in a more upbeat tempo, ending with a mocking 'rom-tiddee-om-pom-pom' which makes his listeners laugh. The old man underscores his point: 'There's no use for that if you're heaving round a capstan. . . . When you're putting all your weight on a heavy capstan bar you can't go jigging like that.'[2]

This insistence upon the defining features of an authentic capstan-song would have struck a chord in Joseph Conrad, also an ex-sailor, who regarded accuracy in the portrayal of maritime life as nothing less than an artistic and ethical imperative. Early in his literary career, he expressed a desire that another sailor read the manuscript of *The Rescue* in order to 'look over the seamanship of my expressions' (*CL* 1: 291), as if terminological exactness in a novel were a matter of maritime professionalism. Many years later, when another former sailor invited him to collaborate in a short musical drama featuring sea shanties, the now established author gave the matter serious consideration. Suggesting that the American composer Henry T. Finck would be 'the man to do justice to these weird suggestive tunes of our young days', Conrad confessed his affection for the singing traditions of the merchant marine: 'That wistful capstan song "Along the Banks of Sacramento" should not be forgotten with its sub-chorus, a great shout "Hurrah! Santa-Anna!" Most effective!' (4: 352).[3]

Although the proposed project came to nothing, the significance that Conrad ascribed to these artefacts of a disappearing way of life can be seen by his insertion of the shanty 'Rio Grande' into 'To-morrow', a short story that, as he explained to his would-be collaborator, he had already adapted for the stage as *One Day More*. The plot of 'To-morrow' centres on a retired master mariner named Hagberd who is awaiting the return of his son who ran away to sea after an argument. Harry does finally come home, just as Hagberd has always predicted, but only to find himself rejected as an imposter by his now unhinged father. Before leaving for good, Harry tries to persuade the girl next door, who also yearns to escape a father's domestic tyranny, to elope with him. While Bessie hesitates, he sings what he tells her is a 'Capstan song':

> Oh, oh, ho! Rio! . . .
> And fare thee well,
> My bonnie young girl,
> We're bound to Rio . . . Grande.
> (*T* 258)

On the face of it, Harry's choice of song seems innocuous and unremarkable. 'Rio Grande' was a favourite among the crews of ships leaving the west coast of England (Hugill, 1961: 88); if he were not already acquainted with it, Conrad would have had plenty of opportunity to learn the shanty by heart during the eight frustrating months he spent in Falmouth harbour in 1882 as second mate of the leaky barque *Palestine*. In 'To-morrow', however, the valedictory nature of the song has a disturbing ambiguity. Even in the act of inviting Bessie to be his companion, Harry seems already to be anticipating the day when he will abandon her, just as he has twice left his father. Since a certain notoriety appears to have attached to South American 'elopements' at this time, Conrad may be suggesting that Bessie acts wisely in refusing this singing sailor who has 'opened [her ears] to the voices of the world' (*T* 257) – this much, at least, is implied by James Joyce's short story 'Eveline', in which a young woman similarly rejects a musical sailor's proposal to leave her overbearing father and elope to Argentina.[4] Indeed, in *One Day More*, Conrad hints that Harry and Bessie's journey together would not have lasted long:

HARRY [*Hums significantly*]:

> Oh, oh, oh, Rio, . . .
> And fare thee well
> My bonnie young girl,
> We're bound for Rio Grande.

BESSIE [*shivering*]: What's that?
HARRY: Why! The chorus of an up-anchor tune. Kiss and go. A deep-water ship's good-bye. . . .   (*T* 286)

And yet Conrad's intentions in directing Harry to hum '*significantly*' are far from self-evident. Some versions of 'Rio Grande' contained crude puns on the maritime metaphor of 'boarding' (accosting) a young girl on the street (Hugill, 1961: 95), and it is perhaps the shadow of this male-dominated environment (the 'we' of the song) and not the cold night air that makes Bessie shiver. Whatever the case, the shanty's appearance at this crucial moment serves to confirm that Harry, though a scrounger and a loafer, ultimately thinks and behaves like a real sailor, singing the chorus as if in reply to the call of an invisible chanteyman. Moreover, he has a repertoire of such songs whose lyrics speak to his own situation with all the force of a revealed truth:

He leaned back again, and hummed thoughtfully a bar or two of an outlandish tune. . . .

'Learned it in Mexico – in Sonora.' He talked easily. 'It is the song of the Gambusinos. You don't know? The song of restless men. Nothing could hold them in one place – not even a woman . . . That's what the song says. It's all about a pretty girl that tried hard to keep hold of a Gambusino lover, so that he should bring her lots of gold. No fear! Off he went, and she never saw him again.'

'What became of her?' she breathed out.

'The song don't tell. Cried a bit, I daresay. They were the fellows: kiss and go. But it's the looking for a thing – a something . . . Sometimes I think I am a sort of Gambusino myself.'   (T 259–60)

Indeed, in *One Day More*, this ironic resemblance between father and son, each a sailor condemned to an unending search, takes on an Ibsenesque dimension when Hagberd declares paradoxically: 'None of us Hagberds belonged to the sea. . . . Harry ain't a sailor at all. And if he isn't a sailor, he's bound to come back – to-morrow' (*T* 276).

'Rio Grande' is significant in another respect, too. Unlike an evening paper or the Bible, the popular song is an unstable, unauthorized and thoroughly adaptable text that normally invites the collective participation of its audience, a factor that may account for the slight differences in how Conrad transcribed its lyrics in 'To-morrow' and *One Day More* as well as his insertion of ellipses seemingly indicative not of pauses but of a tonal shift. Not only is it unclear how Conrad's readers and audience, let alone Bessie, are supposed to understand the words of a song that Harry is described as having 'hummed thoughtfully' (*T* 259) and of which only a fragment is supplied, but the sea shanty seems to have been included in this scene precisely in order to foreground the land-lubber's inability to appreciate its full meaning. Interestingly, shanties were conventionally used as a kind of popular code even among sailors: the ship's officers would tolerate the chanteyman splicing commentaries about them into the lyrics of a shanty since they pretended to be deaf to such profane discourse.[5] This epistemological space of secrecy, a central theme of Conrad's fiction, is here imagined as an opposition between plain speech and sailors' song, and for those willing to countenance such nice distinctions Harry's boast in *One Day More* that he has 'Never yet *told* a lie to a woman' (*T* 287, emphasis added) may actually be true. As he explains with brutal candour:

HARRY: I leave the sneaking off to them soft-spoken chaps you're thinking of. No! If you love me you take me. And if you take

me – why, then, the capstan-song of deep-water ships is sure to settle
it all some fine day.   (*T* 288)

The capstan-song 'Rio Grande' offers a snapshot of the depth and complexity of Conrad's relation to popular culture. It forms part of a vast
corpus of artefacts, many of them non-literary or ephemeral and hence
particularly difficult to identify, of which he had direct personal experience and on which he drew, consciously as well as unconsciously, for his
fiction, essays and plays. Cedric Watts's observation that 'Conrad's treatment of source material . . . tends not only to heighten significance but
also to multiply ironies' (Watts, 1993: 149) is particularly applicable in
the case of popular cultural materials, which assume a variety of functions in Conrad's writing: as indices of character traits or social relations;
as a shorthand for phenomenological or aesthetic experiences; and as
organizing tropes within the narratives themselves. Marginalized yet
still vital, 'Rio Grande' evokes, too, the world of jigs, music, slang, oral
storytelling and shipboard traditions centred on work and the elements
that Conrad saw as the property of a coherent and organic community
just beyond the reach of mechanized communication and urban mass
production. Now in abeyance as a result of the eclipsing of sail, this maritime popular culture would often be counterposed in his writing to the
new and more troubling cultural practices of modernity epitomized by
the globally-distributed newspapers in which Captain Hagberd has been
advertising for his prodigal son. Viewed from this perspective, popular
culture describes a site of historical contestation in which Conrad, not
least as a professional writer reliant upon a transatlantic periodical readership, found himself directly implicated. Hagberd's libidinal investment in the newspaper and his son's identification with sea shanties and
Gambusino songs mark the parameters of Conrad's project to represent
the space of individual negotiation and collective solidarity opened up
by contemporary popular culture.

In December 1900, David Meldrum, a publisher's reader who helped
to establish Conrad as a writer of consequence, lamented to William
Blackwood *à propos* the author whose *Lord Jim* had just concluded a
protracted serialization in *Blackwood's Magazine*: 'I wish I could believe
that he would ever be "popular" in the popular sense, but he is too good
for that' (Blackburn, 1958: 122). The sentiment was to be echoed by
many of Conrad's contemporaries, including the subscribers to influential but small-circulation periodicals such as the *New Review* and the
English Review for whom he long remained a 'writer's writer', someone
who, as a partner in the firm of Heinemann once declared, 'will never

have anything published for the mere sake of making money' (Stape and Knowles, 1996: 34–5). Strikingly, however, Meldrum does not simply bemoan Conrad's inability to survive without the help of grants and loans (that is, to live within his means) but invokes it as a necessary complement of his genius and artistic integrity. Indeed, as his telling use of quotation marks indicates, the category of 'popular' has now become radically incompatible with any quality of entitlement to general appreciation. For Meldrum, to be ' "popular" in the popular sense' is precisely to be the object of unfounded admiration – to pander, in effect, to the reading public's lowest common denominator. Setting aside the fact that Conrad's work always appealed strongly to working-class readers (whether autodidacts, sailors, or, famously, the inmates of Dannemora Prison in New York) and that he would eventually earn considerable sums from serializing his work in mass-circulation periodicals such as the *Daily Mail* and *Harper's Magazine* as well from selling the rights to four novels to Hollywood, Meldrum's remark highlights the slipperiness of the term 'popular' for literary producers of Conrad's generation. Conrad might denounce commercially successful writers for merely expressing 'the common thought', a tactic he described as 'the secret of many popularities' (*CL* 2: 137), but, like James Joyce, he never entirely abandoned the conviction that his own uncompromising style of writing, a style faulted by more than one critic for being both too vulgar and too recondite, might nevertheless find a large audience.

This historical conundrum, which might be called the paradox of popularity, lies at the heart of Conrad's literary enterprise. Whilst the central themes of his novels – colonial life, seafaring and revolutionary intrigue – perhaps failed to engage what one reviewer called 'the great and influential sections of readers who like their fiction to be spiced with topical allusions, political personalities, or the mundanities of Mayfair' (*CH* 119), their inherent drama and exoticism was strengthened by the fact that they had been authored by someone whose experience of the world was exceptionally broad. 'I have had some impressions, some sensations – in my time – impressions and sensations of common things' (*CL* 1: 288–9), Conrad told Edward Garnett modestly; yet many of the most memorable descriptions in his fiction – drifting in an open boat in the South China Seas, a storm off the Cape of Good Hope, the regal Congolese mistress of a white colonist – were based upon events that he had witnessed with his own eyes. Despite this, the arc described by Conrad's literary trajectory has often been seen as fulfilling Meldrum's prediction: the achievement of an enviable reputation through novels such as *Almayer's Folly*, *The Nigger of the 'Narcissus'* and

Lord Jim that did not sell well, followed by commercial success through late works such as *Chance*, *The Rescue* and *The Rover* whose critical standing has never been strong. Indeed, as Scott McCracken points out, the very presence of popular cultural elements in *Chance* has been taken as *prima facie* evidence of the onset of Conrad's artistic 'decline' (McCracken, 1995: 267).

Perhaps unsurprisingly, the topic of popular culture has itself proven less than popular among what the *Times Literary Supplement* once unkindly dubbed 'the Anglo-American Conrad critical-industrial complex', despite the publication of numerous studies illuminating Conrad's relation to subjects as diverse as the Bible, Darwinism, anthropology, travel writing, gender and colonialism.[6] Some scholars, it is true, have referred in passing to popular culture as a significant context for Conrad's writing – Cedric Watts examines the advertisements that appeared alongside *Nostromo* in *T. P.'s Weekly*, Gustav Morf comments upon Conrad's remarkable memory for the work of the Russian fabulist Ivan Krylov, and Tony Tanner highlights the importance of games in his fiction – but with the partial exception of magazine serialization no serious attempt has been made to offer a systematic overview of even a single field of popular culture.[7]

The explanation lies partly in the perceived intractability of the topic itself and partly in the way literary study has been institutionalized in universities in the twentieth century. Conrad seems to have served as a rallying figure for many early academic critics who themselves viewed popular culture as spiritually and intellectually impoverishing. Thus the Polish scholar Gustav Morf, author of the landmark study *The Polish Heritage of Joseph Conrad* (1930), recorded in 1976: 'Being an aristocrat of the mind, [Conrad] did not believe in the infallibility of the mass, nor did he see anything but danger in arousing them. He abhorred mass culture. (How he would have hated TV!)'[8] This perspective, which has shown considerable resilience in the face of the transformation of literary studies in the last twenty-five years, effectively defers to the image of patrician aloofness that Conrad took pains to cultivate: 'I am totally unable to comprehend why hitting a ball with a piece of wood can produce a state of lunacy in people who one would assume were otherwise apparently sane' (Conrad, 1981: 164); 'We went through the depressing ceremony of having tea [in an A.B.C. teashop]; but our interest in each other mitigated its inherent horrors' (*LE* 104); and so on. And yet this mandarin pose was exactly that – a pose. Richard Curle, Conrad's executor and a self-appointed guardian of his posterity, declared confidently, 'He would have been perfectly content never to have seen a daily paper from year's end to year's end. . . . Conrad was absorbed by the realities of life, and though he could amuse himself with trifles, he could not amuse himself with impersonal ephemeralities' (Curle, 1928a: 138); but John Conrad recalled his father being engrossed by newspapers until 10.30 each morning and Norman Sherry's researches have demonstrated that the writer relied heavily upon his wide reading of newspapers.[9]

Pace his claim that 'my face has nothing to do with my writing' (*CL* 2: 458), one suspects that the common perception of Conrad as an austere and humourless early Modernist has been quietly reinforced by the many photographs of his gaunt countenance peering forth. Accordingly, in attempting to present a new face of Conrad to readers familiar with his work, the following study offers itself as the literary-critical corollary to a little-known photograph taken by Alvin Langdon Coburn in 1916 in which the elegantly dressed writer raises his eyes heavenward with an inscrutable expression somewhere between reverie and a smile. More than just a concession to publishers' demands for marketable images of a popular writer or, for that matter, a half-admitted desire to appear 'illustrious' (3: 389), the slightly blurred photograph hints at a very different side to Conrad's personality, one that he preferred to conceal behind the twin façades of Tory squire and elder statesman of letters. This Conrad is patently thinking about something quite different from Russian tyranny, colonial brutality or the trials of the Southern Ocean in winter: reciting Edward Lear's nonsense verse; howling with laughter at John Maskelyne's conjuring tricks; practising tightrope walking in the back garden with his youngest son; or enjoying the innocent pleasures of the *Boy's Own Paper*.[10]

Conrad protested on many occasions (albeit rarely to his agent or publishers) that he had no desire to be popular. The claim implies both a sensitivity to the accusation that he could not make a living from his art and a wider condescension towards the *hoi polloi* that John Carey identifies as a hallmark of avant-garde British intellectuals in the early twentieth century (Carey, 1992). Even so, neither factor accounts adequately for his apparent inconsistency on the subject. In the first place, his acknowledgment to E. B. Redmayne that 'novel-writing may bring reputation without money' did not mean that Conrad viewed the two as mutually exclusive. Not only did he justify his choice of sequel to *Almayer's Folly* in terms of wishing 'to follow my first success ([which] was purely literary) by a more popular achievement' (Stape and van Marle, 1995: 32, 31), but it could even be argued that Conrad's scrupulous attention to the publishing and marketing of his early work paid handsome dividends when he somewhat improbably emerged as a bestselling

author and celebrity in the early 1910s. In the second place, his uncon-
cealed contempt for the fellow citizens whom he variously labelled 'the
herd of idiotic humanity' (*CL* 1: 17), 'a great multitude whose voice is a
shout' (3: 13), 'the Great Public (which has the sails of windmills for
brains)' (5: 165) and 'the Democracy of the book-stalls' (5: 173), coex-
isted with an equally pronounced animus towards being patronized by
a literary elite. As he told Frank Doubleday: 'I am sufficiently of a demo-
crat to detest the idea of being a writer of any "coterie" of some small
self-appointed aristocracy in the vast domain of art or letters. As a matter
of feeling – not as a matter of business – I want to be read by many eyes
and by all kinds of them, at that' (6: 333). Like his increasingly frequent
references to himself in the third person – he once boasted of having
written 'every word' of an interview with himself (6: 123) – Conrad's
ironic supplication during a particularly low point in his finances, 'Oh!
for a success, a beastly popular success!' (2: 73), must be seen in the
context of an overall strategy, as he put it, 'to create a public for myself'
(1: 390). In this light, it becomes possible to see his fictional works as
attempts to realize a quality that he saw as *popular* in something rather
more precise than what Meldrum calls 'the popular sense of the word'.

The origins of these overlapping problematics of individualism versus
collectivity and aesthetic legitimacy versus commercial success lie in a
profound cultural shift that occurred roughly in parallel with Conrad's
literary career. The years 1880–1920 witnessed a series of epochal changes
in the social and political fabric of British life: a steep increase in the size
of the population and a correspondingly ambitious programme of urban
construction; the proliferation of new means of transport such as the
bicycle, the automobile and the aeroplane; the emergence of new communication technologies such as motion photography and radio; the
extension of legislated leisure time; a fundamental transformation of
print media and the publishing industry; the growth of a national
labour movement with representation in Parliament; an increasingly
militant struggle for women's rights and the franchise; a revolution in
Ireland, Britain's oldest and nearest colony; a series of imperial conflicts
that culminated in a world war; and the emergence of a large white-
collar secretariat that historians and modernization theorists consider a
necessary condition for a modern social infrastructure.[11] As the following chapters will show, the impact of these changes was especially manifest in the field of culture. As cultural artefacts of all kinds began to
be produced and distributed on an unprecedented scale, fostering in
the process new kinds of user practices and reaching new audiences, the
industrialization of film production and the emergence of newspaper

monopolies and magazine syndicates provided the first glimpses of an entity that later commentators would designate a 'culture industry'.

This phenomenon, which Modernist writers and their first academic advocates often strove to dismiss as a process of aesthetic debasement and social levelling, now typically figures in scholarly histories as a site of social contestation and a dynamic force that exercised a decisive influence on avant-garde experiments with artistic form and subject-matter. From the newspaper collages of early Cubism to the parodies of advertising language in James Joyce's *Ulysses*, Modernism's artistic innovations are today understood as having their roots in the opening up of a cultural 'Great Divide' around the start of the twentieth century.[12] Clearly, then, any attempt to recover Conrad's relation to popular culture necessarily requires more than just an analysis of the publishing and reception histories of his writings. Rather, such an investigation will have to weigh the possible links between, on the one hand, a hardening opposition between different kinds of cultural practices and, on the other, the constituent elements of Conrad's fictional works such as plot, narrative form, characterization, style and source material. As Fredric Jameson observes: 'In Conrad we can sense the emergence not merely of what will be contemporary modernism . . . but also, still tangibly juxtaposed with it, of what will variously be called popular or mass culture' (Jameson, 1981: 206).

Confusingly, as Jameson's phrase 'popular or mass' indicates, the nomenclature of this topic has long been a matter of debate among critics. Now increasingly used interchangeably, the terms *popular culture* and *mass culture* in academic discourse have at various times presupposed different theoretical or historiographic apparatuses and in some cases even addressed wholly discrete objects of enquiry. To simplify drastically, the distinction might be characterized as being between a traditional, rural and organic folk culture and a modern, urban and manufactured commercial culture.[13] With its obvious debt to Ferdinand Tönnies's classic antithesis between *Gemeinschaft* and *Gesellschaft*, the difficulties of such a definition are immediately clear. Not only is there an inescapably political aspect to any privileging of 'traditional' (however defined) over 'manufactured' – a problem exacerbated by the fact that neither category belongs exclusively to the right or the left, as can be seen by juxtaposing William Morris with Knut Hamsun or Filippo Marinetti with H. G. Wells – but it will readily be granted that terms such as 'organic' come to us already freighted with ideological valuations.

In the last decade or so these questions have been further complicated on several counts. First, any residual distinction between 'popular' and 'mass' has been rendered next to meaningless by an environment in which every cultural development can be instantly recouped and branded for an international consumer audience. The very concepts of 'traditional' and 'organic', which are themselves, as historians such as Eric Hobsbawm and Terence Ranger have insisted (Hobsbawm and Ranger, 1983), often either invented or complicit in reactionary nostalgia, have now been fully integrated into all official and commercial discourse on culture. Second, one no longer needs to deny the manipulativeness of capitalist ideology in order to acknowledge the simplistic and reductive nature of any straightforwardly pejorative connotation of 'mass culture'. (The distinguished critic of cultural and political imperialism, Edward Said, whose own tastes were famously highbrow, recognized that American soap operas can disseminate proto-feminist ideas among television audiences in the Middle East.) And third, it is today widely accepted that 'culture', far from being a neutral label or an ideal category, describes a field of struggle for legitimacy between geographically specific, class-based interests in which a national and metropolitan elite has historically prevailed.[14] What is more, these definitional problems clearly already existed, if only in embryonic form, in Conrad's day. When he recalled passengers aboard the *Torrens* seizing 'the opportunity of learning to dance the hornpipe from our boatswain (an agile professor)' (*LE* 26), was Conrad describing the survival of a popular culture or its commodification? In *The Nigger of the 'Narcissus'* the reader's prejudice about forecastle life are confounded by a vignette of a tattooed helmsman reading Bulwer Lytton's *Pelham* with rapt attention. Is Singleton's love of 'silver fork' society novels an example of what one reviewer of Conrad's work condemned as 'pseudo-culture' (*CH* 119) – or its antidote? Like Conrad's quip in *The Secret Agent* that 'the Italian restaurant is such a peculiarly British institution' (*SA* 115), these are objective contradictions that cannot be resolved by choice of terminology alone.[15]

The following study does not pretend to cut this Gordian knot. On the contrary, it adopts a shamelessly pragmatic attitude in using *popular culture* as a blanket term to describe not just the usual suspects (adventure stories, sport, music-hall entertainment) but also thoroughly commercial artefacts such as advertisements and less definable activities such as the pigeon fancying and dancing dogs to which Marlow alludes in *Heart of Darkness*. As partial justification for this pragmatism, it demonstrates in a variety of contexts that Conrad's own perception of contemporary culture was frequently inconsistent and always contingent upon an array of complicating factors, both personal and professional. As its pairing of seemingly contradictory epigraphs at the head of each chapter is intended to highlight, this study advances the claim that, even when presenting himself as resisting the commodification of a specific dimension of human experience (spectacle, travel, food, storytelling) by a field of popular culture, Conrad can be seen to acknowledge the latter's inevitability and to shape his own writing in response to this historic shift, most often through a strategy of ideological and/or formal recontainment. What Jameson identifies as the presence of 'popular or mass culture' in Conrad's writing will be revealed, therefore, as the product of an historic fault-line that served, in turn, as an endlessly productive source of narrative inspiration for his literary project.

It would be prudent to submit a caveat at this point. Any book with so reckless a title as *Joseph Conrad and Popular Culture* might reasonably be expected to give an overview of several relevant topics: the dialect, sayings and slang of the sailors from whom Conrad proudly claimed to have learned vernacular English (*CL* 4: 409) and about the transcription of which he would later argue with one of his editors (*LL* 2: 247–8); newspapers such as the *Morning Standard*, which, as he enjoyed telling scandalized listeners, had given him his first lessons in the written language (Conrad, 1981: 112); and the varieties of 'popular propaganda' (*CL* 6: 496) that he both read and wrote. Moreover, L. P. Hartley's dictum that the past is a foreign country where they do things differently applies literally to Conrad, who gives tantalizing hints of his experiences of Polish and French popular culture in the reference in 'Amy Foster' to buying 'a ribbon at a Jew's stall on a fair-day' (*T* 156), the detailed descriptions of women's fashions and Marseillais carnival costumes in *The Arrow of Gold*, and his delicate pen-and-ink sketch of a coquettish dancing girl in Champel-les-Bains (Plate 1).[16] Such a study ought, too, to present a strictly chronological account of Conrad's treatment of the subject as it evolved during the various phases of his artistic development. Ideally, it would reveal popular culture as rivalling or even exceeding in importance what critics have hitherto regarded as his main influences: the literatures of France, Poland, Russia and Britain; the political and scientific thought of the nineteenth century; and his twenty years at sea. Adhering to a schematic distinction between popular culture and mass culture, it would show how Conrad's work nuances and deepens our understanding of these vexed theoretical categories, drawing into its discussion his posthumous treatment in twentieth-century popular cultural forms ranging from television to the graphic novel. Lastly, it goes without saying that the demands of this gargantuan task would require that the work be a multi-author collaboration.

Conrad and Popular Culture cannot claim to be that book. Within the limitations of space its more modest goals are, first, to unsettle some received notions about Conrad, above all, that he was indifferent to popular culture and that its technologies and experiences left little or no trace in his writings, and, second, to present case studies of separate but interconnected aspects of this sprawling subject that can collectively encourage a fresh approach to how we read his extensively interpreted texts. Drawing upon archival material, biographies and correspondence, in each of which Conrad students are exceptionally well served, it throws into relief his wide-ranging engagement with contemporary popular culture. Each of its four chapters, on visual entertainment, tourism, advertising and magazine fiction, has a broadly similar organization: an introduction that highlights the historical intersections between Conrad's biography and the particular field of popular culture in order to evoke what the writer once called 'the proper atmosphere of actuality' (*WT* vi); a synoptic account of the subject's treatment in his writings as a whole; a number of longer studies exploring different aspects of the field in question; and, finally, an extended analysis of the topic's significance for one or two of his fictional works. In each case, the choice of text subjected to detailed examination is intended to strike a balance between canonicity and length; like popular culture's own marginal presence, several of them have long been regarded as extraneous to the body of work that comprises Conrad's major phase. In so doing, this study seeks to offset the disproportionate attention directed towards *Heart of Darkness* and to allow a new cast of Conradian protagonists and motifs to step forward – salesmen and shoppers, journalists and newspaper readers, advertisers and consumers, tourists and tour guides, magic lantern exhibitors and spectators.

1
Visual Entertainment

> I aim at stimulating vision in the reader. If after reading the *part I*st you don't *see* my man then I've absolutely failed and must begin again – or leave the thing alone.
>
> Conrad to William Blackwood,
> 6 September 1897 (*CL* 1: 381)

> Imagine an atmosphere of opera-bouffe in which all the comic business of stage statesmen, brigands, etc., etc., all their farcical stealing, intriguing, and stabbing is done in dead earnest. It is screamingly funny, the blood flows all the time, and the actors believe themselves to be influencing the fate of the universe.
>
> *Nostromo* (*N* 152)

In October 1914, while waiting anxiously for visas that would permit them to leave Vienna, where the outbreak of hostilities had left the family stranded, Conrad and his eldest son stumbled into a very peculiar entertainment. Half a century later, Borys could still remember the incident vividly:

[O]ne day as we wandered through the streets, he suggested we should patronize a shooting gallery which seemed to be attracting a lot of customers. When we got inside, however, we were shocked at finding that this was no ordinary shooting gallery: it appeared to be a sort of War propaganda entertainment. Instead of conventional targets there were cinema screens on which were being shown a film of kilted Scottish infantry charging with fixed bayonets, and the marksmen had to fire at the figures as they ran across the screens. When a hit was made the film stopped and the marksman was invited to choose from the trays of junk displayed. My Father paused and uttered a startled exclamation when he saw what we had walked into, and then gripped my arm and urged me forward saying: 'We have to go through with it Boy, to retract now would draw too much attention, but take care you don't hit any of those fellows.'

(Conrad, 1970: 95–6)

Relieved to have 'missed' with his own cartridges, Borys was sternly instructed to do the same with his father's: 'I realized that this action on his part was no gesture of paternal affection – he just felt he dare not fire them himself – so I took another deep breath, and, I am thankful to say, succeeded in "missing" five more times. He would have been terribly distressed if I had hit one of those running figures' (Conrad, 1970: 96). The two foreigners crept out unnoticed.

Shooting at cinema screens was a recent innovation in 1914, pioneered by an exhibit titled 'Big Game Hunting by Cinematograph' at the 1909 World's Fair (Harding and Popple, 1996: 40), and the first of these *Lebende Zielscheiben* or 'living targets' had caused a sensation several months earlier in the German garrison town of Döberitz, attracting interest from army officials and the Kaiser himself. By July, the *Oesterreichischer Komet* was telling its readers that a newly opened cinematic firing range on Berlin's Unter den Linden boulevard promised to amuse 'every fashionable young gentleman in town' for weeks to come.[1] This latest marvel of an 'age of surrogacy', the *Komet's* correspondent explained, could transport patrons to the jungle, the savannah, or the polar circle where they might blaze away with a Winchester rifle at lions, tigers, jaguars, antelopes, zebras, giraffes, polar bears and penguins – a Noah's Ark of virtual canon-fodder that had presumably been filmed in Berlin Zoo – as well as artificial targets such as speeding cars, motor-boats and aircraft. More disturbingly, it also transformed skiers, racing cyclists, marching soldiers and charging cavalry into targets for those 'of a particularly bloodthirsty disposition' so that 'the marksman of the cinema will be able to dream not only of a sensational fairy-tale-like hunt but also of the horrors of war'. By the time the entertainment reached Vienna its exhibitors had evidently decided to capitalize on the mood of virulent nationalism by awarding prizes for direct hits on enemy troops. The presence of civilian and military dignitaries at the grand reopening of Innsbruck's Zentralkino as a cinematic shooting gallery in January 1915 indicates that the diversion even enjoyed the status of an officially approved contribution to the war effort.[2]

The *Lebende Zielscheiben* are a useful coda to the complexity of early twentieth-century popular visual entertainments. Most immediately, there is the startling modernity of this visual practice whose affinities to the latter-day videogame range from its artful topicality and violent realism to its individual screens, authentic weaponry and freeze-frame 'game over' ending. Although half a dozen Austrian war features were already playing at Viennese cinemas by the time the Conrads arrived (Fritz, 1980), the footage described by Borys was most likely a hastily dusted-off 'topical' from the Boer War, possibly James White's 'Capture of a Boer Battery by British' (1900) which purported to show kilted Highlanders in combat. Moreover, in its speedy integration of the short news film and the travel feature into the dual format of a fairground sideshow and a military propaganda event, the show testifies to the protean adaptability and geographical reach of early cinema. Indeed, within just a few years Conrad would have sold the film rights to four of his own novels, watched Maurice Tourneur's adaptation of *Victory* in a cinema in Canterbury and written a Hollywood screenplay titled *Gaspar the Strong Man*, a military drama based on his short story 'Gaspar Ruiz', which contains a number of battle scenes.[3]

It is easy to imagine Conrad's surprise at being suddenly confronted by the sight of Scottish infantrymen in Vienna, a forceful reminder of cinema's ability to present spectators with lifelike animated images of those far away. During the war years, he would have the opportunity to watch newsreels in temporary cinemas in several towns in Kent, doubtless a tense experience for the parent of a soldier on active service at the Western Front, and his declaration in August 1916, 'I am not going to run my life like a cinema-film regardless of anything but time' (*CL* 5: 632), may reflect the outrage of cinemagoers at the grotesque comedy which had resulted the previous month when exhibitors played J. B. McDowell and Geoffrey Malins's actuality film *The Battle of the Somme* (1916) too quickly in order to squeeze in extra performances (Hiley, 1998: 99). Equally understandable is Conrad's dismay at the *Lebende Zielscheiben*'s eliding of cinematic representation with real violence. The macabre show follows the logic of previous innovations that established an affinity between photography and the military, including Etienne Jules Marey's photographic gun, one of the first cameras to capture movement in a series of images, a process termed 'chronophotography'; Conrad would later record testily to having had '14 shots fired at me by [Malcolm] Arbuthnot the photographer' (*CL* 6: 449). A disagreeable feeling of being unpatriotic would have troubled anyone in his position and the dangers attendant upon being identified as British in such a fiercely bellicose milieu were genuine enough (see Figure 2). Even so, there is something deeply irrational about the writer's

Figure 2   Viennese film and magic-lantern show, 10 October 1914. Reproduced with permission of Vienna City Library, Poster Collection.

unwillingness to fire upon what were, after all, mere projected shadows. Borys's comment, 'He would have been terribly distressed if I had hit one of those running figures', contains the implication that his father, like many of the pre-cinematic generation, found the realism of moving photographs deeply uncanny.[4] For all his bluff assertions that film was 'milk for very young children' (*JCIR* 51) and 'just a silly stunt for silly people' (Curle, 1928a: 114), Conrad was clearly susceptible to the medium's sheer power.

The jolt given to Conrad's sensibilities by the *Lebende Zielscheiben* highlights the discursive instability of early cinema, its unpredictable subject matter and exhibition practices, and its continual recalibration of audience experience. In particular, his unease can seen be as a response to the inherently controversial nature of recording or re-enacting historic events for the camera, compounded by what the *Oesterreichischer Komet* aptly called 'surrogacy', that is, cinema's unique capacity to convey convincing impressions of presence, movement and verisimilitude. Conrad's quaint aversion to firing at 'living pictures' dramatizes, too, the contested epistemological status of early film among contemporaries who regarded motion photography as a gimmick promoting a variety of bad faith in producers and viewers alike. In fact, since 'Capture of a Boer Battery by British' had been made for Edison Biograph using costumed actors in New Jersey, the Scottish soldiers who elicited Conrad's sympathies could easily have been nothing of the kind. Whether or not he was aware of this possibility, his distaste for a filmed entertainment that encouraged patrons to identify firing at shadows with bloody military conflicts elsewhere is consistent with his oft-stated contempt for the supposed faithfulness of filmic representation and his emphasis upon the dimensions of experience that cinema failed to replicate, as when he told the *Boston Evening Telegraph*'s reporter James Walter Smith: 'The trouble with moving-pictures is that they don't show, except in a superficial way, what the characters are thinking' (*JCIR* 186). On this view, despite its promises of immediacy and phenomenological plenitude, cinema delivered a mere simulacrum of experience, doubly removing spectators from the viewed object by virtue of the cinematographic process as well as the theatrical staging of the event itself.

The intricacy of Conrad's response to this unusual photographic entertainment is typical of his relation to popular visual culture as a whole. To be sure, a fascination with the visual sense permeates his writing, as perhaps might be expected from someone who spent long hours in isolation reviewing memories of distant places and who was described by his son as having 'a photographic (for want of a better word) mind' (Conrad, 1981: 166). As Marlow remarks in *Chance*, 'Images, visions, obsess with particular force men withdrawn from the sights and sounds of active life' (*C* 267). Arthur Symons recalled the writer telling him, 'I write by images' (Stape and Knowles, 1996: 92), and Conrad insisted to Edward Garnett that *The Rescue* would be 'a kind of glorified book for boys . . . . Pictures – pictures – pictures' (*CL* 1: 392). And yet Conrad repeatedly compared successful literary narrative to visual experiences that, far from being straightforwardly revelatory or 'graphic', were fleeting, difficult and even non-rational. He praised Garnett's prose style for being 'like a flash of limelight on the façade of a cathedral or a flash of lightning on a landscape' (*CL* 1: 198), and he announced elliptically to R. B. Cunninghame Graham: 'Straight vision is bad form . . . . The proper thing is to look round the corner' (1: 370). Unwavering in its author's conviction of the superiority of literary art to all other modes of representation, Conrad's fiction makes, for its own part, a series of appeals to a more profound and counter-intuitive way of seeing, a faculty encompassing not merely sensory perception but a kind of empathetic insight that he once described as 'the inner character of things which demands interpretation, and is, so to speak, personal to the interpreter' (Najder, 1978: 96). The frame-narrator of 'The Partner' records being eyed by an old stevedore 'in an unseeing way, as if engrossed in the thought of the years so easily dealt with' (*WT* 96), just as Marlow speculates in *Chance* that Captain Anthony in the very moment of deciding to rescue young Flora de Barral 'must have suddenly *seen* the girl' (163, Conrad's emphasis).

An examination of Conrad's treatment of contemporary visual entertainments accordingly requires more than just a simple cataloguing of contextual references. Like the crowds drawn to the *Lebende Zielscheiben*, he was fascinated by visual novelties which, as his description of documentary films as simultaneously 'amazing' and 'maddening' (*JCIR* 161) suggests, he found intellectually exciting as well as aesthetically infuriating. In his writing, he sought to address readers in the visual lexicon that such entertainments were bringing into existence even as he strove in exemplary Modernist fashion to integrate and subsume these artefacts of popular culture. As this chapter will show, by invoking the experiences of specific viewing situations – the analogues of what James Joyce once called 'the sixty-miles-an-hour pathos of some cinematograph' (Joyce, 1966, 2: 217) – Conrad created a palette of aesthetic and epistemological reference points with which to confer subtle nuances upon his fictional characters and narratives. Wholly distinct from seeing in its everyday sense as well as from the diversions now being offered by a burgeoning array of visual practices, the artistic intention which he famously emphasized in the Preface to *The Nigger of the 'Narcissus'* (1897) as 'by the power of the written word . . . to make you *see*' (*NN* x) should thus be understood as a sustained engagement with the visual dynamics of contemporary popular culture.

Under the very point of the pen

An extensive secondary literature has documented the central role of visual entertainment and public spectacle in Britain between 1880 and 1920. Indeed, it is scarcely an exaggeration to describe this period as witness to a revolution in the sprawling assortment of phenomena that some media historians now term *visual culture*. Apart from brief periods of political unrest in 1888–89 and 1912–14, the urban crowd became increasingly synonymous with choreographed manifestations of national and imperial pride, large-scale exhibitions and fairs, and sensational publicity stunts. Professional football and cycling emerged as mass spectator sports, the construction of leisure attractions such as zoos and aquaria proceeded apace, and grand displays of organized pageantry came into vogue. At night, the central streets of British cities basked in the glow of powerful electric lights as the massive plate glass windows of department stores such as London's Selfridges (1909), following Paris's Samaritaine (1903) and Berlin's Kaufhaus des Westens (1907), began dazzling their passers-by with a new standard of illumination. The increasing size and number of music halls (London alone boasted 300 at the turn of the century) made performers such as Dan Leno, Harry 'Little Tich' Relph and Marie Lloyd into nationally recognized stars whose appeal extended even to the middle and upper classes. 'We had 3 people to dinner last night and a party of four to get bored at the Alhambra' (*CL* 5: 381), Conrad remarked sardonically in May 1914 of a music-hall variety programme that had included George Grossmith and Cosmo Gordon's hit revue *Not Likely*, starring Eddie Cantor and Beatrice Lillie, 'The Funniest Woman in the World'.[5] In the realm of print media, the perfecting of the monochrome and colour halftone processes in the 1880s and 1890s raised the quality of magazine illustrations and artistic reproductions to new heights, and in January 1904 readers of Alfred Harmsworth's revamped *Daily Mirror* were able to savour the first regular photographs in a daily newspaper.[6] The public début of projected motion photography in 1895–96 famously elicited cries of delight from audiences who had become accustomed to highly sophisticated magic lantern shows as well as a vast array of other visual entertainments, and the launch of George Eastman's Kodak Brownie in 1900 gave additional impetus to the spread of home photography. As if to acknowledge the ubiquity of this new visual culture, Conrad and Ford Madox Ford portray the celebrity novelist Callan in *The Inheritors*, their thinly-veiled burlesque of Hall Caine, as keeping himself permanently 'ready for the kodak wielder' (*I* 16).[7]

In recent years literary historians have begun to scrutinize this visual culture's formative influence on Modernist writing – from Prufrock's plangent cry, 'It is impossible to say just what I mean! / But as if a magic lantern threw the nerves in patterns on a screen' (Eliot, 1989: 16), to Charles Swann's luminous memory of the magic lantern show as 'supernatural phenomena of many colours, in which legends were depicted, as on a shifting and transitory window' (Proust, 2000: 16).[8] In the words of Sara Danius, whose *The Senses of Modernism* (2002) offers one of the most ambitious of these re-evaluations: 'A sustained reconsideration of aesthetic modernism thus has to include a historically reflexive and multi-leveled attempt at incorporating the operations of the perceptual technologies of the second machine age into an understanding of the modernist enterprise' (Danius, 2002: 196). Like Eliot and Proust, Conrad was acutely sensible of these historic changes in the realm of spectacle and visual entertainment. In his short story 'Il Conde', a Neapolitan crowd promenades beneath electric street lamps 'as if in a bath of some radiant and tenuous fluid' (*SS* 277); and in his late novel *Chance* London's nocturnal illumination stands as an emblem of the fractured urban consciousness that, having enabled a swindler to defraud an entire nation, threatens to intrude upon the stolid maritime world of Captain Anthony: 'The night of the town with its strings of lights, rigid, and crossed like a net of flames, thrown over the sombre immensity of walls, closed round him, with its artificial brilliance overhung by an emphatic blackness, its unnatural animation of a restless, overdriven humanity' (257). In his wartime memoir 'Poland Revisited', Conrad similarly describes how the great cargo steamers now plying the North Sea 'spangled the night with the cheap, electric, shop-glitter, here there and everywhere as of some High-street broken up and washed out to sea' (*NLL* 129).

There are, in fact, a striking number of allusions to identifiable visual technologies and popular amusements in Conrad's fiction. 'The Return', an early attempt at magazine melodrama, unfolds within what its main protagonist experiences as 'the convincing illusion of a room' (*TU* 125), a virtual domestic space that is strongly reminiscent of a fairground Hall of Mirrors; and Conrad would later confess to his own puzzlement at the story's insistent detailing of 'physical impressions . . . rendered as if for their own sake' (*TU* viii). *Lord Jim* is especially dense with references to visual culture, including telescopes, electric lights, magic mirrors, Punch and Judy shows, slapstick clowns and wooden puppets. Jim compares a colourful Indian street to a 'damaged kaleidoscope' (*LJ* 157) and a group of 'picturesque' locals to the subjects of a 'chromo-lithograph' (157), and Marlow perhaps has in mind Edison's peep-show Kinetoscope or a hand-cranked flip-book viewer such as the Mutoscope or the Kinora when he recollects: 'All at once, on the blank page, under the very point of the pen, the two figures of Chester and his antique partner, very distinct and complete, would dodge into view with stride and gestures, as if reproduced in the field of some optical toy' (*LJ* 174). In *Under Western Eyes*, too, Razumov contemptuously regards the prospect of the Château Borel as having 'the uninspiring, glittering quality of a very fresh oleograph . . . . odious – oppressively odious – in its unsuggestive finish: the very perfection of mediocrity attained at last after centuries of toil and culture' (*UWE* 203).[9]

More than just evidence of his acquaintance with specific visual entertainments, such references are integral components of a literary project whose purpose Conrad expressly defined as 'stimulating vision in the reader' (*CL* 1: 381). At one level, these entertainments supplied him with convenient analogies if not the actual inspiration for psychological experiences that he sought to convey to the reader, as when Razumov, guilt-ridden at having betrayed his fellow student Haldin and oppressed with surveillance by '[t]he eye of the social revolution', momentarily hallucinates that he is seeing the eyes of General T——and Privy-Councillor Mikulin hanging in the air 'like a vivid detail in a dissolving view of two heads' (*UWE* 222). Dissolving views were a well-known magic-lantern technique whereby exhibitors used one or more multi-lens projectors to create ingenious and often surreal effects of movement and transformation, a context that inflects this charged scene in several ways.[10] Not only does the dissolving view externalize the identity crisis that has just prompted Razumov's schizophrenic reflection, 'Was it possible that he no longer belonged to himself?' (*UWE* 222), it creates a characteristically Conradian moment of epiphanic intensity in which the political-optical thematics of the novel as a whole, something Jeremy Hawthorn has called 'a cumulative and organic system of meaning' (Hawthorn, 2002: xxv), are registered by the visual faculties of its main protagonist.[11] Since Conrad had described the 'spectre of Russia's might' as a 'dreaded and strange apparition' in his 1905 essay 'Autocracy and War' (*NLL* 75), it was doubly appropriate that he should have chosen this dramatic and ironic emblem – as handbooks for projectionists warned, dissolving views of portraits usually produced a comic effect – for a regime whose grasp on power would prove as ephemeral as a phantasmagoric illusion.[12]

The fact that Razumov's fantasy, like the animated figures under Marlow's gaze in *Lord Jim*, occurs while he is sitting at a desk illuminated by a 'lighted lamp' (*UWE* 221) in the very act of reaching for his pen, that is, during a quintessentially Modernist scene of writing, also reconfirms the importance of visual entertainment for Conrad's conception of literary art. At another level, then, such references comprise a meditation upon the reading situation itself, as is suggested by Conrad's treatment of the moving or rolled panorama, a pre-cinematic technology still popular in the early 1890s in which long painted canvases, often depicting river journeys, were unwound horizontally in front of seated audiences.[13] Like his description of *Almayer's Folly* as the result of 'a hallucinated vision of forests and rivers and seas' (*PR* 3), Conrad's memory of how the 'mere scenery' of *An Outcast of the Islands* 'got a great hold on me as I went along' (*OI* ix) attests to the over-determined status of spectatorship in these early novels. *Almayer's Folly* opens with Almayer standing on his verandah watching the Pantai River flow 'before his eyes' (*AF* 5) – 'naturally enough', as H. G. Wells remarked dryly of the novice author's prolixity (*CH* 75) – before embarking upon an 'imaginary voyage' into his own inglorious past and down the stream that 'rolled an angry and muddy flood under his inattentive eyes' (*AF* 5–6). At the climax of *An Outcast of the Islands*, the sight of his daughter sleeping leads Almayer into a similarly ironic reverie about Nina's future: 'And he could see things there! Things charming and splendid passing before him in *a magic unrolling of resplendent pictures*; pictures of events brilliant, happy, inexpressibly glorious, that would make up her life' (320, emphasis added).

That Conrad's novels themselves succeeded in 'showing' Borneo (a country unknown to British readers, as several commentators pointed out) to an audience habituated to visual entertainments like the moving panorama can be measured from contemporary reviewers' praise for their 'scenery' (*CH* 50, 55, 60), 'picturesqueness' (58), 'admirably graphic passages' (61), 'pictures evidently drawn from life' (52), 'scenic descriptions' (63) and 'tropical scenery glow[ing] with life and colour' (78). 'The scenery does not appear behind the characters like the "back cloth" at a theatre – it mingles with them to the end . . .' (*CH* 50), enthused the *Daily Chronicle*; and even the *Sketch's* unimpressed reviewer complained that the author of *An Outcast* 'must needs paint every blade of grass with pre-Raphaelite minuteness, while he observes through a microscope every thought that floats, however casually, through the minds of his personages' (71). The motif would surface regularly in subsequent reviews of Conrad's work, as when the *Daily News* approvingly characterized *Lord Jim* as an 'ever-shifting panorama of the great Pacific, varied by the picturesque islands of the Indian Sea' (*CH* 125), or when

W. L. Courtney welcomed *The Nigger of the 'Narcissus'* as 'a moving panorama of the phases of the ocean' (87).

These considerations raise the important issue of Conrad's engagement with the dramatic arts. His love of Verdi and Bizet is recorded in the memoirs of family members and friends, to whom he suggested at different times that *Nostromo, Victory, Almayer's Folly* and *The Rover* were each suitable for operatic treatment.[14] 'What a tremendous subject for a great a really great Opera!' he enthused to Hugh Clifford of the latter's *The Downfall of the Gods,* declaring extravagantly that their collaboration on its libretto would have produced 'a magnificent achievement' (*CL* 4: 451). Conrad's attitude towards the theatre was more ambivalent, despite the fact that he counted playwrights such as John Galsworthy, Edmund Garnett and James Barrie among his acquaintance, was active in a public campaign against dramatic censorship, and wrote approvingly of 'the sort of contentment the middle plays of Ibsen give one' (4: 218). Even so, and notwithstanding his protestations at having 'no dramatic gift' (2: 34) and 'detest[ing] the stage' (4: 218), he completed theatrical adaptations of several of his works. *The Secret Agent* closed in November 1922 after just ten performances at the Ambassadors Theatre, London, but *Victory* had a profitable ten-week run at the Globe Theatre in spring 1919, possibly helped by the apparent topicality of its title.[15] 'Mr. Conrad is just the sort of person who ought to be coaxed into writing plays,' declared Max Beerbohm in a generous review of the 1905 stage version of 'To-morrow' (Beerbohm, 1953: 384).

A study of the influence of neglected popular cultural forms on Conrad's writing need only mention in passing the substantial body of work treating his relation to the dramatic arts, but it should be noted that the scholarly interest in this topic derives at least in part from the status of opera and theatre as legitimate or 'high' art, as is confirmed by Conrad's own admission that 'it has been my highest ambition to have one of my stories made into an opera' (Randall, 1968: 61n).[16] What is more, it exemplifies a critical tendency to conceptualize his relation to individual fields of popular culture exclusively in terms of narrative. This approach has a number of limitations. For example, a focus upon the intentions, realized or otherwise, behind Conrad's stage adaptations necessarily sidelines the relevance of theatrical themes and terminology, whether of individual plays or dramatic form in general, for his prose fiction as a whole. In writing *Under Western Eyes*, he explained to Basil Macdonald Hastings, 'My artistic aim was to put as much dramatic spirit as possible into the form of the novel . . . . to keep close to scenic effects all the time . . . . to keep always before myself the effect of a "performance" ' (*CL* 5: 696), a declaration that is amply borne out by the teacher of language's abiding sense of watching 'an obscure drama' (*UWE* 251): 'The thought that the real drama of autocracy is not played on the great stage of politics came to me as, fated to be a spectator, I had this other glimpse behind the scenes, something more profound than the words and gestures of the public play' (*UWE* 248). Not only did Conrad take an active part in the set design of his dramas, he repeatedly returned to the dimension of visual and scenic 'effects' when discussing the theatre, and the readers who consider Conrad's plays solely as texts thus risk missing one of their author's principal concerns: the experience of visual spectacle.[17]

In a concession that speaks directly to the mechanics of performance as well as to historically contingent practices of spectatorship, Conrad once told Hastings that 'the stage can never attain for me the necessary force of illusion' (*CL* 4: 207). Like his criticism of theatre as 'the destroyer of all suggestiveness' (4: 432), the comment casts dramatic representation as the antithesis of a quality that he insisted in another letter was 'the mark of a real artist in words' (4: 229) and that he memorably described as 'the light of magic suggestiveness . . . . play[ing] for an evanescent instant over the commonplace surface of words' (*NN* ix). What this seems to imply is that the illusionism on which Conrad modelled his fiction owed as much to more popular kinds of entertainment as to the established theatre. To be sure, his dramatic works are stagey by our own standards. Noting how *One Day More* is weakened by the 'forced exposition' (*T* 269) of Carvil's domestic tyranny – and possibly with an eye to Captain Hagberd's '*throaty, gurgling laugh*' (275), the final scene's lightening storm and the melodramatic directions '*viciously*' (273), '*anxiously*' (274) '*almost hysterical*' (277), '*horrified . . . explodes . . . fiercely*' (279), '*violently*' (286), '*raving to and fro*' (291), '*terrified*' (291) and '*distracted*' (293) – Paul Kirshner speculates that 'a semi-expressionistic production might work' (*T* 269–70). More recently, however, Richard J. Hand has offered a cogent re-evaluation of *Laughing Anne* (1920) which challenges such routine assumptions that Conrad's intentions were frustrated by an ignorance of stagecraft (Hand, 2001, 2002).[18] Hand's contention that the novelist successfully adapted 'Because of the Dollars' as a Guignol play, a violently sensational genre of popular melodrama closer to the modern low-budget horror film than to the respectable theatre, invites us, in turn, to reconsider other moments of stylized tableaux and emotional extremes in works that are conventionally analysed in terms of characterization and narrative: Kurtz's African mistress standing with arms upraised on the bank of the Congo; the suppressed sexual violence of *Victory* and 'The Inn of the Two Witches'; or the references to galvanized corpses in *Under Western Eyes* and 'Because of the Dollars'. With these factors in mind, let us turn to Conrad's engagement with some specific instances of visual culture and, above all, the non-narrative entertainments that danced before him, as Marlow puts it, 'on the blank page, under the very point of the pen' (*LJ* 174).

Democracy of vision

In the tragic dénouement of *Nostromo* (1901), Conrad depicts the Capataz de Cargadores dying from Viola's bullet with only a solitary anarchist at his side. Uncanny as well as out of the ordinary, Nostromo's deathbed attendant clearly deserves the epithet 'weird' (*N* 563). And yet the presence of this hirsute dwarf who perches on a stool 'like a hunchbacked monkey' (562) is also weird in a more oblique sense. No doctor, he is, in fact, a photographer. His physique anticipates that of Julius Laspara, the firebrand editor of *Living Word* in *Under Western Eyes*, just as the tool of his trade anticipates the Professor's concealed bomb in *The Secret Agent* with its trigger mechanism based on 'the principle of the pneumatic instantaneous shutter for a camera lens' (*SA* 55). There is, too, something suspicious about his eagerness to discover the missing silver's whereabouts so as to be able to fight the rich, as he puts it, 'with their own weapons' (*N* 562), certainly an ironic proposal in light of the fact that Emilia Gould has just stopped Nostromo from telling her the location of the ingots. But the pairing of anarchism and photography itself seems puzzlingly arbitrary.

The broader context of Conrad's attitude towards photography goes some way towards accounting for the anarchist photographer's presence at this critical juncture. Despite having been suppressed, the Monterist rebellion begun 'in the name of Democracy' (*N* 242) has let the revolutionary genie out of the bottle, making it likely that the persistence of extreme social inequality will, as Archbishop Corbelán warns, catalyse Sulaco's dispossessed masses into another violent uprising. Conrad once declared that 'the artistic! photographer's aim [is] always to obliterate every trace of individuality in his subject' (*CL* 2: 105, Conrad's exclamation mark), and there is an obvious parallel between *Nostromo*'s spectral embodiment of this communist future, his soul 'dyed crimson by a bloodthirsty hatred of all capitalists' (*N* 528), and photography's own baleful arrival as part of what Conrad calls 'the material apparatus of perfected civilization which obliterates the individuality of old towns' (*N* 96). Every bit as disrespectful and intrusive as the pale vampire at Nostromo's bedside or the revolutionary mob that destroys Sulaco's artistic heritage of canvas paintings, photography constitutes a failure of aesthetic representation that mirrors democracy's own failure as political representation.

In his notorious polemic against the 'imbecile infatuation' of the 'idolatrous multitude', Charles Baudelaire underscored the danger posed by photography's democratizing tendencies (Baudelaire, 1980: 86–7). 'If photography is allowed to deputize for art in some of art's activities,' he warned, 'it will not be long before it has supplanted or corrupted art altogether, thanks to the stupidity of the masses, its natural ally.' Indeed, the overheard boast of a society woman, 'Let me see; nothing shocks me' (Baudelaire, 1980: 87), confirmed for him that its dulling of viewers' sensibilities was already well advanced. Conrad's own opinions on photography, if but a distant echo of Baudelaire's, were hardly less reactionary.[19] Hugh Walpole recalled him having 'cursed the public for not distinguishing between creation and photography' (*JCIR* 135) and the camera's inadequacy is emphasized on several occasions in his writing. In 'The Character of the Foe', he predicted that 'the seamen of three hundred years hence . . . will glance at the photogravures of our nearly defunct sailing-ships with a cold, inquisitive, and indifferent eye' (*MS* 73), and he casually elides photography with 'blind' faith in sensory experience in an orientalizing portrait of the serang helmsman in 'The End of the Tether': 'The record of the visual world fell through his eyes upon his unspeculating mind as on a sensitized plate through the lens of a camera' (*Y* 228).[20] Remarks like these indicate that Conrad saw photography as defined by undiscriminating inclusiveness and relentless equivalence, in effect, as a mere footprint of the visual. Thus *Lord Jim*'s eponymous hero admits to his fatal naivety about the ways of the world: 'My weakness consists in not having a discriminating eye for the incidental . . . . A confounded democratic quality of vision which may be better than total blindness, but has been of no advantage to me' (*LJ* 94).

The special case of spirit photography further complicates this view. Given the popular wisdom that photographs are, in Baudelaire's contemptuous phrase, 'identical to nature' (86), it is a paradox that Conrad's contemporaries continued to accept them as more reliable than human perception even after their vulnerability to fakery had become common knowledge. The Cottingley Fairies hoax of 1917, for example, caused an international sensation despite their use of techniques of double exposure and composite montage whose role in doctoring photographs had long been satirized. In June 1896, an article in *Pearson's Magazine* had facetiously proclaimed of its own absurdly double-exposed and retouched photographs: 'The camera . . . sees things which to the eyes of the ordinary mortal are invisible. It has undoubtedly an intimate association with the phenomena of the spiritualistic world' ('A. W.', 1896: 44).[21] At the same time, Tom Gunning has argued that since all photographs have the uncanny power to preserve the image of their subject beyond the latter's death, the significance of spirit photography goes beyond simple questions of authenticity and credulity. 'As visual spectacles and entertainment,' he notes, 'such manifestations opened the way for the enjoyment of appearances whose very fascination came from their apparent impossibility, their apparent severance from the laws of nature' (Gunning, 1995c: 68). In other words, spirit photography must be seen not just as a symptom of New Age crankiness but, rather, as staging in extreme form the suspension of critical disbelief integral to an array of modern visual entertainments. As a reviewer for *La Poste* declared in 1895: '[W]hen all are able to photograph their dear ones, no longer merely in immobile form but in movement, in action, with their familiar gestures, with speech on their lips, death will no longer be final' (Rossell, 1998: 150).

The issue is an important one because Conrad treats spirit photography in some detail in his short story 'The Black Mate' (1908). This slight tale, which the narrator calls 'a record of a spiritualistic experience' (*TH* 97), concerns a prematurely greying sailor named Bunter who has resorted to dying his hair in order to find work. When Bunter's stock of dye is broken during a storm, he hits upon the ingenious ruse of letting Captain Johns, a believer in spiritualism who only hires younger men, infer that his mate's hair has been turned white by the shock of seeing a ghost. Not only does this expedient allow Bunter to retain his berth for the homeward leg of what will be his final sea voyage, it gives him the satisfaction of deceiving his martinet employer. It would have been natural for Conrad to identify with Bunter's 'tragic position' (93) when he first drafted 'The Black Mate' in 1886, and several commentators have suggested that his own resentment of an intolerable working situation can be discerned behind the story's plot contrivances and comic tone:

A man could not expect much consideration should he find himself at the mercy of a fellow like Johns. A misfortune is a misfortune, and there's an end of it. But to be bored by mean, low-spirited, inane ghost stories in the Johns style, all the way out to Calcutta and back again, was an intolerable apprehension to be under. Spiritism was indeed a solemn subject to think about in that light. Dreadful even!

(*TH* 93–4)

Figure 3 Spirit photograph of William Thomas Stead and 'psychic figure', *Borderland* 2 (1895), 310. Reproduced with permission of Bodleian Library, Oxford.

'The Black Mate' is, among other things, a satire on the spiritualist William Thomas Stead (Figure 3), a campaigning editor whose muckraking exposé of child prostitution had caused a sensation in 1885. Captain Johns's references to the spirit photographs 'published every month in a special newspaper' and 'that newspaper fellow – what's his name – who had a girl-ghost visitor' (*TH* 89) describe, respectively, Stead's illustrated review *Borderland* and his spirit muse and late colleague Julia Ames, whilst 'Professor Cranks' (110) refers to Sir William Crookes, the renowned physicist and President of the Society for Psychical Research, whose activities were promoted by Stead for much of the 1890s.[22] Stead's Radical politics, feminism, pacifism and championing of Tsarist Russia were, of course, anathema to Conrad; the July 1905 number of Stead's *Review of Reviews* had carried a stinging denunciation of Conrad's 'Autocracy and War', an essay which ridicules as 'a sight of disarming comicality' (*NLL* 89) the Permanent Court of Arbitration that Stead had been instrumental in establishing and for which he had been nominated for the first Nobel Peace Prize in 1901 (Stead, 1905).[23] Pique was therefore the likely motive for Conrad's decision to portray Captain Johns's spiritualism as 'clothed in a sort of weird utilitarianism' (*TH* 102). Certainly, the captain's pet topics, which include 'the improvement of morality to be expected from the establishment of general and close intercourse with the spirits of the departed' (100) and the potential for using spirits in 'the detection of crime' (102), recall Stead's own plans for a Borderland Bureau (a spiritualist equivalent to the Labour Bureau), so-called Social Purity campaigns and at times wild speculations about the possible applications of mediumship.[24] For reformers like Stead, Roger Luckhurst has argued, 'Telepathy was a democratic prosthesis, existing somewhere between an emerging organic potential and a new *fin-de-siècle* technology' (Luckhurst, 2004: 129). At the same time, Stead had always seen technological innovation as central to his various projects of societal improvement – for him, magic lanterns represented 'the true direction in which democratic endowment of art should turn' (Stead, 1891: 6) – and spirit photography was no less crucial to his stated intention 'to democratize Psychic study' (Stead, 1897: 339). This democratic agenda may partly explain why the politics of class figure so insistently in Conrad's treatments of spiritualism, as when Johns's desire to make contact with his mate's 'well connected' dead relations provokes Bunter to exclaim: 'It would be an impudent intrusion . . . What is it? A new sort of snobbishness or what?' (*TH* 93).[25]

Conrad would return to mock 'the forcible incantations of Mr. Stead' in 'The Life Beyond' (1910), a review essay in which, after noting tartly that a medium recently exposed by investigators was currently living 'on the top floor of a Neapolitan house', he asked with ill-concealed condescension: 'Can you imagine anything more squalid than an Immortality at the beck and call of Eusapia Palladino?' (*NLL* 58). But despite sending up 'spiritism – or whatever the ghost craze is called' (*TH* 93), Conrad's real target in 'The Black Mate' is less the 'fraudulent mediums' (92) themselves than their victims' faith in photography, as here exemplified by Johns's unshakable conviction that '[t]he sensitized plate can't lie' (101) when remonstrating with his hapless first mate:

> 'Incredulity, sir, is the evil of the age!'
> It rejected the evidence of Professor Cranks and of the journalist chap. It resisted the production of photographs.
> For Captain Johns believed firmly that certain spirits had been photographed. He had read something of it in the papers. And the idea of it having been done had got a tremendous hold on him, because his mind was not critical . . . .
> 'Photographs! Photographs!' he would repeat, in a voice as creaky as a rusty hinge.   (*TH* 100–1)

In a sense, then, the story presents the credulousness engendered by spirit photography, a system of representation that Conrad believed to be predicated on deception and delusion, as synecdochic of a more widespread failure of visual scepticism. Not only was the mate never 'black' to begin with (in which misapprehension the story's readers are as guilty as Johns) but hair colour itself is shown to be doubly unreliable as a guide to physical fitness or even age. In its carelessly 'democratic' conflation of appearance and reality, Johns's ill-conceived rule of hiring only dark-haired crewmen stands revealed as yet another symptom of Conrad's *bête noire*, the 'modern conditions of push and hurry' (*TH* 88). The epistemological problem is encapsulated neatly in Bunter's belligerent reply to a berthing master who wonders aloud whether he has not already met the mate: ' "An individual who calmly tells me to my face that he is *not sure* if he has seen me before, either means to be impudent or is no better than a worm, sir" ' (94, emphasis in original).

Life in visions: *The Secret Agent* (1907)

In his 1920 'Author's Note' Conrad directs readers to the unusually visual quality of *The Secret Agent* (1907). The novel 'delivered to the public gaze' (*SA* 3), he explained, had been his 'largest canvas' (4), the product of an imagination captivated by 'strange forms, sharp in outline but imperfectly apprehended' (6). Even with the passage of time, its violent subject matter remained for him a macabre spectacle: 'I have been forced, so to speak, to look upon its bare bones. I confess that it makes a grisly skeleton' (8). Whilst Conrad's rationale for the novel's setting – 'the vision of an enormous town presented itself, of a monstrous town more populous than some continents' (6) – has often been cited in relation to imperial geopolitics, the metropolitan Gothic and Dickens, critics have had relatively little to say about the first term of his famous declaration.[26] And yet it is entirely appropriate that London should have 'presented itself' to Conrad as a *vision*. Most obviously, the city was the hub of an entertainment industry that had become integral to the routines of work and leisure as well as the rituals of social life. In 'Youth', Marlow recalls how he willingly travelled all the way from Falmouth to London for a five-day spree that included a visit to a music hall; and in *The Secret Agent*, Winnie's mother remembers that Verloc, after becoming engaged to her daughter, 'never offered to take Winnie to theatres, as such a nice gentleman ought to have done' (*SA* 12). The proximity of the capital's entertainment industry presumably accounts, too, for why Inspector Heat likens being grilled by the Assistant Commissioner to how 'a tight rope artist might feel if suddenly, in the middle of the performance, the manager of the Music Hall were to rush out of the proper managerial seclusion and begin to shake the rope' (92). Conrad had recently presented a similar logic at work in 'The Informer' (1906), whose anarchists think it advantageous to live above 'a shabby Variety Artists' Agency – an agency for performers in inferior music-halls' with its to-and-fro of 'foreign-looking people, jugglers, acrobats, singers of both sexes, and so on' (*SS* 82), oblivious to the fact that police infiltration has reduced their own activities to a mere show of subversiveness.[27]

At the same time, London constituted a phantasmagoric experience in its own right. As Ben Singer notes: 'Amid the unprecedented turbulence of the big city's traffic, noise, billboards, street signs, jostling crowds, window displays and advertisements, the individual faced a new intensity of sensory stimulation' (Singer, 1995: 73).[28] The coverage of the real-life Greenwich Outrage of February 1894, Conrad's inspiration for *The Secret Agent*, illustrates how this sensibility was further disseminated by the media to the nation at large. The extensive reporting of the bombing by the *Daily Graphic* and the *Illustrated London News* included half-tone photographic reproductions of gawping crowds near the Greenwich Observatory, in which a white 'X' had been inserted to direct readers to the exact spot where Martial Bourdin had accidentally blown himself up. This dialectic of spectatorship and performance governing street life in the capital is invoked on several occasions in *The Secret Agent*, as when Stevie is 'easily diverted' by the 'comedies of the street' (*SA* 13) or when Ossipon is surrounded by an 'excited crowd' (223) after his treacherous leap from a moving train in Waterloo Station. Conrad even goes so far as to depict Stevie's distress at 'the dramas of fallen horses' as an inability to take part in the normal city dweller's 'enjoyment of the national spectacle' (13).

The Secret Agent alludes to the world of visual entertainment at every turn, from the 'photographs of more or less undressed dancing girls' (*SA* 9) which Adolf Verloc displays in the shop window to his 'automaton's absurd air of being aware of the machinery inside of him' (149).[29] Conrad's memorable description of gas-lit London as 'a slimy aquarium from which the water had been run off' (114) recalls not only the common household ornament but the Aquarium, a world-famous Variety hall in Westminster that was one of the city's top venues for sporting events, moving pictures and living waxwork tableaux as well as the 'jugglers, acrobats, singers of both sexes, and so on' itemized in 'The Informer'.[30] Above all, what Conrad called 'Winnie Verloc's story' (8) has for its subject one of the Victorian media's most enduring obsessions: the woman who murders her husband.[31] Like its satirizing of 'beauties of journalistic style' such as ' "*An impenetrable mystery seems destined to hang for ever over this act of madness or despair*" ' (228), *The Secret Agent*'s refusal to glamorize or mystify Winnie's actions effectively challenges the contemporary romanticization of female killers, a phenomenon described by Judith Knelman as 'a peculiar symbiosis of fact and fiction validated, not by an actual increase in cases, but by the sensation novel of the 1860s' (Knelman, 1988: 14). On several counts, then, it is entirely in keeping with the novel's broader thematics that Conrad should have chosen to structure its bloody climax around three separate modes of popular visual entertainment.

Few readers of *The Secret Agent* can have failed to notice the fact that, as Conrad explicitly points out, Winnie thinks 'in images' (*SA* 198). This peculiar attribute is foregrounded strikingly in the scene in which Winnie, after discovering that Verloc has used Stevie as a bomb courier, fatally stabs the man responsible for her brother's death. In this melodramatic passage, arguably the most ambitious in his fiction, Conrad seeks to represent the 'mental state' (200) that drives his protagonist to this extreme act, offering as the corollary of her visual thought processes (the word 'vision' recurs ten times in three pages) what appears to be another allusion to the moving panorama: 'The exigencies of Mrs Verloc's temperament . . . forced her to roll a series of thoughts in her motionless head' (182–3). In her mind's eye, Winnie sees again her childish efforts to protect Stevie from their abusive father, her youth spent as a slavey in her mother's guest-house, and her pathetically frustrated romance with a jolly young man in a straw boater. These recollections are heavily inflected with the idiom and visual iconography of popular sentiment: that Winnie's sweetheart is a butcher's son recalls the American ballad 'My True Love is a Butcher Boy'; and her fantasy of sharing a boat-trip 'down the sparkling stream of life' with this 'fascinating companion' (183) evokes the ditty 'Row, row, row your boat / Gently down the stream / Merrily, merrily, merrily, merrily / Life is but a dream' as well as the mawkish watercolour on Alvin Hervey's wall in 'The Return' that depicts a 'young lady sprawled with dreamy eyes in a moored boat . . . and an enamoured man in a blazer' (*TU* 124). As Conrad makes scandalously clear, Winnie's marriage to Verloc – 'seven years' security for Stevie, loyally paid for on her part' (*SA* 184) – has been a kind of sexual thraldom, rendered almost unbearable by Ossipon's philandering attentions, to which she has been bound by this 'crushing memory' (183). So powerful, in fact, is this vision of the past that it can physically immobilize Winnie, make the pupils of her eyes 'extremely dilated' (184) and suspend her normal sight as she stares 'fixedly at a blank wall' (185).

And yet Conrad's statement that Winnie 'reviewed the tenor of her life in visions' (*SA* 183) more precisely connects this pivotal scene of spectatorship to another visual mode: the *life review*. In a major reassessment of August Strindberg's relation to *fin-de-siècle* visual culture, Vreni Hockenjos has shown, not only that the writer drew on the life review for his plays *Advent* (1898) and *To Damascus* (1898–1901) and his novel *Legends* (1898), but that the very notion of one's life 'flashing' instantaneously before one's eyes only entered general usage in the 1890s; Inspector Heat, we recall, has been reading in 'popular publications' about 'the whole past life lived with frightful intensity by a drowning man as his doomed head bobs up, streaming, for the last time' (*SA* 71).[32] Citing Friedrich Kittler's provocative axiom, 'Brain phantasms . . . exist only as the correlatives to technological media' (Kittler, 1999: 130), Hockenjos concludes that the life review, far from simply resembling a sped-up cinema film, is in fact a phenomenological artefact of the manipulation and acceleration of time by chronophotography, dissolving views and, in particular, motion photography. A literary trope as well as a notation for a particular visual experience, the life review was itself a common motif in early films such as the Pathé drama *Histoire d'un crime* (1901), in which a prisoner's dream about his criminal past is graphically represented as a series of moving images superimposed on the wall above his bed.[33]

Perhaps because of its partially obscured origins, the life review appealed strongly to Modernist writers (Proust and Joyce are its poet laureates) for whom it seemed to express a new temporal subjectivity and to offer a paradigm for their own innovations in narrative form. And in 'Typhoon', Conrad uses the life review to evoke the surreal mental state that dread and exhaustion have induced in the *Nan-Shan*'s first mate:

> Jukes was benumbed much more than he supposed. He held on – very wet, very cold, stiff in every limb; and in a momentary hallucination of swift visions (it is said that a drowning man thus reviews all his life) he beheld all sorts of memories altogether unconnected with his present situation. He remembered his father, for instance: a worthy business man, who at an unfortunate crisis in his affairs went quietly to bed and died forthwith in a state of resignation. Jukes did not recall these circumstances, of course, but remaining otherwise unconcerned he seemed to see distinctly the poor man's face; a certain game of nap played when quite a boy in Table Bay on board a ship, since lost with all hands; the thick eyebrows of his first skipper; and without any emotion, as he might years ago have walked listlessly into her room and found her sitting there with a book, he remembered his mother – dead, too, now – the resolute woman, left badly off, who had been very firm in his bringing up.
>
> It could not have lasted more than a second, perhaps not so much.
>
> (*T* 93)

However, like the tell-tale allusion to photography in Captain Whalley's 'sudden evocation' of the past in 'The End of the Tether', 'swift and full of detail like a flash of magnesium into the niches of a dark memorial hall' (*Y* 195), Conrad here encourages a readerly scepticism towards the truth value of the life review. Contrary to popular wisdom, the significance of Jukes's vision, whose mixture of the trivial and the important is said to be 'altogether unconnected with his present situation', lies less in its ostensible content than in what it reveals about an unobservant young man who has, we are told, 'no wide experience of storms or of men' (*T* 92).

Although Winnie's vision is similarly defined by montage and compression – glimpsed vignettes that connote her entire life, decades that pass in a 'few seconds only' (*SA* 184) – Conrad uses this popular motif in order to stress, not the possibility of distilling a person's life into a single narrative, but, rather, the inherent chaos and meaninglessness of such pictorial cascades. In *The Secret Agent*, the life review that redeems or expiates the protagonists of early films such as *Histoire d'un crime* instead reveals to Winnie the pointlessness of her many sacrifices, her folly in entrusting Stevie to Verloc and, ultimately, the sheer futility of her life. Whereas Winnie might have accepted Stevie's death had she been able to hold his corpse in her 'protecting arms' while venting her grief in 'a flood of bitter and pure tears' (*SA* 182) – Conrad's ironic adjectives 'protecting' and 'pure' signal her identification with this *Pietà* spectacle – the life review's parade of images forces her to abandon the superficial logic of her visual imagination and, with it, her conviction that the world '"did not stand looking into very much"' (182). She achieves real insight, then, by seeing *through* 'the supreme illusion of her life', an image of Verloc and Stevie walking together which has 'such plastic relief, such nearness of form, such a fidelity of suggestive detail' that it can elicit from her an 'anguished and faint murmur' (184). Literally and figuratively, Winnie must open her eyes in order to see things as they really are:

> She remembered now what she had heard, and she remembered it pictorially. They had to gather him up with the shovel. Trembling all over with irrepressible shudders, she saw before her the very implement with its ghastly load scraped up from the ground. Mrs Verloc closed her eyes desperately, throwing upon that vision the night of her eyelids, where after a rain-like fall of mangled limbs the decapitated head of Stevie lingered suspended alone, and fading out slowly like the last star of a pyrotechnic display. Mrs Verloc opened her eyes.
>
> (196)

In a letter to J. Henry Benrimo, the director of the stage version of *The Secret Agent*, Conrad insisted that the play end with Inspector Heat standing motionless at centre stage with Winnie crouching at his feet and a crowd murmuring in the wings: 'There is a tableau there which must not fail because it is on that impression the audience will leave the theatre' (*LL* 2: 277). Seemingly an index of his reliance upon the kinds of conventional theatrical devices which would be reimagined by innovative writer-producers such as Harley Granville-Barker, Conrad's choice of the *tableau* to create a visual 'impression' here is, in fact, less a clumsy adaptation of the novel than a recognition of one of its constituent elements.[34] When Inspector Heat breaks the news of Stevie's death, Conrad dwells upon the effectiveness of Winnie's frozen position as a visual signifier, almost as if it were her intention to communicate physically the distress she cannot articulate verbally: 'The perfect immobility of her pose expressed the agitation of rage and despair, all the potential violence of tragic passions, better than any shallow display of shrieks, with the beating of a distracted head against the walls, could have done' (*SA* 160). Her striking resemblance to a mannequin during her fatal conversation with Verloc is likewise underscored by narratorial remarks such as 'Mrs. Verloc's lips, composed in their usual form, preserved a statuesque immobility' (185) and 'Her cheeks were blanched, her lips ashy, her immobility amazing' (186). As Verloc complains irritably: '"One can't tell whether one is talking to a dummy or to a live woman"' (193).

The *Secret Agent*'s climactic murder scene is, indeed, a triptych of artfully arranged *tableaux*. In the first, which is set at just after 8.30 p.m. Greenwich Mean Time, Winnie is standing 'mysteriously still' (*SA* 196) at the mantelpiece looking at her husband, who is lying on a sofa from which, we are told, he 'did not stir' (196). In the second tableau, a moment of 'immobility and silence' (198) set at about 8.49 p.m., Winnie is leaning over Verloc's corpse in an 'easy attitude' from which, as Conrad twice notes, 'she did not move' (198). In the third, which is set at about 8.52 p.m., Winnie is pausing at the door after having knocked a joint of meat to the floor in her haste to escape. As narrative devices, the tableaux allow Conrad to manipulate time, an underlying theme of the novel, in a way that anticipates the philosophical assaults upon unitary conceptions of time by Henri Bergson and Wyndham Lewis. But why should this fundamentally static form of entertainment be at the heart of a novel that otherwise attests to its author's preoccupation with moving visual experiences – rolled panoramas, proto-cinematic life reviews, fireworks and the phantasmagoria of urban bustle?

In the 1890s waxwork tableaux became very popular as a spectacular mode of representing murders, thanks in part to two sensational cases involving women. After a public outcry in 1889 led to the commuting of the death sentence passed upon the poisoner Florence Maybrick, McLeod's Waxworks in Glasgow opened a tableau entitled 'The Last Moments of Mr. Maybrick' and Madame Tussaud's in London put an effigy of the killer herself on display in its famous Chamber of Horrors (Knelman, 1988: 119–20; Munro, 1931: 117). The following year, the conviction of Eleanor Pearcey for the double-murder of a mother and child, dubbed 'The Hampstead Horror' by the press, resulted in a media frenzy of which Judith Knelman has observed: 'All of London was trying to find out what made her tick' (Knelman, 1988: 112). The wretched Pearcey had paid for her legal defence by selling her furniture and personal effects (including an infamous perambulator) to Madame Tussaud's, where they were inserted into a forensically accurate facsimile of the domestic crime-scene (Chapman, 1984: 118–19). Opened within an hour of Pearcey's sentencing and attracting over 30,000 visitors in its first month, the tableau encouraged John Theodore Tussaud to create a new kind of waxwork in 1891, a six-scene Hogarthian account of an imaginary murderer's life-story entitled 'The History of a Crime'. The success of this second tableau inspired the Musée Grévin in Paris to create its own 'Histoire d'un Crime', a waxwork display that the catalogue described as '*un journal plastique*' or three-dimensional newspaper; this latter formed, in turn, the basis for the 1901 Pathé feature titled *Histoire d'un crime*, already mentioned, that cinema historians now regard as the prototype of the realistic crime film (Schwartz, 1995: 305, 310–11; Ceram, 1965).[35] Although Conrad's own familiarity with the murder tableau genre is suggested by a description in *The Arrow of Gold* of an articulated tailor's dummy as 'prostrate, handless, without its head, pathetic, like the mangled victim of a crime . . . . the model of some atrocious murder' (*AG* 189), he adopted a diffident tone when replying to the organizer of a fund-raising evening of *tableaux vivants* based on characters from his work.[36] Claiming that 'neither my people nor the situations in my novels lend themselves to pictorial grouping', Conrad politely declined to propose a specific tableau: 'It's the static quality of a grouping that disconcerts my imagination. When writing I visualise the successive scenes as always in motion – a flow of closely linked effects; so that when I attempt to arrest them in my mind at any given moment the first thought is always: that's no good!' (*CL* 6: 72, 117).

Critics have often commented upon the black humour of *The Secret Agent*'s murder scene and its effective use of narrative devices such as delayed decoding (Verloc's 'discovery' that a knife has already been planted in his chest, Winnie's realization that the 'ticking' of the clock is actually blood dripping). But Conrad is also satirizing the inductive habits fostered by the modern waxwork tableau, something Vanessa Schwartz characterizes as an ability to 'read' intertextually by 'moving not only across media (from newspapers to wax tableaux) but also through shifting modes of perception (from the written word to the three-dimensional wax sculpture)' (Schwartz, 1995: 128). As with the life review, Conrad mocks the notion that an onlooker might succeed in reassembling a coherent narrative from the spectacle's fractured semiotics. Thus, in the first tableau, ironic remarks such as 'Anybody could have noted the subtle change on her features' (*SA* 196) and 'the resemblance of her face with that of her brother grew at every step' (197) serve to parody not only the pseudoscientific anthropometry of Cesare Lombroso but also the superficial epistemology that had authorized *Pearson's Magazine* to declare confidently in 1897: 'there is hardly one in the fifty or so men and women criminals in the Chamber of Horrors whose looks do not stamp them as miscreants' (Howard, 1897: 392). Conrad reiterates this point in the second tableau by presenting Winnie as 'a woman enjoying . . . endless leisure, almost in the manner of a corpse' (*SA* 198), a 'pose of idleness' that is seemingly mirrored by the dead man's own 'attitude of repose' (199). And in the third tableau, which depicts her arrested flight not only through the parlour but also 'through long years' (200), Winnie confronts the dismal prospect of becoming the misunderstood object of a collective gaze: 'The only murderer that would be found in the room when people came to look for Mr. Verloc would be – herself!' (200).

This is exactly what happens when Ossipon arrives at 32 Brett Street. At first, Winnie's ravings lead the anarchist to think that he has blundered into a domestic quarrel in which he risks being 'murdered for mysterious reasons by the couple Verloc' (*SA* 213). He is quickly disabused of this misconception by entering the crime scene, which, as Conrad's awkward use of 'disclosed' (199) in an intransitive sense makes clear, has itself now become a penny gaff or cheap waxwork tableau for paying viewers. Lying in the middle of the floor, Verloc's round hat exemplifies the tableau designer's practice of foregrounding small objects through which spectators could imaginatively enter into the display (Sandberg, 1995: 345):

> But the true sense of the scene he was beholding came to Ossipon through the contemplation of the hat. It seemed an extraordinary thing, an ominous object, a sign. Black, and rim upward, it lay on the floor before the couch as if prepared to receive the contributions of pence from people who would come presently to behold Mr Verloc in the fulness of his domestic ease reposing on a sofa. From the hat the eyes of the robust anarchist wandered to the displaced table, gazed at the broken dish for a time, received a kind of optical shock from observing a white gleam under the imperfectly closed eyelids of the man on the couch. Mr Verloc did not seem so much asleep now as lying down with a bent head and looking insistently at his left breast. And when Comrade Ossipon had made out the handle of the knife he turned away from the glazed door, and retched violently.
>
> (*SA* 213–14)

In this extraordinary passage Conrad acknowledges the spectacle's hyper-realism (Ossipon's convulsion by the 'optical shock' of seeing Verloc's eyes betrays his inability to imagine so lifelike a corpse) even as he insists upon its failure to convey a 'true sense' of what has taken place. Ossipon cynically assumes that Winnie has murdered Verloc from motives of greed and adulterous desire but Conrad's readers know that, on the contrary, she has acted in self-defence, albeit a mistaken belief that the man who intentionally killed her brother was about to turn on her.

The third visual artefact of this overdetermined scene is introduced when Winnie, weighing the implications of her act, confronts for reasons that are not immediately apparent a *woodcut* of a 'gallows' (more accurately, a gibbet):

> Mrs Verloc, who always refrained from looking deep into things, was compelled to look into the very bottom of this thing. She saw there no haunting face, no reproachful shade, no vision of remorse, no sort of ideal conception. She saw there an object. That object was the gallows. Mrs Verloc was afraid of the gallows.
>
> She was terrified of them ideally. Having never set eyes on that last argument of men's justice except in illustrative woodcuts to a certain type of tales, she first saw them erect against a black and stormy background, festooned with chains and human bones, circled about by birds that peck at dead men's eyes.   (*SA* 201)

Whether a memory of Thomas Bewick's often-reproduced 'Gibbet' of 1821 or, as seems more probable, an illustration from a mid-century morality tale, Winnie's woodcut attests to the peculiar power of monochrome shading and simple design to evoke a condemned criminal's end. The popular appeal of even crude broadside woodcuts, something historian Vic Gatrell has termed 'image magic' (Gatrell, 1994: 176), lasted well into the second half of the nineteenth century. Thus Robert Louis Stevenson, a major influence on Conrad, pays tribute to the visual dynamism of this folk art in *Kidnapped* (1886) by having his Highland Rebellion hero David Balfour declare: 'Of all deaths, I would truly like least to die by the gallows; and the picture of that uncanny instrument came into my head with extraordinary clearness (as I had once seen it engraved at the top of a pedlar's ballad)' (Stevenson, 1925: 149). Conrad, too, presents woodcuts as formally superior to photographs in a telling parenthesis in *The Arrow of Gold* when M. George recollects Marseilles during the early years of the Third Republic: '[Don Carlos] caught my eye on that spiritedly composed woodcut. (There were no inane snapshot-reproductions in those days)' (*AG* 8).

The key to the woodcut's appearance at this moment in *The Secret Agent* lies in a statement that Conrad made two years earlier when responding to the inadequacy of newspaper accounts of corpse-strewn battlefields in Manchuria. 'Direct vision of the fact, or the stimulus of a great art,' he wrote, 'can alone make [our imagination] turn and open its eyes' (*NLL* 71). By the logic of this formulation, which implicitly denies photography a documentary or aesthetic value, the woodcut that forcibly wakens Winnie's own long-dormant imagination is not merely the relic of a bygone visual mode but a work of art. Stylized without being stereotyped, it embodies a truly popular culture for Conrad, whose repetition of the word *ideal* serves to highlight Winnie's transition from a superficial worldview based upon 'ideal conception' (*SA* 201) – her naïve attempt to form an 'ideal conception' of a burglar (152), for example, or Stevie's 'ideal conception for the metropolitan police as a sort of benevolent institution for the suppression of evil' (133) – to a properly Modernist moment of self-knowledge in which she finds herself 'terrified . . . ideally' by ideograms of unspeakable fears. This opposition between what might be called mass cultural reification and popular cultural immediacy is signalled even more graphically when Winnie, in a grim parody of pyrography, the pastime of burning images onto wooden blocks that was especially popular among Victorian women, experiences the sensation of having the text of the newspaper cliché '"The drop given was fourteen feet"' (201) physically scorched onto her brain with a hot needle. In a defiant gesture that neatly summarizes *The Secret Agent*'s refusal of the new culture of spectacle, Winnie chooses to throw herself from a passenger ferry, thereby ensuring that her own death will always remain an 'impenetrable mystery', safe from the prying gaze of newspaper readers and visitors to waxwork tableaux.

Justice to the visible universe: *The Nigger of the 'Narcissus'* (1897)

By a coincidence that is seldom pointed out, Conrad's literary career began during what has come to be seen as the *annus mirabilis* of visual culture. *Almayer's Folly* was published in April 1895, just two weeks after the Lumière brothers presented their invention to the Sorbonne in Paris, and *An Outcast of the Islands* appeared in print in March 1896 a few days before the Cinématographe-Lumière began its main London engagement at the Empire Theatre of Varieties on Leicester Square. Conrad's upcoming wedding likely left him little time for such diversions and he could well have missed the *Times*'s inauspicious paragraph on 22 March 1896 on the first public projection of moving pictures in Britain. But he would have returned from his Brittany honeymoon in September that year to find the country in the grip of cinema fever, thanks to a hugely popular film of the Prince of Wales's horse 'Persimmon' winning the Derby in June, a Royal Command Performance in July and ubiquitous booming of a novelty that Birt Acres's Kineopticon, now at Piccadilly Circus, was proclaiming in its programme as 'the sensation of the nineteenth century' (Barnes, 1996–98, 1: 79).

This historical juncture raises a series of questions about the relation between moving pictures and *The Nigger of the 'Narcissus'*, a work that Conrad composed between June 1896 and January 1897 immediately after abandoning *The Rescue* in what can best be described as a state of visual crisis. Of this sudden loss of faith in his ability 'to master both the colours and the shades' of his subject, he later wrote, 'comparison of any page of "The Rescue" with any page of "The Nigger" will furnish an ocular demonstration' (*Res* viii). Though largely absent from school and university curricula today thanks to its offensive treatment of race, *The Nigger of the 'Narcissus'* played a crucial role in establishing Conrad's early reputation. After being serialized in the avant-garde *New Review*, the novel was published in book form in December 1897 and garnered particular approval from the critics for its narrative realism: 'figures that live and move before our eyes' (*The Scotsman*); 'a wonderful picture . . . [whose] vivid colouring bites into the mind of the spectator' (*The Speaker*); 'Never . . . has a storm at sea been so magnificently yet so realistically depicted' (James Payn).[37] '[W]e doubt whether the state of a sailing ship during a storm at sea has ever been described with greater truth and power,' declared the *Daily Chronicle*, and in the *Academy* Israel Zangwill pronounced the novel's 'sea-pictures' to be 'beyond praise' (*CH* 91, 94). Tributes like these lent weight to Conrad's autograph inscription in the fly-leaf of Richard Curle's copy: 'By these pages I stand or fall' (Curle, 1928a: 92).[38]

Conrad could hardly have remained unaware of the arrival of projected motion photography. Resident in or near London and a regular visitor to France, he was ideally placed to follow the emergence of cinema during the early 1890s. In October 1892 Émile Reynaud launched the Théâtre Optique, moving hand-painted pictures that delighted over a million people by the decade's end, and two years later Thomas Edison franchisees in London and Paris opened parlours for the Kinetoscope, a peepshow device of the kind evoked in *Lord Jim* by

Marlow's fantasy of seeing animated figures in the field of an optical toy. Conrad's known movements during these years show him to have been in close proximity to these dramatic developments. In December 1896, he asked Edward Garnett to meet him behind the Palace Theatre of Varieties on Cambridge Circus (*CL* 1: 323), soon to become the American Biograph's London home, and later that month he arrived, hot on the heels of the touring Cinématographe-Lumière, in Cardiff, a city whose summer Art and Industrial Exhibition had featured daily Kineopticon shows. Moreover, in his memoir of Stephen Crane, Conrad describes how the two men strolled through central London in October 1897, a route that would have taken them past billboards for the Palace Theatre's 70 mm film of the view from an express train, before parting in front of 'that monumentally heavy abode of frivolity, the Pavilion' (*LE* 106), that is, the Pavilion Music Hall at Piccadilly Circus, an exhibition space for cinematic devices where Alberto Duran had exhibited his Vivagraph in August the previous year and where Conrad would one day watch Frank Lloyd's filmatization of *Les Miserables* in preparation for his own efforts at screenwriting.[39] Lastly, it is hard to believe that so fervent a patriot would have missed the cinematic event of 1897, the Diamond Jubilee parade of 22 June, whose popularity, according to film historian John Barnes, meant that 'by the end of the year there could hardly have been a person in England who had not seen this historic scene on the screen' (Barnes, 1996–98, 2: 7).

Conrad's friendship with H. G. Wells, especially the timing of their first contact, is no less suggestive. Wells had recently become involved with the new medium by the time that he 'descended from his "Time-Machine" ' to contact the fledgling author, as Conrad told Garnett excitedly in May 1896 (*CL* 1: 281). The previous year, as film pioneer Robert Paul explained in *The Era* on 25 April 1896, Wells and Paul had designed and provisionally patented a cinematic spectacle based on *The Time Machine*, their plan being to seat an audience in mechanically rocked chairs and to project sequences of moving images so as to simulate a journey through time (Barnes, 1996–98, 1: 38–41). One of film history's more famous what-might-have-been incidents, the project ultimately fell through, but nothing would have been more natural than for Wells to enthuse to a fellow writer about the peculiar quality of surrogacy that enabled cinema to mediate directly the sensory experiences to which literature could only allude.

To these circumstantial pieces of evidence can be added Conrad's documented interest in optical entertainments and new technology around the time that he composed *The Nigger of the 'Narcissus'*. In September 1898, he attended a dinner party at the house of Dr John McIntyre at which guests discussed wave theory, listened to a phonograph and tried a Röntgen X-ray machine (*CL* 2: 94–5; Munro, 1931: 113–14). The latter had made its British début in January 1896, enjoying a brief run at Crystal Palace and Olympia while being hailed as the 'New Photography' by an enthusiastic press. A commentator in *Photography* noted in late 1896 that 'the poor x-rays are now being trotted out at every bazaar' (Harding and Popple, 1996: 25), and one year on they were still sufficiently novel to justify a demonstration by James Williamson to Hove Camera Club (Barnes, 1996–98, 2: 93). Although Frederick Karl has described McIntyre as 'one of the first radiologists' (Karl, 1979: 429), the word 'radiologist' was only coined in the mid-1900s, and something of its original identity of optical entertainment still clung to the X-ray machine, as is suggested by the doctor's use of it to entertain visitors and Conrad's description of his host as a 'scientific swell' (*CL* 2: 94). Conrad was similarly well informed about innovations in cinema. In later years, he admitted to having seen 'certain experiments' in sound and colour film (*JCIR* 186).[40]

For many of Conrad's contemporaries, motion photography and X-rays posed a collective challenge to the seeming stability of the visual universe, whose ramifications extended well beyond their initial application as a mode of entertainment and a tool of medical diagnosis. Both raised questions of surveillance and privacy, as illustrated amusingly by the advertisements for 'X-ray proof' underwear (Chanan, 1980: 124), and both, as Richard Crangle observes, 'were perceived to have functions in revelation of the invisible' (Crangle, 1998: 142). X-rays thus made a natural subject for early scientific films such as McIntyre's own *X-Ray Cinematography of a Frog's Legs* (1897) as well as for naughty comedies such as G. A. Smith's *The X-Ray Fiend* (1897) (Barnes, 1996–98, 2: 198–9, 2: 235) and until the grim consequences of exposure to radiation became apparent, several commentators concurred that the discovery of X-rays had, in one journalist's words, 'opened a new and most promising field of scientific research, even suggested a new science, perhaps a new art' (Barnard, 1896: 75). As *The Sketch* asked: 'When practice has brought about perfection, where will the invention stop?' (Harding and Popple, 1996: epigraph). Not only did periodical contributors speculate freely about their potential uses – 'The cinematograph . . . appears about to enter on a path of usefulness the extent and value of which it is impossible to estimate', declared *Chambers's Journal* in May 1900 (Winter, 1900: 391) – they repeatedly pointed out that these new visual technologies had effected a fundamental change in how people looked at the world.[41]

The nature of the epistemological revolution unleashed by the cinema and X-rays was registered with particular sensitivity by the literature of these years. As Simon Popple notes, 'Stories about people recognising missing relatives, or people caught in compromising situations by the camera became the standard plots of fictional stories about the cinema' (Popple, 1996: 101).[42] Fictional treatments of the X-rays likewise shared common features. The protagonist of Grant Allen's short story 'Miss Cayley's Adventures' (1898) relates his discomfort at an old lady who 'peered right through me, as if she were a Röntgen ray' (Allen, 1898: 426) in much the same way as Etchingham Granger, the protagonist of Conrad and Ford's *The Inheritors*, recalls being scrutinized by a sinister politician: 'I seemed to feel his glance bore through the irises of my eyes into the back of my skull . . . as if some incredibly concentrant reflector had been turned on me' (*I* 63). Indeed, Conrad's own exposure to the unnatural perceptual mode of X-rays seems to have left a lasting impression, to judge from his exclamation *à propos* the dreary task of rewriting an accidentally destroyed manuscript: 'Imagine trying to clothe in flesh a naked skeleton, without the faith to help you in the impossible task!' (*CL* 2: 440). In a bold reinterpretation of *Heart of Darkness*, Martine Hennard Dutheil de la Rochère has even proposed that the prominence of metaphors of physical vacuity and transparency in the novella – supreme knowledge, Marlow concludes, is granted during 'that inappreciable moment of time in which we step over the threshold of the invisible' (*Y* 151) – constitutes an attempt to imagine the monstrous body of Belgian colonialism in the disturbing light of X-ray photography.[43]

Given his hostility towards still photography, it is hardly surprising that Conrad's recorded opinions of motion photography were overwhelmingly negative: Vio Allen recalled him telling her that he 'loathed the movies' (Allen, 1967: 86); Muirhead Bone noted his anger at being pestered by a pushy 'kinema operator' (*JCIR* 167); and the portraitist Walter Tittle remembered his subject denouncing Chaplin as unfunny and vulgar before launching into a 'real tirade' against films:

> 'They are absolutely the lowest form of amusement. I hate them!' he said, with quite a considerable show of heat. 'They are stupid, and can never be of real value. The cinema is not a great medium. It merely affords entertainment for people who enjoy sitting with thought utterly suspended and watching a changing pattern flickering before their eyes.'   (*JCIR* 161)

This uncompromising perspective informs, too, the sole reference to cinema by name in Conrad's fictional *œuvre*: the callow and unperceptive magazine-writer in 'The Partner' who betrays his distance from the maritime world of oral storytelling by describing a retired stevedore as keeping 'his eyes on the wall as if not to miss a single movement of a cinematograph picture' (*WT* 93). Like his declaration to the *Boston Evening Telegraph*, 'Before the cinematograph was invented . . . fiction-writers tried to make moving pictures' (*JCIR* 186), Conrad effectively presents literary narrative as historically antecedent and formally superior to motion photography. It is, to be sure, a posture of intransigence that seems to deny outright the idea that early cinema might have been a significant context for *The Nigger of the 'Narcissus'*.

Noting the decision of the Moscow Art Theatre to base a staging of Pushkin's *Boris Godunov* on the cinematograph show's 'staccato rhythm of unrelated items', film historian Ian Christie has asked: 'How many other works and projects of the 1900s may have been influenced in similar ways, without leaving any evidence of the fact?' (Christie, 1994: 11). Certainly, it would be reasonable to expect to find the traces of moving pictures in Conrad's writing. It is, after all, hardly credible that an author who modelled his fiction, explicitly as well as implicitly, on particular kinds of visual experience and who, as we have seen, attributed epistemological and aesthetic values to photography, moving panoramas, life reviews and tableaux, could have remained unaffected by one of the most momentous innovations in visual culture of his lifetime. For instance, it is surely more than coincidence that Conrad chose to open 'The Return', a story he wrote in summer 1897, with a description of a train arriving at a station that could serve as a thumbnail sketch of the Lumières' much imitated film *Arrival of a Train at Ciotat Station* (1895). Even so, the task of reconstructing the specific influence of early cinema on *The Nigger of the 'Narcissus'* remains daunting, not least because Conrad's relation to motion photography was both more intimate than he was willing to admit and more complicated than the condescension or outright antipathy towards cinema of Modernist writers such as D. H. Lawrence or the anti-Modernist critic Karl Radek, who once notoriously dismissed *Ulysses* as 'a heap of dung, crawling with worms, photographed by a cinema apparatus' (Radek, 1977: 153).

A rare indication of Conrad's indebtedness to cinematographic technology is to be found in the manuscript notes for a private lecture entitled 'Author and Cinematograph' that he gave at the offices of his American publisher during a visit to New York in May 1923.[44] Its central thesis, he explained in a letter to Eric Pinker, was that 'the (apparently) extravagant lines of the imaginative literary art [are] based fundamentally on scenic motion, like a camera; with this addition that for certain purposes the artist is a much more subtle and complicated machine than a camera, and with a wider range, if in the visual effects less precise' (*LL* 2: 302). In the lecture, Conrad gave a crucial inflection to this by now familiar assertion of the superiority of literary art as a 'machine' for communicating 'scenic motion'. He began by offering a definition of the novelist's aim as 'to present humanity on the background of the changing aspects of nature and a series of acted scenes', a formula that he had used on previous occasions and that, like his identification of 'visuality' as a 'fundamental condition' of all great fiction, would have surprised few in the audience. But in clarifying the nature of literary artistry, he made a far more revealing admission: 'Trusting then in your sense not to condemn me I will repeat that fundamentally the creator in letters aims at a moving picture' (Schwab, 1965: 346). Lest it be objected that Conrad's description of literary art as quintessentially cinematic was merely a concession to the enthusiasms of his transatlantic public or the American journalists who had eagerly sought his opinion of a medium that was growing in status, it should be stressed that this address was given in private, not to Hollywood people, but to a thoroughly bookish audience of editors and publishers. (His public comments upon cinema during this tour were, in any case, equivocating when not actually critical.) Conrad was, in other words, under no pressure to recognize the aesthetic importance of film. Rather, his startling claim to have used cinema as a model invites us to rethink his much-analysed promise 'to make you *see*' (*NN* x) in terms of the challenge posed to literary representation by moving pictures.

Conrad's brushes with the world of spectacular theatre further suggest that he was aware of the new representational demands being made by audiences in the era of motion photography. Sometime prior to 1900, he recalled, Stephen Crane and he had begun collaborating on a play, only to abandon the project after becoming frustrated with the difficulty of presenting the protagonists standing by their dead ponies after a 'furious ride': 'A boundless plain in the light of a sunset could be got into a back-cloth, I admitted; but I doubted whether we could induce the management of any London theatre to deposit two stuffed horses on its stage' (*LE* 115–16). As well as fuelling such demands for dramatic verisimilitude, cinema was uniquely suited to conveying the spectacle and the sensation of movement, whether realistic or fantastic, and although the chase sequence did not establish itself as a pre-eminently cinematic form until Edwin Porter's hit melodrama *The Great Train Robbery* (1903) and Biograph's *The Escaped Lunatic* (1904), this future was already anticipated by the Kinetoscope film *Chinese Laundry Scene* (1894), G. A. Smith's

The Miller and the Sweep (1898) and James Williamson's *Stop Thief!* (1901) (Musser, 1991: 259–60).[45] For Conrad and Crane to find themselves wrestling with the problem of depicting a 'furious ride' thus had every-thing to do with the emergence of new cinematic genres and standards of realism. 'Recalling now those earnestly fantastic discussions,' Conrad declared, 'it occurs to me that Crane and I must have been uncon-sciously penetrated by a prophetic sense of the technique and of the very spirit of film-plays, of which even the name was unknown then to the world' (*LE* 116).

Whether the culmination of decades of optical innovation or, as Conrad's remark disingenuously implies, a wholly new development, projected motion photography reconfirmed the power of seeing as never before, dangling the prospect of unimagined visual pleasures before a public which, as Michael Booth remarks, 'craved concrete images of historical and contemporary reality . . . . actualised and made visually familiar and accessible' (Booth, 1981: 14). Discussing a proposal for a short musical with a maritime theme, Conrad recognized the pub-lic appetite for spectacular realism that had led the Drury Lane Theatre to construct a life-size deck of a sinking ship for its staging of Cecil Raleigh's *The Price of Peace* in 1899.[46] To create a 'purely animated pic-ture' of everyday life at sea, he explained, 'The representation of a ship's forecastle-head trois-quarts to the audience would have to be contrived somehow – *as near to truth as possible*' (*CL* 4: 352, emphasis added). It is as the heir to this tradition of visual spectacle, therefore, as well as an amalgam of old and new technologies, that cinema should be under-stood by those who would isolate its influence on *The Nigger of the 'Narcissus'* (also a drama featuring a half-submerged ship).

As an early response to projected motion photography, *The Nigger of the 'Narcissus'* must be situated, above all, in a climate of radical uncer-tainty. Cinema in 1896 and 1897 bore only a faint resemblance to the stable, conventional, and primarily narrative system of entertainment into which it would evolve. Mostly single-shot, less than a minute long and reliant on natural lighting, the features of the Victorian 'cinema of attractions' were overwhelmingly presentational, their subject matter consisting for the most part of trains, boxing matches, street scenes, children playing, military parades, and the like (Gunning, 1990). Touring projectors, not dedicated buildings, were the basis for exhibition, with billings typically being headed by the name Cinématographe, Theatrograph, Biograph, or a rival apparatus, rather than by the title of a specific film. In their temporary home in the music hall, moving pictures were usually combined with magic lantern slides and accompanied by a spoken commentary. Not only was cinema's possible evolution into what Christian Metz calls a 'machine for telling stories' barely considered at this stage (Metz, 1974: 93), its future, as another film historian has noted, seemed almost entirely unclear:

> Would the new technical marvel become an instrument for instruction? For entertainment? For communication? For news? Would the cinema be a scientific instrument? Would it be seen in the home? Or only by individuals? Would it be the opening, closing, or starring act in theatres? Would it be absorbed into existing entertainments to become simply another piece of technical stagecraft for dramatists? For magicians? For lectures? Who would make the films? Professionals? Photographers? Amateurs? Would it become a mass experience with the appearance of a 'Kodak' for moving pictures that could claim, 'You press the button, we do the rest'?   (Rossell, 1998: 134)

The action of *The Nigger of the 'Narcissus'* centres on the crew of a sailing ship on a journey from Bombay to London, their exposure to the psychological strain of a dying West Indian crewmate named James Wait, the machinations of a villainous labour agitator named Donkin, and a terrific storm off the Cape of Good Hope during which the ship capsizes. Gripping enough for an audience of non-sailors, Conrad underscores the fact that these events also present a mesmerizing spectacle for the protagonists themselves. 'Twenty-six pairs of eyes' (*NN* 27) watch the tug-boat pull away from the *Narcissus* in Bombay in a scene of visual wonder that prefigures the extraordinary moment at the storm's climax when, we are told, 'Perhaps for the first time in the history of the merchant service the watch, told to go below, did not leave the deck, as if compelled to remain there by the fascination of a venomous violence' (55). At the dawn of a day that few of them expected to see, the men turn their eyes on cue 'to the eastward', the heroic helmsman Singleton remains at his post 'with open and lifeless eyes', and Captain Allistoun stares 'unblinking' into the rising sun (84). When the captain refuses to allow Wait to report for duty, a ploy which would entitle the latter to wages for the entire voyage, he finds himself confronted by a crowd of onlookers whose 'row of eyes gleaming' (119) coalesce into the mutinous gaze of a 'staring crowd' (120). Responding in kind, Allistoun exercises his natural authority by meeting the 'eager looks of excited men who watched him far off' (119) with a 'quiet and penetrating gaze' (119) and by publicly humiliating Donkin with the same 'worn, steely gaze, that by an universal illusion looked straight into every individual pair of the twenty pairs of eyes before his face' (133). As with the novel's many other scenes of spectatorship – the officers watching 'the weather and the ship as men on shore watch the momentous chances of fortune' (50), the Scandinavians staring as their crewmates squabble with 'the dumfounded and distracted aspect of men gazing at a cataclysm' (129), and Donkin's 'scrutinizing watchfulness' (151) at the dying Wait's bedside – Conrad continually reminds his reader that all the events being narrated have already unfolded before a keenly attentive audience.

Despite drawing loosely on his experiences aboard a ship of the same name in 1884, Conrad's first extended treatment of life at sea was a condition of England novel, a condition he saw as marked by what one critic has termed 'the advent of mass society with all its attendant ethical and political ills' (McDonald, 1997: 59). Correctly anticipating that *The Nigger of the 'Narcissus'* would fail to sell in large numbers, Conrad nonetheless told Garnett that 'the thing – precious as it is to me – is trivial enough on the surface to have some charms for the man in the street' (*CL* 1: 321). It is a significant detail. *Pace* the *Spectator's* opinion that Conrad's choice of themes and methods 'debar him from attaining a wide popularity' (*CH* 93), the novel not only engaged with the newest developments in visual culture at the level of narrative form and prose style, it addressed two topics that, having featured regularly in magic lantern shows, stereoscopic views and moving panoramas, were now enjoying a vogue with the 'man in the street' watching early cinema films.

The first of these was the representation, albeit offensive and stereotyped, of people of colour: *The Picaninny's Bath* was a popular item on the Edison Biograph's new programme in March 1897; the Lumières' British catalogue for 1897 included the film *Negro Street Dancers*; and by September of that year the Cinématographe-Lumière was exhibiting a series of 'exotics' featuring colonial black African subjects (Barnes, 1996–98, 2: 144). Minstrelsy, too, was a favoured topic of early cinema, forming the subject of a French film being shown in Britain by June 1896 and James Wait's 'frantic dumb show' (*NN* 151) and 'rolling eyes' (152), which appear in mid-air 'glimmer[ing] white, and big, and staring' (34) and 'blaz[e] up . . . like two lamps' (155), bear more than a passing resemblance to Mr Chirgwin, 'The White-Eyed Kaffir', a music hall comedian whose recorded image had been delighting cinema audiences since September 1896 (Barnes, 1996–98, 1: 118).

The second topic was the sea. Waves made excellent material for early films even when projected too slowly, and reviewers and audiences almost unanimously pronounced *Sea Bathing* the most successful item on the first Cinématographe-Lumière programme. 'Nothing could have been more realistic than the breakers rolling in', enthused the *St Paul's Magazine*, whilst the *British Journal of Photography* declared it 'the *piece de resistance*', a subject depicted 'so faithfully to life that one "longed to be there"' (Barnes, 1996–98, 1: 94, 1: 98). As film historian Thelma Gutsche remarks: 'To have captured the movement of so fluid a medium as water for the purposes of reproduction seems to have struck the public as peculiarly wonderful' (Gutsche, 1972: 14).[47] *The Nigger of the 'Narcissus'* attests to Conrad's own painstaking rendering of the play of light on waves – 'the blackness of the water was streaked with trails of light which undulated gently on slight ripples, similar to filaments that float rooted to the shore' (*NN* 15) – and, above all, of the sea's ability to present viewers with 'a strange optical delusion' (*MS* 145), as he elsewhere described the silent plunge of a swamped ship. The *Daily Telegraph* voiced a consensus among reviewers when it praised the novel's evocation of the 'changing aspects and beautiful metamorphoses' of the sea (*CH* 87).

Since the first cinema audiences found the sight of stormy seas particularly compelling, the insistently monochromatic world of *The Nigger of the 'Narcissus'* in which 'the stars, coming out, gleamed over an inky sea that, speckled with foam, flashed back at them the evanescent and pale light of a dazzling whiteness born from the black turmoil of the waves' (*NN* 77) could well have recalled a prospect of the sea glimpsed, not from the deck of any ship, but in the darkness of a music hall. At the second public projection in Britain on 24 January 1896 Birt Acres's *Rough Sea at Dover* received an ecstatic reception, with the *Amateur Photographer* reporting that 'the final slide – a study of waves breaking on a stone pier – was simply wonderful in its effect' (Barnes, 1996–98, 1: 66). At the Broadway début of Edison's Vitascope on 23 April, one witness recorded, the scene of storm-tossed waves was 'totally unlike anything an audience had ever before seen in a theatre. When it was thrown upon the screen the house went wild' (Barnes, 1996–98, 1: 142). The *Era* greeted Robert Paul's popular film *Sea Cave Near Lisbon* with similar enthusiasm in October 1896: 'The foam-crested waves rush into the recesses of the rocks, clouds of spray are hurled into space, and the grandeur and beauty of the scenes are remarkable' (Barnes, 1996–98, 1: 131). 'Animated photography is perhaps better at the portrayal of the multifarious movements of water than of anything else', declared Cecil Hepworth, and many years later the film pioneer could still remember vividly his amazement at *Sea Cave Near Lisbon* (Barnes, 1996–98, 4: 208).

The narrative basis of *The Nigger of the 'Narcissus'*, a voyage during which, as one reviewer complained, 'Nothing particular happens'

(*CH* 89), also had a corollary in contemporary cinema and the environment of visual entertainment from which it emerged in the 1890s.

Filmmakers had effectively marketed virtual travel well before Hale's Tours, a simulated journey in a replica railway carriage, was launched at the 1904 World's Fair in St Louis; and filmic boat trips led the evolution of a well-established moving panorama entertainment into the new cinematic genre of 'phantom rides'.[48] The Lumières' *Grand Canal, Venice* (1895), Paul-Acres's *Oxford & Cambridge University Boat Race* (1895) and Birt Acres's travelling shot in *Practising for the Oxford and Cambridge University Boat Race* (1897) were quickly followed by Edison's *Going Through the Tunnel* (1898) and Paul's *A Phantom Ride* (1897). As Wells and Paul had intuitively grasped, projected motion photography was exceptionally well suited to conveying the experience of travel. Thus a contemporary film poster advertised a series of short features: 'You can MEET THE PARIS EXPRESS, at CALAIS . . . . Then back to WESTMINSTER . . . . after that to HAMPSTEAD HEATH . . . then with the crowd to THE DERBY – A Grand Race!!' (Low and Manvell, 1948: 11). The public's enthusiasm for virtual sea travel was unbounded. Combining projected film with compressed air and a moving platform, Louis Régnault's 'Maerorama', a visual entertainment that opened in Paris in 1898, created a simulacrum of ocean travel so convincing as to induce seasickness in some visitors, and during the Paris Exposition of 1900 huge crowds flocked to the Maréorama, a steamship simulator featuring a reconstructed ship's deck and a complex system of hydraulic pistons and rolled panoramas (Schwartz, 1998: 170–3; Oettermann, 1997: 177–81).

The reach and appeal of such simulacra of maritime experience are discernable in contemporary responses to *The Nigger of the Narcissus*. The *Daily Telegraph*, while faulting the novel for recording 'in infinite detail . . . what sky and sea were doing', explained that Conrad's sailors 'stand out with vivid and lifelike presentment; we know them all as though we, too, had partaken in the lengthy cruise' (*CH* 86–7). The *Saturday Review* declared of the storm sequence: 'We know nothing else so vivid and so convincing in contemporary fiction as the way in which the reader is forced, along with the crew, to hang on for dear life to the perilously slanting deck' (*CH* 99–100). Indeed, Conrad would invoke this fascination with simulating life at sea in *The Shadow-Line* by having his narrator liken the experience of being becalmed to a theatrical or proto-cinematic entertainment: 'I remain on deck, of course, night and day, and the nights and days wheel over us in succession . . . . The effect is curiously mechanical; the sun climbs and descends, the night swings over our heads as if somebody below the horizon were turning a crank' (*SL* 97).

By the time Heinemann published *The Nigger of the 'Narcissus'* sailing ships at dock had already been the subject of successful films. The 60 mm Gaumont-Demeny Chronophotographe had exhibited an item in this class at its premiere in April 1897, and films recording the experience of ships in storms soon followed, including James White and Fred Blechynden's *S.S. 'Coptic' Running Against the Storm* in February 1898, W. K. -L. Dickson's *Tug in a Heavy Sea* in March 1898, White's *S.S. 'Deutschland' in a Storm* in 1902 and an early Kinora film whose exact date is unknown (Musser, 1991: 111, 198; Anthony, 1996: 34–5). The subject's intrinsically spectacular nature would even be thematized in Edison's *A Storm at Sea* (1900), a film advertised as 'the most wonderful storm picture ever photographed', in which two cameramen stand at the rail of a ship as mountainous waves sweep past, almost as if they, too, are watching a film show. In 1897, however, life aboard a ship at sea had not yet been captured by cinema.[49] For the brief period of Conrad's writing of *The Nigger of the 'Narcissus'*, therefore, the visual spectacle presented by this subject still belonged exclusively to the imaginative artist:

> The ship began to dip into a southwest swell, and the softly luminous sky of low latitudes took on a harder sheen from day to day above our heads . . . . The sunshine gleamed cold on the white curls of black waves . . . . She drove to and fro in the unceasing endeavour to fight her way through the invisible violence of the winds: she pitched headlong into dark smooth hollows; she struggled upwards over the snowy ridges of great running seas; she rolled, restless, from side to side, like a thing in pain.   (*NN* 49)

> At night, through the impenetrable darkness of earth and heaven, broad sheets of flame waved noiselessly; and for half a second the becalmed craft stood out with its masts and rigging, with every sail and every rope distinct and black in the centre of a fiery outburst, like a charred ship enclosed in a globe of fire.   (*NN* 104)

At the same time, the phenomenological universe of *The Nigger of the 'Narcissus'*, in which thoughts are said to cross men's faces 'like the shadow of a travelling cloud over the light of a peaceful sea' (*NN* 114), is markedly reminiscent of early cinematic experience. As in *The Shadow-Line*, even the passage of time takes on an almost hallucinatory quality: 'The days raced after one another, brilliant and quick like the flashes of a lighthouse, and the nights, eventful and short, resembled fleeting dreams' (*NN* 30). From its opening vision of 'silhouettes of moving men . . . without relief, like figures cut out of sheet tin' (3) to the vignette of Singleton standing 'watchful and motionless in the wild saraband of dancing shadows' (26), the novel offers an extended meditation upon the aesthetic and philosophical qualities of light and dark, one of whose premises is that the visual faculty by itself cannot give a truthful or complete account of the material world.[50] When the first English lighthouse finally appears, it merges with the lanterns of a fishing fleet to give the illusion of being 'an enormous riding light burning above a vessel of fabulous dimensions' (162), just as the very stones of the Tower of London seem to 'stir in the play of light' (172) for the dazzled sailors emerging from the gloomy Board of Trade offices into bright sunshine.

The numerous references to ghosts in *The Nigger of the 'Narcissus'*, in which a 'black phantom' (*NN* 151) haunts 'a shadowy ship manned by a crew of Shades' (173) under the authority of a 'phantom above a grave' (30), also have filmic echoes.[51] Maxim Gorky was not alone in thinking that cinema's first subjects resembled spectral shadows; the fairground exhibitor Randall Williams reinvented his celebrated Ghost Show as a cinematic 'Phantoscopical Exhibition' in late 1896, and the double-exposed 'ghost' quickly became a staple of trick films such as G. A. Smith's *Photographing a Ghost* (1897) (Harding and Popple, 1996: 5). Likewise, contemporary discussion of the *unheimlich* nature of cinematic light, or the peculiar qualities of X-rays that Sylvanus Thompson detailed in his *Light Visible and Invisible* (1897), could have inspired Conrad's descriptions of 'rays of sinister light [cast] between the hills of steep, rolling waves' (*NN* 53), the 'invisible sun' with its 'blurred stain of rayless light' (104), the 'lifeless flames without rays' (128) in the forecastle lamps, or the vessel herself: 'In the magnificence of the phantom rays the ship appeared pure like a vision of ideal beauty, illusive like a tender dream of serene peace. And nothing in her was real, nothing was distinct and solid but the heavy shadows that filled her decks with their unceasing and noiseless stir . . .' (145).

Conrad stages the class-political conflict at the heart of *The Nigger of the 'Narcissus'* as an allegorical clash between two visual cultures. In the same way as Winnie Verloc flees the easy yet bankrupt representational logic of the life review and the modern waxwork tableau in *The Secret Agent*, the crew of the *Narcissus* are portrayed as the inheritors of an organic popular culture now under siege, her imaginative identification with the older woodcut print finding a corollary in their enthusiasm for traditional sailors' songs, jigs and tall tales. The maritime community, whose unity derives from its 'dependence upon the invisible' (*NN* 146) and preference for symbolism and ritual over the explicitness that Conrad once described as 'destroying all illusion' (Curle, 1928b: 143), faces its sternest challenge, not in the ocean's elemental fury, but in the predations of what might be called a scopic régime of modernity: a mode of vision whose facile habits of interpretation and superficial exposition make it the natural tool of cynics and interlopers. Conrad defined the novel as a study in microcosm of 'the psychology of the mass' (*LE* 95) but, like the more famous contemporary students of this phenomenon, Gustave Le Bon and John Hobson, his focus might more accurately be said to be the *manipulation* of the mass. Wait and Donkin's skilful deception of the crew is thus 'a manifestation grand and incomprehensible that at times inspired a wondering awe' by which, quite simply, 'Falsehood triumphed' (138).

In this, as the narrative makes abundantly clear, vision plays a pivotal role. Each sailor's individuality finds expression in an unseen spectacle that is replayed in his mind's eye: the Russian Finn 'contemplating, perhaps, one of those weird visions that haunt the men of his race' (*NN* 13); young Creighton's daydream of a girl in a country lane under 'the caressing blueness of an English sky' (21); the boatswain's 'acute and fleeting visions of his old woman and the youngsters in a moorland village' (93); and the men's contemplation, as they cling to the capsized ship, of 'known faces and familiar things . . . . the aspect of forgotten shipmates . . . . the scorching sunshine of calm days at sea' (78). Even Wait, who, for all his grievous failings, never ceases to be a sailor, sees in his delirium 'strange things that resembled houses, trees, people, lampposts' (113). And if the sole exception to this principle is the wretched Donkin, whose prosaic materialism apparently does not allow of an inner life, it finds its supreme exponent in his antithesis, Singleton. A visual repository of maritime experience, the old sailor impresses his shipmates with having 'a sharper vision and a clearer knowledge' as befits one who has 'already seen all' (129). In portraying his intense absorption by one of Bulwer Lytton's stories of aristocratic life, Conrad not only equates the helmsman's visual integrity with imaginative literature but implicitly suggests that novels such as *The Nigger of the 'Narcissus'* are uniquely capable of mediating between the far-removed worlds of land and sea:

Or are the beings who exist beyond the pale of life stirred by [Lytton's] tales as by an enigmatical disclosure of a resplendent world

that exists within the frontier of infamy and filth, within that border
of dirt and hunger, of misery and dissipation, that comes down on all
sides to the water's edge of the incorruptible ocean, and is the only
thing they know of life, the only thing they see of surrounding land –
those life-long prisoners of the sea? (*NN* 6–7)

In stark contrast to these private epiphanies, Donkin and Wait are
repeatedly characterized in terms of public performance. A ' "Reg'lar
Punch and Judy show" ' (*NN* 16) to his mates, the scrawny agitator
reminds the narrator variously of a 'consummate artist' (100) and a sort
of magician's assistant who 'appear[s] alone before the master as though
he had come up through the deck' (135). Meanwhile, in one of Conrad's
most dismally racist formulations, Wait is said to present 'the repulsive
mask of a nigger's soul' (18) and 'a fantastic and grimacing mask' (151).
Their joint connivance, the reader comes to appreciate, is a kind of
show that distracts the members of the crew from their duties even as it
draws them together in a thoroughly spurious and reprehensible solidarity (that of mutineers) which jeopardizes both the ship's safety and
their own. It is interesting to note, therefore, that Donkin, whom the
sailors nickname 'Whitechapel' and 'East End', hails from a district that
was proving extremely popular for early cinema shows – in 1896 Robert
Paul's Theatrograph was playing at the Paragon music hall on Mile End
Road and at Wonderland on Whitechapel Road – at a time when middle-
class commentators were expressing unease at the social unruliness,
what Simon Popple calls 'a growing tendency towards a rejection of the
values of class and duty' (Popple, 1996: 104), that such shows appeared
to encourage among working-class audiences. For critics like Robert
Buchanan, who denounced the popularity of Kipling's Cockney verse as
a symptom of creeping vulgarity (Buchanan, 1899: 783), Donkin's dialect
was synecdochic of the new and debased culture of the music hall.[52]
Appropriately, then, Conrad has Donkin takes charge of Wait like a professional entertainer, whether a cinematograph lecturer-commentator or
a magic lantern exhibitor:

[Crewmen] stood astride the doorstep discoursing, or sat in silent
couples on his sea-chest; while against the bulwark along the spare
topmast, three or four stared meditatively; with their simple faces lit
up by the projected glare of Jimmy's lamp. . . . Donkin officiated. He
had the air of a demonstrator showing a phenomenon, a manifestation bizarre, simple and meritorious that, to the beholders, should be
a profound and an everlasting lesson. (*NN* 105)

The balefully narcotic qualities of the visual culture personified by Donkin are confirmed shortly after when 'an addled vision of bright outlines' makes the *Narcissus*'s evangelizing cook feel 'delighted, frightened, exalted – as on that evening . . . when as a young man he had – through keeping bad company – became intoxicated in an East-end music-hall' (115).

This imposture, which is, fundamentally, a visual con (Wait acts the part of an invalid, Donkin that of a long-suffering patriot and labour advocate), suffers a double defeat at the hands of the *Narcissus*'s embattled crew. Most obviously, Allistoun, the ship's titular head, reasserts the superior faculty of discernment required by a master mariner when he declares contemptuously to Wait, ' "You have been shamming sick . . . . Why, anybody can see that" ' (*NN* 120), a phrase that precisely echoes the malingerer's earlier admission, ' "I am as well as ever" ', and Donkin's reply, ' "In course . . . any one can see that" ' (111). More subtly, the duo's faith in their power to create a simulacrum of actuality for their own purposes receives a fatal blow from Singleton, the novel's ultimate bearer of authority, who quietly identifies the truth behind what Wait represents as infirmity and what Allistoun dismisses (in front of the men, at least) as dissembling: the mortal illness that Wait believes himself to be faking is, in fact, real. When Wait dies following the appearance of land, Singleton's verdict delivers, in turn, a final vindication of traditional nautical wisdom in this contested realm of the visual: 'the old seaman became quite cheery and garrulous, explaining and illustrating from the stores of experience how, in sickness, the sight of an island (even a very small one) is generally more fatal than the view of a continent' (156).

In a groundbreaking study of *The Nigger of the 'Narcissus'*, Peter D. McDonald has argued persuasively that Conrad planned the novel as a bid to secure the endorsement of William Henley, conservative editor of the *New Review* and a 'symbolic banker' of literary capital (McDonald, 1997: 31). If Henley's patronage was really as crucial as McDonald claims, we can be confident of Conrad having read and taken to heart the Henley circle's *ex cathedra* pronouncement on motion photography, which was delivered by O. Winter in the *New Review* of February 1896. Titled simply 'The Cinématographe', the article polemicizes vigorously against the notion that M. Lumière's 'ingenious toy' might have aesthetic value. Far from achieving verisimilitude, Winter argued, film's putative realism was inherently false and constituted no more than a 'mechanical and intimate correspondence with truth'; lacking the designing imagination of an artist and being fatally 'incapable of selection', cinema could only ever present the viewer with a barrage of undifferentiated and therefore meaningless visual data (Harding and Popple, 1996: 13–15). Winter ostentatiously proclaimed his conservative loyalties through disparaging references to Zola, modern journalism, popular novels and even the Lumière films themselves: the subject of *Arrival of a Train at Ciotat Station* was a 'common drama of luggage and fatigue'; *Workers Leaving the Lumière Factory* depicted 'a mob happy in its release'; and the children frolicking in *Sea Bathing* were 'a crowd of urchins'. And yet what clearly disconcerted the would-be man of letters most was not the camera's 'fecklessly impartial eye' and the mechanical gimmickry that it shared with chronophotography, phonographs and the X-ray machine, but the palpable authority of images that could make the 'ignorant' spectator gasp: ' "Ain't it lifelike!" ' (Harding and Popple, 1996: 14–15). It is a blanket denial of cinema's value as documentary or pedagogical representation that Conrad would echo until the very end of his life. As he told Walter Tittle:

> There is no value in a gesture except at full speed. I like to see a blow delivered in boxing, but I hate to see it analysed. As for golf, no two swings are ever alike, anyway. One kind of motion picture might be of some value if the producers would not spoil it. I have seen several so-called educational films that pretended to show a process of manufacture, beginning with the raw material and ending with a finished product. But no stage of the thing was ever completed. As soon as I began to be interested the scene would invariably change, skipping most essential steps in the sequence of production, and taking the thing up again at an advanced stage. It was most amazing, maddening, and not in the least informing. (*JCIR* 161)

This notion of cinematic spectacle as a debasement of genuine art forms a central strand of Conrad's discussion of aesthetics in the Preface to *The Nigger of the 'Narcissus'*, an essay that he drafted after finishing the novel and that was published in the *New Review* in December 1897. Too familiar to require paraphrasing in full, Conrad's manifesto rests upon the unstated premise that modern art (specifically, fiction) now has to justify the visual truth of its representations. Art, Conrad declares, 'may be defined as a single-minded attempt to render the highest kind of justice to the visible universe, by bringing to light the truth, manifold and one, underlying its every aspect' (*NN* vii). He contrasts this endeavour to a wholly inadequate, realist kind of fidelity: 'the unveiling of one of those heartless secrets which are called the Laws of Nature' (xi–xii).

Unlike the scientist or philosopher, the artist responds to the 'enigmatical spectacle' (vii) of life by delving into 'that part of our nature . . . necessarily kept out of sight' (viii), thereby recovering 'a glimpse of the truth for which you have forgotten to ask' (x). In turn, Conrad's claim in 'Author and Cinematograph', that the written word possesses 'a strange power both *in its shape and in its sound* of suggestion which [cinema and the stage] somehow miss' (346, emphasis added), seems to have originated in his assertion in the Preface: 'it is only through an unremitting never-discouraged care for *the shape and ring of sentences* that an approach can be made to plasticity, to colour, and that the light of magic suggestiveness may be brought to play for an evanescent instant over the commonplace surface of words' (*NN* ix, emphasis added). Likewise, his definition of the artist's aim in the manuscript of the Preface as being 'to find . . . in the aspects of [changing] matter and in the [flashing] facts of life what of each is fundamental' (Smith, 1966: 35) finds an echo in his subsequent condemnation of cinemagoers for being content to watch 'a changing pattern flickering before their eyes' (*JCIR* 161). Here and elsewhere, Conrad revisits both the argument and the terminology of Winter's review of the Cinématographe-Lumière.

Conrad's emphasis in the Preface upon visual experience – fiction's 'beholders' (*NN* x) and art's duty to 'compel men . . . to glance for a moment at the surrounding vision of form and colour, of sunshine and shadows' (xii) – certainly becomes less mysterious when restored to the context of early cinema. The brevity of films in 1896–97, the transience of performances and even the opinion of observers such as Cecil Hepworth that 'the present boom in these animated palsy-scopes cannot last for ever', all throw into sharp relief Conrad's call for a representation of 'what is enduring and essential' (vii), an art whose 'effect endures forever' (viii) and qualities that are 'permanently enduring' (viii), just as his vignette of watching 'the motions of a labourer in a distant field' during an 'idle hour' (xi) recalls the Cinématographe's display of 'the actions of a man at work' in April 1896 as well as the numerous films of 1897 that featured men ploughing, felling trees, sawing wood and shoeing horses (Barnes, 1996–98, 1: 226, 1: 101).[53]

Jonathan Crary has suggested that early cinema was regarded as 'an extension of existing forms of verisimilitude' and 'a *validation* of the authenticity of the perceptual disorientations that increasingly constituted social and subjective experience' (Crary, 1999: 344–5, emphasis in original). However, this may be something of an overstatement since these years also saw the development of a position deeply hostile towards the new medium. Indeed, Winter's denigration of cinema as a kind of aesthetic false consciousness – a statement of Henleyite orthodoxy that has far-reaching implications for Conrad's treatment of the visual sense in *The Nigger of the 'Narcissus'* – is recognizably the first in a long line of polemics against cinema as *lacking* verisimilitude. Even the humorous contributor to *Chambers's Journal* in June 1900 who declared that 'these strangely fascinating pictures . . . record life and motion so vividly that they seem to represent an opening in the canvas through which we look on the real thing rather than pictures' also felt compelled to acknowledge: 'So much has been said of the occasions when the animatograph does not tell the truth, the whole truth and nothing but the truth, that the result may have been to convey an exaggerated notion of its capacity for setting forth the thing that is not' (Cook, 1900: 487, 489). Seen in this light, the Preface to *The Nigger of the 'Narcissus'*, a work that marks the threshold of Conrad's major phase, takes on the rather different status of a literary counter-manifesto, as it were, to Year One of the New Photography.

The intersections between Conrad's literary project and popular visual entertainment at the level of theme, narrative and lexical style find iconic expression in *The Nigger of the 'Narcissus'*, above all, in the character of Donkin, who represented for the Henley circle what McDonald calls 'modernity in its most repellent incarnation' (McDonald, 1997: 62). Donkin's presence, like that of the communist photographer in *Nostromo*, serves as a warning of the danger posed to the crew's robust individualism by a new kind of mass experience; this, perhaps, is the real albeit unintended significance of the 'profound and . . . everlasting lesson' (*NN* 105) given by his exhibition of Wait. Certainly, Conrad would return on numerous occasions to the incompatibility of these two kinds of visual fidelity, one documentary and 'realist', the other selective and imaginative. In *Heart of Darkness*, the treacherous shallows of the Congo lead Marlow to reflect upon the epistemological distinction between 'the mere incidents of the surface' and the 'inner truth' (*Y* 93), a point that Conrad reiterated even more forcefully in *A Personal Record*: 'And what is a novel if not a conviction of our fellow-men's existence strong enough to take upon itself a form of imagined life clearer than reality and whose accumulated verisimilitude of selected episodes puts to shame the pride of documentary history?' (*PR* 15). In a move with which we will become increasingly familiar as we turn now to his treatment of tourism, advertising and magazine fiction, Conrad defines his literary project in opposition to popular culture's core features – in this case, the distortion and spurious plenitude (as he saw it) of contemporary visual entertainment – even as he seeks to counter its ever-expanding reach with his own attempt to render 'the highest kind of justice to the visible universe' (*NN* vii).

2
Tourism

Between the five of us there was the strong bond of the sea, and also the fellowship of the craft, which no amount of enthusiasm for yachting, cruising, and so on can give, since one is only the amusement of life and the other is life itself.

'Youth' (*Y* 3)

The man Marlow and I came together in the casual manner of those health-resort acquaintances which sometimes ripen into friendships.

Author's Note, *Youth and Other Stories* (*Y* vi)

Only Max Beerbohm could have imagined Conrad on a beach. In his 1921 cartoon, he has the monocled novelist pose in a dandyish summer suit while watching a snake slither through the eye-socket of a skull on a deserted stretch of sand. 'What a charming beach!' Conrad muses grimly. 'One has the illusion that here one could be always almost merry!'[1] Beerbohm titled the caricature 'Somewhere in the Pacific' but 'Conrad on the Beach' would have been even better since the joke draws its force in part from the irreconcilability of Conrad and the seaside. By the end of the nineteenth century, cheap rail tickets and shorter working hours had transformed Britain's seaside resorts into familiar spaces of popular culture that offered visitors not just swimming and sailing but musical shows, ornamental gardens, fairground rides and the latest innovation in visual entertainment, moving pictures. As Conrad informed Alfred Knopf in 1913, even the herring port where he had first set foot on English soil was 'Now [a] rather fashionable sea-side place' (*CL* 5: 280). Like Lowestoft, popular resorts such as Margate, where Adolf and Winnie Verloc honeymoon in *The Secret Agent*, and Brighton, where the scheming governess insists on being lodged in *Chance*, energetically recommended themselves to Conrad's contemporaries as brimming with health and the potential for romance (Walton, 1981), something James Joyce scandalously commemorated in *Ulysses* by having Leopold Bloom ogle Gerty McDowell on Dublin's Sandymount Strand. In stark contrast, Beerbohm's cartoon has Conrad standing alone in the harsh glare of a featureless and vaguely colonial beach. More than just a parody of the seaside idyll or the novelist's early reputation as 'the Kipling of the Malay Archipelago' (*CH* 69), it invites us to see the beach through Conrad's eyes – as an existential desert.

After Conrad's death, Beerbohm described him as a genius 'whom the world had for many years neglected . . . [and] at last made much of' (Stape and Knowles, 1996: 247), and beneath the mock-heroic tone of 'Somewhere in the Pacific' can be discerned Beerbohm's reverence for a fellow artist who espoused a moral seriousness at odds with his immediate surroundings. Beerbohm's Conrad is not so much on a beach as *beached*, stranded in an alien space of levity and triviality, his immaculate suit the civilian equivalent of a captain's uniform that implicitly sets its owner apart from the beach's more popular, knotted-handkerchief-wearing visitors of whom Jean-Didier Urbain has remarked: 'On the beach, society puts itself on display, looks at itself as a whole and in parts, and stages itself for itself, outside of any context' (Urbain, 2003: 193). It is not hard to see how Beerbohm formed this impression. Marlow, Conrad's cantankerous alter-ego, comments grumpily in *Chance* that 'leisure must be got through somehow' (*C* 102) and damns the Fynes' family dog: 'His sharp comical yapping was unbearable, like stabs through one's brain, and Fyne's deeply modulated remonstrances abashed the vivacious animal no more than the deep, patient murmur of the sea abashes a nigger minstrel on a popular beach' (108). Conrad's fictional beaches, too, are disconcertingly liminal spaces that leave his protagonists, and particularly sailors, physically and psychologically vulnerable. In *Nostromo*, Martin Decoud is seized by a 'sudden desire to hear a human voice' (*N* 301) after being left on the Great Isabel's empty beach by Nostromo, who will himself be shot there by the new lighthouse-keeper Viola, and in *The Rescue*, the likely inspiration for Beerbohm's cartoon, Captain Jörgensen remembers how the owner of the derelict schooner *Emma* had 'cut his throat on the beach below Fort Rotterdam' (*Res* 101). When the schooner-yacht *Hermit* runs aground on a mud bank, it sets in motion a train of violent events that leads d'Alcacer to refer to the so-called 'Shore of Refuge' as 'that horrible beach' (408).

Conrad once characterized his literary career as a 'quest without end' in which he felt like an 'unequip[p]ed traveller stumbling in a desert in pursuit of a mirage' (*CL* 1: 336), and critics have often remarked upon the close relation between narrative and movement through space in his writings. The sea voyage, Daniel R. Schwarz points out, 'provided a correlative *within Conrad's own experience and imagination* for the kind of significant plot that he sought' (Schwarz, 1992: 176, emphasis in original). Noting that Conrad's novels are less centred upon the sea than his novellas, Con Coroneos observes that 'the more "novelistic" Conrad's writing, the drier its tendency . . . a tendency accompanied by a difference in narrative protocol' (Coroneos, 2002: 9). And yet tourism in the broadest sense of leisure travel has largely been relegated to the margins of the several studies of Conrad and travel.[2] This chapter will accordingly present an account of Conrad's treatment of the cluster of popular cultural practices and texts that constitute tourism, ranging from the world tour and the provincial walking holiday to the armchair tourism of the middle-class women in *The Inheritors* who pore gravely over 'a volume of views of Switzerland' (*I* 64). As with popular visual entertainment, it will be seen that tourism supplied Conrad with plot settings and ideas as well as influencing the form of his narratives. Justifying his short story 'Karain' to William Blackwood, he declared: 'there's not a single action of my man (and a good many of his expressions) that can not be backed by a traveller's tale – I mean a serious traveller's' (*CL* 2: 130). This chapter builds upon this distinction between 'serious' and 'unserious' travel to show how Conrad equates tourism with a peculiarly flawed mode of storytelling, a spatial-narrative logic that can be seen in his short story 'The Partner' where day-trippers are pulled along in boats from the shore while hearing about the loss of the *Sagamore* and her captain's supposed suicide – travesties of sailing and of the truth, respectively. A symptom of growing commercialization, technological development and class mobility, tourism was necessarily a fraught subject for Conrad, and, as the first epigraph to this chapter suggests, he harboured particular resentment towards leisure travel at sea, something he felt had perverted and even jeopardized the craft of the professional mariner. In his fictional treatment of this topic, Conrad would seek to call into question a field of popular culture that he saw as occupying the vanguard of modernity even as he incorporated into his narratives some of its defining experiences.

Ambassadors and nightmares of the future

'My first novel was begun in idleness – a holiday task' (*PR* 68), Conrad once recalled. In letters to friends he similarly joked that a holiday in Aix-les-Bains hung upon the whim of the book-buying public, 'a kind of inferior Providence for the use of Authors' (*CL* 2: 67) and complained about the difficulty of marketing novels to an audience either in search of 'holiday reading' (4: 372) or already 'away on its holidays' (6: 460). He also gave the impression of rarely taking or enjoying holidays himself. In his memoir *A Personal Record* he claimed that 1873 was 'the very last year in which I have had a jolly holiday' (*PR* 37), and in July 1914 he told Alfred Knopf that an upcoming vacation in Poland would be his first in five years (*CL* 5: 405). But even a perennial shortage of funds did not prevent Conrad from taking holidays: a six-month honeymoon in Brittany; a series of health cures at Champel-les-Bains in Switzerland; pleasure trips to Marseilles, Montpellier and Corsica; a literary tour of New York and New England; and shorter excursions to Paris, Cardiff, Edinburgh and the Belgian coastal resort of Knocke-sur-Mer. September 1904 found him busy planning a winter break to the Palm Tree Hotel in Mogador, Morocco, whose proprietor was offering a reduced rate '*by special favour*' (3: 168, Conrad's emphasis). Since they were often financed by his agent, James Pinker, Conrad understandably preferred to portray these holidays as therapeutic and professional necessities, what he liked to call 'health and business' (Stape and Knowles, 1996: 28).[3] Two in particular, however, linked him to some historic developments in tourism.

In May 1873, the fifteen-year-old Korzeniowski was sent by his guardian Tadeusz Bobrowski on a twelve-week tour of Europe, accompanied by a tutor, Adam Pulman, who had been instructed to dissuade the youth from a career at sea – that is, a life of working travel. As well as visiting Munich, Milan, Venice and Vienna, Pulman and his charge spent several days walking in the Swiss Alps where they rubbed shoulders with tourists taking in the spectacular views from the summit of Mount Rigi, recently made accessible by the construction of the world's first rack railway (Morf, 1976: 68). Thirty years and 100,000 nautical miles later, Conrad could still remember two incidents from the tour with luminous clarity. In the first, he and Pulman had chanced upon an 'unexpected building', a lonely Alpine hotel in the Reuss valley. 'It was clear that no travellers were expected, or perhaps even desired, in this strange hostelry', Conrad noted, 'Even the live tourist animal was nowhere in evidence' (*PR* 38). The appearance of a party of English engineers at breakfast had allowed him to 'listen my fill to the sounds of the English language . . . . my first contact with British mankind apart from the tourist kind seen in the hotels of Zurich and Lucerne – the kind which has no real existence in a workaday world' (39). He underscored the 'workaday' aspect of the foreign guests: 'Not one of them looked like a tourist' (39).

The second incident, which one critic has extravagantly described as a 'seemingly trivial detail without which we should never have had *Almayer's Folly*, nor all the sequence of magic volumes which followed it' (Cooper, 1912: 6–7), occurred at the top of the Furka Pass when Conrad glimpsed an 'unforgettable Englishman' leading his two daughters and a Swiss guide up the mountain: 'He was clad in a knickerbocker suit, but as at the same time he wore short socks under his laced boots, for reasons which, whether hygienic or conscientious, were surely imaginative, his calves, exposed to the public gaze and to the tonic air of high altitudes, dazzled the beholder by the splendour of their marble-like condition and their rich tone of young ivory' (*PR* 40). Just as crossing the Alps on foot marked a turning-point in Wordsworth's life, Conrad imagines this epiphanic moment as an augury of his own literary destiny: 'Was he in the mystic ordering of common events the ambassador of my future, sent out to turn the scale at a critical moment on the top of an Alpine pass, with the peaks of the Bernese Oberland for mute and solemn witnesses?' (41). Once again, he was careful to point out that the English walking enthusiast had been no mere tourist but 'an ardent and fearless traveller' (41).

Conrad's encounters with Englishmen occurred at a key moment in the history of European tourism. The construction of the St Gotthard tunnel for which the engineers had been engaged was one of several projects that decisively opened Switzerland and Italy to mass tourism in the 1880s. As the canny Swiss began offering their mainly British visitors a holiday to fit every budget, Lynne Withey notes, 'Switzerland became a kind of microcosm of leisure travel, with a little something for everyone' (197), boasting luxury enclaves such as the Burgenstock in Lucerne as well as cheap *pensions* for the new 'package' tourists. Upper- and middle-class Britons such as Conrad's 'unforgettable Englishman' embraced mountain walking and climbing, not least as a means of escaping the compatriots whom Leslie Stephens had snobbishly dubbed 'Cockney travellers' in his influential guide to Switzerland, *The Playground of Europe* (1871). By the time Conrad returned in 1907 to arrange sanatorium treatment for Borys's lungs, a 'damnable outing' that provoked him to announce, 'No more trips abroad. I am sick of them' (*CL* 3: 459–60), the country had established itself as an efficient provider for the full range of visitor needs, from the winter sports made popular by Cook's in the 1890s to the healthcare industry of Davos-Platz where, as Conrad remarked to Pinker, 'the modern Dance of Death goes on in expensive hotels' (*CL* 3: 420).[4]

For all that Conrad's sober professionals and comical eccentrics are familiar stereotypes of Englishmen abroad, the incidents connect tourist experience to some central themes of his writing: the English language, British national identity and the meaning of different kinds of travel. There is, too, a distinctly Nietzschean quality to his division of 'British mankind' into 'the live tourist animal' and 'men who do not believe in wasting many words on the mere amenities of life' (*PR* 38–9), an echo of the antithesis between taciturn individuals and chattering crowds that colours his treatment of the popular voice more broadly. From his vantage point thirty years later, Conrad represents the reticent engineers and the manly 'leader of a small caravan' (*PR* 40) as exemplars of the purposive and meaningful travel that has all but disappeared in an era of touristic superficies. During a recent family holiday, he had referred to himself as just such a 'leader of a caravan' (*CL* 3: 202) and begun work on a novel that, as the final section of this chapter will show, re-imagines the popular pastime of leisure walking as a coda to the corrosive effects of modernity.

A similar range of issues is raised by Conrad's trip to Capri in early 1905, a journey that would have taken him through the completed St Gotthard tunnel.[5] Although he justified the four-month holiday as a much-needed opportunity for his wife Jessie to recover from a knee operation, he had in fact been thinking about spending a winter in the Bay of Naples since November 1900. Famed for such geological wonders as the Arco Naturale, the Faraglioni Islands and the Blue Grotto, as well as its Roman imperial ruins, Capri was no ordinary destination but a place of romance and fable. Before departing, Conrad confessed to Henry-Durand Davray that Jessie, like her husband, 'dreams of Capri' (*CL* 3: 190); and the inscription 'Jph Conrad 1905 Jany' inside his copy of Axel Munthe's *Letters from a Mourning City* (1899) suggests the couple's familiarity with the island's most charismatic resident (van Marle, 1991: 73). By the 1900s, the island had become a magnet for millionaires and royalty as well as artistic luminaries such as Nietzsche, Hauptmann, Rilke, Wilde and Henry James; the plentiful advertisements for luxury hotels, multilingual doctors, international property agents and chic art galleries in Harold Trower's *The Book of Capri* (1906) attest to the range of amenities available to the well-heeled visitor. (The Caprese, meanwhile, continued to live for the most part in picturesque poverty in two villages riven by a centuries-old hatred.) Capri's vogue among the rich increased the popular appeal of an island described by *Cook's Tourist's Handbook for Southern Italy* as 'one of the most favourite spots in the Bay of Naples, frequented by some 30,000 visitors annually' (Cook, 1905: 359). Even so, Capri seems an almost incredible choice of destination for the Conrads given that its steep rocky terrain was wholly unsuited to an invalid and its isolated location all but guaranteed high living costs and unforeseen expenses. In the event, freak weather, special porterage requirements and visits to a Neapolitan dentist helped Conrad to spend over £200 on the trip, a colossal sum. By the time he returned home, a holiday initially undertaken as a 'mad extravagant thing' (*CL* 3: 205) had turned into a 'cruel and expensive affair' (3: 255).

Although Zdzisław Najder is correct in describing early twentieth-century Capri as 'neither as commercialized and crowded nor as expensive as it is today' (Najder, 1984: 306), the peculiar social and political composition of its tourists must have rankled with Conrad. In the first place, the island's smallness forced visitors from very different backgrounds into close proximity. The Conrads' tiny holiday home, the Villa di Maria, lay in a narrow alley just below the magnificent Hotel Quisisana; Conrad referred to another sumptuous hostelry, the Hôtel Capri, as 'a place where one can hang out well enough for a small ransom' (*CL* 3: 218). Conditions at the Villa were extremely frugal: Borys remembered being teased by the daughter of the large peasant family with whom they lodged that lunch would be '*Zoupa de aqua calde* [sic] *e niente*' – hot-water-and-nothing soup (Conrad, 1970: 45). Worse still from Conrad's point of view, Capri was virtually a German tourist colony. Contemporary photographs show most shop and hotel signs in German and the authors of German guidebooks proudly directed their compatriots to the luxurious Hotel Germania and the wine merchant Herman Moll. Kaiser Wilhelm II himself visited Capri in April 1904 and the Grand Duke of Saxony was resident on the island throughout the Conrads' stay. On her visit to Capri a few years earlier, the Swedish writer Ellen Key had shunned the main village entirely, recording waspishly in her diary: '[I]t is where all the Germans go who want to sin against the Ten Commandments . . . . and, above all, against what I regard as the most important: Thou shalt not bellow!'[6] Conrad could not be so choosy. A reference to buying hot chocolate from 'big Mrs. Morgano' (*CL* 3: 241) indicates that he patronized the nearby Café zum Kater Hiddigeigei, a popular hangout for German expatriates owned by Lucia Morgano. Their nightly carousing would likely have been all too audible from the Villa di Maria.

Capri tourism left its mark on Conrad in several ways. The sight of the Mediterranean awoke memories of his youthful escapades there, and it may have been the stranding of the schooner *Raffaello* on the rocks of Marina Piccola directly below the Conrads' villa in January 1905 that encouraged him to write his 'Mediterranean paper' (*CL* 3: 280), an embellished account of the wreck of the *Tremolino* that subsequently appeared in *The Mirror of the Sea*. What is certain is that Conrad was desperate to convert tourist experience into literary material. 'After all,' he told Pinker plaintively, 'my mind must have been refreshed by new sights and impressions' (3: 229). Capri's rich literary and historical associations – in legend it was home to the Sirens – conferred a special aura upon the island for writers and artists. Conrad recorded his own fascination with Homer's Mediterranean in 'Initiation', another *Mirror of the Sea* paper written at this time, and he claimed to have found 'the subject of my Mediterranean novel' (3: 219) in the letters, songs and pamphlets about the Anglo-French struggle for Capri in the library of Dr Ignazio Cerio, a local man of letters. (He would gather additional material while holidaying in Corsica in 1921.) Interestingly, Conrad conceived of this novel, of which an incomplete draft was published posthumously as *Suspense* in 1925, not merely as having a touristic location for its setting but as deriving commercial value from this fact. As he explained to his long-suffering agent, 'A book treating of the bay of Naples, Capri, Sorrento etc – places visited every year by the English and Am[eri]can tourists – stands a better chance of popularity' (3: 219).

To Edmund Gosse, however, Conrad confided that his writing was suffering badly from the absence of 'the moral support, the sustaining influence of English atmosphere' (*CL* 3: 227), and the essay 'Autocracy and War' that he completed on Capri in April 1905 shows the traces of this insecurity about national identity in its nostalgia for 'close-knit communities' and, above all, in its final caveat: 'Le Prussianisme – voilà l'ennemi!' (*NLL* 93). Although the essay has been described by Avrom Fleischman as 'one of the most accurate predictions of the aggressive tendencies and vacuums of power that produced the world wars' (Fleishman, 1967: 32), its invective can only have been sharpened by a more immediate factor – the notorious British prejudice against German tourists. Conrad's denunciation of the 'German Eagle' for being 'inclined to look *intemperately* upon the waters of the Mediterranean when they are blue' (*NLL* 93, emphasis added) recalls his jaundiced account of Capri to Ford Madox Ford:

> All this is a sort of blue nightmare traversed by stinks and perfumes, full of flat roofs, vineyards, vaulted passages, enormous rocks, pergolas, with a mad gallop of German tourists *lâchés à travers tout cela* [let loose through it all] in white Capri shoes . . . . from the top of Monte Solaro (where the clouds hang) to the amazing rocky chasms of the Arco Naturale – where the Lager beer bottles go pop. It is a nightmare with the fear of the future thrown in.   (*CL* 3: 241)[7]

It could not have pleased Conrad to discover that Capri's other tourists included a significant Russian contingent. A stone's throw from the Villa di Maria lay a boarding-house for Russians that would later host Lenin and, when Maxim Gorki moved to Capri after the St Petersburg uprising, Dr Cerio unwisely asked Conrad for an introduction. Subversive fellow-tourists like these may well have led Conrad's thoughts towards the idea of 'a bomb in a hotel' (*CL* 3: 326), the subject of a story that has not survived, just as his reading of newspaper articles about the Russo-Japanese War while on Capri, with their 'veil of inadequate words' (*NLL* 71), appears to have prompted him to project a series of short stories based on a war correspondent's letters to his sweetheart, 'the inner truth of his feelings – things that *don't* go into his war corresp[ondence] that *can't* go into it' (*CL* 3: 243, Conrad's emphases).

The perils of Neapolitan tourism provided Conrad with the theme of 'Il Conde' (1908), a short story about a frail aristocratic visitor to the city who, after being robbed by a local gangster, feels compelled to return to Central Europe and what he believes will be an early grave. The tale stands in a complicated relation to what might be called tourist epistemology. If its plot seems to anticipate the modern holiday 'horror story' by ironically reinterpreting the famous Neapolitan invitation to 'see Naples and die' (*Vedi Napoli e poi mori*, the tale's epigraph) as a literal warning to avoid the city on pain of death, the narrative's many inconsistencies encourage a readerly scepticism towards this particular tourist's tale. As Douglas Hughes points out, the elderly count's claim to have been blackmailed by a young *cammorrista* who threatened to report him for assault makes little sense (Hughes, 1975: 19). On the contrary, his homoerotic descriptions of the assailant's red lips, white teeth and 'liquid black eyes' (*SS* 278), his reference to possible exposure by 'some dishonouring charge' (281) and his habit of 'pick[ing] transient acquaintances of a day, week, or month in the stream of travellers from all Europe' (271) all suggest a very different explanation for what the count characterizes as an 'abominable adventure' (274). Like his idea of basing a series of stories on what a war correspondent must omit from dispatches, 'Il Conde' is typical of Conrad's interest in narratives that take their readers, as it were, inside a shared experience of popular culture. Indeed, the tale presupposes a special kind of tourist knowledge since only a reader aware of the Bay of Naples's reputation as a favourite holiday destination for gay men – it was on Capri that Conrad met Norman Douglas, a writer who was later prosecuted for his homosexuality – would grasp the possible significances of the count's enthusiasm for strolling alone around the grounds of the Villa Nazionale at dusk.[8]

(Its modern equivalent would be the backpacker who disingenuously relates a 'mysterious' experience that befell him in an Amsterdam coffee shop.)

In his 1920 Preface to *A Set of Six*, Conrad claimed that 'Il Conde' was 'an almost verbatim transcript of the tale told me by a very charming old gentleman whom I met in Italy' (*SS* v). Although this holiday acquaintance has been identified as a Polish nobleman, Count Zygmunt Szembeck, the tale's basis remains obscure. Conrad was studiously vague about his source: '[W]here [my informant] left off and where I began must be left to the acute discrimination of the reader who may be interested in the problem. . . . it is not to be solved, for I am not at all clear about it myself' (v). More relevant than whether or not Szembeck was a victim of blackmail – holiday horror stories are, after all, invariably related by someone who claims to have heard them from the lips of the person concerned – is the affinity between 'Il Conde' and Capri's own tourist tales. In fact, the 'deucedly queer story' (281) at the heart of 'Il Conde' resembles nothing so much as the kind of gossip that flourished in the island's peculiar atmosphere of class tension and moral decadence, what Conrad described to Ford Madox Ford as '[t]he scandals of Capri, atrocious, u[n]speakable, amusing, scandals international, cosmopolitan and biblical, flavoured with Yankee twang and the French phrases of the *gens du monde* . . .' (*CL* 3: 241).

At the time of the Conrads' visit in early 1905, two of Capri's freshest scandals related to homosexuality. In the first, W. C. Allers, a wealthy Hamburg portrait painter fond of using Caprese youths as artistic models, fled to Germany hours before *carabinieri* came to arrest him. Although the details were never made public, local rumour had it that his exposure was the result of a botched attempt at blackmail. The other concerned Friedrich Alfred Krupp, Germany's richest man and a grandson of the arms-maker. Krupp was a fishing enthusiast who had surveyed Capri's marine life and financed the building of a road on the island's eastern cliff face. After he refused to pay off a journalist who was threatening him with publicity, a Neapolitan newspaper ruined Krupp by publishing a poisonous article about his bacchanalian parties; its title 'Il capitone' (the eel) was selected for its obscene secondary connotation. Krupp's enemies claimed that his death from heart failure shortly after was suicide.[9] Conrad would have had ample opportunity to hear first-hand accounts of all these proceedings from either his local café owner Lucia Morgano, who had helped Allers to escape, or from his literary host Dr Cerio, who had been a close friend of Krupp's. In turn, the subjects of these scandals have an obvious relevance to the protagonist of 'Il Conde' (also a fishing enthusiast) of whom the narrator dolefully concludes: 'To go home really amounted to suicide' (*SS* 288).

An age of bewildered travellers

The root of the word 'travel' in the Old English word *travail*, meaning work, has a special relevance to Conrad's writings, in which meaningful or 'authentic' travel necessarily demands laborious effort. Thus Marlow reports his introduction to the captain of the *Judea* in 'Youth': 'He said to me, "You know, in this ship you will have to work." I said I had to work in every ship I had ever been in' (*Y* 4). For Conrad, the off-duty or unemployed sailor occupies a state not of leisure but of idleness – 'the indolence of a sailor away from the sea, the scene of never-ending labour and of unceasing duty' (*PR* 73) – and leisure time in works such as 'Falk' and *Heart of Darkness*, far from being beneficial or pleasurable, typically involves a debilitating physical and mental stasis.[10] His World War I propaganda essay 'Tradition' opens with an approving paraphrase of Leonardo da Vinci on the deleterious nature of inactivity: 'Work is the law. Like iron that lying idle about degenerates into a mass of useless rust, like water that in an unruffled pool sickens into a stagnant and corrupt state, so without action the spirit of men turns to a dead thing' (*NLL* 153). Labour and duty, degeneration and stagnation; like a ship in dry dock, a sailor on shore-leave does not rest but, figuratively speaking, *rusts*. This unease about the nature of holiday time – as, so to speak, dead time – runs through Conrad's fiction. In *Nostromo*, Charles Gould's fateful meeting with the San Francisco financiers, like Holroyd's disastrous visit to Costaguana, takes place under the exceptional circumstances of a holiday. In *The Secret Agent*, Winnie thinks contentedly of Stevie as enjoying 'a damp villegiature in the Kentish lanes under the care of Mr Michaelis' (*SA* 148) when in reality his blasted remains are lying in the morgue, a disjunction that is echoed by the fate of Captain Harry Dunbar in 'The Partner', who reluctantly allows his wife to talk him into taking a shore holiday during which he loses both his ship and his own life and of Maggie Colchester in 'The Brute', who is drowned while taking a 'sea-trip for the benefit of her health' (*SS* 119). And in 'Il Conde', as we have seen, a holiday taken on health grounds ultimately results in the mental collapse of the main protagonist, whose departure in the 'train de luxe of the International Sleeping Car Company' leads Conrad's narrator to doff his hat 'with the solemn feeling of paying the last tribute of respect to a funeral *cortège*' (*SS* 289).

To follow Conrad's association of leisure with danger and death in this way is to begin to appreciate why tourism, that is to say, leisure travel, should have troubled him as deeply as it did. Both singly and *en masse*, tourists struck him as intrinsically suspect, their hectic schedules evincing an underlying frivolity even as their zeal for sightseeing betrayed a deeper failure of vision. In *The Inheritors*, the Duc de Mersch's New Palace, modelled on Leopold II's palace at Tervuren, produces 'the stupefaction of swarms of honest tourists' (*I* 74) who nonetheless fail to connect metropolitan opulence with colonial brutality. In 'The End of the Tether', the tragedy of blind Captain Whalley reveals the caprices of an invisible network of financial forces (lottery tickets and bank failures) in a world now being criss-crossed by a new class of paying travellers: 'the periodical invasions of tourists from some passenger steamer in the harbour flitted through the wind-swept dusk of the apartments with the tumult of their unfamiliar voices and impermanent presences, like relays of migratory shades condemned to speed headlong round the earth without leaving a trace' (*Y* 184). In an image with powerful resonances in this tale of literal as well as figurative blindness, their departure in a 'sightseeing hurry' leaves Whalley feeling 'more and more like a stranded tourist with no aim in view, like a forlorn traveller without a home' (184).

The same dismal perspective is invoked casually, indeed, almost axiomatically, in 'Typhoon' when the senior partner in a shipbuilding firm tells Captain MacWhirr that they have recommended him to their client in Siam, only to receive the mumbled thanks of a man 'to whom the view of a distant eventuality could appeal no more than the beauty of a wide landscape to a purblind tourist' (*T* 59). Later on, Mrs MacWhirr blithely informs her friends that the climate of the Far East 'agrees' with her husband – it has, in fact, almost killed him – 'as if poor MacWhirr had been away touring in China for the sake of his health' (126).[11] In fact, the portrayal of tourism as *ersatz* travel and self-deception functions as an organizing principle in Conrad's work. For all his self-ironic quips about leading his family on 'the conquest of Corsica' or making 'a small invasion' of a friend's Spanish holiday home (*LL* 2: 252–3), Conrad repeatedly casts his fictional tourists as gawping fools, unwitting troublemakers and deadly interlopers. 'Occupation?' asks Mr Jones, the murderous vagabond in *Victory*: 'Put down, well – tourists. We've been called harder names before now; it won't hurt our feelings' (*V* 103).

Disdain for other tourists was a deeply entrenched cultural reflex among the British middle classes, who preferred to conceal the recent provenance of their own mobility behind what one contributor to *Cook's Traveller's Gazette* called 'the usual air of supercilious superiority of the British tourist' (Anon, 1909b, 15). Holidaying in Greece in 1907, a young Virginia Woolf recorded in her diary: 'A hoard [*sic*] of Teutons invaded us, & had the audacity to pose themselves in the midst of the Temple of Pluto; it was a photographer's shop to them' (Woolf, 1990: 324–5). Even a well-travelled American such as Stephen Crane could make passing reference in his 1899 novel *Active Service* to 'depressing maps with the name of a tourist agency luridly upon them' (Crane, 1926: 281). The prejudice was wittily satirized by Noël Coward in *Sail Away*: 'Why do the wrong people / travel travel travel / and the right people / stay at home?' Conrad's own accommodation to this perspective is evident from his claim, made while honeymooning in Brittany in 1896, to have a 'mortal terror' of 'absurd French tourists' (*CL* 1: 269); Jessie, meanwhile, recalled them giving tea and a friendly send-off to the lone British walker who passed by their cottage.

As with other aspects of contemporary popular culture, Conrad's treatment of tourism is a more complicated issue than mere hostility or rejection, the latter being in any case an attitude that Felix Driver describes as 'utterly conventional' at this time (Driver, 2001: 5). Like Forster's *Room With a View*, Eliot's 'Burbank With A Baedeker: Bleistein With A Cigar' and Woolf's *Jacob's Room*, Conrad's fiction is both a document of and a Modernist commentary upon an epochal shift in the nature of travel.[12] An avid reader of Jules Verne in his youth, he had witnessed in his own lifetime the realization of Verne's fantasies of high-speed global travel and near-instant communication. Verne had written *Around the World in Eighty Days* in 1872 to coincide with the publicity generated by Thomas Cook's first world tour, and some measure of the pace of change can be gauged from the fact that in 1894 an English tourist named George Griffiths succeeded in replicating Phileas Fogg's journey in sixty-five days using only Cook's tickets and scheduled services (Williamson, 1998: 63). Thus an editor at Harper's once remarked to Conrad, '[W]e have almost forgotten that the stagecoach used to be our only conveyance at long distances, and the steamship and Transatlantic cable were undreamed of' (Stape and Knowles, 1996: 38). By 1911, Conrad could invite a friend to land his plane on the field in front of Capel House and during the war he even went up in a biplane himself, an experience he described in his 1917 essay 'Flight'. As emblems of this annihilation of distance, the tourists who stroll around Captain Hagberd's village in Kent in the manuscript version of 'To-morrow' have come, not from another part of England, but the United States.

What did it mean to call oneself a traveller when such vast distances had become traversable by anyone? Conrad's perplexity in the matter is clear from the shifting terms of his account of returning to Cracow in 'Poland Revisited' (1915). Claiming as his motive 'simply the desire to travel' (*NLL* 116), Conrad cast himself in the role of a reluctant traveller persuaded to embark upon a romantic 'adventure' to which the presence of his sons lent 'something of a migratory character, the invasion of a tribe' (117). In a tacit concession to the wartime mood, he professed to have seen nothing of Germany from his express train window, likening his previous crossings of the country to 'pilgrimages when one hurries on toward the goal for the satisfaction of a deeper need than curiosity' (118). Far from having indulged a tourist's desire for novelty, Conrad mawkishly claimed to have 'carried off in my eye . . . [a] tiny fragment of Great Britain' (119), a talismanic vision of Kent. For him, this return to Poland had been 'a retracing of the footsteps on the road of life' (130), a kind of time-travel that had activated memories of young Korzeniowski entering London in June 1878 'with something of the feeling of a traveller penetrating into a vast and unexplored wilderness' (121), but also, more disconcertingly, an awareness of having become in Polish eyes 'the grizzled foreigner holding forth in a strange tongue' (131). Here and elsewhere, the energy expended by Conrad on affixing specific meanings to his journeys attests to his refusal to be labelled as a tourist. As he admitted of this most symbolically overdetermined of vacations, 'These were strange as if disproportionate thoughts to the matter in hand, which was the simplest sort of a Continental holiday' (119).

In *The Seven Lamps of Architecture* (1847), John Ruskin famously complained that rail travel 'transmutes a man from a traveller into a living parcel' (Ruskin, 1849: 111), and one need only recall the day-trippers being hauled along Westport bay in 'The Partner' to appreciate that Conrad's fiction makes a similar claim about the pernicious effects of modern tourism. The travel that requires the crews of the *Narcissus* and the *Nan-Shan* to confront their inner fears and weaknesses as well as the elements and the high seas can only be experienced by tourists as empty and meaningless disengagement, mere transit. Interestingly, this perspective neatly reverses the growing emphasis that contemporary tourists were placing upon the journey as a valuable and enjoyable component of their holiday, a tendency that owed much to a series of technological and cultural developments: the longer trips enabled by falling transportation costs; the construction of trains and ships to new standards of comfort and hygiene; the appearance of travel agencies offering advance bookings, fixed prices, translation services, guides and money-wiring facilities; the proliferation of tourist brochures and specialist magazines; the marketing of middle-distance destinations such as the French Riviera and Norway; and the popularity of foreign holidays, both winter and summer, among even those of modest means. Consider the hotel, for example. Conrad treats hotels, a rarity in Europe until the second half of the nineteenth century, with a scepticism that verges on scorn. The antithesis of properly communal lodgings such as the London Sailors' Home, which he praised in 'A Friendly Place' for having 'no ulterior aims behind [its] effective friendliness' (*NLL* 203), the hotel epitomized for him the alienated, anonymous and profit-driven nature of modern travel. (His own taste in hotels, which included the Savoy in Cannes and the Grand in Deal, nevertheless tended towards the opulent.) Accordingly, Conrad's fictional hotels have unpleasant affinities to markedly different kinds of establishments. After mistaking Inspector Heat for a fugitive anarchist, Winnie Verloc recommends him to the 'Continental Hotel' (*SA* 150), presumably a safe-house for bomb-throwers.[13] In *Under Western Eyes*, Geneva is 'the serious-minded town of dreary hotels, tendering the same indifferent hospitality to tourists of all nations and to international conspirators of every shade' (*UWE* 356). The teacher of languages explains how, while escorting Natalie Haldin to the Hotel Cosmopolitan, 'the emptiness, the silence, the closed doors all alike and numbered, made me think of the perfect order of some severely luxurious model penitentiary on the solitary confinement principle' (326). And in *Victory*, the despicable Schomberg arranges all-female concert performances at his 'respectable hotel' (*V* 47) for the titillation of lonely bachelors whose reasons for patronizing his seedy establishment are a mystery even to the narrator.[14]

It is all the more significant, therefore, that Conrad represented tourism as having transformed sea travel into the bland occupancy of a maritime hotel.[15] 'I abhor hotels and steamboats,' he declared to John Quinn in February 1913 (*CL* 5: 175), and the juxtaposition recurs frequently in his later writings. In his essay 'Some Reflections on the Loss of the *Titanic*', he levels a diatribe against the '45,000 tons hotel of thin steel plates' intended to satisfy 'a vulgar demand of a few moneyed people for a banal hotel luxury' (*NLL* 171, 174). In 'The *Torrens*: A Personal Tribute', he praises life aboard the celebrated clipper for being 'far removed from the ideals of the Ritz Hotel' (*LE* 25). And in an essay written aboard the S.S. *Tuscania* en route to New York (Figure 4), which the *Evening News* published in May 1923 under the mischievous heading 'My Hotel in Mid-Atlantic', he laments the conditions under which 'travelling multitudes' now cross the high seas and the accompanying change in 'the whole psychology of sea travel' (*LE* 35). In place of the calm afforded by the sailing ship's isolation from 'the sound of the

Figure 4 Muirhead Bone, 'Conrad and David Bone on "Tuscania" in the Atlantic', April 1923. Pen and pencil drawing with watercolour wash. Reproduced with kind permission of Mr Gavin Sprott.

world's mechanical contrivances' (38), he notes, the steamship now pampers its passengers with 'sham comforts' and 'sham shore conditions' (36). Like Ruskin's rail-travelling parcel, Conrad's passenger is literally human cargo, his ability to walk the liner's deck 'the only thing which differentiates him from the bales of goods carried in the hold' (38). In turn, the passivity and superfluousness of passengers generally functions as a source of narrative tension in Conrad's narratives: the pilgrims travelling to Mecca in *Lord Jim*; the indentured labourers returning home in 'Typhoon'; Hermann's niece in 'Falk'; and the stowaway Legatt in 'The Secret Sharer'. Indeed, in *Chance*, de Barral's troublesome status as a passenger makes itself felt at two levels: on the one hand, his threat on Captain Anthony's life directly parallels that posed by the *Ferndale*'s deadly cargo of dynamite; and, on the other, his and Flora's presence on board necessitates an unseamanlike refurbishing of the captain's saloon, a concession to the needs of the leisure traveller that not only echoes a major theme of the novel but, as will be seen, plays an important role in its dénouement.

If modern travel increasingly resembled a freighting of goods in Conrad's eyes, he also recognized that the experiences sought after by tourists were themselves becoming ever more stable and stereotyped. As he enquired politely of a young correspondent recently returned from Corsica: 'Did Cook's people show you a vendetta? I haven't seen one but I saw a bandit' (*LL* 2: 300). The holidaymakers in 'The Partner' similarly enable the economic survival of a community that their very presence promises to fix as a picturesque item for the consumption of tourists and magazine readers, just as it did in Conrad's likely model for Westport, the Devon village of Sidmouth which his friend Stephen Reynolds had recently written about in *A Poor Man's House* (1908).[16] Conrad's frame narrator equates a tourist's sheltered experience with a magazine reader's narrow tastes, and he concludes his tale of maritime sabotage and murder with the ironic comment: 'it is too startling even to think of such things happening in our respectable Channel in full view, so to speak, of the luxurious continental traffic to Switzerland and Monte Carlo' (*WT* 128). Like its references to advertising and the cinematograph, the story's tourists stand as markers of something historically new, a popular cultural practice with profound, if not revolutionary, implications.

The epochal nature of this development is highlighted in the opening paragraph of *Victory* where Conrad defines 'the age in which we are camped like bewildered travellers in a garish, unrestful hotel' (*V* 3). In his study of Conrad's relation to contemporary anthropology, John W. Griffith suggests that this statement articulates its author's view of colonial travel as fraught with 'psychological and cultural anxiety' (Griffith, 1995: 13). And yet its immediate context is a meditation upon the battery of transformative processes that form the backdrop to the novel: concentration (of coal into diamonds); representation (coal and diamonds as signifiers of value); integration (the invisible financial bonds between metropolis and colony); and disintegration (the instant and inexplicable liquidation of those bonds). Modernity is here imagined as a force of relentless dynamism, bringing the peoples of the world together even as it alienates and disorients them. Neither anthropologists nor colonists, the world-historical subject whom Conrad evokes as a 'bewildered traveller' is, properly speaking, a circulating consumer or tourist. Indeed, *Victory* is very much a tale of 'the age in which we are camped like bewildered travellers in a garish, unrestful hotel'. Axel Heyst, who is introduced as living 'out of everybody's way' (*V* 3) in Samburan, rescues from a touring orchestra a girl so bewildered as to have 'no definite idea where she was on the surface of the globe' (79), only to fall victim to a gang of self-styled 'tourists' who have been camping in a tawdry hotel without paying.[17]

Conrad treats the transformative impact of global tourism at both the macro- and micro-levels in his writing. On *Nostromo*'s world-historical stage, the new mode of travel stands as a signifier of the various elements of capitalist modernity that are revolutionizing Costaguana, including the insertion of the Occidental Province into a global financial system, the adoption of new technologies (rail, electric lighting, telegraphy, ballistics) and the importing of foreign ideologies and methods of social control (communism, newspaper propaganda). Conrad uses the biographies of several key characters to locate pre-revolutionary Costaguana precisely in an era of heroic travel: the Montero brothers owe their education to 'the munificence of a famous European traveller, in whose service their father had lost his life' (*N* 39), whilst the assimilation of young Charles Gould gives the lie to his outward appearance of being 'more English than a casual tourist, a sort of heretic pilgrim . . . [at that time] quite unknown in Sulaco' (47). Post-revolutionary Sulaco is then firmly identified with tourism, most explicitly in the chapter in which Captain Mitchell, now indulged by his employers in a discretionary 'leisure' (473), is shown regaling visitors with an incomplete and self-serving account of Sulaco's recent history. Mitchell's 'relentless' (481) sightseeing programme is an obvious parody of the tedious tourist guide who points out the imported plate glass in local shops, compares the town plaza to Trafalgar Square, extols the local coffee, and brightly announces everything to be 'picturesque' (475) – a farrago of information that leaves his victims 'as it were annihilated mentally' (486). But Conrad also takes pains to present this touristic scene as symptomatic of a more seismic change. Just as Mitchell's own future has become expressible as a dollar value, his retirement nest-egg of 17 thousand-dollar shares in Consolidated San Tomé Mines, so, too, has Sulaco's revolutionary past become a fixed quantity, its narrative packaged for easy consumption by the desultory visitors: 'The phrase, "In my delicate position as the only consular agent then in the port, everything, sir, everything was a just cause for anxiety," had its place in the more or less stereotyped relation of the "historical events" which for the next few years was at the service of distinguished strangers visiting Sulaco' (473). Thanks to the *Times*'s special correspondent, whose series of letters have made the Occidental Republic internationally famous as 'The Treasure House of the World' (480), these bored tourists – ' "Abominable Pedrito! Who the devil was he?" would wonder the distinguished bird of passage' (487) – have already heard a reified version of Sulaco's history even before they arrive. Oblivious, Mitchell directs their attention to 'the famous Hernandez' and 'the renowned Carabineers of the Campo' (480) as if the Minister of War and his militia are costumed actors in an open-air heritage museum.

At the other extreme, Conrad anatomizes the psychological impact of tourism on the individual in 'The Planter of Malata' (1914). This long short story opens with Geoffrey Renouard being introduced to a party of English travellers at the home of a colonial politician who once enjoyed the hospitality of his guests while on his own tour of Europe. Disastrously, Renouard agrees to a proposal to escort them back to his island on a kind of 'pleasure cruise' (*WT* 52). Although Professor Moorsom, his sister and his daughter Felicia are searching for the latter's fiancé (Renouard's assistant, who, unbeknownst to them, has been killed in an accident), Conrad highlights their status as would-be tourists. Ultimately indifferent to the object of their 'sentimental pilgrimage' (40) and openly confessing 'his impatience to complete the circuit of the globe and be done with it' (37), Moorsom longs for 'the cool spaces of the Pacific, the sweep of the ocean's free wind along the promenade decks, cumbered with long chairs, of a ship steaming towards the Californian coast' (39). Upon arrival at Malata, he is described as resembling 'a banal tourist more than was permissible to a man of his unique distinction' (81). Meanwhile, Renouard, who has by this point developed a hopeless attachment to Felicia, finds himself in the role of unwilling guide to guests who behave like 'a personally conducted party of tourists' (63). Tellingly, his invented excuse for the assistant's absence, 'a short tour of the island, to the westward' (63), not only elides touring with death (the euphemism 'gone West') but echoes the local legend about a colonial governor who drowned himself while 'on official tour' (44), a fate that anticipates Renouard's own suicide after he is rejected by Felicia. Conrad here imagines tourism as a network of phantasmic relations that produces a kind of destructive alterity in the individual. One night, Renouard has a dream in which he follows a 'startling image of himself' (31) around an empty palace and stumbles over a marble statue of Felicia that crumbles in his hands. In the light of day, he tries to reassure himself that 'the reflection of himself in the mirror was not really the true Renouard' (32) and that there must be a more rational explanation. But in this story thematizing the uncanny – the Moorsoms are convinced spiritualists, the plantation workers see ghosts, and Felicia threatens to 'haunt' (82) Renouard – the return of the repressed prefigured by Renouard's dream is clearly the arrival of the tourist party, just as what he sees in his unrecognisable other self, 'the frightened guide of his dream' (31), is the part he will be forced to play for them. Renouard's fantasy about the fragmentation of his personality is, in short, a nightmare of tourist experience.

Globetrotting with Thomas Cook: *Lord Jim* (1900)

The sheer ease with which the Moorsoms trek 12,000 miles in search of Felicia's fiancé can easily escape the attention of the modern reader for whom intercontinental travel has become an everyday matter, as can the fact that they have represented their journey to friends back in England as 'a trip round the world *of the usual kind*' (*WT* 22, emphasis added). And yet, as this arresting qualifier indicates, the global tour had already become so commonplace for people of the Moorsoms' social class by the 1900s that, far from attracting unwelcome curiosity from their acquaintances, it could serve as the cover for an extraordinary journey. Conversely, in 1860, the year in which *The Rescue* is set, taking a private yachting party from Manila to England via the Dutch East Indies and the Cape would have been considered remarkably ambitious, an excursion only within the means of the *Lightning*'s upper-class travellers.[18] By the time Conrad began writing the novel, Cook's was opening its *Annual Tour Round the World* brochure with the words: 'A tour round the world has become such an everyday affair . . .'

Conrad expounds at some length upon this new mundanity of global tourism in 'Travel', an essay written as a preface for Richard Curle's travelogue *Into the East* (1923) that paradoxically announces the passing of 'the days of heroic travel' (*LE* 89) and, with it, the demise of the travelogue. 'Nowadays many people encompass the globe' (85), Conrad observes, adding that, in consequence, 'a traveller of our day [is] condemned to make his discoveries on beaten tracks' (92).[19] The tourist parties of the 1870s, among them the authors of a travel literature 'more devastating to the world's freshness of impression than a swarm of locusts in a field of young corn' (86), had brought into existence a network of steamship routes catering for 'an enormous company of people who go round the world for a change and rest, either suffering from overwork (whatever that may mean) or from neurasthenia' (86).[20] Significantly, he identifies a literary dimension to this inexorable process of popularization. As a legacy of the Suez Canal's completion and the 'inanity of the mass of travel books' (86) that had followed, the world was now witnessing the subjugation of even the remotest parts of Africa to 'fatuous daily photographs and even more fatuous descriptive chatter' (89).[21]

If many of the terms of this jeremiad – pampered leisure, purposeless travel, stereotyped experience – are by now familiar, one stands out. Taking his cue from Curle's choice of epitaph, the Arabic proverb 'Travelling is victory' (a phrase also used by a character in *An Outcast of the Islands*), Conrad likens modern tourists to the Arab explorers of old who 'did much of their travelling sword in hand . . . . personally conducted parties, as destructive to the peace and the spiritual character of the places they visited as any crowd from a tourist agency invading the shades of Vallombrosa' (*LE* 85). On first sight, it seems a provocative but superficial comparison between two military and cultural imperialisms: the armed travellers of the past and latterday visitors to a famous Umbrian convent.[22] Conrad's reference to the tourist agency as charging 'so many pounds per head for a certain number of days' (85) hints at an obscure congruence between the slave-raider and the tour operator, an image of organized travel as a violation of the world being surveyed that recurs in his allusion to the safari tourists who bore their readers with 'descriptive statistics of slaughter and as to the shortcomings of their "boys"' (87).[23] Nonetheless, Conrad records an important distinction between the Arab explorers of old and their 'successors' (85), the global tourists. Where the former had travelled 'with the name of the One God on their lips' (85) – that is, had embarked on a journey inspired by a sacred text, the Qur'an – the latter had set forth with precisely the opposite, 'blank minds and, alas, blank notebooks where the megalomania, from which we all more or less suffer, got recorded in the shape of "Impressions"' (86). As his praise for Curle's commitment to 'the ultimate truth of travel' (92) suggests, Conrad sees the tourism produced by this 'world in transition' (92) as irredeemably materialist, a parodic version of older forms of sacral or idealist travel whose practitioners fully deserved the designation 'heretic pilgrims' that he had coined in *Nostromo*.[24] In place of the Arab explorer whose maxim *'expresses . . . a romantic conception'*, the prosaic modern tourist seeks merely the 'mastery of first *impressions'* (85, 92, emphases added).

Pilgrims, romance, the ultimate truth of travel . . . we have entered the moral universe of *Lord Jim*. And tourists? Most immediately, there is Marlow's mordant sketch of the mail-boat passengers thronging the dining-room of the Malabar House Hotel, a locale that has been identified by Norman Sherry as Singapore's Hôtel de l'Europe:

> An outward-bound mail-boat had come in that afternoon, and the big dining-room of the hotel was more than half full of people with a hundred pounds round-the-world tickets in their pockets. There were married couples looking domesticated and bored with each other in the midst of their travels; there were small parties and large parties, and lone individuals dining solemnly or feasting boisterously, but all thinking, conversing, joking, or scowling as was their wont at home; and just as intelligently receptive of new impressions as their trunks upstairs. Henceforth they would be labelled as having passed through this and that place, and so would be their luggage. They would cherish this distinction of their persons, and preserve the gummed tickets on their portmanteaus as documentary evidence, as the only permanent trace of their improving enterprise. The dark-faced servants tripped without noise over the vast and polished floor; now and then a girl's laugh would be heard, as innocent and empty as her mind, or, in a sudden hush of crockery, a few words in an affected drawl from some wit embroidering for the benefit of a grinning tableful the last funny story of shipboard scandal. Two nomadic old maids, dressed up to kill, worked acrimoniously through the bill of fare, whispering to each other with faded lips, wooden-faced and bizarre, like two sumptuous scarecrows.   (*LJ* 77)

Despite being singled out by Cunninghame Graham as an example of 'the subtlest and most sarcastic humour that no reviewer ever seems to have observed' (*TH* x), most critical studies of *Lord Jim* have passed without comment over this extraordinary passage. It is a doubly puzzling omission in light of the fact that its foregrounding of the presence of non-auditors is almost unique among Conrad's many stagings of scenes of narrative. What is more, despite their ostensible irrelevance, these tourists repeatedly interrupt Jim's tale, in effect, as a kind of imbecilic chorus to his private tragedy:

'Do you think I was afraid of death?' he asked in a voice very fierce and low. . . . There was a burst of voices, and several men came out in high good-humour into the gallery. They were exchanging jocular reminiscences of the donkeys in Cairo. A pale anxious youth stepping softly on long legs was being chaffed by a strutting and rubicund globe-trotter about his purchases in the bazaar. 'No, really – do you think I've been done to that extent?' he enquired very earnest and deliberate. (*LJ* 87)

He had thrown himself back and was shaking with laughter. . . . It fell like a blight on all the merriment about donkeys, pyramids, bazaars, or what not. Along the whole dim length of the gallery the voices dropped, the pale blotches of faces turned our way with one accord, and the silence became so profound that the clear tinkle of a teaspoon falling on the tesselated floor of the verandah rang out like a tiny and silvery scream. (*LJ* 100)

A feeble burst of many voices mingled with the tinkle of silver and glass floated up from the dining-room below; through the open door the outer edge of the light from my candle fell on his back faintly; beyond all was black; he stood on the brink of a vast obscurity, like a lonely figure by the shore of a sombre and hopeless ocean. (*LJ* 173)

That those tourists occupy a parallel universe to Jim's is underscored by their cultural philistinism, their zeal for being labelled and their dreary lack of sensuality. For them, loss of honour is the stuff of 'shipboard scandal', not existential despair, let alone a despair voiced calmly in tones suited to 'discussing a third person, a football match, last year's weather' (*LJ* 78). Marlow's affirmation that 'he was one of us' (*LJ* 78), which most critics gloss as simply the salute of a fellow British sailor, precisely dissociates Jim from these other expatriates whom the older man twice disparages as 'globe-trotters' (*LJ* 78, 116).[25]

Although the word *globe-trotter*, which came into general use in the early 1880s, could denote any world traveller, Conrad has a particular variety in mind here: the Cook's tourist. Specifically, these are holders of second-class round-the-world tickets, prices for which started at £105 in

Cook's *Programme of Independent Tours Round the World* for 1890. Conrad's anxious youth is fussing about his bazaar purchases in Cairo but since most transport, porterage, guide and hotel costs were usually paid for in advance in a Cook's office in Britain, it is probably the only expense he has had to negotiate for himself during the entire trip. Moreover, since they have already passed Egypt, these are clearly 'independent' tourists, the name given by Cook's to the individual travellers who now constituted ninety per cent of its business (Williamson, 1998: 96): personally conducted tourist parties always travelled westward from London via New York, San Francisco, Hong Kong, Singapore, Bombay, Aden, Suez, Florence and Paris.

It is barely an exaggeration to say that for the late-Victorian holiday-maker, foreign travel, particularly Egyptian holidays and world tours, was synonymous with the Thomas Cook agency. By 1891, Thomas Cook and Sons had established itself as the authorized agent of every major steamship company in the world, boasting a staff of 2,500 and over 30,000 varieties of ticket, annual sales of which approached three and a half million (Williamson, 1998: 21, 96). Cook's became the world's largest travel agency through a campaign of vigorous expansion intended to make foreign travel convenient and affordable for tourists of every social class. The firm's importance in domesticating the exotic was incalculable. 'Thomas Cook & Son is one of the monumental achievements of the Victorian era,' enthused an anonymous contributor to *The Young Man* in December 1900: '[T]o-day you can ride to the Sphinx in a tram-car, with as little to-do as if you were riding from Charing Cross to the Bank' (Anon, 1900: 159). Key innovations included the all-in-one ticket (later printed bilingually), the traveller's cheque and the local representative, this latter a veritable Cook's institution. Arriving in Naples at 2 a.m., Conrad was relieved to find that the Cook's interpreter, though a 'very picture of misery', had heroically held their carriage and porters in the snow for two-and-a-half hours (*CL* 3: 209). Once installed on Capri, he wasted no time in making use of the company's money-wiring services. 'Cook's office,' he explained to Pinker during a later trip to Champel, 'lay themselves out for that kind of thing' (3: 442).

Cook's was thus the dominating presence behind the varieties of long-haul tourism that Conrad portrays in his fiction. Any of its eighty-five offices could have sold the Moorsoms their tickets to Sydney in 'The Planter of Malata' or arranged shore excursions in Singapore for the global sightseers in 'The End of the Tether', and by the time Conrad began writing *The Rescue* in 1896, Cook's had been offering £500-a-head world cruises on the luxury private yacht *Victoria* for almost a decade.[26] Indeed, no tourist party or destination seemed impossible to Cook's. On 10 March 1894, barely four months after the troops of Cecil Rhodes's British South Africa Company had defeated King Lobengula's impis, Cook's monthly magazine *The Excursionist* began advertising a five-month tour of Matabeleland for £395. On 2 April 1900, it publicized the launch of a South African battlefields tour, and on 10 September that year it reported the opening of a Cook's office in Cape Town, 'now that the war is almost over'.

There is even a shadowy connection between the world's largest tourist agency and Conrad's most formative journey. In *Heart of Darkness*, Conrad famously re-imagined his ascent of the Congo in 1890 as an epic voyage into the unknown 'like travelling back to the earliest beginnings of the world' (*Y* 92). As John Griffith rightly observes, 'No *Baedeker's* exists to guide [Marlow] where he is going' (Griffith, 1995: 29). However, only six months before Conrad began writing the novella, Cook's had in fact taken a party of tourists on precisely this route. The Conducted Tour to West Africa and the Congo, *The Excursionist* announced on 16 April 1898, would 'enabl[e] those who are interested in that great development of civilization to take part in the inauguration of the railway from Matadi to Stanley Pool, the laying of which has occupied some nine years'.[27] Mr Stanley would be there in person, it promised, and interested parties should consult the specially illustrated Cook's brochure. In *Heart of Darkness*, Marlow describes having been captivated by a map of Africa in a shop window on 'Fleet Street' (*Y* 53), an address famous the world over as the home of the British press. But Fleet Street was also the world headquarters of Thomas Cook and Sons, whose 'Round The World By Steam' sign on Ludgate Circus had long been a London landmark. As Jack London observed satirically in *The People of the Abyss* (1903): 'Thomas Cook & Son, pathfinders and trail-clearers, living sign-posts to all the world, and bestowers of first aid to bewildered travellers – unhesitatingly and instantly, with ease and celerity, could you send me to Darkest Africa or Innermost Thibet, but to the East End of London, barely a stone's throw distant from Ludgate Circus, you know not the way!' (London, 1978: 11). In a photograph of its offices taken in around 1902 and now preserved in the company's archives (Figure 5), what appears, under the magnifying glass at least, to be two large maps can just be made out in its Fleet Street windows. Conrad's contemporaries nicknamed the Nile 'Cook's canal' in recognition of the company's near-monopoly of traffic on the river, and during the 1885 Sudan campaign Cook's had even transported Kitchener's

Figure 5   Thomas Cook's Ludgate Circus offices, Fleet Street, London, *c.*1902.
Reproduced with permission of Thomas Cook UK Ltd, Company Archives.

army to Khartoum. It is not inconceivable, therefore, that its Fleet Street
offices were displaying a map of Africa in 1890 and, in the year of its
Conducted Tour to West Africa and the Congo, perhaps even of the river
Congo itself.

For Conrad, as we have seen, the 'personally conducted party'
typically denotes a superficial or destructive mode of tourist travel, and
he was no less slighting about the agency that had done most to popu-
larize the concept. Complaining to Edward Garnett in August 1908
about the terms in which *A Set of Six* had been reviewed, he explained:
'I have approached things human in a spirit of piety foreign to those
lovers of humanity who would like to make of life a sort of Cook's
Personally Conducted Tour – from the craddle [*sic*] to the grave' (*CL* 4: 112).
A jibe at the protection offered by Cook's against what Frederick Karl
and Laurence Davies call 'rude surprises' (*CL* 4: 112n), the remark also
reveals that Conrad envisaged his writing as the inverse of a particular
category of tourist experience. To his fury, Robert Lynd in the *Daily News*
had described him as 'without either country or language' and as

articulating 'the vision of a cosmopolitan' (*CH* 211), whilst the *Daily Telegraph*'s W. L. Courtney had similarly dwelt upon his foreignness and synoptic vision, noting his 'large experience of the world' and 'a certain quality about him which makes him a thing apart . . . . He sees the world as a whole' (214). Even Garnett had reminded readers of the *Nation* that Conrad had 'sailed to the ends of the earth on English ships' (*CH* 221), declaring that 'his cosmopolitan vision transports us straightaway to the Marañon cattle estancia in a South American country' (222).

More than just irritation at being branded a rootless alien – 'cosmopolitan' was commonly used as an anti-Semitic slur at this time[28] – Conrad's sardonic reference to Cook's Tours should therefore be seen as expressing his resentment at the perception of his work as literary globetrotting, that is, as a series of fictional tours of exotic destinations led by an experienced guide. Such concerns were not entirely without foundation. Geographically and thematically disparate, the stories in *A Set of Six* could well be said to take the reader on a personally conducted world tour via London in 'The Informer', Australia in 'The Brute', French Guiana in 'An Anarchist', Naples in 'Il Conde', Russia and France in 'The Duel' and, in the case of 'Gaspar Ruiz', what Conrad describes in his own Author's Note as 'all the South American Continent' (*SS* vi).[29] We are, perhaps, hearing Conrad's own defensiveness on this score when the lepidopterist-narrator of 'An Anarchist' protests: 'I travelled at that time, but strictly for myself and with a moderation unknown in our days of round-the-world tickets. I even travelled with a purpose' (137).

Coming back to *Lord Jim*, it will be observed that there is something incongruously touristic about the self-imposed nomadism which makes Jim into a 'rolling stone' (*LJ* 197) in the novel's middle section, moving continually from one port to the next in a melancholy parody of 'independent' travel. In turn, Marlow's attempt to break this pattern and 'get him out of the way' (221) involves finding him employment with Stein, who, as the former assistant of 'a Dutch traveller – a rather famous man' (205), embodies a bygone era of heroic travel.[30] From this perspective, Jim's voluntary exile to Patusan, an idealized space of romance out of the sight of tourists and sailors alike, represents his return to what John Urry defines as the 'romantic' gaze of middle-class tourists for whom the 'collective' gaze is a disconcerting and even repulsive experience (Urry, 1990: 46–7).

Even so, and as Conrad drives home by having Jim tell Marlow in a hotel full of sleeping guests about how he abandoned a steamship full of sleeping passengers, the real counterparts to the Cook's tourists in the novel are the Muslim pilgrims. Literally and metaphorically, the Hajji are travelling in the opposite direction to the tourists, seeking spiritual redemption in place of cheap souvenirs and the cultural capital of globetrotting's 'improving enterprise' (*LJ* 77) that James Buzard has defined as the conversion of ' "culture" encountered through travel into exchangeable items, tokens of cultural accomplishment that are legal tender in the sign-market of personal acculturation at home' (Buzard, 1993: 225). The autobiographical echoes in Jim's description leave little doubt as to Conrad's own respect for the pilgrims' motives for travelling: 'Eight hundred men and women with faith and hopes, with affections and memories. . . . At the call of an idea they had left their forests, their clearings, the protection of their rulers, their prosperity, their poverty, the surroundings of their youth and the graves of their fathers' (*LJ* 14). In sharp contrast to the noisy tourists disgorged by the mail-boat, these humble travellers file on board the *Patna* 'without a word, a murmur, or a look back' (14), the 'unconscious pilgrims of an exacting belief' (15) for whom the voyage to Mecca is itself a religious act. When their leader recites aloud 'the prayer of the travellers by sea', not only does he invoke Allah's blessing 'on men's toil and on the secret purposes of their hearts' (15) but he signals, in this context, crucially, that they have begun a journey upon which, as the *Times* had noted in its account of the *Jeddah* scandal on 14 August 1880, even their own death would be considered a divine blessing (Moser, 1996: 323).[31] The pilgrims accept the discomforts and dangers of their 'pious voyage' (*LJ* 15) in the same 'spirit of piety' invoked by Conrad when describing his own refusal to make life into, as he put it, a Cook's personally conducted tour from cradle to grave.

Strictly speaking, the 'unconscious' pilgrims in *Lord Jim* are nonetheless tourists. Their journey by chartered steamer has been undertaken for holiday (literally, holy day) purposes and their skipper is little more than an unscrupulous tour operator. Indeed, the captain's contemptuous epithet 'dese cattle' (*LJ* 15) would find an echo in Conrad's satirical reminder to the *Titanic*'s owners that 'men and women . . . are not exactly the cattle of the western ocean trade that used to be thrown overboard on an emergency' (*NLL* 189). The religious significance of the *Patna*'s passengers has been debated by critics (Jameson, 1981: 244–6; Berthoud, 1985), but it follows logically from Conrad's descriptions of ordinary tourists as 'heretic' or 'sentimental' pilgrims that he saw the latter, *mutatis mutandis*, as 'faithful' or 'serious' tourists. And if equating pilgrims with tourists sounds fanciful, it has an intriguing corollary in Conrad's source material. In 1887, a string of shipping disasters involving Indian pilgrims prompted the Government of India to appoint Thomas Cook, who had been transporting Christians to the Holy Land for almost twenty years, as national travel agent for the Hajj. Between 1887 and 1893, when the government's withdrawal of its subsidy made the line unprofitable, company-chartered steamers carried Hajjis from Bombay to Jeddah and back. It was a high-profile contract. John Cook's in-house report, *The Mecca Pilgrimage*, noted that the appointment of Cook's as the Indian Government's official agent for Hajji pilgrims had been the subject of 'a large number [of] . . . leading articles in the chief papers of India and England' (Cook, 1886: 19).

For the central episode in *Lord Jim*, the abandoning of Hajji pilgrims in the Red Sea, Conrad drew on his first-hand experiences of abandoning the fire-damaged *Palestine* in 1882 as well as on his second-hand knowledge of the *Jeddah* scandal of 1880, a pilgrim ship which continued to transport Hajjis under another name until 1894 (Sherry, 1971: 41–64). But he also had an indirect and hitherto unknown connection to Hajji tourism. Between November 1893 and January 1894, Conrad served as second mate on the *Adowa*, an emigrant ship chartered by the Franco-Canadian Transportation Company. Of these seven weeks, most of which were spent idling in Rouen harbour, he later recalled: 'I was always in evidence in my best uniform to give information as though I had been a Cook's tourists' interpreter, while our quartermasters reaped a harvest of small change from personally conducted parties' (*PR* 12). Given Conrad's strong interest in the histories of ships, it is quite possible that during this period he heard about an incident that had occurred a few years earlier when this same vessel had been chartered to take Hajji pilgrims from Bombay to Aden.[32] According to the private journal of Jaffir Ali Najuf Ali, included as an appendix to the 1887 Government of India Report on conditions in the pilgrimage industry, the *Adowa*, bound for Aden with 797 Javanese and Indian Muslim pilgrims on board, had begun to founder in calm seas in the Indian Ocean on 21 July 1886. Declaring that the ship would sink in less than twenty-four hours, the captain and his crew had attempted to set off in the boats to find help, only to be forcibly restrained by the pilgrims, who, as Hajji Jaffir Ali recorded, 'came on deck with their arms on, may be to stab the captain, thinking that he meant to escape with officers and crew and leave them to perish with the ship'.[33] At this wretched moment, the *Adowa*'s ship's doctor, like the *Patna*'s second engineer, went and got drunk. By labouring for three days to pump out the water, the *Adowa*'s passengers and crew managed to restart the flooded engines and the steamer limped into port with the loss of only nine lives.

It was precisely the scandalous condition of ships like the *Adowa* – which had, incredibly, already picked up the crew of another distressed vessel – that forced the Indian Government to turn to Thomas Cook and Sons the following year. The seaworthiness of the refitted *Adowa* when Conrad signed up as her second mate in 1893 is not known, but the ambiguity of his only recorded statement on the matter certainly gives grounds for doubt: 'Four hundred and sixty bunks for emigrants were put together in the 'tween decks by industrious carpenters while we lay in the Victoria Dock, but never an emigrant turned up in Rouen – of which, being a humane person, I confess I was glad' (*PR* 11). Among the inexplicably equivocating and untruthful answers that Conrad gave six months later to a Board of Trade Committee on the Manning of Merchant Ships, was an admission that the *Adowa* had been dangerously short-handed (Bojarski, 1968: 20).

In conclusion, *Lord Jim* can be seen to record the impact of tourism in two ways: firstly, as a deformation of the true nature of sea travel, here staged in terms of Jim's loss of honour as a sailor; and, secondly, as a spatial closing-off of the high seas to romance, a shift symbolized by the odious presence of globetrotters – 'A sailor isn't a globe-trotter' (*C* 30), Marlow would insist in *Chance* – and reflected structurally by the novel's much discussed move to onshore action and colonial melodrama in its second half. Whilst the humiliating memory of ending his maritime career as a glorified tourist guide on the ill-fated *Adowa* could only have exacerbated Conrad's resentment towards the new breed of leisure traveller, it is worth noting that one consequence of Cook's foray into transporting Indian pilgrims was to improve safety standards in the merchant marine, a development that ultimately removed the need for the Indian government to subsidize an official agent. Given that his skills as a sailing ship captain were rendered obsolete by the advent of steam, it is doubly ironic that the last berth of Conrad's sea career – as the *Patna* is for Jim – was aboard a steamer whose own career as a pilgrim ship had been terminated by the new safety standards required for tourist travel.

Excursus: Conrad on the road

Perhaps surprisingly, Conrad's distaste for mechanization – the steamship's encouragement of globetrotting and the 'new seamanship' that he summarized as 'when in doubt try to ram fairly – whatever's before you' (*NLL* 171) – restricted itself to sea travel. His enthusiasm for motoring has a number of explanations. The automobile was, in theory at least, more convenient and comfortable than the horse-drawn carriage that Conrad found both dull and carrying the risk of 'a dismal death in a ditch' (*CL* 1: 434). Early twentieth-century motoring was also unpopular in the double sense of being an elite activity and an object of regular public censure. No longer required to mix with public transport users, the affluent motorist was free to do and drive as he liked. No less importantly, as Lynne Withey points out, motor travel promised to replace the 'modern obsession with speed and schedule' with what Edith Wharton, a keen motorist, extolled as 'the romance of traveling . . . [without] the compulsions and contacts of the railway, the bondage to fixed hours and the beaten track' (Withey, 1997: 337). In an interview given half a century later, Conrad's eldest son suggested, intriguingly, that his father had seen the motor car as a 'substitute ship'.[34]

Whatever the case, Conrad acquired the first in a series of increasingly expensive cars in 1912. A thirty-horse-power second-hand Cadillac, affectionately dubbed 'the puffer' by the family, was followed by a Model 'T' Ford, a Daimler, a Humber, a Studebaker and a Panhard (though not, one suspects, the 'Roi des Belges' model).[35] Appropriately enough, Conrad bought a new Cadillac with the money from selling his film rights to Hollywood in 1919. In addition to its obvious practical benefits in rural Kent, car ownership was a powerful marker of social status; his last purchase, he told a correspondent proudly in January 1924, had been 'acquired from H. R. H. the Duke of Connaught' (*LL* 2: 332). Arthur Symons might mock Conrad's 'childish enjoyment' at driving 'the funniest little car I ever saw' but even portly Henry James confessed to being in 'fond awe of your possession of a (I won't say life-saving, but literally life-making) miraculous car' (Stape and Knowles, 1996: 82, 90). When the motoring fanatic Lord Northcliffe came round for tea, Conrad could not refrain from admiring 'the great man's Rolls-Royce' and joked about buying one for himself (*CL* 5: 638, 6: 397). His invitation to Sidney Colvin in May 1916 to go for 'a cruise in the car' (5: 588) attested to the new mobility conferred on car-owners (not least, those prepared to ignore wartime appeals for fuel conservation), whilst a drive to the South of France in 1921 confirmed his membership of the class-within-a-class of motorists able to afford the hefty deposits being demanded by French customs officials, who wished to prevent tourists from selling their cars in France (O'Connell, 1998: 90–1).[36]

Conrad evidently had a taste for the speeding that formed a central part of Edwardian car culture. John Conrad remembered his father crashing into a gate during a bravado attempt to pass a tight corner at

30 m.p.h. as well as his delight upon reaching 60 m.p.h., three times the national speed limit that had been imposed by the 1903 Motor Car Act in a climate of public anger at motorists' apparent disregard for other road-users (Conrad, 1981: 193). Conrad even confessed to having forced a baker's cart into the hedge: 'The road was covered with bread. After the first scare it was rather funny (the baker's man was a stutterer) but I couldn't sleep for three nights afterwards' (*CL* 4: 380). Humour, danger and excitement also featured prominently in the representation of the automobile in contemporary culture, ranging from C. N. and A. M. Williamson's 'motoring novels' (*CL* 4: 381), as Conrad called them, to a popular cinematic sub-genre with titles such as *Explosion of a Motor Car* (1900), *Car Ride* (1903), *The Motor Hooligans* (1905), *Motor Mad* (1906), *The '?' Motorist* (1906) and *The Motor Bandits* (1912).[37] The most famous of these, *How It Feels To Be Run Over* (1900), positions spectators directly in the path of an approaching car that proceeds to 'crash' into their field of vision, followed by an inter-title comprising large exclamation marks and the punch-line 'Oh! Mother *will* be pleased'.[38] Being run over for real was no joke, however, and Conrad's claim to have been going 'dead slow' – the standard plea of early motorists – in the car that knocked down a bricklayer named George Field in Chatham village on 27 August 1904 belies his subsequent reference to a '[c]rowd around cursing and howling' (*CL* 3: 158). The previous week, a child had been knocked down and killed in the neighbouring village of Meopham, prompting the coroner to declare that 'Motors were very dangerous things, and they were not popular'. Although Conrad recorded that Field had only been 'shaken' (3: 158), the local newspaper stated that he had been admitted to hospital suffering from 'bruises and shock'.[39]

A familiar icon of modernity in the work of Rudyard Kipling, Marcel Proust and Filippo Marinetti, the automobile makes two appearances in Conrad's *œuvre*. In an essay written a fortnight before his encounter with the Chatham bricklayer, he praised Anatole France's 'The Military Manœuvres at Montil', a farcical story about two motorists hopelessly lost in a landscape of quaintly-named French villages, for capturing what he called 'the very spirit of automobilism': 'the absurd rushing about of General Decuir in a 30 horse power car, in search of his cavalry brigade becomes to you a more real experience than any day or night run you may ever have taken yourself' (*NLL* 36).[40] And in Conrad and Ford's *The Nature of a Crime*, the narrator devises a suicide in which a new car belonging to the young man whose inheritance he has embezzled will be 'arrested in a long rush, by my extinction' (Najder, 1978: 134) – a grisly echo of the comic trick film *How to Stop a Motor Car* (1902) in which a policeman is mangled by a speeding vehicle. During the 1900s, notes Sean O'Connell, 'the car frequently became a metaphor for the shallowness of materialistic modern society' (188); and Conrad later recalled the story's themes as reflecting the 'crudely materialistic atmosphere of the time' (Najder, 1978: 117). Like the steamship, the motor car was a key agent of touristic modernity, and he acknowledged its 'vast topographical range' (*NLL* 35) in 'Anatole France' as well as showing a pair of newly-weds planning to drive to Italy for their honeymoon in *The Nature of a Crime*.

Motoring's impact on tourism was two-fold. Its speed engendered a new sensibility of travel akin to the 'stimulus shock' that Wolfgang Schivelbusch has shown to have both disturbed and thrilled nineteenth-century train travellers (Schivelbusch, 1986: 113–23). The motor car, A. B. Filson Young explained breathlessly in *The Complete Motorist* (1904), 'flattens out the world, enlarges the horizon, loosens a little of the bonds of Time, sets back a little the barriers of Space' (Young, 1904: 311).[41] Filson Young quoted Kipling's description of driving as 'projecting one's imagination a hundred yards ahead of one's nose down an apparently empty road' and of the motor car as making possible nothing less than 'the discovery of England', 'a time-machine on which one can slide from one century to another at no more trouble than the pushing forward of a lever' (Young, 1904: 286). Conrad's own experience of this phenomenon is evident from his observation after taking a ride in Pinker's coach-and-four: 'The countryside seemed lazy this afternoon, turning round much more slowly than when we are in the car' (Conrad, 1981: 185). Like the bicycle decades earlier, the motor car not only physically connected individuals and communities through the road network but created a new epistemology of those relations. The 'supreme charm' of the motor car, according to *The Complete Motorist*, consisted in 'tak[ing] us from one world to another . . . open to, and conscious of, the things that connect those worlds with each other' (Young, 1904: 312). Introducing 'The Inn of the Two Witches', a Gothic tale about a diabolical bed used to murder unwary travellers, Conrad observed ironically that 'of course no motoring tourist can hope to find such an inn anywhere, now' (*WT* 133). It is to this spatial transformation of rural England into an object of tourist inquiry that the final section of this chapter will turn as we metaphorically leave the road and enter – on foot – Conrad's pastoral.

Senseless pedestrianism and the path of life: *Chance* (1914)

The English, as Conrad was well aware, have a particular fondness for walking. In *The Secret Agent*, Tibbles explains to Inspector Heat that the Home Secretary likes to stroll to and from the House of Commons 'for the sake of a little exercise' (*SA* 105), and in *Under Western Eyes* Nathalie Haldin tells the teacher of languages, 'I did come out for a walk . . . for exercise, as you English say' (*UWE* 195). When Ford Madox Ford caricatured Conrad as Simeon Brandetski in *The Simple Life Limited* (1911), he was careful to include chronic laziness among the hack-writer's vices of racism, womanizing and egoism: 'He hated to walk, he hated to get on to the back of a pony, he disliked even standing still. He wanted to be in a hammock for ever and ever . . .' (Ford, 1911: 73). Ford's elision of moral degeneracy with slothfulness says as much about his own prejudices as the cultural significance attached to walking in Edwardian Britain; implicitly, Brandetski's unpopularity among the local villagers and his aversion to physical exercise are the natural corollary of his misanthropy, narcissism and un-Englishness. Both charges were, of course, slurs on Conrad's character. Neighbours may have seen him as a crusty squire but he enjoyed the trust of local trades people, most of the village came to listen when the great pianist Ignacy Paderewski played in his house, and even the village hall in Bishopsbourne was named in his honour (Conrad, 1981: 153, 161). Nor did Conrad hate walking. In the first place, many of his closest friends were energetic walkers. 'We are ready for you whenever you like to come for a few days on the plan of country walks,' he told Galsworthy in June 1902 (*CL* 2: 426), and he noted that Arthur Marwood 'walks the ten miles religiously every Tuesday' (4: 414) in order to call at his house.[42] Moreover, Conrad himself enjoyed regular walks, as Robert Hampson has pointed out (Hampson, 1992: 170–1) and even regarded them as a key element of his creative method. 'I will think of it as I take my daily walk' (*CL* 4: 62), he told Pinker in March 1908, referring to the title of what would become *Under Western Eyes*. It makes perfect sense, then, that walking should have emerged as a central theme of a work that its author described as 'my bid for popularity' (*CL* 5: 290) and that Thomas Moser has called 'Conrad's most *English* novel' (Moser, 1975: 207).

The bipartite structure of *Chance*, the first half of which is set in South-East England and the second aboard the Australia-bound *Ferndale*, suggests that by the time he began redrafting it in 1909 Conrad had come to envisage the novel as a comparison of life on shore with life at sea, the latter representing a space of moral and emotional integrity capable of overcoming the deceit and self-interest generated on land. To be sure, this reading of the novel as dramatizing what Juliet McLaughlan calls 'a sustained antithesis: land "values" (all negative) *versus* sea values (which in the context are true values)' (McLaughlan, 1992: 69) is supported by the relatively simple plot. After being variously neglected and exploited by her father, her governess, her relatives and a sexually predatory employer, Flora de Barral languishes in a holiday cottage rented by John and Zoe Fyne, from which she unexpectedly elopes with Zoe's brother, Captain Anthony. On board Anthony's ship, Flora and he are joined by Flora's father, a confidence trickster newly released from prison. De Barral's attempt to poison Anthony is thwarted by the intervention of the young second mate, Charles Powell, but Anthony dies a hero's death on a subsequent voyage when the *Ferndale* is involved in a collision at sea. By this time, a mutual attraction has developed between Flora and Powell that nonetheless remains strictly decorous. The several narrative strands are woven together by Marlow, Powell and the frame-narrator during spare moments while cruising on the Thames estuary, a suitably intermediary location between land and sea as well as a figurative middle-ground between what Marlow calls 'the now nearly vanished sea-life under sail' (*C* 21) and its amateurish successor, yachting. It is here, too, that the first happy ending in a Conrad novel takes place when, after a decent interval of years, Flora is reunited with Powell, who has taken to sailing his cutter on the Essex creek near her house.

Conrad saw *Chance*'s setting rather differently. Revising the version serialized in the *New York Herald* the previous year, he told Methuen in March 1913 that 'the novel I am now writing has no more sea in it than the ordinary citizen can enjoy from the end of Brighton pier' (*CL* 5: 201). Like his summary of *Heart of Darkness* as a 'wild story of a journalist' (2: 407), this estimation differs substantially from the terms in which the novel is often discussed today. As Susan Jones has shown, reinventing Conrad's public image was a necessary strategy for successfully marketing *Chance* to a female readership, and his reference to Brighton pier undoubtedly attests to his desire to shake off the label of writer of sea-stories. At the same time, the comment defines the novel's maritime component as literally subordinate to a land-based and touristic sensibility. On Brighton's waterfront, Flora remembers fondly, 'the band was playing; and there was the sea – the blue gaiety of the sea' (*C* 171). Significantly, *Chance*'s seaside resorts straddle an uneasy intersection of personal freedom and leisure time, particularly that of women: Zoe Fyne recuperates from childbirth in Brighton; Flora is a failure as the companion of an old lady holidaying in Bournemouth; and Brighton is where the governess and her companion toy with and then abandon Flora. The bystanders who witness Fyne's clumsy rescue of Flora see only 'the spectacle of a shameless middle-aged man abducting headlong into the upper regions of a respectable hotel a terrified young girl obviously under age' (97), the sight of an older man accompanied by a girl young enough to be his daughter clearly prompting murky associations ('shameless', 'obviously under age') in the minds of Brighton residents, perhaps those 'ordinary citizens' whom Flora remembers having stared at her and de Barral during their walks along the Parade.[43]

Unlike the working worlds of metropolitan espionage and policing in *The Secret Agent* or the colonial settings of Marlow's other narratives in 'Youth' and *Lord Jim, Chance* is firmly located in provincial space and holiday time. Indeed, the story which Marlow dismissively characterizes as 'an episode of one of my humdrum holidays in the green country' (*C* 79) is, more accurately, a Conradian variation on the holiday romance. The Fynes, who themselves eloped in a 'runaway match' (52) after a holiday encounter in the countryside, take into their home a girl who marries first one vacationing sailor and then, eventually, a second. Explaining the unusual circumstances of his involvement with the Fynes, Marlow emphasizes to his listeners, 'You must understand that I cultivated the Fynes only in the country, in their holiday time. Of their existence in town I knew no more than may be inferred from analogy' (34). And when he runs into Flora on a London street, he is insistent on the matter: 'You understand that I am not their friend. I am only a holiday acquaintance' (151).

Crucially, Flora has inadvertently joined the Fynes on a walking holiday, a mixture of sport, recreation and tourism whose modernity parallels that of the themes of Suffragism and financial fraud that critics often cite as evidence of *Chance's* topicality. John Fyne's professional status as, in Marlow's patronizing phrase, 'a good little man in the Civil Service' (*C* 36), is less important for the purposes of the novel than his leisure identity as a zealous practitioner of the new activity of *pedestrianism*. Ostensibly a mere hobby, Fyne's relation to walking in fact more closely resembles membership of a New Age movement, involving a costume of 'knickerbocker suit' (33) and 'cycling stockings' (38) as well as a physical regimen that builds 'muscular arms' (39) and 'great pedestrian's calves' (68). His 'pedestrian genius' (43) is nothing less than a worldview that structures every human interaction, from the casual to the most intimate:

> Little Fyne's marriage was quite successful. There was no design at all in it. Fyne, you must know, was an enthusiastic pedestrian. He spent

his holidays tramping all over our native land. His tastes were simple. He put infinite conviction and perseverance into his holidays. At the proper season you would meet in the fields, Fyne, a serious-faced, broad-chested, little man, with a shabby knap-sack on his back, making for some church steeple. He had a horror of roads. He wrote once a little book called the 'Tramp's Itinerary,' and was recognised as an authority on the footpaths of England. So one year, in his favourite over-the-fields, back-way fashion he entered a pretty Surrey village where he met Miss Anthony. Pure accident, you see. They came to an understanding, across some stile, most likely. Little Fyne held very solemn views as to the destiny of women on this earth, the nature of our sublunary love, the obligations of this transient life and so on. He probably disclosed them to his future wife. Miss Anthony's views of life were very decided too but in a different way. I don't know the story of their wooing. I imagine it was carried on clandestinely and, I am certain, with portentous gravity, at the back of copses, behind hedges . . .   (31–2)

With its curiously syllogistic trio of opening sentences – success in marriage and an absence of 'design' both imply and are implied by the practice of pedestrianism – this passage lends itself to a number of interpretations. To begin with, it anticipates the rationalization of individual leisure time at mid-century that Theodore Adorno would dissect in his classic study of the 'rugged' conformism promoted by the *L.A. Times* astrology column (Adorno, 1994: 94–8). On this view, the renaming of walking as pedestrianism, like its investment with the professional virtues of 'conviction', 'perseverance', and 'authority', marks its evolution into a modern mass cultural artefact. Less walking than working, the pedestrianism that Marlow repeatedly describes as 'severe exercise' (*C* 41, 42) is thus a form of self-discipline, a voluntary equivalent to the prison régime in *The Secret Agent* that Michaelis experiences as 'tyrannical' interruptions 'for the odious purpose of taking exercise' (*SA* 94). What is more, as an instance of what Pierre Bourdieu has termed 'the legitimate art of living' (Bourdieu, 1984: 179), Fyne's pedestrianism exemplifies the stratifying role of aesthetic judgements and recreational preferences in modern class society. Despite seeming to refuse social convention in the name of a serendipitous individual freedom, Fyne's eschewing of 'design' in his marriage (or his choice of spouse) in fact signals his conformity to the middle-class values of independence and self-confidence that, as Marlow notes ironically, he and his wife have since reproduced in their offspring: 'the Fyne marriage was perfectly successful . . . being blessed besides by three healthy, active, self-reliant children, all girls. They were all pedestrians too. Even the youngest would wander away for miles if not restrained' (33). Just as the 'respectable vulgarity' (100) of de Barral's repellent cousin confirms his moral and social inferiority to Fyne – tellingly, the civil servant refuses to recognize the petit bourgeois factory owner as anything more than 'lower middle class' (100) – so, too, does the statement 'His tastes were simple' (31) effectively raise Fyne above the crass materialism of the grasping cousin's 'false simplicity' (100). Unsurprisingly, the Fynes speak of their children's 'rude health' as if it were 'a result of moral excellence' (105). On several counts, then, Flora's insertion into a family of avid pedestrians is more than just a plot device for introducing her to Captain Anthony.

What exactly was pedestrianism? Coined in the early nineteenth century and thereby predating the arrival of the term *automobilism* with which it is now usually paired, pedestrianism in Edwardian Britain covered two related activities. The first was competitive speed and endurance walking, whose semi-professional athletes had attracted large crowds on both sides of the Atlantic since the 1880s. Before becoming an Olympic sport, this plebeian variety of pedestrianism, also known as footracing, was practised by both sexes and often accompanied by unlicensed gambling and a boisterous theatricality akin to latterday professional wrestling. Feelings of cultural inferiority likely prompted C. Lang Neil to insist in his shilling handbook *Walking: A Guide to Pedestrianism for Athletes and Others* that pedestrianism was 'manly competition' and 'The Most Healthy and Least Artificial Sport' (Neil, 1903: 13, 15) as well as gravely instructing readers on the right way to put one foot in front of the other.

The second of these activities was firmly participatory. Indeed, the pioneers of this precursor of modern rambling or hiking frequently spoke in near-evangelical tones of the physical and mental benefits of regular walking. By 1907, pedestrian clubs had sprung up in Surrey, Yorkshire, Glasgow, Dundee, Liverpool, Manchester and many other cities, including a dozen in London, whose Federation of Rambling Clubs founded a national organization shortly afterwards (Hill, 1980: 18–38). The clubs' membership included large numbers of city-dwellers for whom statutory holidays and cheap rail transport had recently made possible regular excursions to the countryside. 'It is a good sign of the times to find so many young men of the working classes employing their Saturday afternoons in a ramble in the country,' noted an editorial in *The Gipsy Journal and British Tourist* in July 1895. Countryside residents, particularly those who, like the Conrads, lived in areas popular with the new walkers, were predictably less sanguine. The 1904 guide *How to Walk: The Whole Art of Training Without a Trainer* (Figure 6) contains a map titled 'Picturesque Walks Round London' showing the towns and villages that an ambitious pedestrian tourist could hope to reach in a day (Anon, 1904). Its suggested route to Southend (40½ miles) ran through Stanford-le-Hope, the Conrads' home from 1896 to 1898, and its routes to Sittingbourne (41 miles) and Tonbridge (31 miles) took the walker to within a few hours of each of the five houses occupied by the Conrads between 1898 and 1924 (Figure 7). With thick black lines radiating from it in every direction, the metropolis resembles a gigantic octopus stretching out to embrace its diminutive neighbours.[44]

As befits a London bureaucrat with a taste for country life, Fyne is an amalgam of both kinds of pedestrian. Like the amateur sportsman, he has developed his own 'pedestrian style' (*C* 41) – a technique Conrad variously describes as 'a rapid striding rush' (69) and an 'efficient pedestrian gait' (178) – and routinely covers distances that would exhaust a casual walker.[45] As the author of *How to Walk* enthused: 'Once the amateur walker has experienced the pleasure of seeing the miles slip by, almost without conscious effort, he will never be content to fall back into the flabby, nerveless condition that so many people remain in all their lives' (59–60). Fyne's ensemble of knickerbocker suit, tweed cap and knee-length stockings advertises the prowess that marks him off from the general population, leading Marlow to admit his own inability to match the civil servant's athletic vigour: 'Once clear of the garden Fyne gathered way like a racing cutter. What was a mile to him – or twenty miles?' (43).

Fyne also exhibits the characteristics of the second kind of pedestrian. Affecting a 'horror of roads' (*C* 31), he has written a guide to rural footpaths, a modest contribution to the growing body of literature aimed at the tourists now tentatively exploring the countryside beyond the reach of motor cars. Among the first regions covered by such pedestrian guides were the south-eastern counties of Surrey, Sussex, Kent and Essex, where much of *Chance* takes place; the highly successful *Field-Path Rambles* series by Edmund Taylor ('Walker Miles') began with *West Kent* in 1893, and was followed by the *Eastbourne Series* and *Canterbury and Kent Coast* in 1904.[46] At times Taylor's wealth of instructions, historical background and photographs gives the impression of a meticulously planned orienteering course rather than a casual stroll along rural byways, and the title of Fyne's own 'Tramp's Itinerary', with its very different connotations of vagabondage and sightseeing, similarly embodies the contradictoriness of attempting to reinvent the countryside as a touristic space of 'natural'

Figure 6 Cover illustration, *How To Walk* (1904). Reproduced with permission of Bodleian Library, Oxford.

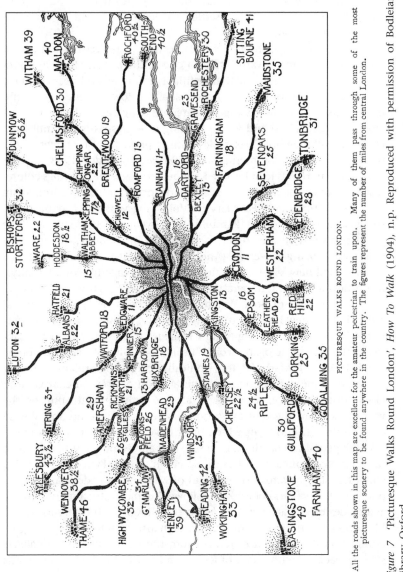

PICTURESQUE WALKS ROUND LONDON.

All the roads shown in this map are excellent for the amateur pedestrian to train upon. Many of them pass through some of the most picturesque scenery to be found anywhere in the country. The figures represent the number of miles from central London.

Figure 7 'Picturesque Walks Round London', *How To Walk* (1904), n.p. Reproduced with permission of Bodleian Library, Oxford.

freedom and spontaneity for city-dwellers. As Rebecca Solnit observes astutely in her excellent history of walking: '[T]o play at tramp or gypsy is one way of demonstrating that you are not really one. You must be complex to want simplicity, settled to desire this kind of mobility' (Solnit, 2001: 123–4).

In several respects, then, Conrad's portrait of pedestrian tourism in *Chance* is a straightforward satire on one of the popular 'fads and proprieties' (*C* 165) of shore life that justifiably infuriate level-headed sailors like Captain Anthony. Even Fyne's dog, Marlow remarks, goes into paroxysms of rage at passing wayfarers 'having the audacity to walk along the lane' (108) and at the buzzing of a 'trespassing bumble-bee' (114). Like all such novelties, pedestrianism proved an easy target for the mockery of genteel commentators. In *The Perfect Holiday* (1908), a series of sketches in the style of Jerome K. Jerome, the *Sunday Pictorial*'s columnist burlesqued the pursuit of 'pedestrian glory' as mindless automatism ('G', 1908: 19), and in February the following year *Punch* published a spoof account of 'correct Rambling (not walking)' that ridiculed the pedestrian's slavish adherence to maps and his blindness to the very countryside being traversed (Anon, 1909a: 114–15). Undeterred, the exponents of new leisure activities in the 1900s eagerly promoted physical fitness as a moral imperative, their resolve strengthened by revelations that a third of Boer War recruits had been rejected on medical grounds. 'The new interest in walking exercise is not a craze or an affectation,' announced C. Lang Neil in *Walking*, 'it is surely a return to sanity, in the best sense of the word, "health" – health of mind and body' (Neil, 1903: 17). Marlow refers ironically to this investment of bodily toning with mental distinction in his account of how Fyne, anxious at Flora's disappearance, contrives to fall into company with him on the way home from the railway station: 'Fyne caught me up and slowed down to my strolling gait which must have been infinitely irksome to his high pedestrian faculties. I am sure that all his muscular person must have suffered from awful physical boredom' (*C* 39). Fyne's ill-concealed condescension towards other modes of walking – a pedestrian anthropometry that echoes Robert Baden-Powell's famous strictures on posture as an index of 'character' in *Scouting For Boys* (1908) – is further satirized in Marlow's account of how the Fynes indignantly watch Charley, the governess's rakish accomplice, return from the bank 'strolling, *absolutely strolling* back . . . with an air of leisure and satisfaction' (*C* 85, emphasis added).

As his phrase 'awful physical boredom' implies, Marlow sees the disparity in the two men's rates of walking as symptomatic of a more profound intellectual incompatibility. With an eye to his auditors, he represents his contempt for Fyne's pedestrianism as a sailor's natural suspicion of landlubberly diversions: 'You know how I hate walking – at least on solid, rural earth; for I can walk a ship's deck a whole foggy night through, if necessary, and think little of it.... But to tramp the slumbering country-side in the dark is for me a wearisome nightmare of exertion' (*C* 42). '[T]he one good in pedestrian exercise,' he concludes grimly, 'is that it helps our natural callousness' (50). Behind this studied hostility towards pedestrianism lies a very different conception of what walking should be, especially as it relates to the imagination. Tellingly, Marlow twice remarks that Fyne's brand of pedestrianism, far from stimulating his perceptual faculties, appears to have impaired his ability to deal with new people and situations. When Fyne cannot remember the colour of Flora's hair and eyes, Marlow comments pointedly, 'He was very unobservant except as to the peculiarities of footpaths' (40). Later, he describes him as dodging an oncoming horse-cart 'with a purely instinctive precision; his mind had nothing to do with his movements' (179). Like his dreary conversational topics of 'Indian and colonial affairs, matters of trade, talk of travels, of seaside holidays' (32), Fyne's tedious allusions to his brother-in-law as 'the son of Carleon Anthony, the poet' confirm him as a cultural philistine, a point Marlow drives home with a series of heavy puns on his surname: 'a fine day . . . perfection for remaining indoors' (51); 'fine days are the best for stopping at home' (69); and 'a day much too fine to be wasted in walking exercise' (103).

In stark contrast, Marlow's conception of his own 'strolling gait' (*C* 39) as the physical corollary of 'contemplative aspirations' (69) – 'To drift is the only reposeful sort of motion (ask any ship if it isn't) and therefore consistent with thoughtfulness' (49) – attests to his nostalgia for an older, Romantic view of walking as an exercise of the imagination as much as of the body.[47] First expressed in the writings of William Wordsworth, Samuel Taylor Coleridge and Thomas De Quincey, this philosophy had been revived at the end of the nineteenth century by Robert Louis Stevenson's *Travels With a Donkey* (1879), Leslie Stephen's manifesto 'In Praise of Walking' (1902) and A. H. Sidgwick's *Walking Essays* (1912). As Marlow explains:

> What really jarred upon me was the rate of his walking. Differences in politics, in ethics and even in aesthetics need not arouse angry antagonism . . . . But a temperamental difference, temperament being immutable, is the parent of hate. That's why religious quarrels

are the fiercest of all. My temperament, in matters pertaining to solid land, is the temperament of leisurely movement, of deliberate gait. And there was that little Fyne pounding along the road in a most offensive manner; a man wedded to thick-soled, laced boots; whereas my temperament demands thin shoes of the lightest kind. Of course there could never have been question of friendship between us; but under the provocation of having to keep up with his pace I began to dislike him actively.   (*C* 44)

Here is a model of walking as 'temperament', that is to say, less sport or exercise than peripatetic philosophy, with which Conrad, mulling over literary problems on his daily stroll, would surely have identified. Indeed, his circle of acquaintance included some of its best-known practitioners: the poet William Davis, author of the unsentimental *Autobiography of a Super-tramp* (1907); Hilaire Belloc, whose *The Path to Rome* (1902) and *The Old Road* (1904) effectively established the pedestrian travelogue as a modern genre; and literary walking enthusiasts such as G. K. Chesterton, E. V. Lucas, Ford Madox Ford, John Galsworthy and H. G. Wells (whom Jessie Conrad identified as her husband's model for Fyne).[48] After the *Daily Mail* published 'A Happy Wanderer', his favourable review of C. Bogue Luffmann's walking memoir *Quiet Days in Spain* (1910), Conrad had to decline an invitation to contribute to *The Tramp*, a new magazine devoted to literature and walking, adding politely, 'tho' I should like to' (*CL* 4: 394). Predicated upon spontaneity, individualism and temperamental expression, *The Tramp*'s brand of culturally exclusive walking was as far removed from the foot racers and itinerary followers of popular pedestrianism as pompous 'little' Fyne is from Conrad's 'unforgettable Englishman' in the Furka Pass. In Marlow's dismissive comment, 'senseless pedestrianism was Fyne's panacea for all the ills and evils bodily and spiritual of the universe' (*C* 69), the crucial qualifier 'senseless' directs the reader towards this alternative mode of walking, that is, untouristic and doubly *sensible* in being moderate as well as impressionable.

From the thematizing of pedestrianism as an Edwardian popular culture we come, finally, to its function within a narrative that misleadingly insists upon the aleatory. In the instalment of *Chance* that appeared in the *New York Herald* on 18 February 1912, Conrad has Marlow declare a preference for 'the tale one can watch, pursue, lose track of, pick up afresh and lose again, and then in the silence, in the stillness of a tracker at fault listen to its distant sounds' (Jones, 1996: 76). An allusion to the scouting vogue popularized by Ernest Thompson Seton and Baden-Powell, the metaphor also invites us to think of movement through space as a narrative coda, a pedestrian unconscious, so to speak. To be sure, almost every character or social interaction in the novel is rendered in terms of walking: Marlow's exchanges with John Fyne and Flora in the countryside and London; Charles Powell's wanderings, by turns dejected and ecstatic, in and around the Shipping Office on Tower Hill; the de Barrals parading 'hand-in-hand' (*C* 70) by the sea; the hurried departure of the governess and Charlie, whom Fyne precisely recalls as 'walking independently' (96); Flora's 'ugly pilgrimage' (158) on foot from Whitechapel Station to East India Dock Road; Anthony's endless 'pacing [of] the poop' (206) aboard the *Ferndale*; de Barral choosing to 'toddle off for a solitary walk' (283) to avoid his son-in-law; and the seemingly extraneous detail that 'After leaving the Registry Office Flora de Barral and Roderick Anthony had gone for a walk in a park' (255). It is, moreover, only because Anthony is not a pedestrian that Fyne abandons him in order to visit an invalid colleague, thereby unwittingly ensuring that the captain's 'slow casual stroll' (118) will bring him into contact with the unchaperoned Flora. As Marlow explains, 'They had met somewhere accidentally (which of them crossed the other's path, as the saying is, I don't know)' (119). Indeed, at times almost everything in *Chance* seems to be on its feet, from Marlow's mental image of 'three trained dogs dancing on their hind legs' (46) to the prostitutes taken in by de Barral's swindle: 'the word Thrift was out in the streets walking arm in arm with righteousness . . . . The very drabs of the pavement, poor things, didn't escape the fascination' (58); even time itself advances in 'leaden-footed minutes' (130). In *Chance*'s central chapter, 'On the Pavement', the metropolitan humanity surging around Marlow and Flora, 'an unsmiling sombre stream not made up of lives but of mere unconsidered existences' (157), is a pedestrian crowd worthy of Eliot's *The Waste Land*.

Importantly, not just streetwalking but all walking in *Chance* is heavily inflected by gender. Anthony tells Flora that he has 'not been for a walk with a lady for years and years' (*C* 164); Zoe Fyne's 'ruddy out-of-doors complexion' and 'blouses with a starched front like a man's shirt' (33) parallel the depiction of Suffragettes as mannish pedestrians in contemporary newspapers and advertisements; and from his chauvinistic perspective even Marlow has to concede that 'Women can't go forth on the high roads and byways to pick up a living even when dignity, independence, or existence itself are at stake' (131).[49] As if in confirmation of this principle, Flora's confession of having met her husband 'in the country, on a road' (269) elicits a groan from her father and the accusation of having sold herself 'as much as if you had gone on the streets' (284–5). And so it is precisely in the open air and on foot that the women of *Chance* seek their freedom. Abandoned by her husband, Mrs de Barral wanders forlornly around the village until she meets young Zoe Anthony, who, in defiance of her father, accompanies her on 'melancholy strolls to and fro in the great avenue of chestnuts' (57). The reader learns that Zoe, as Mrs Fyne, 'always walked off directly after tea' (35) with her arm around the latest girlfriend whom she seeks to 'befriend, counsel, and guide . . . on the path of life' (40), and that she enjoys 'strolling aimlessly on the road' (168) with her daughters at dusk. In fact, Zoe views spatial transgression as integral to feminism, a doctrine that Marlow summarizes brusquely: 'no scruples should *stand in the way* of a woman . . . from *taking the shortest cut* towards securing for herself the easiest possible existence. She had even the right *to go out of existence* without considering anyone's feelings' (47, my emphases). In this way, *Chance* can be seen to stage both extremes of gendered authority – Zoe's militant feminism and Carleon Anthony's patriarchal tyranny – as attempts to control pedestrian space.[50] Thus Marlow explains: 'Her father had kept her strictly cloistered. Marriage with Fyne was certainly a change but only to another kind of claustration' (52).

As with Conrad's meditations upon consumption and speculation in 'An Anarchist' and 'The Partner', which will be examined in the next chapter, *Chance* attaches a meaning to pedestrian movement that constantly shifts between the metaphorical and the literal. The frame-narrator's bland observation that '[i]ntelligence leads people astray as far as passion sometimes' (C 31) finds an ironic echo in Marlow's comment that 'a menaced passion . . . . is capable, for its own ends, of walking backwards into a precipice' (81) as well as in his suggestion that Flora 'be given some sort of footing in the world' (148). He recounts being upbraided by Fyne 'as though he had been on the watch for a lapse from the straight path' (144), and Powell regrets the spoiling of 'a quiet watch on deck when one may let one's thoughts roam in space and time' (301). Similarly, the German who attempts to seduce Flora is said to have been 'straying from the path of virtue' (137), whilst she herself elects not to 'enter on the path of confidences' (270) with her father. In this unstable cultural landscape, with its emphatic rejection of the discipline of organized pedestrianism, real walking becomes the truthful expression of a state of mind – Fyne's 'distracted gait' (146), Flora's 'walking slowly . . . [from] caution or reluctance' (184), Anthony's 'roam[ing] the streets . . . in the manner of a happy and exulting lover' (252) – rooted in individual temperament rather than pedagogical guidebooks or frenetic competition. As Marlow asks rhetorically: 'Our mental conclusions depend so much on momentary physical sensations, don't they?' (45). This ambulatory logic is dramatized in exemplary fashion in the two climactic scenes around which Conrad organizes the novel, each of which symbolically reclaims a particular kind of space from tourism. In the first, Flora crosses a field and two post-and-rail fences in order to reach the edge of a deep quarry.[51] Having decided upon suicide in preference to a life of economic or sexual exploitation, probably what Marlow has in mind by 'dead souls lying so to speak at the foot of high unscaleable places' (C 43), she is deterred at the last minute by a fear of the dog jumping after her and she turns back to join Marlow on the road below. Marlow is impressed by Flora's courage and perhaps also by the anti-pedestrian and anti-feminist aspects of her plan to leave John Fyne's footpath once and for all while clutching Zoe Fyne's walking-stick. Indeed, during their second meeting 'walk' develops into a codeword for this supreme moment of self-assertion:

'And so you gave up that walk you proposed to take?'
'Yes, I gave up the walk,' she said slowly before raising her down-cast eyes. When she did so it was with an extraordinary effect. It was like catching sight of a piece of blue sky, of a stretch of open water.
(C 173)

Appropriately, the second scene takes place aboard the *Ferndale* on precisely such a stretch of open water when Powell glimpses de Barral, the landlubberly supercargo whom he earlier described as walking 'as if he were carrying a glass full of water on his head' (C 286), surreptitiously putting poison into Captain Anthony's glass of brandy-and-water. The topography of the cabin that Powell painstakingly explains to Marlow has attracted the attention of several critics, who see in its disordered spatial layout a metaphor of social or sexual subversion. In the context of pedestrianism, however, the crucial detail is that Powell takes up his viewing position beside the saloon skylight while stooping to pick up some rope on his 'regular officer-of-the-watch tramp' (303). It is, in other words, a triumphant proof of Marlow's earlier diatribe against pointlessly tramping the countryside at night: the purposive and observant walk of the night watch officer effectively saves the lives of his captain and, ultimately, the woman who will become his wife. In an epilogue that echoes both scenes, Anthony and Powell conceal de Barral's own death as a heart attack in order to spare Flora from the shadow of suicide, as Marlow puts it, 'falling upon her path' (322).

Chance's extended engagement with the popular cultural politics of walking recapitulates many of the central features of Conrad's treatment of tourism in his novels and short fiction, particularly their thematic emphasis on tourism's disquieting reconfiguration of social relations and their narrative recycling of actual tourist experiences and texts. Far from simply capitulating to a putatively feminine readership's predilection for romantic plot lines and pastoral settings, the novel seeks to represent and in some sense to rescue an England that its author saw as falling prey to modern tourists – people like the Fynes, who impress Marlow with their air of having 'annexed the whole country-side' (145) – in much the same way as the spontaneous and attentive walking of the sailors Anthony and Powell saves Flora from the dreary prospect that awaits her 'outside the pale' (158). As Conrad declared in one of his last essays, 'The *Torrens*: A Personal Tribute': 'A passage under sail brings out in the course of days whatever there may be of sea love and sea sense in any individual whose soul is not indissolubly wedded to the pedestrian shore' (*LE* 23).

At the same time, *Chance* explicitly acknowledges literary convention – Marlow quips about Fyne having to make '[a] sort of anti-sentimental journey' (*C* 114), an allusion to Laurence Sterne's *A Sentimental Journey* (1768) – and Conrad's portrayal of pedestrianism as physically and intellectually dulling makes a Sterne-like rejoinder to the sentimental popular narratives being generated by this new kind of tourism: works like James Winifred's short pedestrian romance, 'A Serious Afternoon', published in the first number of *The Tramp* in March 1910, or the 'Romances of the Road' fiction feature that had appeared in *The Rambler: A Penny Weekly Devoted to Out-door Life* since 1897. And whereas *Chance*'s shipboard setting, foregrounded by the officer-and-a-lady motif of the cover illustration of the first English edition, has long been recognized as integral to its commercial appeal, the seemingly unmotivated choice of location for its shore episodes should be seen in the context of an extension of tourism to the more obscure corners of the English countryside. Despite its reputation for being irredeemably prosaic, the county of Essex was enjoying a steady growth in tourism in the early twentieth century, thanks, in part, to the publication of illustrated walking guides such as Reginald Beckett's *Romantic Essex: Pedestrian Impressions* (1901) and reliable sailing charts such as that provided in the Essex volume of Frank Cowper's *Sailing Tours* (1892, revised 1909). In every respect, then, it is entirely fitting that *Chance* should end on the Essex marshes with Powell conveying his intention of proposing to Flora in terms of a desire 'to see Mrs. Anthony home' (*C* 330) and that Marlow should leave the couple to walk, not into the proverbial sunset or towards a shining hill-top, but into their own private gloaming.

3
Advertising

> The public's so used to the guidance of Advertis[e]ment! Why!
> even I myself feel the spell of such emphasis.
>
> Conrad to James Pinker, 14 January 1901
> (*CL* 2: 319)

> In various parts of the civilized and uncivilized world I have
> had to swallow B.O.S. with more or less benefit to myself . . . .
> But I have never swallowed its advertisements.
>
> 'An Anarchist' (1906) (*SS* 136)

A witty cartoon in *Punch* in September 1890 acknowledged the howl of genteel protest that had greeted the erection of an advertising billboard on Ludgate Hill the previous month. Drawn by the talented Edward Tennyson Reed, 'Picturesque London' presents a Swiftian panorama of monstrous umbrellas, boots, collars, bottles, gloved hands and top hats, at the centre of which stands an oddly two-dimensional St Paul's Cathedral, as if to suggest that the capital's tallest building has itself become a kind of hoarding (Figure 8).[1] Below, a pair of enormous opera-glasses scrutinize the city's ant-like inhabitants as they pass along Fleet Street beneath a colossal articulated mannikin, advertising's own Gulliver. Above, stretching towards the horizon like the augury of a dismally commercial future, a huge banner flies the single word 'Blowvril' in an obvious allusion to the food manufacturer Bovril, the cartoon's only identifiable brand. In an accompanying poem titled 'Sky-Signs of the Times', Reed updated Thomas Carlyle's classic jeremiad against mechanization and profit-worship in 'Signs of the Times' (1829):

> Colossal bottles blot the air, to tell
> That MUCKSON's Temperance drink is a great sell.

Here's a huge hat, as black as sombre Styx,
Flanked by the winsome legend, 'Ten and Six.'
Other Sky-signs praise Carpets, Ginghams,
Mugg's Music-hall, and 'Essence of the Ox.'

(Anon., 1890: 119)

For all its mockery of the commercializing of public space, 'Picturesque London' attests to the aura of dynamism and limitless possibility surrounding advertising at the turn of the century, particularly in the capital city of what economic historians P. J. Cain and A. G. Hopkins have called 'the warehouse and shop-window of the world' (Cain and Hopkins, 1993: 89). In this metropolitan landscape of animation and disfigurement, advertising has become metonymic of modernity, its disappearance or eradication almost unimaginable. George Gissing might present the poster-covered underground station in *In The Year of Jubilee* (1894) as '[a] battle-ground of advertisements . . . a symbol to the gaze of that relentless warfare which ceases not, night and day, in the world above' (Gissing, 1994: 259), and H. G. Wells gave an honest assessment of the medium's indispensability for contemporary urban life by having his awestruck Time Traveller explain of London in the eight hundredth millennium: 'There were no signs of struggle, neither social nor economical struggle. The shop, the advertisement, traffic, all that commerce which constitutes the body of our world, was gone' (Wells, 1977: 37).

Conrad's own experience of London was profoundly shaped by advertising. An advertisement for 'respectable youths' first brought him to the capital in 1878, he later recalled, and he had navigated the 'wonder city' while clutching a newspaper notice for a shipping agent whose address lay 'as if graven deep in my brain' (*NLL* 122). The capital's commercial bustle evidently continued to fascinate and disorient him in equal measure. He told Elsie Hueffer in 1902 that a recent holiday there had been 'a week of what to rustics of our sort was a Whirl – (with a capital W)' (*CL* 2: 450), and in his fiction London's shop windows are unsettling meeting-places between the beholder's gaze and the strange aura of objects on display: Bland's gun-shop on the Strand in 'Karain' presents a ghostly face peering out from among the 'dark and polished tubes that can cure so many illusions' (*TU* 54); the map of an African river on Fleet Street in 'Heart of Darkness' mesmerizes Marlow 'as a snake would a bird' (*Y* 52); and readers of *The Secret Agent* are given an inventory of the inflammatory and pornographic contents of the 'mysteriously dim window' (*SA* 148) of Adolf Verloc's stationery shop in Soho.

Figure 8 Edward Tennyson Reed, 'Picturesque London', *Punch* (6 September 1890), 119. Reproduced with permission of Bodleian Library, Oxford.

Coincidentally, just two months before the incident that inspired *Punch*'s cartoon, Conrad spent a hectic fortnight in London buying supplies for what he expected would be a long tour of duty as a steamboat captain in the Congo Free State. In a letter to Karol Zagórski, he recorded his impressions of the city as a frenetically commercial space:

> If you had only seen all the tin boxes and revolvers, the high boots and the tender farewells . . . and if you knew all the bottles of medicine and all the affectionate wishes I took away with me, you would understand in what a typhoon, cyclone, hurricane, earthquake – no! – in what a universal cataclysm, in what a fantastic atmosphere of mixed shopping, business, and affecting scenes, I passed two whole weeks. (*CL* 1: 52)

Conrad's choice of terms – 'typhoon', 'hurricane', 'earthquake', 'universal cataclysm' – betrays an underlying unease about the 'fantastic atmosphere' of commodity retail. These fears were to be confirmed during his six-month stint in King Leopold's killing-fields, where the severed hands of *Punch*'s three-shilling glovist had found a ghastly echo in the punishment meted out to Congolese labourers who failed to deliver their quotas of ivory and rubber, the raw materials for the umbrella handles and boot heels now dominating the London skyline. Writing from Kinshasa in September 1890, Conrad described the Société Belge du Haut-Congo's manager as someone 'who considers himself a merchant although he is only a kind of African shop-keeper' (*CL* 1: 62), and in his fictionalized account of these events in *Heart of Darkness* he places special emphasis upon the baleful semiotics of the Belgian administration. When he tries to comfort a dying worker, Marlow is unexpectedly confronted by a scrap of cotton around the man's neck that raises awkward questions about the link between exploitative production and conspicuous consumption: 'He had tied a bit of white worsted round his neck – Why? Where did he get it? Was it a badge – an ornament – charm – a propitiatory act? Was there any idea at all connected with it? It looked startling round his black neck, this bit of white thread from beyond the seas' (*Y* 67). Although Marlow is disturbed by the rag's sheer incongruousness – a visual shock that anticipates the photographs in our own era of drought victims in T-shirts bearing the logos of soft drinks companies – the object's shape and location raise the spectre of a far older instrument of enslavement. Again, when the Eldorado Exploring Expedition's 'sordid buccaneers' (87) arrive with a consignment of imported goods at the Central Station, Conrad's name for Kinshasa, Marlow sees only 'their absurd air of disorderly flight with the loot of innumerable outfit shops and provision stores, that, one would think, they were lugging, after a raid, into the wilderness for equitable division' (87). And as he talks with the Russian just moments before finally meeting Kurtz, he realizes that the colony's implausibly skewed balance of trade – the anomaly that, in real life, had first roused the suspicions of campaigner Edmund Morel – conceals a diabolic zero-point of commodity exchange:

> 'But [Kurtz] had no goods to trade with by that time,' I objected. 'There's a good lot of cartridges left even yet,' he answered, looking away.
>
> (*Y* 128)

Conrad's fraught relation to the phantasmagoric world of commodity circulation provides the starting point for this chapter. As with the earlier chapters' treatment of his relation to visual entertainment and tourism, it offers an overview of Conrad's attitude towards advertising in general before going on to make close readings of several works in which he addresses specific aspects of the medium. Following Jennifer Wicke's *Advertising Fictions* (1988), Ellen Gruber Garvey's *The Adman in the Parlor* (1996) and Garry Leonard's *Advertising and Commodity Culture in Joyce* (1998), it is premised upon the view that literary texts can bear the imprint of advertising at several discrete levels: as material artefacts such as the Congo propaganda that Marlow dismisses as 'rot let loose in print' (*Y* 59) or the 'empty Huntley and Palmer biscuit-tin' (85) to which he compares his steamer; as a less tangible discourse regulating the inner-most desires of individuals such as the Russian who praises ' "the excel-lent English tobacco" ' (123); and, most abstractly, as a semiotic system expressive of the new global economy in which the starched head-covering of a Brussels secretary and the large cotton handkerchief of Kurtz's cousin have unsettling counterparts in the rags of Congolese slaves, the meticulously starched linen of the Company accountant, and what Marlow calls 'ghastly glazed calico that made you shudder only to look at it' (84).[2]

Theorists have long debated the extent to which a professionalized system for stimulating consumer demand can justifiably be considered a field of popular culture. Rather than seeking to adjudicate in the matter, this chapter focuses on the stakes in Conrad's own identification of adver-tising as an expression of popular culture. Its central section offers a reap-praisal of 'An Anarchist' (1906) and 'The Partner' (1911), two relatively neglected magazine stories written during the difficult years preceding the commercial success of '*Twixt Land and Sea* (1912) and *Chance* (1914).

In these stories, which evince a critical incisiveness and a topicality that belies their weak standing in the canon, Conrad situates advertising at the cutting edge of a capitalist system organized around *speculation* and *consumption* – figurative terms whose literal connotations of seeing and eating provided the inspiration for these two tightly constructed satires. Conrad's specific choice of a patent medicine and a patent food as themes, it is argued, reflects not just the ubiquity of these products in contemporary advertisements but also his dim view of advertising's impact upon the realms of health and nutrition. More than just melodramatic pot-boilers, the stories represent attempts to demystify aspects of advertising and commodity circulation: in 'An Anarchist', branding and the new global corporation; and in 'The Partner', venture capital investment and the modern adman. The chapter closes by examining Conrad's exploration of advertising's role in fusing popular culture and (unsound) business in *Chance*, a novel whose own success, appropriately enough, owed much to the booming of its author by the mass-circulation *New York Herald*.

Abominable advertisements and the meaning of things

Conrad made little secret of his contempt for advertising. 'I must strongly protest against the abominable advertisement being put opposite my dedication,' he admonished T. Fisher Unwin in January 1896 after finding an 'Opinions of the Press' page at the front of *An Outcast of the Islands* (*CL* 1: 261). Behind his mocking alliteration – 'this blighting bill, this pernicious placard, this abominable advertisement,' thunders Dickens's union agitator Slackbridge in *Hard Times* – lies the genuine concern of a writer confronted by a medium whose power over literary production could no longer be ignored or denied. He might tell Pinker that he had no wish to encourage the 'absurd and debasing practice' (*CL* 3: 38) of advertising authors via interviewing, but lacklustre sales of *The Secret Agent* led him to instruct his agent, 'I expect to be made *a feature* of [Methuen's] advertising' (*CL* 4: 44, Conrad's emphasis), and by August 1919 he was authorizing his American publisher to use photographs from a recent *Vanity Fair* photo-shoot 'for publicity purposes' (*CL* 6: 479). He even blamed the poor reception of *The Rover* on the 'confounded prenatal publicity' (*LL* 2: 337) surrounding his much-anticipated Mediterranean novel *Suspense*. And so it is a nice paradox that disdain for advertising became an integral part of Conrad's public image, itself the object of careful promotion in later years. He might confess to Gérard Jean-Aubry that he feared being laid 'open to the charge that "Conrad looks after his own advertisements"' (*CL* 6: 314) – Henry James and Edith Wharton had sniggered privately at his claim to have no part in Booth Tarkington's campaign to boost his American reputation – but to readers of newspapers and magazines he appeared in quite another light. On 12 May 1923, a month after Conrad's portrait had graced the cover of *Time* magazine, the *Boston Evening Transcript* solemnly informed readers of its full-page illustrated interview with the author: 'Joseph Conrad is honest in his dislike of publicity. He is a shy man, seeking no advertisement.'

Love it or hate it, there was no escaping the new medium. Describing a visit to Conrad's home in Kent in 1912, the critic James Huneker recalled seeing from his train window 'American liver-pill advertisements pinned to the landscape' (*JCIR* 22). Whether or not Conrad, who was himself afflicted periodically by liver trouble, had these eyesores in mind when he wrote 'The Partner', a tale about an American advertiser bent on launching a patent medicine, Huneker's observation confirms the omnipresence of advertisements in late Victorian and Edwardian Britain. These were years in which advertising grew at breakneck speed, led by a vanguard of manufacturers eager to forge a new kind of relationship between consumers and 'repeat purchase' commodities such as soap, cigarettes and medicines. Precise statistics on the growth of late-nineteenth-century advertising are scarce but its scale can be measured by the fact that the London Motor Show attracted £250,000 worth of advertising during a single week in 1907. When Conrad began his writing career in the mid-1890s, a large firm like Mather & Crowther could already afford to retain a staff of 100, and by the time of his death the industry was reckoned to employ over 100,000 people in Britain alone, an expansion that had led to the formation of professional bodies such as the Advertisers' Protection Society (1900), the Incorporated Society of Advertising Consultants (1907) and the Association of British Advertising Agents (1917).[3]

Advertisers were quick to exploit new technologies such as the neon sign and colour lithograph printing as well as marketing innovations such as publicity stunts, sports sponsorship and mail-order selling. Advertising's tightening grip on the retail economy was mirrored by its spectacular entry into formerly inaccessible or restricted areas. Long a vital source of revenue for newspapers and periodicals, manufacturers and retailers began flexing their muscles in the late 1890s, just as Conrad's work began appearing in serial form and even succeeded in forcing the staid *Times* to lift its restrictions on column size and its ban on display advertisements. 'During the last year or two there has been a marked expansion in advertising enterprise, and an equally striking change in advertising methods,' observed the *Yorkshire Post*'s editor H. J. Palmer: 'In newspaper history the year 1896 will be said to have witnessed the successful revolt of the advertiser from the stifling bondage in which he has been enchained for over a century' (Nevett, 1982: 80). Five years later, the London *Star*, a paper that would later serialize Conrad's *Victory*, sold half of an entire number to the British tobacco company Godfrey Phillips for what it trumpeted as 'the most costly, colossal and convincing advertisement ever used in an evening newspaper' (Williams, 1980: 178).

Advertising's importance for the late nineteenth- and early twentieth-century economy has been a subject of heated controversy among economic and cultural historians. The influential model of advertising as a response to overproduction, which Terry Nevett and others have advanced, has recently been challenged by Roy Church (Church, 2000), who argues that the creation of a mass market in Britain resulted from active decision-making on the part of corporate executives. Church also contests several of the claims made by Thomas Richards's influential cultural history *The Commodity Culture of Late-Victorian England* (1990), specifically, that the Great Exhibition of 1851 triggered a national shift towards commodity consumption, that advertisements usually depicted the commodities themselves, and that the working class remained largely untouched by advertising until the 1880s.

A similar absence of consensus characterized the debate over advertising's economic role among commentators in Conrad's day. In one corner, Ernest Calkins and Ralph Holden declared in *The Art of Modern Advertising* (1905) that advertising had developed from 'an untrustworthy instrument of quacks and charlatans' into 'an engine in the conduct and expansion of business' (Calkins and Holden, 1905: 1). More extravagantly, William Stead, Jr boasted in *The Art of Advertising* (1899) that progress itself would inevitably grind to a halt without what he called 'the vital force which animates society' (Stead, 1899: 11–12). In the opposing corner, sceptics lambasted advertising as a blot on the landscape, a public nuisance and a parasite on the national economy – views that, as will be seen, were shared by Conrad. As Richardson Evans noted scornfully in the *National Review* in October 1890, 'the cost of wholesale puffing is included in the price, and there is hardly a case in which, by proper inquiry, a substitute or equal, perhaps identical quality, may not be procured at a reduction of 25 per cent' (Evans, 1890: 180). Even the definition of an advertisement was a matter of dispute. Advertisers' promises, for example, did not become legally binding until 1892, when a customer successfully sued the Carbolic Smoke Ball Company for reneging on an offer to pay 1,000 guineas to anyone who contracted influenza after buying its product. Meanwhile, cash incentives such as the gold coins which Thomas Lipton hid in lumps of cheese narrowly escaped prosecution as gambling, and other ingenious marketing ploys such as bulk telegrams were repeatedly accused of violating individual privacy.

The resourcefulness of advertisers was exemplified by one of the period's most heavily marketed products, Pear's Soap, whose infuriatingly catchy slogan 'Good Morning! Have you used Pear's Soap today?' entered the popular idiom in the 1880s. (In *Ulysses*, Joyce's wiseacre Bantam Lyons is still quoting it in 1904.) *Tit-Bits* might joke about the London visitor whose unfashionably high collar had attracted an offer from a bill-sticking firm, but no one could say with any confidence where advertisers would actually draw the line.[4] Since the visitor was said to be 'stopping at the Langham Hotel', a real hotel near Regent Street that published tourist guides, even this gag could have been a covert puff. As commentators often remarked, advertising was capable of cannibalizing other media with impressive ease: Beecham's, for example, juxtaposed the titles of popular songs to create dire product puffs such as ' "The Anchor's Weighed" in the "Bay of Biscay" with a supply of BEECHAM'S PILLS'. 'The more an advertisement appears not to be an advertisement, the better it is,' explained Nathaniel Fowler in his handbook *About Advertising* (1889) by way of preface to a handy list of commercially useful literary quotations such as 'DENTISTS. For there was never yet philosopher / That could endure the toothache patiently. *Much Ado About Nothing*' (Fowler, 1889: 50, 110).

Small wonder, then, that Derwent Miall chose to depict the hero of his comic novel *Disclosures of a Press Agent* (1912) as effortlessly converting the most improbable situations into bankable publicity. By the time the 'art' of advertising had become a talking-point in the press, its most fervent exponents were already confident enough to echo the *Times*'s advertising manager, Howard Bridgewater: 'Advertising has so recently come to be regarded as a science that many people still fail to recognise it in that – its proper – light' (Bridgewater, 1910: 1). Indeed, for the late Victorian public, advertising was now not only a science but the rightful preserve of science fiction. In the advertiser's untiring quest for new audiences, nothing was truly unthinkable. Jules Verne's story 'In the 29th Century' (1889) presents a global media tycoon ordering the projection of vast advertisements onto the clouds; George Allan England's

'A Message from the Moon' (1907) conjured up the prospect of a Lunar Advertising Company. A few months after the appearance of Conrad and Ford's *The Inheritors*, a fantasy in which advertising serves as the main tool of a conspiracy against capitalism itself, a contributor to the *Monthly Review* stated in all seriousness: 'Pears or Monkey Brand or Elliman or some of their enterprising compeers will eventually cover the entire dome of St Paul's with pictorial placards' (Cholmondeley, 1901: 79).

Advertising messages were even projected onto the safety curtain during the interval in theatrical performances, prompting Conrad's ironic response to suggestions by Basil Macdonald Hastings for changes to the script of *Victory: A Drama*: 'No doubt it would be "Grateful and comforting" (you remember Epps' [cocoa] adver[tisem]ents) to the audience' (*CL* 6: 3). Few could have denied W. Teignmouth Shore's observation in the *Fortnightly Review* in February 1907:

> Our daily life is permeated with advertising: advertisements in our paper and in our correspondence at breakfast; advertisements in the train, throughout the stations, on omnibuses, hoardings, shopfronts, and on the sky-line; advertisements in the office correspondence, probably on the blotting-pad and the hanging almanac; advertisements on the table, if we dine at an hotel or a restaurant; advertisements blazing from the housetops as we drive home from theatre or concert, where the programme was disguised in advertisements . . .
>
> (Shore, 1907: 307)

Although, as Shore's remarks suggest, much of the criticism of advertisements focused on their location, advertising content could also be highly provocative: moral reformers secured a ban on placards and pamphlets depicting the female acrobat Zaeo in 1890; and a storm of criticism forced the Quaker Oats Company to remove its name from Dover cliffs in 1897 (Fraser, 1981: 136). The game of cat-and-mouse continued, with anti-advertising campaigners successfully blocking an attempt to parade sandwich-board men in British army uniform, only for advertisers to deploy men in German uniform to advertise Walter Wood's invasion thriller *The Enemy in Our Midst*. Advertisers dressed sandwich-board men as country bumpkins, blacked-up 'minstrels', and escaped convicts, and on at least one occasion even painted slogans directly onto the bald heads of some hapless employees. 'One set of men was dressed to represent corpses until the public protested', the *Daily Graphic* recorded on 7 January 1891, one of numerous incidents that hastened the founding of the Society for Checking the Abuses of Public

Advertising (SCAPA) in 1893 and the passing of the Advertisement Regulation Act of 1907, which empowered local authorities to control the height of hoardings and commercial signs on public view. Advertising's popularity, however defined, was a prominent feature of such controversies. To be sure, Conrad's hostility towards the medium typifies the fact that resistance to advertising on aesthetic grounds came overwhelmingly from the upper and middle classes. (SCAPA pointedly titled its house journal *Beautiful World*.) And yet, as their nickname 'the poor man's picture gallery' reminds us, advertisements also made a strong appeal to the working class; the Royal Academician John Millais did not scruple to invoke this democratic argument when defending his widely censured decision to allow his painting *Bubbles* to be used in a poster for Pear's Soap (Garvey, 1996: 102–3). Moreover, although its aesthetic status would always remain contentious, the 'art' of advertising underwent a degree of cultural legitimation during these years, with some of its posters becoming collectables and the subject of specialist magazines and international exhibitions. As Aubrey Beardsley, himself a designer of advertisements for such mundane products as Bovril, announced with his customary panache: 'London will soon be resplendent with advertisements, and against a leaden sky skysigns will trace their formal arabesque. Beauty has laid siege to the city . . .' (Beardsley, 1894: 54).[5]

Conrad's rather bleaker view of this development is evidenced by his insistent depiction of advertising's physical artefacts as shabby or sordid: the 'line of yellow boards with blue letters on them' in 'Karain' that resembles 'some queer wreckage adrift upon a river of hats' (*TU* 55); the garishly coloured election poster in *The Inheritors* that seeks to smear a rival candidate by asking, 'Who starved her governess?' (*I* 42); the newsbills in *The Secret Agent* that appear 'maculated with filth' (*SA* 65); and in *Victory* the '[t]orn and fluttering bills, intimating in heavy red capitals "Concerts every night"' fly-posted by the sleazy hotelier Schomberg (*V* 35).[6] Beyond such narrowly aesthetic concerns, however, Conrad's writing can be seen to express his anxiety at the process of mutual interpellation and interpretation through advertisements that Michael Schudson has described as 'the establishment and reflection of a common symbolic culture' (Schudson, 1993: 210). Just as advertising's circulation of images reflects or, more precisely, offers a distorted representation of capitalism's own circulation of goods, so, too, does Conrad's resentment towards this field of popular culture have its roots in a more acute unease about the ascendancy of the commodity itself.

Conrad often uses the term 'commodities' when alluding to saleable goods in his fiction: gunpowder in *Almayer's Folly*; coconuts in

An Outcast of the Islands; silver in *Nostromo*; potatoes in 'A Smile of Fortune'; and coal in *Victory*, 'the supreme commodity of the age' (*V* 3). Like his frequent mention of patented products, including 'a patent tray for sea use' (*C* 305) and a 'patent taffrail-log' (*PR* 75), or his references to tariffs and rates of profit, the habit displays the familiarity with commerce that prompted him to rebuke a correspondent who had dared to impugn his financial acumen: 'I am no stranger to business, and know the meaning of things' (*CL* 3: 259). But Conrad also understood that commodities are more than just inert objects or bearers of monetary value, and he repeatedly points out that 'the meaning of things' always involves a relation between human beings. From the Jubilee sixpence in 'Karain', whose 'image of the Great Queen' (*TU* 49) has the power to exorcise ghosts, to the sentient billiard balls in Macassar's Sunda Hotel in *An Outcast of the Islands*, which 'stood still as if listening' (*OI* 6), his fiction can be seen to echo Marx's famous description of the commodity as a 'social hieroglyphic' in which 'the relationships between the producers . . . take on the form of a social relation between the products of labour' (Marx, 1976: 167, 164). In *Nostromo*, the champagne, boots, ironware, muslins, patent medicines and French paperback novels stocked by Sulaco's 'universal storekeeper' (*N* 271) appear as so many components of the same global system for organizing humanity that lets Don José Avellanos sit in 'a rocking-chair of the sort exported from the United States' (51) and Costaguanan army officers buy 'Swedish punch, imported in bottles' (161) or a 'brown tweed suit, made by Jews in the slums of London' (527). As if in acknowledgement of this phenomenon, Emilia Gould and the Costaguanan labourers refer openly to the San Tomé silver mine as a 'fetish' (221, 398), the very epithet that Belgian administrators and their Congolese subjects give to the colonial storehouse in 'An Outpost of Progress' – 'perhaps,' as Conrad suggests satirically, 'because of the spirit of civilization it contained' (*TU* 93). Numerous asides of this kind throw into relief what Patrick Brantlinger describes as 'Conrad's conservative belief in the decay of heroic adventure, eroded by technology and a dishonorable commercialism' (Brantlinger, 1988: 262).

'I am not . . . one of your saleable people' (*CL* 2: 370), Conrad protested to Pinker as he struggled to complete 'To-morrow' (1902), a cautionary tale about how commodity fetishism and advertising can corrupt even the closest human bonds. As mentioned earlier, the story's plot centres on Captain Hagberd's compulsive advertising in London newspapers for his estranged son Harry. When Harry finally returns after sixteen years, the now deranged Hagberd accuses him of being an impostor on the grounds that his real son is 'coming home to-morrow'

(*T* 250). At one level, 'To-morrow' presents advertising as straightforwardly exploitative, wasting Hagberd's half-crowns week after week whilst transforming his 'disease of hope' (242) into a pathology of infinite deferral.[7] When his neighbour Bessie tries to persuade him that 'the expense of advertising was unnecessary' (247), Hagberd discloses just how tightly he has become ensnared by the chimera of newspaper advertising:

> These sheets were read in foreign parts to the end of the world, he informed Bessie. . . . 'They all do it,' he pointed out. There was a whole column devoted to appeals after missing relatives. He would bring the newspaper to show her. He and his wife had advertised for years; only she was an impatient woman. The news from Colebrook had arrived the very day after her funeral; if she had not been so impatient she might have been here now, with no more than one day more to wait. (*T* 247–8)

Indeed, whatever his personal failings, even Harry is a victim of such advertising since the 'loving parent' (258) announced in the missing relatives column turns out to be nothing of the sort.

Yet Hagberd's accommodation to the rhythms of newspaper publication, the central conceit of 'To-morrow', points towards the real culprit. By the early 1900s, complete economic reliance upon advertising had made the periodical, which Margaret Beetham has described as 'the first date-stamped commodity . . . designed both to ensure rapid turnover and to create regular demand' (Beetham, 1990: 21), into a potent symbol of the commodity's supremacy.[8] In Conrad's story, the advertisement does not force Hagberd and Harry into the cash-nexus; rather, it reflects the fact that each has already been contaminated by materialism. Both men are signally incapable of treating others in anything but instrumental fashion. The father is an 'awful skinflint' (*T* 242) who wears canvas in preference to shop-bought clothes and who tells Bessie, his tenant, that he will force his son to marry her or 'cut him off without a shilling' (262). The prodigal son is no better, a self-styled fortune-hunter who calculatingly invests in a 'twopenny shave' (252) to create a good impression and leaves Bessie, whom he has seduced and relieved of a half-sovereign, with the parting words: 'You can't buy me in . . . and you can't buy yourself out' (263). Even Bessie cannot help but fantasize about the vacant cottage, which Hagbard has been furnishing surreptitiously with purchases for his son and prospective daughter-in-law, in terms of commodity retail: 'She imagined it all new, fresh with varnish, piled up as in a warehouse. There would be tables wrapped up in sacking; rolls of carpets thick and vertical, like fragments of columns; the gleam of white marble tops in the dimness of drawn blinds' (244). In this minor domestic tragedy of 'saleable people' Conrad reveals advertising as commodity fetishism writ large, a fatal separation of the thing itself from its interchangeable sign. Where commodities express relations that are real but invisible, advertising expresses relations that are visible but unreal: a father who believes himself to be making a declaration of forgiveness; a son who sees only the monetary expression of that sentiment in the chance to cadge five pounds from a newspaper's 'Loving Parent'.

Commodities in fiction perform a number of distinct functions. Most immediately, as Ellen Garvey notes, they supply the literary realist with 'a universe of domestic minutiae' (Garvey, 1996: 14), that is, a set of stage properties that denote, metonymically or synecdochically, the public and private lives of their owners. Thus Conrad opens 'The Return', a melodrama about marital infidelity in the style of Maupassant, with a snapshot of commuting office-workers that instantly evokes the story's themes of social propriety and grubby morality: 'They had high hats, healthy pale faces, dark overcoats and shiny boots; they held in their gloved hands thin umbrellas and hastily folded evening papers that resembled stiff, dirty rags of greenish, pinkish, or whitish colour' (*TU* 118). In turn, Alvin Hervey registers the news of his wife's betrayal as a seismic shock to this stable world of commodity signification: 'For a moment he ceased to be a member of society with a position, a career, and a name attached to all this, like a descriptive label of some complicated compound' (133–4). And yet, as the phrase 'descriptive label' implies, commodities signify most effectively not through the adjectival compounding of 'greenish, pinkish, or whitish' but through name recognition proper. In 'Typhoon', the sobriquet that Captain MacWhirr gives to his umbrella, 'the blessed gamp' (*T* 56), evinces Conrad's willingness to indulge a Christmas magazine readership in the fantasy that British sea captains speak in Dickensian slang. Brand names executed this task with particular efficiency, becoming, in Garvey's words, 'a short-hand version of this type of realism. . . . [that] quickly indicated to readers that the characters inhabited the same universe as their own' (Garvey, 1996: 15). When he describes Doña Rita as having 'taken root in that thick-pile Aubusson carpet' (*AG* 311), a Continental brand famous for its luxurious texture, Conrad not only flatters the implied discernment of his readers but offers an objective correlative to *The Arrow of Gold*'s own sensuous exoticism.

By invoking public perceptions of trademarked products such as Yorkshire Relish, a condiment stocked by Alfred Jacobus in 'A Smile of Fortune' (*TLS* 31) and heavily advertised at the time as 'The Most Delicious Sauce in the World', an author can pass judgement on real-life and fictional consumers alike. Conrad uses this device on several occasions to create an effect of layered irony. In 'The End of the Tether', the colonial trader Van Wyk sits at a piano 'generally out of tune' (*Y* 279), playing to himself new music from damp score-sheets that are periodically delivered to his remote outpost. Ownership of a piano, as Richard Ohmann points out, became a 'cultural imperative' at the end of the nineteenth century, as much a social symbol as a means of home entertainment (Ohmann, 1998: 90) and Van Wyk's upright 'cottage piano' (*Y* 278) is typical of the inexpensive mail-order models advertised in magazines such as the *Weekly Graphic*, which sits in colourful piles on his veranda.[9] However, far from marking his participation in the familial domesticity that these magazine advertisements sought to project onto readers – Captain Whalley, we are told, ordered *his* piano from London on the day he got engaged – Van Wyk's purchase is the act of a man completely isolated from his kind, literally at the end of the line. (Conrad originally titled the story 'The End of the Song'.)

A similar pathos attaches to the advertised commodity in 'Il Conde', a story in which a young *mafioso* attempts to rob an aristocratic tourist who turns out to be carrying only small change, an inexpensive timepiece and some gold rings that he refuses to part with. The count pays dearly for his decision to stroll about Naples with an empty wallet and an inferior watch instead of his 'valuable gold half-chronometer' (*SS* 282) since the gangster, infuriated by the thought of having been tricked, returns to threaten his victim with revenge. The narrator offers a plausible reason for the count's precise identification of his watch as a 'Waterbury fifty-franc thing' (282): 'Every small fact and event of that evening stood out in his memory as if endowed with mystic significance. If he did not mention to me the colour of the pony which drew the carozella . . . it was a mere oversight arising from his agitation' (284). But the brand also resonates suggestively with the tale's motif of deceptive appearances. During the late 1800s, the Waterbury Watch Company's products acquired a commercially disastrous reputation for cheapness that was exacerbated by their frequent use as giveaways in advertising promotions for tobacco and newspapers.[10] Since the firm had, in desperation, renamed itself the New England Watch Company in 1898, 'Waterbury' had been a dead letter for some time when Conrad wrote 'Il Conde'. Despite this, the count's assailant has no difficulty in recognizing 'the nature of this booty' (282) and immediately rejects the 'distained object' (283) as worthless. The gilt or nickel watch – possibly a model from Waterbury's grandly titled 'Duke' and 'Duchess' series – and its solid gold counterpart stand as emblems of the doubleness or duplicity that, as several critics have noted, characterizes the count's narrative of his 'abominable adventure' (285).[11] Like its dapper owner, who has perhaps been taking precautions lest rough trade turn violent, there is both more and less to this over-advertised watch than meets the eye.

Time and again, Conrad's fiction records the facility with which commodities now traverse the globe: the copies of *Punch* in Emilia Gould's drawing-room in *Nostromo*; the replacement billiard cue that Schomberg must order from Europe in *Lord Jim*; and the Colt revolvers and Dutch crockery being hawked around Borneo by American and German salesmen in *The Rescue*. However, Conrad's approval of such 'civilizing' enterprise is invariably tinged with irony. Despite having been encouraged to become 'a sailor combined with a salesman' by Tadeusz Bobrowski, who asked his nephew to investigate the prospects of importing 'Liqueurs des Isles' from Marseilles and cigars from Havana (Najder, 1983: 59), Conrad's view of the relation between professional sailing and commerce more closely resembles Captain Whalley's in 'The End of the Tether': 'For his own part he had always preferred sailing merchant ships (which is a straightforward occupation) to buying and selling merchandise, of which the essence is to get the better of somebody in a bargain – an undignified trial of wits at best' (*Y* 181). For Conrad, the unequal bargain that lay at the heart of commodity circulation and that was encapsulated in advertising, a cultural space dedicated to the struggle between buyer and seller, threatened to exact a terrible price from both individual and nation. Thus he argued in his essay 'Autocracy and War' that the new era ushered in by the Russo-Japanese War had been presaged by the Great Exhibition of 1851, a meta-advertisement for 'that variegated rubbish which it seems to be the bizarre fate of humanity to purchase for the benefit of a few employers of labour' (*NLL* 88). Fifty years on, and in the absence of any treaty modelled on 'the territorial spheres of influence in Africa to keep the competitors for the privilege of improving the nigger (as a buying machine) from flying prematurely at each other's throats' (107), Europe had committed to waging endless war in the name of commerce. '*Il n'y a plus d'Europe*,' Conrad concluded sombrely, 'there is only an armed and trading continent, the home of slowly maturing economical contests for life and death' (112).

Brand loyalty: 'An Anarchist' (1906)

'An Anarchist' is the story of a convict named Paul who escapes from an island prison off the coast of French Guiana during a riot, only to find himself a *de facto* prisoner on another island. After rescuing him from being trampled by cattle, Harry Gee, manager of the Marañon estate, cynically spreads a rumour that Paul is an anarchist as a way of forcing the former mechanic to stay on without salary. Unknown to Gee, Paul has in fact associated with anarchists, albeit through bad luck rather than conviction, and a fear of being murdered by his old comrades makes him decline the narrator's offer of passage home on a steamer. Tormented by frustration and insomnia, he lives out his days as 'the anarchist slave of the Marañon estate' (*SS* 161).

Published in *Harper's Magazine* in August 1906, the story, Conrad confessed to John Galsworthy, was written 'carelessly in a temper of desperation' (*CL* 3: 300). Such feelings possibly prompted him to append the subtitle 'A Desperate Tale' to the version collected in *A Set of Six* (1908), although it may also recall the French expression *une histoire désespérée*, a bleak or hopeless story. The South American setting of 'An Anarchist' further echoes that of two recent works, *Nostromo* (1904) and 'Gaspar Ruiz' (1906), for which Conrad had gleaned information from extensive secondary reading and conversations with R. B. Cunninghame Graham. Although Norman Sherry has shown that Conrad adapted material from anarchist newspaper reports of a convict uprising on Ile St Joseph on 21 October 1894 (Sherry, 1971: 220–7), no contemporary source has been identified for the cattle estate, which does, however, bear a resemblance to the Brazilian island of Ilha de Marajó in the Amazon delta.[12] By contrast, Paul's frustration and despair at the prospect of unending servitude to a colonial company manager were emotions that Conrad had known at first hand. In a letter to Marguerite Poradowska written in Kinshasa in September 1890, he had lamented the vindictiveness of Camille Delcommune, local manager of the Société Anonyme Belge pour le Commerce du Haut Congo and referred to 'the white slaves (of whom I am one)' (*CL* 1: 63). Returning to manage Barr, Moering & Company's warehouse in London the following year, he again complained to Poradowska that 'disagreeable work. . . . is too much like penal servitude, with this difference, that while rolling the stone of Sisyphus, you lack even the consolation of thinking of the pleasure you had in committing the crime' (*CL* 1: 91).

Most reviewers were favourably disposed towards the story. Robert Lynd in the *Daily News* called it 'whimsical', W. L. Courtney in the *Telegraph* praised it as a 'fine achievement' and Edward Garnett in the *Nation* pronounced it 'a gem of Mr. Conrad's art' (*CH* 212, 217, 222). H. G. Wells was curious as to whether the name Harry Gee was a reference to his own initials, a suggestion Conrad strenuously denied. Since then, 'An Anarchist' has attracted scant attention from critics, many of whom would probably echo Sherry's view that anticipation of the themes of *The Secret Agent* constitutes the main interest of 'a strange story, crude and uncomfortable in some of its implications' (Sherry, 1971: 227). Daniel R. Schwarz, noting its narrative affinities with 'Il Conde' and 'The Informer', nevertheless suggests that 'An Anarchist' 'while certainly not one of Conrad's finest stories, deserves more attention than it has received' (Schwarz, 1971: 333). Sherry discerns a parallel between 'the gullibility of mankind in the face of modern devices of advertisement . . . and the gullibility of the working man in the fact of anarchist propaganda' (Sherry, 1971: 219), a point repeated by Carol Vanderveer Hamilton who further notes that the proverbial wisdom invoked by the narrator to explain Paul's predicament – 'Warm heart and weak head' – is itself 'a verbal formula, a cliché, reminiscent of a commercial jingle . . . suggest[ing] that the narrator participates in the gullibility that he criticizes' (Hamilton, 1994: 35). And in her discussion of how Conrad represents naming as a tactic common to anarchists and capitalists, Jennifer Shaddock argues that the story reveals the latter as needing anarchists both as a source of cheap labour and as a pretext for 'the state surveillance that makes a capitalist state possible' (Shaddock, 1994: 59). Much, however, remains to be said about the political and popular cultural contexts of the story, which, as will be seen, are integral to its satire.

The first of these concerns the firm that employs Harry Gee and indirectly enslaves Paul. In the latter half of the nineteenth century, the real-life counterparts of B.O.S. Ltd played a pivotal role in South America's economic modernization, successfully establishing close client-patron relationships between former colonies and European powers. The abolition of slavery by French Guiana and Venezuela in the 1850s and Brazil in 1888 was a key stage in this process. As Cain and Hopkins observe, 'Britain achieved in Brasil what she failed to bring about in Africa: the conversion of a slave-holding state to one capable of sustaining new and much expanded forms of "legitimate" commerce' (Cain and Hopkins, 1993: 299). The shadow of this recent history falls briefly on 'An Anarchist' in the scene where Paul is rescued from the high seas by a ship crewed entirely by black sailors, what the racist Gee calls 'a small schooner full of niggers' (*SS* 140). But the 1900s also saw a series of scandals over of the use of restrictive labour practices by precisely such 'legitimate' enterprises. Roger Casement's searing exposé of concession-aire companies in the Congo Free State provoked a storm of controversy in 1903, as did his investigation of the Peruvian Amazon Rubber Company in 1910. With the General Election of January 1906 dominated by the issue of 'Chinese slavery' in the Transvaal gold mining industry, British firms such as Cadbury's, owner of several West Indian cocoa plantations, and Lever Bros, owners of the Société des Huileries du Congo Belge, loudly defended their records on colonial labour.[13] These controversies spawned, in turn, numerous literary polemics against plutocracy, monopolistic combines and labour exploitation, and Conrad's story has an obvious indebtedness to what later commentators would call 'the literature of exposure', a sub-genre of fiction and reportage that included Robert Sherrard's *The White Slaves of England* (1897) and *The Child-Slaves of Britain* (1905), Frank Norris's *The Octopus* (1901), Jack London's *The Iron Heel* (1908) and Robert Tressell's *The Ragged Trousered Philanthropists* (1914). In his short story 'Bloody Niggers', published in the *Social-Democrat* in April 1897, Conrad's friend R. B. Cunninghame Graham had satirized the British South Africa Company's 'money-grubbing miscreants', and renamed Cecil Rhodes's newly-won territory 'Fraudesia' (Cunninghame Graham, 1897: 109).

Conrad wrote 'An Anarchist', then, in a climate of growing cynicism about modern business and, in particular, the unchecked might of a new industrial entity: the vertically integrated corporation, supported by vast capital reserves and exercising direct control over every stage in the production process. Andrew Carnegie's US Steel, the world's first corporation to be valued at one billion dollars, had been involved in several violent disputes in the 1890s, notably the Homestead strike in Pittsburgh in 1892 and the 'labour war' that convulsed Pennsylvania in 1894. Widely reported in the British press, such conflicts may have prompted Conrad's inquiry to E. B. Redmayne, whose wife was visiting the United States in 1897, 'Are there any prospects of peace in the industrial world?' (Stape and van Marle, 1995: 37). Yet his suspicion of millionaires was fuelled as much by their seeming affinity with anarchists as by what Shaddock sees as their exploitation of anarchists as bogeymen. With their radical republicanism, opposition to state regulation and insistence upon the primacy of the economic sphere, some libertarian capitalists must have sounded remarkably like anarchists to Conrad. To be sure, he had already made the violence and injustice of colonial corporations a central motif in earlier works: in 'Heart of Darkness', the reality of indentured labour under the legal fiction of 'time contracts' (*Y* 66); in *The Inheritors*, the unregulated financing of colonial joint-stock companies; in 'Typhoon', the slave-like transport conditions of the Bun Hin Company's 'seven-years'-men' (12); and in *Nostromo*, the conspiratorial role of financiers and industrialists in national revolutions. Carnegie's career led Conrad to wonder aloud, 'God knows what flaws *he* too in his dazzling career he may be groaning over in the secret of his heart' (*CL* 2: 436), and he remarked waspishly of 'that plutocrat [Julius] Wernher' (3: 470), his diamond-dealing (and gentile) neighbour in Kent: 'A flavour of South Africa and Palestine hangs about our old walled garden' (3: 489–90).[14] Joseph Lyons, a food manufacturer who for a while considered buying the *English Review*, could be simply dismissed as 'a cheese-monger or something nearly equivalent' (4: 275). As Conrad declared in 1907, 'By Jove! If I had the necessary talent I would like to go for the true anarchist – which is the millionaire' (3: 491).[15]

Pace Harry Gee's talk of making arrangements 'in justice to my company' (*SS* 138), B.O.S. no longer bears the imprint of any individual: even the cowboys he works with 'had no definite idea of the B.O.S. Co., Ltd., which paid their wages' (137). Instead, anonymous shareholders head an organization whose day-to-day running has devolved onto a managerial class of hard-pressed men like Gee, who candidly explains: 'I am bound to do my best for the company. They have enormous expenses. . . . One can't be too economical in working the show' (140). Such personal tyranny, Conrad implies, is the iron-bound rationale of modern corporations for whom all moral issues can be settled by the Occam's razor of profitability – Gee's watchword, 'It's good for the company' (140). On the state-within-a-state of the Marañon *estancia*, 'an island as big as a small province' (137), capitalists are, like Paul's anarchist 'comrades' back in Paris, a law unto themselves.

So far, so anarchist. But it is a crucial detail that this particular capitalist produces meat. To be sure, Conrad's setting of 'An Anarchist' on a cattle ranch seems self-explanatory in terms of theme: the dehumanized convict, having been 'corralled' (*SS* 141) and reduced to a kind of 'breed' (143), lives under the shadow of execution like the beef cattle around him. The moral, too, seems simple: modern companies view men as beasts. Indeed, given the narrator's scorn for the crude allegory of B.O.S.'s advertisements, Conrad is somewhat heavy-handed in driving home his story's allegorical nature, having the narrator liken the Marañon estate to 'a sort of penal settlement for condemned cattle' whose lowing is 'a deep and distressing sound under the open sky, rising like a monstrous protest of prisoners condemned to death' (137). Yet by the time the story was published the dire conditions of the meat industry were internationally notorious, thanks largely to Upton Sinclair's highly publicized investigation of Chicago slaughterhouses, which were already infamous for using 'every part of the pig except the squeal'. Conrad had a low opinion of *The Jungle* (1906) – Sinclair's realistic exposé of the industry belonged to 'a damnable category of more or less pretentious emptiness' (*CL* 4: 127) – but the scandal was unavoidable. By May 1906 an editorial in *The World's Work*, a New York magazine that had published a portion of Conrad's *Mirror of the Sea*, was noting that the matter had been in the public eye for over a year (Anon, 1906: 7469). Closer to home, the impounding of a shipment of American meat at Brighton in June 1906 led Conrad to reflect: 'my long Anarc[hist] Story . . . is becoming topical. Query: Which is really more criminal? – the Bomb of Madrid or the Meat of Chicago' (3: 333).

The first decade of the new century saw, on the one hand, a seven-fold increase in the amount of South American meat being imported to Britain and, on the other, growing public criticism of price-fixing and disregard for consumers' health among the North American meat trusts (Fraser, 1981: 153–4). As Conrad protested to Pinker in 1908, 'I am not a sausage machine that takes rotten scraps in at one end and turns out the marketable sausage at the other' (*CL* 4: 44). It would thus be reasonable to assume that the scandal of the North American meat industry affected British perceptions of its South American counterparts. Certainly, the narrator's description of the Marañon cattle herd as 'condemned' (*SS* 137) seems to insinuate that B.O.S.'s meat, even when fresh, is unfit for human consumption: 'When I got back to Horta from Cayenne and saw the "Anarchist" again, he did not look well. . . . Evidently the meat of the company's main herd (in its unconcentrated form) did not agree with him at all' (161). The activities of South American meat producers had, moreover, been in the news even before Conrad wrote 'An Anarchist': the *Times* reported on 26 May 1905 that production at Liebig's famous factory at Fray Bentos on the River Plate in Uruguay was continuing despite a recent revolution; and another article detailing the role of '[a]narchists and professional agitators' in a strike wave that was paralysing the country appeared on 12 August 1905. In the late 1900s, Liebig's capitalized upon public interest in its activities with a series of documentary films about Fray Bentos that featured employees at work in the factory as well as cowboys driving and branding cattle.[16]

B.O.S. Ltd is not merely a beef supplier but 'a famous meat-extract manufacturing company' (*SS* 135), the producer of a processed and patented foodstuff. As with genetically manipulated crops today, early twentieth-century consumers were highly suspicious of new processes such as concentrating, freezing and tinning as well as of manufactured patent foods. Conrad was no exception, lambasting the designers of the *Titanic* as grocers who poison their customers with tinned salmon and noting ironically that 'the tinning of salmon was "progress" as much at least as the building of the *Titanic*' (*NLL* 246). A similarly negative perspective informs much of his fiction. The anonymous narrator of 'The Secret Sharer' recounts feeding his stowaway companion 'tins of fine preserves', presumably a mocking quotation of their label, that he defines more precisely as 'stewed chicken, pâté de foie gras, asparagus, cooked oysters, sardines . . . all sorts of abominable sham delicacies' (*TLS* 127), just as Mr Travers in *The Rescue* alludes to the prospect of living off preserved food as 'distinctly unpleasant' (*Res* 146).[17] In 'Falk' a young captain sardonically describes how in a tropical slum '[a]n empty Australian beef tin bounded cheerily before the toe of my boot' (*T* 199), and in 'A Smile of Fortune' another master mariner recalls a sumptuous breakfast of 'shore provisions' that contained 'butter which plainly did not come from a Danish tin' (*TLS* 8). More than just realistic stage props, these references to tinned comestibles attest to Conrad's awareness of the growing market for 'new' foods, produced, as he saw it, to service advertising-created needs, and packaged and transported in a mechanized fashion appropriate to their intrinsic unnaturalness.

Conrad's point is not subtle: whatever the seductive claims of manufacturers, only someone facing imminent starvation would eat these products willingly. As the narrator of 'An Anarchist' notes, 'In various parts of the civilized and uncivilized world I *have had to* swallow B.O.S. with more or less benefit to myself, though without great pleasure' (136, my emphasis). Of course, poisoning by unhygienic or adulterated foods was a real danger in late Victorian Britain – according to Jessie, the Conrads got food-poisoning when they went out to lunch after getting engaged in February 1896 – and resulted in a series of far-reaching Acts of Parliament. To be sure, rotten and alien foodstuffs recur frequently in Conrad's *œuvre*: rancid hippo meat in 'Heart of Darkness'; human flesh in 'Falk'; 'foreign preserved milk' (*SA* 13) in *The Secret Agent*; and dog meat in *A Personal Record*.[18] At the same time, whatever their nutritional merits or hazards, processed and patent foods differ from ordinary foodstuffs in that they rely entirely on advertising to announce their existence and to direct consumers (rather than retailers) towards specific brands; 'An Anarchist' and 'The Partner' kept company in *Harper's Magazine* with advertisements for Bermaline Bread and Brand's Beef Essence. This core attribute of the edible manufactured commodity – patent food producers, as Roy Church notes, naturally gravitated towards advertising's vanguard – structures Conrad's parallel scepticism towards patent foods and modern business methods. In 'The Partner', he depicts two entrepreneurs as graduating naturally from the manufacture of wood pulp and tinned fruit (itself a comic juxtaposition akin to Monty Python's 'Holiday Homes for Pets Pie Company') to a promotional scheme for a patent medicine. De Barral's advertising-fuelled fiascos in *Chance* include 'a canning Factory on the banks of the Amazon' (*C* 63), and Conrad's first draft of the novel, titled 'Explosives', contains a comic scene in which Marlow accuses a waiter of having poisoned a fly with a bottle of 'stale Worcester Sauce'.[19] In his preface to Jessie's *Handbook of Cookery for a Small House*, written in January 1907, Conrad ironically contrasts the 'conscientious cook' whose 'labours make for the honesty . . . of our existence' (*LE* 148) with the 'fraudulent medicine men' who keep entire nations 'in abject submission' (147) by steeping them in 'the gloom of vague fears' (148) or what would today be called *scare copy*.

Conrad repeatedly foregrounds the new power of advertising in 'An Anarchist.' The narrator prefaces his tale with the words: 'B.O.S. Bos. You have seen the three magic letters on the advertisement pages of magazines and newspapers, in the windows of provision merchants, and on calendars. . . . Of course everybody knows the B.O.S. Ltd.' (*SS* 135). Harry Gee explains that his motive throughout has been to defray the 'enormous expenses' of his company: 'Why – our agent in Horta tells me they spend fifty thousand pounds every year in advertising all over the world!' (140). After he repeats this excuse, the narrator comments dryly that 'for a company spending fifty thousand pounds every year on advertising, the strictest economy was obviously necessary' (144). Like the 'statistics of slaughter and bloodshed enough to make a Turk turn faint' (135) supplied by B.O.S.'s pamphlets that recall Liebig's grisly boast of butchering 200,000 cattle annually, enough, if stacked, to dwarf St Paul's Cathedral, Conrad's complaint would appear to be that meat extract advertising is in poor taste. Yet his critique of commodity culture extends beyond aesthetics and even politics. Advertising's truly disturbing feature is the intellectual debasement that follows upon its reification of the English language. No longer the brain, it is now the stomach that processes this kind of language, metaphorically *consuming* it just like the B.O.S. promoted by the latter. 'I have had to swallow B.O.S.,' the narrator insists. 'But I have never swallowed its advertisements' (135). This point is reiterated in 'The Informer', where the anarchist revolutionaries pack propaganda sheets into old boxes labelled 'Stone's Dried Soup,' an unappetizing yellow powder 'once rather prominently advertised in the dailies, but which never, somehow, gained the favour of the public' (*SS* 82). Whether an ideological or a nutritional sham, each depends upon its rhetoric 'catching on' to succeed. The anarchist mastermind of 'The Informer' is thus not merely a political demagogue but also 'the greatest destructive publicist that ever lived' (74), just as in 'An Anarchist' the socialist lawyer who defends Paul gives a 'magnificent' (*SS* 148) speech that advertises himself but damns his client.[20] Advertising, Conrad insists, ultimately circulates not products but a popular language distorted and stripped of meaning.

Importantly, B.O.S. is not just any company. As explicitly as libel laws permitted, Conrad directs readers to recognize it as the meat-extract manufacturer Bovril.[21] There are plenty of clues. Harry Gee charges the butterfly-collecting narrator two dollars per day but the reference to his company's 'capital £1,500,000, fully paid up' (*SS* 138) establishes that B.O.S. is a British firm. *Bos*, as several critics have pointed out, is Latin for ox, but it also formed the first element in Bovril's composite name, the second being *vril*, the mysterious 'life force' in Bulwer Lytton's science fiction fantasy *The Coming Race* (1871).[22] Like B.O.S., Bovril's advertising prominently featured a black bull and although it did not acquire cattle estates of its own until after 1905 the firm repeatedly alluded to its product's geographical origins: 'BOVRIL AS A BEVERAGE is Meat and Drink at one draught, containing in an easily digestible form the entire nourishment of Prime Ox Beef from selected Cattle reared in Australia and South America.' Sales of Bovril tripled during 1894–97 alone and Conrad's catalogue of B.O.S.'s 'unrivalled products: Vinobos, Jellybos, and the latest unequalled perfection, Tribos' (*SS* 135) accurately parodies the synergy and product extensions of Wild Cherry Sauce, Kudos Cocoa and Virol ('Recommended For the Young') which were pushing Bovril to the fore of Britain's food concentrate industry at the turn of the century.

Above all, Conrad chose Bovril because of its unique status as an advertised commodity. In fact, he could not have found a better exemplar of the hallmarks of modern advertising that his narrator identifies as 'enterprise, ingenuity, impudence, and resource' (*SS* 135). Guided by Samuel Benson, a former employee who became the most innovative advertising agent of his day, Bovril spent a fortune on a range of promotional stunts that included sand design contests on Bournemouth beach, bales of vouchers dropped from hot-air balloons and displays of leaflet-packed fireworks that, copying anarchism's own headline-grabbing tactics, warned the public: 'Look Out For THE BOVRIL BOMBS Are About To Be Discharged!' A sponsor of sporting events, temperance magic lantern shows and charity fundraisers, Bovril even organized an independent news service during the Boer War, announcing in one startling advertisement that the bloody route taken by Lord Roberts's army spelt out the word 'Bovril', 'one more proof of the universality of Bovril, which has already figured so conspicuously throughout the South African Campaign.' These marketing ploys reached huge audiences. In his official company history, Peter Hadley takes seriously Bovril's claim that by 1906 over a million Britons had seen Tom Barton, 'Champion Log Roller of the World', literally log-roll Bovril by balancing on a floating cylinder made from empty tins.[23] By the early 1900s Bovril was, like B.O.S., advertising 'all over the world' in countries as far-flung as Chile and Siam, producing illustrated calendars in Chinese, supplying ingenious window-displays to the trade and putting its name on domestic hoardings, magazines, newspapers, musical albums, omnibuses, golfing score cards and theatre programmes. Even Jessie Conrad's *Handbook of Cookery* contained a recipe for game soup that includes 'a teaspoon of Bovril' (Conrad, 1923: 67), the book's only mention of a branded product, as if in obedience to the company's injunction that 'No Kitchen Should Be Without Bovril'.

B.O.S.'s claim to supply everything short of 'everlasting youth' and 'the power of raising the dead' (*SS* 136) also closely parodies Bovril's tireless invoking of medical exhibitions, hospital contracts, doctors' endorsements, and the importance of calorific 'body-building.' 'Bovril for Influenza' blared its two-column boxed advertisement in the *Times* of 21 January 1905, and another blithely promised: 'Bovril prevents "catching colds." Ask your Doctor!' Bovril's opportunism did not stop there. From Henry Stanley and Nottingham Forest Football Club to Queen Victoria and Pope Leo X, it vigorously exploited the images of the greatest celebrities of the day – with or without their permission. In the *Times* of 15 February 1905, it even went as far as announcing a 'Complete Political Creed' whose 'policies' made the brand simultaneously Liberal Unionist, Protectionist, Conservative, Radical, Free Trader, Colonial Preference and Imperial. Working incessantly to persuade consumers of the symmetry between the nation's interest and its own, the company coined slogans like 'Bovril Is British' to convince people that being British meant buying Bovril. As Cunninghame Graham humorously explained in *Justice* on 22 July 1911, the substitution of Bovril for the consecrated oil in George V's coronation was the only possible explanation for the 'extreme materialism' of a spectacle devised by '[d]ullards, with Bovril in their heads instead of brains' (Cunninghame Graham, 1911: 8). Conrad's satirical allusion to 'the love that Limited Company bears to its fellowmen – even as the love of the father and mother penguin for their hungry fledglings' (*SS* 135) echoes, too, the firm's efforts to cloak itself in an aura of patriotic selflessness, such as the 1903 Bovril advertisement titled 'The Organisation of the Land Forces' (a quotation from a ministerial address on military preparedness) in which one bull says to another, 'I Hear They Want More'.

The lepidopterist narrator of 'An Anarchist' anatomizes in some detail an example of B.O.S.'s advertising:

> The 'art' illustrating that 'literature' represents in vivid and shining colours a large and enraged black bull stamping upon a yellow snake writhing in emerald-green grass, with a cobalt-blue sky for a background. It is atrocious and it is an allegory. The snake symbolizes disease, weakness – perhaps mere hunger, which last is the chronic disease of the majority of mankind. (*SS* 135)

The sketch unmistakeably describes the style of contemporary Bovril advertisements. The company's logo, designed by W. H. Caffyn in 1896, was a large and defiant black bull, and Bovril's fixation with heavy puns and symbolic imagery in advertisements such as 'A Tower of Strength' (the explorer Henry Stanley standing beside a miniature castle labelled 'Bovril') and 'Con-*tent*-ment' (a soldier enjoying a cup of Bovril under canvas) is echoed in B.O.S.'s 'atrocious' allegory. Nevertheless, it would appear that Conrad, despite drawing inspiration from Bovril's advertisements, stopped short of identifying one in particular, as might be expected from a writer who regarded the concealment of traceable sources as a cornerstone of his artistic method. As he once remarked: 'Didn't it ever occur to you . . . that I knew what I was doing in leaving the facts of my life and even of my tales in the background? Explicitness, my dear fellow, is fatal to the glamour of all artistic work' (Curle, 1928b: 143).

But this specimen of B.O.S.'s 'art', far from being an invention or a composite of beef-extract advertising, was in fact modelled on a real advertisement. Filed away in the Bodleian Library's John Johnson Collection of Victorian ephemera lies perhaps the only surviving example of a handbill titled 'Bovril is Liquid Life' (Plate 2) that depicts a black bull in a field under a cloudless sky in a colour scheme of bright yellow, cobalt blue and emerald green. This near-perfect match for Conrad's advertisement was likely produced in a large print run in the early 1900s as an enclosure for trade circulars, Christmas calendars, or one of the special publicity pamphlets that Conrad's narrator describes as 'written in a sickly enthusiastic style and in several languages' (*SS* 135).

The modernity of its design is paralleled by its high print quality, truly 'vivid and shining' colours that testify to the superior images made possible by the perfection of colour lithography and improvements in ink manufacture. Boldly proclaiming Bovril's latest slogan, its caption 'Liquid Life' creates an effective visual pun on the motifs of river and bull – 'Liquid' and 'Life', respectively – whilst paying tribute to the hot beef drink that Conrad's narrator damns with faint praise as 'not really unpalatable' (136).

Conrad's contemptuous quotation marks around the word 'art' are particularly significant since the artistic status of display advertisements, as already mentioned, was the focus of heated debate during this period.[24] Writing in *Art Journal* in February 1897, the British designer Lewis F. Day spoke for many genteel commentators in complaining that 'the bluster, swagger, [and] self-assertion, calculated to attract popular attention, are in flat contradiction to the modesty and reticence of art worth the name' (Day, 1897: 49). In Day's opinion, the problem was three-fold: the imaginative poverty of the advertisers, an excessively ornamental style, and, above all, 'the mediocrity of popular taste' (Day, 1897: 50). Successful advertisements of the future, he predicted, would contain a bare minimum of text incorporated into a bold graphic design so as to induce the consumer to buy products 'not because he believed them to be the best, but because, by dint of advertisement, their names had been *branded* into his memory in connection with those particular wares' (Day, 1897: 52, emphasis added). What is significant about Conrad's representation of Bovril's 'Liquid Life' advertisement is that he entirely ignores its adherence to these forward-looking prescriptions. Where Day and others called for greater sophistication and creativity in advertising – a recognition, in effect, of the medium's special semiotic and aesthetic status – Conrad implies that 'the modern system of advertising' is merely a feeble substitute for genuine art, just as beef concentrate is for real meat. Thus his narrator explains that the unpalatability of B.O.S.'s meat-extract and its advertising stems from accommodation to a wholly inferior, popular standard:

> But being animated by feelings of affection towards my fellow-men, I am saddened by the modern system of advertising. Whatever evidence it offers of enterprise, ingenuity, impudence, and resource in certain individuals, it proves to my mind the wide prevalence of that form of mental degradation which is called gullibility. . . . Whatever form of mental degradation I may (being but human) be suffering from, it is not the popular form.　　　　　　　　　　　　　(*SS* 136)

There is also an intriguing discrepancy between Conrad's description of B.O.S.'s 'atrocious allegory' and his original source, namely, that Bovril's bull is not stamping on a snake. Admittedly, this could be merely a case of oversight or faulty memory on Conrad's part, but closer scrutiny of the Bovril handbill suggests a more interesting explanation: for a viewer unable to read the advertisement's depth cues correctly, one of the bull's foreshortened legs might well appear to be stamping on something yellow. The narrator protests his superiority to the weak-minded consumers targeted by B.O.S.'s advertising but the fact is that he – and, I would argue, Conrad – could equally have misread the 'art' of this particular advertisement in a way that its 'gullible' popular audience would not. The narrator is obviously adept at deciphering the advertisement's coded message, that hunger will be eradicated by making B.O.S. available to the starving 'majority of mankind' (*SS* 135), yet his imperfect grasp of advertising's new visual grammar has perhaps prevented him from fully understanding its dissociation of commodity and image.

Conrad's quotation marks around 'literature' are no less suggestive of a writerly resentment towards advertising and, in particular, towards Bovril advertising. During Conrad's years as a writer, Bovril became what Peter Hadley calls a 'national institution' (Hadley, 1972: 3) whose influence reached deep into the cultural sphere. In 1903 the company announced to great fanfare that Bovril had entered the English language as a synonym of 'concentrated force', and when it balloted the nation four years later on how to pronounce that name, it claimed that 'Bov'ril' had beaten 'Bo'vril' by 95,000 votes. In addition to recruiting celebrity designers such as Beardsley and organizing national competitions for the largest collection of Bovril advertisements and photographs, Bovril had a visible impact on the literary world. The beef extract was endorsed by such prominent writers as Rudyard Kipling, the military novelist John Strange Winter (Henrietta Stannard) and the poet Edwin Arnold, as well as making appearances in fictional works ranging from E. E. Nesbit's *The Story of the Treasure-Seekers* (1899) to Horace Newte's *Sparrows: The Story of an Unprotected Girl* (1909).[25] In Robert Hichens's *The Green Carnation* (1894), the Wildean dandy Amarinth declares satirically, 'I feel so delightfully vicious when I drink it, so unconventional!' (Hichens, 1895: 14) and in the 'Oxen of the Sun' episode of *Ulysses*, a drunken medical student thinks to himself, 'Jubilee mutton. Bovril, by James' (Joyce, 1986: 348). Bovril was ascribed even closer affinities to literary production in Sydney Fane's popular song 'A Novel on the Bovril Principle' (1905) as well as in a letter that Conrad wrote to a fellow writer in 1912:

> Don't forget that the E[nglish] R[eview] is meant for the most con-
> temptible part of the populace, that which fills the more respectable
> streets. They have neither minds nor gullets. You must dilute your
> stuff. I am perfectly serious. It's like too strong Bovril. Nine people out
> of ten won't get it down and the tenth man will feel qualmish.
>
> (*CL* 5: 148)

For Conrad and his contemporaries, then, Bovril's overwhelming
presence in the media had made the company indistinguishable from
the general public. No longer just a meat product manufacturer, Bovril
was now concentrating and selling the British people themselves.

Latter-day opponents of this process of creeping commodification
know it simply as *branding*. The obvious exponent of this tendency in
'An Anarchist' in Harry Gee, literally a cattle brander, whose sense of
humour comprises 'the wearisome repetition of descriptive phrases
applied to people' (*SS* 138). To him, the narrator is 'Desperate butterfly-
slayer' (138) and Paul either 'Escaped Convict' (141) or 'Crocodile' ('he
lives half in, half out of the creek. Amphibious – see?') (139). Jennifer
Shaddock notes that the word 'anarchist' that delivers Paul into
the manager's power functions as a kind of maleficent brand name: 'The
capitalists in the story . . . create anarchists through advertising'
(Shaddock, 1994: 59). Or, in Gee's banal formulation: 'I gave him the
name because it suited me to label him in that way' (*SS* 140). Yet this is
only half the story. Although branding was then in its infancy – as
evinced by scattered references in Conrad's letters to Waterbury watches
(*CL* 3: 357), Waterman and Swan pens (3: 405), Brand's Meat Essence
and Valentine's Meat Juice (3: 456), British Linen Bank paper (4: 230),
Rowntree's Cocoa (5: 626) and Jaeger clothing (6: 548) – its presence was
beginning to be felt even in rural Kent.[26]

It is here that the historical significance of Conrad's choice of model
for B.O.S. lies. By dropping the name Johnston's Fluid Beef, Bovril joined
the ranks of Tatcho (a hair restorer), Odonto (a dentifrice) and Tablones
(indigestion pills) whose depersonalized, wholly advertising-created
identities were replacing traditional proprietor-endorsed products such
as Mrs S. A. Allen's World's Hair Restorer, Himrod's Cure for Asthma and
Keating's Powder (like Bovril, all advertisers in the August 1906 number
of *Harper's*). The brand name B.O.S. leaves British consumers with as little 'definite idea' of its maker as the South American *vacqueros* have of
the B.O.S. Company, Ltd that employs them, just as Bovril's customers

knew it only through the starburst logo, black bull symbol and catchphrases such as 'Who Said BOVRIL?' and 'Alas My Poor Brother!'

Branding neatly illustrates the rise of the advertised commodity. Originally denoting a maker's mark on a box or cask, the term acquired its modern sense in the 1880s when, as Michael Schudson writes, 'the world was changing so that available products were less often local and known and local retailers were more often large institutions serving a wider public than before' (Schudson, 1993: 159). Captain Mitchell's endorsement of Costaguanan coffee in *Nostromo*, for example, reflects the vigorous advertising of brands like Brazil's 'Fazenda' coffee in British magazines of these years:

> The black coffee you get at the Amarilla, sir, you don't meet anywhere in the world. . . . It arrives on three mules – not in the common way, by rail; no fear! – as right into the patio, escorted by mounted peons, in charge of the Mayoral of his estate, who walks upstairs, booted and spurred, and delivers it to our committee formally with the words, 'For the sake of those fallen on the third of May.' We call it Tres de Mayo coffee.[27]   (N 479)

Conrad left readers in no doubt as to his own views. 'I do not know into what brand of ink Mr. Henry James dips his pen but I know that his mind is steeped in the waters flowing from the fountain of intellectual youth' (*NLL* 12), he remarked loftily, a comment clearly intended to underscore his own distance from branding's world of sordid materialism.[28] Indeed, if manufactured commodities acquired a phantasmic individuality in branding, it sometimes seemed to Conrad as if everything and everyone now risked being reduced to a brand. As he quipped to Edward Garnett: 'my full name [is] Joseph Theodor Konrad Nałęcz Korzeniowski, the underlined word being the appelation of our trade mark . . . without which none are genuine. As a matter of fact I and Alfred Borys Konrad Korzeniowski are the only two of that particular brand of Korzeniowski in existence' (*CL* 2: 244).[29] In *The Rescue*, d'Alcacer replies laconically to Mrs. Travers's observation that no two men are stupid in quite the same way: 'Yes, our brand presents more varieties' (*Res* 314).

For Bovril, the holy grail of branding – a quest for what Naomi Klein has dubbed 'corporate transcendence' (Klein, 2001: 21) – was the quintessentially British institution of the cup of tea. As the quotation marks in its own advertisement indicate (Figure 9), Bovril aspired to make 'a cup of hot Bovril' the branded equivalent of a national drink that is as

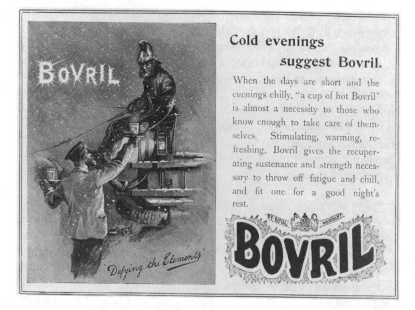

Figure 9 Bovril advertisement, *Illustrated Dramatic and Sporting News* (December 1902), 41. Reproduced with permission of General Research Division, The New York Public Library, Astor, Lenox and Tilden Foundation.

much a symbol of friendship and comfort as a form of refreshment. In the words of another of its advertisements: 'A cup of Bovril taken after the play, on the golf-links, on the football field, or in any circumstance of deprivation or exposure, not only warms, thrills and stimulates, but . . . gives the sustaining, vitalising power that continues and knows no reaction.' That even Conrad had been touched by Bovril's grand ambition is clear from a scene in 'The Partner' in which the American conman Cloete seeks to comfort the distraught Mrs Harry Dunbar: ' "We are all going together," cries Cloete, all of a sudden. He rushes out, sends the woman *a cup of hot bovril* from the shop across the road, buys a rug for her, thinks of everything . . . .' (*WT* 109, emphasis added). Cloete's decision to order this hot drink is not merely proof of Bovril's success in marketing its product as the one to reach for in a crisis; it is, like B.O.S.'s 'three magic letters' (*SS* 135) in 'An Anarchist' and the 'magic word Thrift, Thrift, Thrift' (*C* 61) in *Chance*, the invoking of brand aura.[30] How appropriate, then, that the only reference to Bovril by name in Conrad's *œuvre* should fall from an ad-man's lips.

'An Anarchist' is much more than a hastily-written melodrama in which Conrad settled scores with a company whose advertisements affronted his aesthetic sensibilities and whose product offended his palate. Rather, it performs an ingenious act of imaginative decommodification, penetrating the advertising sheen of B.O.S.'s bull (no pun intended) in order to reveal its brutal exploitation of labour and cynical manipulation of consumers. (In real life, it should be stressed, Bovril was at no point associated with either the meat scandals or repressive labour practices.) With its politically subversive message and refusal of narrative closure or easy moralizing, 'An Anarchist' signally fails to follow the requirements of fiction magazines, then under pressure from advertisers to publish up-beat tales – what Ellen Garvey calls 'fictional worlds as much as possible continuous with the concerns of the ads' (Garvey, 1996: 14) – that would put readers in the mood to buy. In his last years, Conrad became increasingly frank about the commercial factors that dictated narrative form, reminding Pinker in December 1918 that 'buying a Conrad work' was not the same thing as 'buy[ing] a pig in a poke' and instructing his agent to 'assure the representative of the Cosmopolitan Magazine that [*The Rescue*] will end as romantically as it began, and that no one of any particular consequence will have to die' (CL 6: 339). There is, then, a delicious irony in the contemptuous term Conrad's contemporaries gave to this process: Bovrilization.[31]

Lively pills: 'The Partner' (1911)

Written in autumn 1910 and first published in *Harper's Magazine* in November 1911, 'The Partner' tells the story of a botched insurance fraud. George Dunbar, a failing entrepreneur, becomes the partner of an American con-man named Cloete who proposes that they raise capital for a lucrative business project by arranging to wreck a ship owned by George and his brother Harry. When George loses his nerve, Cloete secretly goes ahead with the plan, which ends in disaster. Captain Harry is murdered and half the insurance money goes to his widow. Inadequately funded, George and Cloete lose most of what remains in the business scheme, only to see investors with deeper pockets take over and make a fortune.

The tale has enjoyed a mixed reputation among readers. Possibly relishing its satire on capitalism, George Orwell pronounced it 'very fine' but marred by 'the queer shyness or clumsiness which made it difficult for Conrad to tell a story straightforwardly in the third person' (Orwell, 1968: 388). After languishing on the fringes of the Conrad canon, the story has recently been reappraised by critics who discern an intriguing self-reflexivity in both its double narrative structure – a professional magazine-writer relating a story told to him by a stevedore – and the narrator's reference to the necessity of 'cooking' such tales 'for the consumption of magazine readers' (*WT* 128). John Batchelor finds 'a surprisingly high level of narrative sophistication and self-consciousness' in the tale, which he describes as 'an interesting and under-regarded narrative experiment' (Batchelor, 1994: 221–2). Seconding this view, Robert Hampson argues that its narrative can be read as a complicated parable of writing for serials, 'designed to open the reader's eyes to various aspects of the "business" of magazine-fiction' (Hampson, 1998: 127).

In his 1920 Preface to *Within The Tides*, Conrad hinted that 'The Partner' had a basis in ' "fact". . . derived from my personal knowledge' (*WT* ix), perhaps a reference to the case of Lawrence Wood Cloete whom the *Daily Graphic* reported in February 1891 as found guilty of promoting fraudulent companies, including a South American silver mine. Fraud was a popular topic in contemporary novels such as R. L. Stevenson's *The Wrecker* (1892) and E. Phillips Oppenheim's *A Millionaire of Yesterday* (1900) and H. G. Wells had satirized the patent medicine Lacto-Peptine in *Tono-Bungay* (1909). Conrad, too, had portrayed unscrupulous financiers in *Nostromo* as well as in his and Ford's *The Inheritors* and *The Nature of a Crime*, and he would return to the theme at greater length in *Chance*. As Richard Curle recalled, the swindler epitomized 'a kind of amoral attitude to life and contempt for humanity which interested him as a novelist' (Curle, 1928a: 159).

And yet the most intriguing aspect of the fraud in 'The Partner' is its relation to legitimate business. In directing Stafford, his on-board conspirator, to sabotage the *Sagamore*'s anchor chain, Cloete does more than put lives at risk. He gives himself the edge in a financial contract with Lloyd's which ought to reflect a statistical probability – 'They take every risk into consideration' (*WT* 99), he notes – but which now rests upon a predictive certainty.[32] Marine insurance, it should be remembered, is essentially a kind of financial speculation rather like a share option. Possessed of certain facts such as a ship's age and the nature of her cargo, an underwriter guarantees to pay to an owner the insured value of a ship in the event of her not reaching her destination by a certain date. During the voyage, the policy may be sold to other brokers, and if the vessel fails to arrive on schedule the parties may draw up another contract, known as *reinsurance*, based upon the new circumstances. Conrad devotes a whole chapter of *The Mirror of the Sea* to this 'market of risks' (*MS* 61), explaining wryly how when a ship posted as 'overdue' finally arrives, 'The reinsurer, the optimist of ill-luck and disaster, slaps his pocket with satisfaction' (*MS* 62).

In a sense, then, the intended scam of 'The Partner' can be seen a bizarre variety of insider trading, that is, dealing on the basis of privileged information that, if generally known, would affect the price. For his part, Cloete is quite at ease with the white-collar nature of this crime, and remonstrates with George: 'Do I want you to rob the widow and orphan? Why, man! Lloyd's a corporation, it hasn't got a body to starve' (*WT* 99).[33] In a grotesque inversion of an insurance deal, Cloete negotiates a price for wrecking the *Sagamore* with Stafford – 'I don't mean this to have any future – as far as you are concerned. It's a "once for all" transaction. Well, what do you estimate your future at?' (104) – after which the two men seal their arrangement with a drink. Later, the slippery Cloete even tries to default on the terms of this compact by challenging Stafford's claim to have engineered the shipwreck, a quite unnecessary betrayal that he soon realizes to have endangered 'the whole business he had set his heart on' (115).

The word *speculation*, derived from the Latin *specĕre* (to see), acquired its economic meaning in the late eighteenth century, and its residual connotation of a special kind of seeing has an obvious relevance to maritime business. (Famously, Galileo used the first telescope to spot incoming ships in order to help Venetian commodity brokers outmanœuvre their rivals.) Speculations, both honest and crooked, are a recurrent motif in Conrad, as when Martin Decoud in *Nostromo* reminds his Costaguanan listeners of their ancestors: 'Thieves, of course. Speculators, too. Their expeditions, each one, were the speculations of grave and reverend persons in England' (*N* 174). Similarly, in 'The End of the Tether', Conrad fuses the themes of blindness, financial investment, gambling and commodity trading in a tragic story of deliberate shipwreck and a captain's betrayal by his business partner. In 'The Partner', however, speculation is repeatedly literalized as a disjunction between how something is represented or advertised and its true nature. The stevedore begins by explaining contemptuously how tourists 'Stare at the silly rocks' (*WT* 91) while boatmen unwittingly regale them with false accounts of the loss of the *Sagamore* and Captain Harry's 'suicide.' Upon seeing Stafford's 'nasty-handsome' face for the first time, George thinks to himself, 'Is that how such a man looks! No, the thing's impossible' (105), as if a less repulsive conspirator would somehow mitigate the crime. When the ship does founder, Captain Harry experiences the curious sensation that 'if he were to take his eyes off her she would fall to pieces' (114). Stafford, after shooting Harry and getting into the life-boat, tells the coxswain that the captain has not reappeared on deck because he wants to go down with his ship. The whole drama unfolds, meanwhile, before the transfixed but uncomprehending gaze of Captain Harry's wife, who instructs Cloete to 'Tell him I am here – looking on . . .' (112), and whose later derangement originates in the mistaken belief 'that her husband should take his own life, with her, as it were, looking on' (123). Again and again, Conrad presents guesses as to the meaning of what is seen, that is, attempts at speculation, as irredeemably wrong. After awkwardly casting about for visual metaphors such as 'a Whistler' (92) and 'a cinematograph picture' (93), the magazine-writer explains that 'I was incautious enough to breathe out another "I see," which gave offence again, and brought on me a rude "No, you don't" – as before' (109).

Conrad identifies advertising with this world of insubstantial speculation in two ways. The first is the nature of the proposed business scheme which Cloete presents as 'a patent medicine . . . which with capital, capital to the tune of thousands to be spent with both hands on advertising, could be turned into a great thing – infinitely better paying than a gold-mine' (*WT* 97). Given the promotion budgets of pharmaceutical manufacturers at the start of the twentieth century, Cloete's description of a patent medicine demanding 'pouring thousands into advertising' (97) seems unremarkable. Nevertheless, the magazine-writer presses the stevedore to disclose the product's name:

> 'I am curious,' I said, 'to learn what the motive force of this tragic affair was – I mean the patent medicine. Do you know?'
> He named it, and I whistled respectfully. Nothing less than Parker's Lively Lumbago Pills. Enormous property! You know it; all the world knows it. Every second man, at least, on this globe of ours has tried it.
> (*WT* 125–6)

On the surface, it is an odd question. What difference can the brand make to this sorry tale? Admittedly, the fictitious name does evoke the names of real drugs widely advertised in contemporary magazines – Conrad may well have been thinking of Carter's Little Liver Pills whose advertisements ('Carter's Little Liver Pills Cure All Liver Ills') had punctuated the serial version of *Nostromo* in *T. P.'s Weekly* in 1904 – and there is an obvious irony in the idea of marketing 'lively' pills with the proceeds of a fatal shipwreck. More importantly, the patent medicine's name supplies a pretext for the narrator to interpellate the reader directly, allowing Conrad to connect the fictional narrative of

'The Partner' to the advertisement-dominated world of magazine readers. This is advertising's true 'motive force'. Not merely can it convince millions of the medicinal value of a quack salve – every other person has *tried* it – but it also creates an illusion of community among an anonymous mass of global consumers. In fact, given a different format, the narrator's thumbnail description of the drug would make excellent advertising copy:

PARKER'S LIVELY LUMBAGO PILLS.
YOU KNOW IT.
ALL THE WORLD KNOWS IT.
Every second man on the globe has tried it!

The second link between advertising and speculation is Cloete himself. Not only has he worked in the patent medicine trade, he is a former copywriter whom Conrad takes pains to portray as an advertiser to the very fibre of his being. A careful newspaper reader, Cloete is in his element when buttonholing strangers in the pub in 'American fashion' (*WT* 103) or charming barmaids with his animated expression and 'jocular way of speaking' (93), the latter presumably a reference to his casual profanity and use of Americanisms such as 'cozy' (95) and 'funkiest' (102). Crucially, his skill as a raconteur of 'little tales' (93) is presented as another facet of his professional vocation. As the stevedore remarks: 'Writes advertisements and all that. Tells me funny stories' (94). This copywriter's talent for persuasion, whose similarity to writing fiction has a fascinating resonance in this context, enables Cloete to tempt his cash-strapped partner into crime. 'A man who's been in the patent-medicine trade will be up to anything from pitch-and-toss to wilful murder. . . . Don't mind what they do – think they can carry off anything and talk themselves out of anything,' opines the stevedore, explaining that 'Some of his tales must have opened George Dunbar's eyes a bit as to what business means' (94).[34] In an extraordinarily dense metaphor of literal and figurative consumption, he likens the advertiser's patter to the testimony of a practised perjurer: 'These patent-medicine chaps don't care what they say or what they do. They think the world's bound to swallow any story they like to tell . . .' (116).[35] As often in Conrad, power is shown to reside in the material force of language. What makes Cloete a killer is precisely what makes him a good ad-man: a limitless capacity to lie, that is, to make people believe – once again, literally 'to swallow' – anything. Even so, and notwithstanding the narrator's view of Cloete as 'A plausible fellow' (95), Conrad indicates that advertisers could not succeed without the naivety and greed of ordinary people. What Cloete pitches to George as the 'Chance of a lifetime' (99) consists only of the doubtful proposition that no-one will be hurt if the *Sagamore* is sabotaged in a port, and the ludicrous claim that insurers are less zealous when investigating the loss of ships on which premiums have been paid 'for so many, many years' (99). Indeed, his glib reassurance that the 'Wrecking . . . could be managed with perfect safety' (98) sounds like a self-help pamphlet: *Wrecking With Perfect Safety*.

The theme of 'The Partner' reflects Conrad's own negative experience of patent medicines.[36] 'I am not like Homocea. I don't touch the spot' (*CL* 2: 119), he once quipped, alluding to the slogan of a popular cure-all (Figure 10). More disturbingly, he related in 1906 how Borys had been 'poisoned (through the skin) with the new disinfectant *Lisol* a most damnable stuff' (*CL* 3: 308), and later claimed that the painkiller CBQ (Post's Tablets) was making him feel 'imbecile' (4: 187). Patent medicine appears in a correspondingly bad light in his fiction: in *Lord Jim* a patient ignores his doctor's advice in order to indulge in 'secret debaucheries of patent medicine' (*LJ* 12); the narrator of 'A Smile of Fortune' has an unwelcome feeling that Alfred Jacobus wants to sell him some bottles of 'Clarkson's Nerve Tonic' (*TLS* 40); and an offer of two bottles of patent medicine is described by the narrator of *The Shadow-Line* as an 'atrocity' (*SL* 7). In *The Secret Agent*, patent medicine even stands as a repellent emblem of modernity itself. The prophylactics and indecent photographs in Verloc's shop window are 'nondescript packages in wrappers like patent medicines' (*SA* 3), and, in a markedly caustic aside, Conrad portrays the shopkeeper as having

> the air of moral nihilism common to keepers of gambling hells and disorderly houses; to private detectives and inquiry agents; to drink sellers and, I should say, to the sellers of invigorating electric belts and to the inventors of patent medicines. But of that last I am not sure, not having carried my investigations so far into the depths. For all I know, the expression of these last may be perfectly diabolic. I shouldn't be surprised.   (*SA* 13)

Later, Vladimir declares ominously that 'What we want is to administer a tonic to the Conference in Milan' (*SA* 27), the narrator likens Winnie's ride in a bone-shaking carriage to 'some very new-fangled invention for the cure of a sluggish liver' (126), and the Professor mocks Ossipon's revolutionary ideal as a vision of 'humanity universally putting out the tongue and taking the pill from pole to pole' (228).

Figure 10 Homocea advertisement, c.1905. Author's collection.

Particularly revealing in 'The Partner' is the way that Cloete's scheme is defined as 'the motive force of this tragic affair', since the phrase shifts responsibility for the disaster from an individual to advertising itself, a system that holds out the promise of fantastic profits to the reckless investor, in sharp contrast to the low-risk 'consols' (*WT* 125) purchased on behalf of Captain Harry's widow. Cloete's American provenance further reinforces the impression that Conrad regarded the real culprit as an influx of new money and alien business practices, epitomized in the stevedore's reference to British ships being sold to 'foreigners' (96). (More than one reviewer of 'An Anarchist' identified Harry Gee as American, despite the absence of evidence.) Richard Curle remembered Conrad telling him that ' "Everybody in America is trying to sell something to somebody" ' and maintaining that United States was 'commercialized to the point where nothing else really mattered' (Curle, 1928b: 209). Seen in this light, 'The Partner' can be understood as a fable about venture capital investing whereby one business speculation directly enables another, an appropriate sequel to the theme of 'commercial venture' (*TLS* 85) in 'A Smile of Fortune'. There may even be an ironic echo of the notion of company 'floatation' and product 'launches' in Captain Harry's concern that the crew might 'attempt to launch one of the ship's boats' (*WT* 114) and Cloete's fear that George Dunbar's half of the money will 'not prove sufficient to launch the medicine well' (125).[37]

'The Partner' is, then, a microcosm of a society in which every human relationship has become distorted, or, more precisely, commodified, by absorption into the cash nexus. Stafford exemplifies this process: a disgraced master mariner reduced to scrounging from a boarding-house landlady, he sells himself to Cloete for £500 over 'sixpennyworth of Scotch hot' (*WT* 104). When he later fails to blackmail his way into doubling this figure, he threatens: 'I would shoot you now for tuppence. . . . You low Yankee fiend – I'll pay you off some day' (125). In fact, as Cloete realizes, Stafford has already 'paid him off' (125) by causing him to lose a fortune 'by the price of a revolver-shot' (126).[38] This pecuniary logic also governs Cloete's interaction with the proprietor of a hotel where, posing as a considerate ship's agent, he has lodged Stafford at his own expense. His detection of the proprietor's lie about having given Stafford drinks on the house – 'I don't mind doing that much for a shipwrecked sailor' (123) – is deeply embarrassing to the publican who, having hoped to advertise his generosity, now risks exposure as a fraud. What matters to Cloete, though, is the realization that Stafford has murdered Captain Harry for his gold. The same principle operates throughout the story: the tourists on the beach buy overdiluted 'weak lemonade' (89); the shipping firm of Mundy and Rogers continues to fly 'the firm's *house-flag*' (95), as the stevedore remarks scornfully, as a self-advertisement on a vessel it no longer owns;[39] and the magazine-writer thinks only in terms of what 'pays' (92) and deems the stevedore's tale, picked up in a bar, as 'not worth many thanks' (128). The only exceptions are Captain Harry and his wife for whom the *Sagamore* has not merely a commercial value but is 'our home' (113). The last figures of moral integrity in this sordid world, they are marked out as its victims.

On this view, advertising and the dubious business practices that it encourages are more than just a narrowly commercial evil: they express something fundamental about the changed way in which people relate to each another. Advertising has become, in Raymond Williams's phrase, 'no longer merely a way of selling goods . . . [but] a true part of the culture of a confused society' (Williams, 1980: 191). Thus Conrad presents the 'motive force' of patent medicine advertising as having a necessary corollary in the consumer, personified by George Dunbar's young wife whose 'expensive tastes' (*WT* 97) indirectly bring about the catastrophe. Anatomizing her as 'silk dress, pretty boots, all feathers and scent,' the stevedore describes her house in the new London suburb of Norwood as 'More like the Promenade at the Alhambra than a decent home' (100).[40] That this refers to a location popular with prostitutes advertising their services is confirmed by his brutal comment, 'that piece of goods ought to have been walking the streets' (100).[41] Tellingly, the consumer herself is just another 'piece of goods', a commodity in a commodity-dominated world.

This insight constitutes the real sting in the narrator's oft-quoted closing remark, understandably absent from the serial version, that 'This story to be acceptable should have been transposed to somewhere in the South Seas. But it would have been too much trouble to cook it for the consumption of magazine readers' (*WT* 128).[42] There is, of course, a clever *mise-en-abyme* in the idea of retelling a supposedly unprintable story. But this is to miss the target of Conrad's thinly-veiled jibe: the fact that where others may simply read, magazine readers must always also *consume*. As John Steuart noted soberly in the *Fortnightly Review* in February 1898, 'In America, as everybody is now aware, popular works . . . have long been used as bait for customers expected to invest in millinery, soaps, pills, perfumery, cosmetics, and so forth' (Steuart, 1898: 259). By 1911, *Harper's* and its competitors had long since ceased paying printing and distribution costs with revenue from the cover price but had embraced a system that enabled them to buy 'The Partner', a 13,000-word story, for £40, twice as much as Conrad received for the rights to his first novel ten years earlier. Indeed, it is scarcely an exaggeration to say that neither 'An Anarchist' nor 'The Partner' would ever have seen the light of day without the twenty pages of advertisements – for soaps, hair restorers, underwear, coffee, tobacco, baking powders, cocoas, whiskies, disinfectants, toothpastes and fountain pens – that bracketed the literary contents of *Harper's*. In the process, as Conrad realized, something fundamental had changed. Once the wares that a literary magazine retailed to its reading customers, short stories were now merely the window-dressing, so to speak, of its real business: selling readers' attention to advertisers.

Successful advertising: *Chance* (1914)

Towards the end of 'The Black Mate', a story about a sailor driven to deception by the loss of his hair dye, Conrad's now white-haired mate urges the narrator to convey some important information to the dye's maker: ' "By the way, that fellow's got a fortune when he likes to pick it up. It is a wonderful stuff – you tell him salt water can do nothing to it. It stays on as long as your hair will" ' (*TH* 117). Despite the testimonial's strangeness – there is no reason why the narrator should know the pharmacist personally – Bunter's words make an apt conclusion to a tale that Conrad first submitted to *Tit-Bits* in 1886, probably in hopes of winning its hefty twenty-guinea 'Special Prize' for a short story by a sailor (Carabine, 1988), and that he eventually sold to Alfred Harmsworth's *London Magazine*, a journal notorious for paying good rates for inferior work by its few established writers.[43] In this climate of what Conrad's narrator calls 'modern conditions of push and hurry' (*TH* 88), an author could surely be forgiven for thinking that, with the right kind of endorsement, small fortunes were there for the taking.

It is a nice irony, then, that Conrad's own commercial breakthrough with *Chance* in 1912 hinged upon an advertising campaign in the *New York Herald* that proclaimed him to be the 'World's Most Famous Author of Sea Stories' (Jones, 1999: 145). In the preceding years, Conrad had become highly conscious of the power of effective advertising, even asking his agent to ensure that Heinemann would 'make a certain amount of fuss' about 'Typhoon': 'The public's so used to the guidance of Advertis[e]ment! Why! even I myself feel the spell of such emphasis' (*CL* 2: 319); by the end of his career, opportunists such as Francis Warrington Dawson and Francis McCullagh would be using his correspondence in advertisements for their own work. We do not know whether Conrad's involvement with the floatation of Rorke's-Roodepoort

Gold Mine in 1895 included helping to draft its share prospectus (Figure 11), but he certainly wrote advertising copy on a number of occasions. Typescript revisions in his hand confirm his authorship of the self-congratulatory copy in a publisher's circular for *The Secret Agent: A Drama in Three Acts* (1923): 'This play is . . . an illustration of the corrupting nature of the Anarchist doctrine; a study which Mr Conrad is perhaps, of all English writers, the most qualified to undertake because of his extraordinary capacity for divining human motives and penetrating hidden depths of emotion' (Rude, 1984: 28).

---

602   SOUTH AFRICA.   September 14, 1895.

The Subscription List will open on Thursday, the 12th inst., and close for Town on Friday, the 13th inst., and for the Country and Continent on Monday, the 16th inst., at 12 noon.

RORKE'S ROODEPOORT,

LIMITED.

(WITWATERSRAND GOLD FIELDS, S.A.R)

Incorporated under the Limited Liability Acts, 1862-1893.

CAPITAL -   -   -   -   - £130,000,

IN 130,000 SHARES OF £1 EACH,

Of which 40,000 credited as fully paid will be allotted to the Vendor in part payment of the purchase, and 50,000 are reserved for Working Capital.

ISSUE OF 60,000 SHARES OF £1 EACH,

Payable as follows :—2s. 6d. on Application ; 7s. 6d. on Allotment ; and the Balance two months after Allotment.

DIRECTORS.	SOLICITORS.
EDWARD CHAPMAN, Esq., Devonshire Chambers, Bishopsgate Street, E.C., Director Gem of Cue Gold Mining Company, Limited.	Messrs. MELLOR, SMITH, & MAY, 1, Moorgate Place, E.C.
GEORGE GRIFFITH, Esq., J.P. (late of Cardiff, Colliery Proprietor), Fitzjohn's Avenue, N.W.	CONSULTING ENGINEERS.
F. W. NORTH, Esq., F.G.S., Director of the Scottish African Corporation, Limited (late Government Engineer for Natal and the Cape Colonies).	Messrs. BAINBRIDGE, SEYMOUR, & CO., 13, St. Helen's Place, E.C.
SAMUEL SPENCER, Esq., C.C. (J. E. & S. Spencer), 14, Great St. Thomas Apostle, E.C.	BROKERS.
Major-General E. HARDING STEWARD, C.M.G., Director of the Heidelberg Gold Mines, Limited, and Pardy's Mozambique, Limited.	London : Messrs. JOHN GIBBS, SON, & CO., 31, Threadneedle Street, E.C. and Stock Exchange, London.
	CARDIFF : Messrs. CHARLES MASSY & CO., Cory's Corner, Bute Docks, Cardiff.
JOHANNESBURG AGENTS.	JOHANNESBURG : HENRY LEVY, Esq., 11, City Chambers, and Stock Exchange, Johannesburg, S.A.
THE TRANSVAAL TRADING COMPANY, LIMITED.	AUDITORS.
	Messrs. WARD & WILDING, Chartered Accountants, Clement's Inn, Strand, W.C.
BANKERS.	LONDON—Secretary and Offices (pro tem.) :—
London : Messrs. BROWN, JANSON, & CO., 32, Abchurch Lane, E.C.	A. H. HARDY, Esq., 13, St. Helen's Place, E.C.
JOHANNESBURG : THE STANDARD BANK OF AFRICA.	JOHANNESBURG—Secretary and Offices :—
	HUGH MEHARG, Esq., Simmons Street.

Figure 11 Share prospectus for Rorke's Roodepoort Limited, *South Africa* (14 September 1895), 602. Author's collection.

The professional writer's reliance on publicity explains but also complicates Conrad's oft-stated antipathy towards advertising. Driven by the collapse of the three-decker novel system, the spread of serialization and international syndication, and the burgeoning sale of cheap editions, advertising assumed paramount importance for publishers and booksellers in the early 1900s. Conrad observed cynically that bookselling was now open to 'any man with enough money to take a shop, stock his shelves, and pay for advertisements' (*NLL* 67), and in his letters he applied the terms of his critique of patent food advertising in 'An Anarchist' to the literary market, deriding publishers' advertisements as a mixture of huckersterism and falsehood. 'I don't care for his advertising' (*CL* 4: 503), he remarked of Methuen, and when the publisher misleadingly claimed that a sixth edition of *Chance* was in press, Conrad vehemently denounced the 'lying adv[er]tis[men]t' to Pinker, and declared himself 'sick' of such 'untruthful protestations' (*CL* 5: 348); *Chance*'s promotion was, he complained, 'a ridiculous advertising splash (which was jeered at in the provincial press)' (5: 365). Notwithstanding such disavowals, Conrad was evidently discomforted by fiction's family resemblance to what Daphna Erdinast-Vulcan has dubbed its 'sister art' of 'rhetorical persuasion' (Erdinast-Vulcan, 1999: 115–16), in particular, their joint dependence upon the reader's suspension of disbelief. In 1898, when popularity still seemed an impossible goal, Conrad gave Cunninghame Graham a telling description of the artistic challenge ahead: 'My own life is difficult enough. . . . I could never invent an effective lie – a lie that would sell, and last, and be admirable' (*CL* 2: 60).

Fittingly, Conrad's long-awaited 'lie that would sell' features a protagonist whose identity is almost wholly the product of mendacious advertising. Despite his apparent marginality in *Chance*, it is the trajectory described by the swindler de Barral's journey from bank clerk to fêted entrepreneur, object of national vilification and humbled ex-convict that constitutes, to echo the narrator of 'The Partner', the motive force of this affair. At the level of plot, de Barral's abandonment of Flora, first to her governess and then to an odious cousin, effectively forces her upon the Fynes' charity and thereby introduces the young girl to her future husband. Similarly, the father's sinister presence aboard the *Ferndale* creates the extraordinary circumstances in which Charles Powell can prove his worth to Anthony and Flora. At the level of characterization, de Barral's heartless and domineering treatment of Flora during childhood is the reason for her gullibility and insecurity, qualities that fatally determine the kinds of adult relationships she is capable of sustaining.

Like George Ponderevo in H. G. Wells's *Tono-Bungay* (1909) and Denry
Machin in Arnold Bennett's *The Card* (1911), de Barral's rise into the
upper echelons of society originates in an advertising epiphany: 'one
day as though a supernatural voice had whispered into his ear or some
invisible fly had stung him, he put on his hat, went out into the street
and began advertising' (*C* 61). Conrad's explanation of how the former
bank-clerk hit upon the idea for his savings-and-loan scheme is revealing, implying as it does that the rationale behind advertising more
closely resembles demonic possession or poison-induced delirium than
sound business logic. Although several historical models have been
advanced for de Barral, including the company promoter Whitaker
Wright, the jingo journalist Horatio Bottomley and the former Bovril
publicist Ernest Hooley (Moser, 1975: 209–13), Conrad portrays the
entrepreneur as a nobody, a cipher-like repository of second-hand words
who fails to grasp either the purpose or the significance of his actions.
Far from being a criminal mastermind, de Barral is 'totally unable to
organize anything, to promote any sort of enterprise [even] if it
were only for the purposes of juggling with the shares' (*C* 62); cross-
examination reveals him to have been 'more gullible than any of his
investors' (63). Moreover, as with patent food manufacture in 'An
Anarchist', de Barral's dependence on advertising is more important
than the nature of his business: the Orb Bank, the Thrift and
Independence Association and the Sceptre Trust are, Marlow stresses,
not businesses at all but 'mere names' devised 'for advertising purposes'
(61–2).[44] Without a product in which to invest, de Barral can only use
his capital 'to publish more advertisements and open more branch
offices . . . for the receipt of deposits' (62). Adapting Fredric Jameson's
well-known definition of postmodernism as the 'cultural logic' of late
capitalism, one might say that *Chance* represents advertising as pyramid
selling: as the cultural logic of a simulacrum of capitalism. For Conrad,
de Barral's fraudulent business schemes are not distortions of advertising's real nature but its quintessence.

Advertising, Raymond Williams has argued, is 'a highly organized
system of magical inducements and satisfactions, functionally very
similar to magical systems in simpler societies' (185). By directing consumers to fantasize about commodities in carefully prescribed ways, it
reframes a broader choice of the capitalist mode of production as a set of
more limited choices about its goods and services. Conrad, albeit from a
very different political standpoint, also identifies a coercive dimension
to advertising's 'magic'. Where 'An Anarchist' portrays B.O.S.'s brightly
coloured advertisements and brand aura of 'three magic letters' (*SS* 135)

as simply concealing the reality of labour conditions on company ranches, *Chance* reveals advertising as an insidious form of social hegemony that deceives and disempowers its own participants, the investing public whom Marlow disparagingly calls 'a credulous multitude not fit to take care of itself' (*C* 182).

Crucially, whilst de Barral's advertisements peddle a double deception – ten per cent on invested capital (twice the normal rate) and a financial speculation that profits everyone – their force derives not from any rhetorical skill or imagination on his part (he has neither) but from their recycling of vernacular fragments. Not only does de Barral take as his catchphrase 'the word of the time' from popular idiom 'in the streets', he places 'the magic word Thrift, Thrift, Thrift, thrice repeated' at the head of his 'first modest advertisements' (61) in a kind of incantation calculated to inspire blind trust in his victims.[45] When challenged to justify his blunt description of de Barral's business as the elimination of wealth, Marlow protests: 'I have merely stripped the rags of business verbiage and financial jargon off my statements' (*C* 62–3). Advertising, Conrad would have us believe, is a popular language whose lies and mystifications can only alienate its users. This view of advertising as literally fraudulent is underscored by the portrayal of advertisers as criminal in both 'The Partner' and *Chance*. Tellingly, since a fraud's success or failure is always total, neither Cloete nor de Barral hesitates to resort to extreme measures in defence of his interests, thereby neatly reversing the axiom of Dorothy Sayers's classic whodunnit *Murder Must Advertise* (1933). As what Fyne calls an 'advertising shark' (182), de Barral must murder.

That de Barral is at his most mercenary when at sea provides narrative confirmation of Conrad's belief in sailing as the litmus test of moral fibre. Even so, the incongruous presence of an advertiser on board ship suggests that Conrad wished to lend *Chance*'s sea-scenes an allegorical quality. De Barral's passage aboard the *Ferndale*, which culminates in his attempt to poison Captain Anthony, whom he reviles as a jailor, enacts a key theme of the novel: the transformation of all human activity into business. To be sure, *Chance* is leavened with references to 'business' in both its everyday senses of private matter and professional activity: on the one hand, Marlow's aside that 'the affairs of Captain Anthony were none of my business' (*C* 150) and Fyne's description of Flora's elopement as a 'very painful business' (180); and, on the other, Marlow's mention of being 'called to town on business' (38) and his observation that a financier acquaintance 'would have done business . . . with the devil himself' (59). Standing in a central London street, Marlow feels 'as if the whole world existed only for selling and buying and those who had nothing to do with the movement of merchandise were of no account' (157–8). And yet the line between personal and public 'business' remains indistinct for much of the novel. 'Is it ever the business of any pressman to understand anything?' (68), asks Marlow rhetorically, and when the narrator (whom Conrad identified as a novelist in an earlier draft) offers an opinion of women, he retorts: 'You make it your business to know them – don't you?' (120). As for women themselves, Marlow ironically concedes 'the extreme arduousness of the business of being a woman. . . . a terribly difficult trade since it consists principally of dealings with men' (271), a chauvinist joke that sits awkwardly with the novel's several references to prostitution.

At the centre of *Chance's* network of literal and figurative business relations stands de Barral, who declares solemnly, 'I am a business man' (*C* 268), and whose professional ambition leads him to contemplate disposing of a daughter through marriage and a son-in-law through murder. Such unrelenting instrumentality even governs his own sense of self. Seemingly an expression of megalomania or schizophrenic delusion, his repeated references to 'the great Mr. de Barral' (268, 319) actually show him to be hopelessly in thrall to the discourses of advertising and journalism. 'The start is really only a matter of judicious advertising,' he tells Flora in allusion to his planned return to business: 'After all I am still de Barral, *the* de Barral' (273). The mirror images of this exemplar of advertising-driven business are *Chance's* sailors, who personify an older code of commercial enterprise that is bound by honour, based on the circulation of tangible commodities, and observant of the law (at least in spirit, to judge from Powell's experience at the Shipping Office). In having de Barral sneer, 'But what does a silly sailor know of business? Nothing. No conception' (285), Conrad directs readers to draw precisely the opposite conclusion.

Chance's dramatizing of a clash between two irreconcilable business cultures – one traditional, reliable and patrician, the other modern, speculative and popular – is underscored by Powell's declaration on the novel's opening page: 'If we at sea . . . went about our work as people ashore high and low go about theirs we should never make a living. No one would employ us. And moreover no ship navigated and sailed in the happy-go-lucky manner people conduct their business on shore would ever arrive into port' (*C* 7). The analogy lends itself to more than one interpretation. Read literally, it reiterates Conrad's professional bias towards sailors as well as his warnings in 'Certain Aspects of the Admirable Inquiry into the Loss of the Titanic' about the folly of trusting 'advertising people' (*NLL* 181) in matters of maritime business such as ship design, cargo and route. But since the reflection is prompted by a restaurant waiter's incompetence, Powell's real point would appear to be that 'business on shore' lacks the merchant service's reliability and good sense.[46] Similarly, when Marlow describes de Barral as having been 'carried away out of his depth by the unexpected power of successful advertising' (*C* 198), his intention is not to excuse the fleecing of small investors but rather to suggest that business is subject to 'natural' laws: the businessman who thinks himself empowered by advertising to defy these laws is, in effect, like the novice swimmer or sailor who pays no heed to tidal currents. There is therefore a trenchant irony in Marlow's attribution of de Barral's swindle to 'successful advertising' since it is only when advertising represents the perverting of legitimate business principles that its promotion of an enterprise injurious to everyone can meaningfully be called 'successful'.

More obliquely, the phrase 'successful advertising' also recalls the popular guide *Successful Advertising*, first published in 1885 and still being issued annually in the 1910s, which, in addition to offering advice to professional advertisers and lay people on the design and distribution of advertisements, unblushingly recommended readers to the advertising agency managed by its author, Thomas Smith. Conrad could conceivably have come across *Successful Advertising* during one of his ventures into commodity trading, company floatation, or warehousing, in which case we are perhaps hearing echoes of Thomas Smith's precepts about the 'three primary characteristics or instincts. . . . Self-Preservation, The Acquirement of Food, Curiosity' (Smith, 1902: 61) in the assertion by *Chance*'s narrator that 'Curiosity is natural to man' (*C* 210) and Marlow's definition of the first condition of life as 'the instinct of self-preservation' (*C* 134).[47] Particularly suggestive is the way that *Successful Advertising*'s first chapter offers an account of the 'good ship S.S. Business' being guided by advertising into the 'Port of Success'. Prefacing his maritime allegory with an paean to advertising's universality, 'the subject of advertising. . . . stares us in the face at every turn; in remote and isolated places it appears quite unexpectedly', Smith invites his readers to imagine themselves 'privileged passengers' on this 'Voyage to Success' (Smith, 1902: 18, 22). None too subtly, he reiterates the message that advertising is synonymous with progress, declaring sagely that steam is 'as indispensable to an engine as advertising is to a good paying business' and explaining that many businesses are 'submerged and drowned out of existence because they are not efficiently navigated, and run without the all-powerful aid of advertising and the advertising specialist'

(Smith, 1902: 26, 34). Conrad's take on the pairing of advertising and maritime modernity could hardly be more negative. Powell's intervention prevents Captain Anthony from being murdered by the advertiser who is travelling as *his* privileged passenger but nothing can save Anthony and the sailing ship from being destroyed by a steamer that the mate condemns as a 'cursed, murderous thing' (*C* 324).

Whether or not Conrad consciously intended it as a riposte to *Successful Advertising*, *Chance's* treatment of 'successful advertising' makes a fitting conclusion to this survey. For Conrad, as we have seen, advertising is an irredeemably debased mode of popular culture, creating a false epistemology among its consumers and licensing the very worst cynicism among its practitioners. Far from humanizing a system of commodity circulation that now stretches from metropolitan high street to colonial backwater, advertising epitomizes the most destructive aspects of modernity; it is, in the words of *Chance's* 'serious paper' (evidently the *Times*), 'a deplorable sign of the times' (*C* 83). Having equated advertising with literal and spiritual obliteration – the murder and mayhem unleashed by Cloete in 'The Partner', Comrade Ossipon's bowing his head in *The Secret Agent* 'to receive the leather yoke of the sandwich board' (*SA* 231) – Conrad exacts a symbolic revenge in *Chance*. De Barral dies not only by his own hand but from a poison acquired by his advertising alter-ego. As Marlow notes sombrely, 'It was not Mr. Smith who obtained the poison. It was the Great de Barral' (*C* 323).

Balzac is reported to have settled overdue bills by inserting discreet advertisements for local merchants into his stories, and it might be argued that Conrad simply does the reverse: settling scores with a culture of product endorsement that he despised. Certainly, he appears on occasion to have indulged in some inside jokes: the frivolous wife of Captain MacWhirr in 'Typhoon' announces her intention of going to 'a sale at Linom's' (*T* 126), presumably a reference to John Linom's drapery store on Rendezvous Street in Folkestone; and it is an odd coincidence that 'Falk', a story thematizing eating that begins with an allusion to the 'flavour of salt water which for so many of us had been the very water of life' (*T* 165), should feature a protagonist who shares both his name and nationality with one of the best-known brands of table salt (Figure 12). And yet this chapter has sought to make a case that advertising played a more substantial role in how Conrad understood his historical moment. In works such as 'An Anarchist', 'The Partner', and *Chance*, he offers a meditation on advertising's new importance for a system of business whose products, be they patent foods, pharmaceuticals, or get-rich-quick schemes, can no longer simply be announced but must, whatever

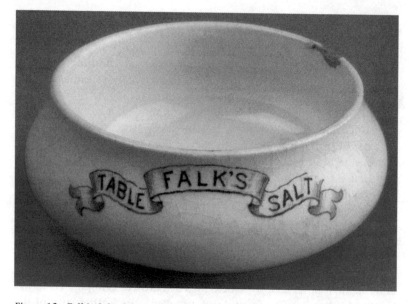

Figure 12   Falk's Salt china salt bowl. Reproduced with permission of The Salt Museum, Northwich, Cheshire.

their real origins, be woven into a persuasive discourse of mutual benefit and progress. Like the fact of Paul's slave labour in 'An Anarchist', the narrator's remark about the petty $2 per diem charge for the 'hospitality of the B.O.S. Co., Ltd. . . . in whose balance-sheet for that year those monies are no doubt included' (*SS* 138) defetishizes the commodity to reveal relations between things as thoroughly exploitative relations between people. By satirizing one of the most innovative and prominent advertisers of his day, Conrad gave warning of the advertising-colonized world to come. In William Morris's futuristic fantasy *News From Nowhere* (1888), a dusty pub sign reminds the narrator how commodity signifiers had once ruled supreme 'in the days when hospitality had to be bought and sold' (Morris, 1986: 374). More pessimistically, Conrad imagined a twentieth century in which advertisements – popular, plausible and familiar – would make willing slaves of us all.

4
Magazine Fiction

> It's quite good magazine stuff, quite Conradesque (in the easier style) . . . .
>
> Conrad describing 'Freya of The Seven Isles' to Warrington Dawson, 15 February 1911 (*CL* 4: 413)

> 'Maroon you! We are not living in a boy's adventure tale,' I protested. His scornful whispering took me up.
> 'We aren't indeed! There's nothing of a boy's tale in this.'
>
> 'The Secret Sharer' (1909) (*TLS* 131)

'Do you know anything about another Joseph Conrad who has published a novel some time ago?' (*CL* 6: 425), Conrad asked his agent in May 1919 following an enquiry from the booksellers W. H. Smith, who had received a request for thirty copies of *The Waitress Bold* by a writer supposedly bearing his name. The absence of any records of Conrad's mysterious namesake or his improbably titled novel, coupled with the fact that the same customer had also ordered a copy of *The Bald-Headed Man*, a novel by Andrew Simpson (*CL* 6: 423n), suggests that Conrad may have been the victim of a humorous prank. Then again, perhaps the unidentified customer was simply mistaken. James Joyce was once provoked to fury when the *Frankfurter Zeitung* erroneously attributed to him a story by Michael Joyce, a minor novelist whose work the established writer denounced in a rare burst of intolerance as 'a fraudulent shoddy piece of journalese' (Joyce, 1966, 3: 227).

Whether a confusion or a canard, the idea of Conrad having a secret other existence as the author of popular works such as *The Waitress Bold* and *The Bald-Headed Man* (this latter also the title of a comic song) is less absurd than it sounds.[1] With the exception of *Almayer's Folly, An Outcast*

161

of the Islands and two short stories, all of Conrad's fiction made its first appearance, if not its second and third, in a periodical publication. Moreover, most of his novels, including major works such as *The Secret Agent* and *Under Western Eyes*, began life as a short story intended for a magazine and were completed on more than one occasion in weekly or monthly instalments that he wrote against a publishing deadline: *Lord Jim* in *Blackwood's Magazine* in 1899–1900; *Nostromo* in *T. P.'s Weekly* in 1904; *The Secret Agent* in *Ridgway's Magazine* in 1906; *Chance* in the Sunday magazine section of the *New York Herald* in 1912; and *The Rescue* in *Land and Water* in 1919. Downplayed by earlier generations of critics, these core features of his literary project are at last beginning to receive the recognition that they deserve. As Sid Reid notes in the conclusion to his valuable survey of the textual history, readership composition, marketing, illustration and even paper quality of Conrad's work in American serials between 1906 and 1912: '[W]hat once appeared to be a matter of an individual artistic temperament has acquired a collective dimension' (Reid, 2003: 75). Nevertheless, the ephemerality of periodicals and their often fragmentary or haphazard preservation in far-flung archives continue to skew our reading of Conrad's work. The only version of his essay 'Hyde Park Mansions' was published in *The Minesweeper's Gazette*, a wartime magazine of which not one copy survives, and another essay on Rudyard Kipling that he submitted to *The Outlook* has similarly vanished without trace. According to the *Oxford Reader's Companion to Conrad*, only in 1993 did scholars discover that Conrad's incomplete novel *Suspense* was first read by subscribers to *Hutchinson's Magazine*, a shilling colour-illustrated fiction magazine studded with full-page advertisements for Ovaltine, Bile Beans and Lyons confectionery. And even Peter McDonald's magisterial analysis of the *New Review* as a publishing context for *The Nigger of the 'Narcissus'* nowhere mentions that the novel was also serialized in abridged form under the rather more humble auspices of the *Illustrated Buffalo Express* (Rude et al., 1977).

Unlike visual entertainment, tourism and advertising, Conrad's relation to contemporary magazine fiction has been the focus of considerable critical attention such that it is a truism to say that the latter now constitutes a significant context for his writing. At the same time, magazine fiction undoubtedly remains one of the richest veins for further work on Conrad and popular culture. We are fortunate in having several studies that have illuminated his indebtedness to short-story writers such as Guy de Maupassant, Alphonse Daudet and Anatole France. And *Heart of Darkness*, in addition to generating a mountain of textual exegesis, has produced a number of important studies that review the novella in terms of popular genres such as the imperial gothic and the colonial romance.[2] Even so, and despite the textual histories supplied in recent scholarly editions and a handful of critical studies of *The Nigger of the 'Narcissus', Nostromo, Under Western Eyes* and *Chance*, students of Conrad still await detailed analyses of most of the periodicals in which his other works were serialized and into whose agendas and marketing strategies they were often integrated. Conrad himself had no illusions about the supplementary identity that his work assumed in periodical format, as he indicated to Algernon Methuen: 'A piece of literary work may be defined in twenty ways. The people [*Ridgway's Magazine*] who are serializing the Secret Agent in the U.S. now have found their own definition. They described it (on posters) as "A Tale of Diplomatic Intrigue and Anarchist Treachery." But they don't do it on my authority and that's all I care for' (*CL* 3: 370–1).

Sea stories are a case in point. Despite Conrad's claim that 'No one cares about [the sea] really, or I would have had as much success here as [Pierre] Loti in France' (*CL* 4: 89), stories with maritime themes were staple features of turn-of-the-century magazines, a fact that makes them a promising subject for examination in their own right. Remarkably, however, there has been no detailed survey of Conrad's treatment of life at sea that addresses the *œuvres* of predecessors such as Mayne Reid and Frederick Marryat or contemporaries such as Edward Noble, W. Clark Russell, Morley Roberts, or Frank Bullen, all of whom published extensively in popular serials. Nor has there been any comprehensive attempt to situate Conrad's sea writings – including serial fiction such as *Lord Jim* and 'The End of the Tether' as well as periodical articles on topics such as the Dogger Bank Incident, the Royal Naval Reserve, the loss of the *Titanic* and the protection of ocean liners – in the context of the changing representation of maritime life in British culture more broadly, an ideological trajectory that may well be reflected in the transition in Conrad's own fiction from the motif of exotic adventure on the main in early tales such as 'Youth' and 'Typhoon' to the darker subjects of atrocity and violence at sea in later works such as 'The Tale' and 'The Secret Sharer'.[3] That no comparative study has been made of W. W. Jacobs's inshore sea stories is a doubly curious omission given that these tales, which were first published in *Strand Magazine* and *Harper's Magazine* and regularly offered with Maupassant's stories as models for aspiring writers, were praised by Conrad as 'most entertaining' (*PR* 136) – an adjective he also applied to his own short fiction at about this time.[4] Critics typically point out that T. Fisher Unwin was unable to place 'The Return', a story described by its author as 'not a tale for puppy dogs nor for maids of thirteen' (*CL* 2: 11), and that Conrad failed to persuade George Blackwood to accept 'Falk' for publication; yet the precise nature of his miscalculations remains unclear. Matters were presumably not helped by Conrad's choice of a magazine editor as the cuckolding villain of 'The Return' but just how far ahead of the moral evolution of British and American periodicals were these stories thematizing adultery and cannibalism? Conrad was certainly insistent enough on how to place 'The Return', telling Fisher Unwin in November 1897: 'If I send it to You at once perhaps You could place it *serially* in some *advanced* Am. Mag: Fossils won't care for it' (*CL* 1: 405, Conrad's emphases).

The view that publication in a popular magazine is a problem requiring justification or apology was for a long time axiomatic among Conrad scholars, allowing perceived weaknesses in his work to be blamed upon the debasing influence and generic conventionality of commercial fiction. Thus Thomas Moser's influential *Joseph Conrad: Achievement and Decline* presents the early magazine stories 'Falk', 'The End of the Tether', and 'Freya of the Seven Isles' as suffering from the same defects of sentimentality and melodrama that mar late novels such as *The Arrow of Gold* in which Conrad similarly chose 'to pander to a popular audience' (Moser, 1957: 111). And in his analysis of Conrad's first story, 'The Black Mate', Lawrence Graver refers casually to the audience for *Tit-Bits* as being 'mindless' (Graver, 1964–65: 164). In the teleology of these book-oriented accounts, popular magazines of the late-nineteenth and early-twentieth century are an inferior and moribund field of literary ephemera that has little or no relevance for our reading of masterpieces by a major writer. And yet, with their connotations of triviality and poor execution, labels such as 'light literature' or 'potboiler' may obscure more than they illuminate about popular magazine fiction and the reading public that Conrad charged with being 'incapable of fixing its attention for five consecutive minutes' (*CL* 2: 418). They evoke, on the one hand, an intrusion of crassly economic factors into the realm of high art – as epitomized, perhaps, by the *World's Work's* proposal that Conrad submit an article on 'the commercial aspect of London' (3: 141) – and, on the other, the mutation of writing into manufacture implied by the narrator's aside in 'The Partner': 'It was some time before I discovered that what he would be at was the process by which stories – stories for periodicals – were *produced*' (*WT* 90, emphasis added). Above all, such pejorative labels fail to explain how Conrad believed that he could publish high-quality fiction in a magazine format, a contradiction that is encapsulated in his comment to R. B. Cunninghame Graham: 'I am glad you like *Karain*. I was afraid you would despise it. There's something magazine'ish about it. Eh? It was written for Blackwood' (*CL* 2: 57).

The present chapter starts from the very different premise that popular magazine fiction is historically significant both in its own right and as a context for Modernist writing. That magazine fiction can now be reassessed in such terms is largely a consequence of two parallel developments. One is the wholesale transformation of how we conceptualize literary Modernism, a movement that has come to be thought of less as a rejection or sublimating of popular culture than as thoroughly saturated with the latter's rhythms or artefacts and, to some extent, as having acquired a public identity through its media.[5] Modernism, Lawrence Rainey has argued, 'marks neither a straightforward resistance nor an outright capitulation to commodification but a momentary equivocation that incorporates elements of both in a brief, necessarily unstable synthesis' (Rainey, 1998: 3). The other development is a fuller recognition of the scale, diversity and complexity of popular fiction and periodical reading. As Michael Hayes astutely observes: '[P]opular fiction is a cultural nexus for a historically determined and evolving relationship [between producers, the literary critical establishment and book readers] whose understanding requires us to reflect on the period, the people and the state of book production as well as the books themselves' (Hayes, 1993, 77). This recognition has been accompanied, in turn, by a growing scepticism towards postlapsarian evocations of what Janice Radway has termed 'a utopian golden age of cultural production unsullied by the forces and concerns of the market' (Radway, 1986: 8).[6] In each case, the result has been to remind us of the necessity but also the interpretative value of connecting literary texts to the precise historical circumstances of their composition and publication.

In place of the customary focus upon magazines as a vehicle for serialization – that is, as an issue primarily of textual history – this chapter considers their serial fiction as a freely accessible repository of popular fantasies upon which Conrad drew for the plots and narratives of his own writing. Contemporary reviews remind us of the dangers of imposing a false inevitability upon Conrad's literary career and posterity. By 1898 he had already been included by one reviewer in the ranks of the nation's 'popular story-writers . . . with great ability of the narrative kind' (*CH* 97), and as late as 1919 he could still be described as 'the only living man who can make a work of atmosphere and character as exciting as a penny blood' (*CH* 322).[7] In keeping with the central argument of this study, that Conrad's work makes a sustained engagement with the experiences, themes and epistemology of popular cultural forms, this chapter seeks to reimagine magazine fiction as a kind of popular cultural spectre that haunts even his most ambitious and austerely Modernist writing. The first of its two longer case studies examines 'Typhoon', a novella that is here considered as a hybrid of popular and high Modernist literary modes, in relation to formal convention and ostensibly marginal references to Christmas and various British towns. The second shows how 'The Brute', a tale regarded as an exemplary magazine story by editors in Conrad's day, responds directly and indirectly to the new narrative demands of popular periodicals. Each case study is intended to restore a measure of contingency to Conrad's relation to magazine fiction and to throw into relief the parallels between his relation to magazine fiction and the fields of popular culture treated in previous chapters, notably advertising and tourism.[8]

Silly fiction

Conrad's economic reliance upon magazine publication has been well documented. Not only did he receive double and even triple payment by serializing his work on both sides of the Atlantic but the rates of remuneration for periodical publication were far more lucrative than those of novels or essay collections. As commentators often point out, without the existence of this market for articles, serialized novels and short stories Conrad would likely have been forced to abandon his ambition of living by the pen.[9] Although he seems not to have appreciated it, he was in fact extraordinarily fortunate to have embarked upon his literary career during a period of rapid expansion in magazine publishing and short fiction in particular. As Frank Mott explains of the American market: 'The wave of magazine prosperity that came with the growth of national advertising and increases of circulation from about 1885 to 1892 caused thousands of adventurers to invest their money in new periodicals' (Mott, 1957: 15). By 1900, the monthly magazine had become, in Richard Ohmann's words, 'the major form of repeated cultural experience for the people of the United States' (Ohmann, 1998: 29). A similar conjunction of factors obtained during these years in Britain, where, as Kate Jackson notes: 'Magazines began to be targeted positively towards specific classifications such as female readers of various types, juvenile readers and those with special interest areas such as art, music, science, travel and sport' (Jackson, 2001: 201). Central to the growth of this cultural-industrial behemoth was fiction, for which the public appeared to have an insatiable demand. As Conrad wrote reassuringly to his long-suffering agent in 1905 after extracting yet another cash advance: 'Short stories – is the watchword now' (*CL* 3: 243).

Critics often represent Conrad's involvement with magazines as sheer expediency or a struggle to resist the downward pull exerted by the dross alongside which his writings were published. Gail Fraser's chapter on short fiction in *The Cambridge Companion to Conrad* (1996), for example, confines its examination of the issue of serialization to two periodicals for which Conrad wrote specifically, *Blackwood's* and *Pall Mall Magazine*, and concludes: 'Conrad's rejection of patriotic rhetoric in "Typhoon" illustrates the limited influence of serial readers on the ideology of his fiction as a whole. To any significant degree, it begins and ends with "Youth" ' (Fraser, 1996: 34). In Fraser's account, popular magazines are a force of pure negation, their division of a work into parts 'destroy[ing] the reader's sense of uninterrupted communion with the author and his work' and their generic stereotyping forcing Conrad to defend both 'the integrity of the modern short story as an art form' and his own 'imaginative integrity' (Fraser, 1996: 30–1, 35). From such a perspective, it would be wilfully perverse to imagine that magazine fiction might have had anything to teach Conrad, or that his surreptitious reading of popular serials like the *Boy's Own Paper* might have provided him with anything other than specimens of bad writing. It is a view of literary production that owes much to Conrad's own high Modernist portrayal of magazine publication as an intolerable artistic compromise in letters to friends and fellow writers, for whom his frequent laments must have become a familiar refrain. When Fisher Unwin tried to have *An Outcast of the Islands* serialized, Conrad told Ted Sanderson, 'I hate the idea but have given in to his arguments' (*CL* 1: 240), and to Edward Garnett he insisted: 'I *would not* have [*The Rescue*] published unless You see and pass it as fit for the twilight of a popular magazine' (1: 284). In similar fashion, Conrad's protestations that 'I am not anxious to fling myself on sixpenny or even shilling magazines' (2: 196), 'All magazines now are short and snippy' (4: 86), and 'Conrad wants special terms for prostituting his intellect to please the Metropolitan [Magazine]' (5: 322) are echoed by his characterization of 'Tomorrow' as ' "Conrad" adapted down to the needs of a magazine' (2: 373), 'Gaspar Ruiz' as 'that infernal magazine fake!' (4: 108) and *Victory* as 'Strictly proper' and 'Nothing to shock the magazine public' (5: 114).

To be sure, Conrad's desire to gloss over the role of magazine serialization in his career is nicely illustrated by 'The Duel', a swashbuckling tale of deadly rivalry between two cavalry officers in Napoleon's army. In 1907, he privately called the tale 'a longish (and stupidish) story ready for the Pall Mall [Magazine]' (*CL* 3: 471), a tone of disparagement that possibly reflected the popularity of duelling tales in contemporary magazines; C. J. Cutcliffe Hyne, for example, had already published two short stories on the subject in the American edition of *Pearson's Magazine* in March 1901 and January 1907. Conrad was similarly dismissive of the special book edition of 'The Duel' commissioned by S. S. McClure, which he haughtily referred to as a 'silly little form – with silly illustrations' (4: 317). In the Author's Note to *A Set of Six*, however, which he wrote in 1920 at the height of his career and with an eye to the Nobel Committee, he gave a very different account of the text's history: 'That story attained the dignity of publication all by itself in a small illustrated volume, under the title, "The Point of Honour." . . . It has been since reinstated in its proper place, which is the place it occupies in this volume, in all the subsequent editions of my work' (*SS* viii). No mention was made of its earlier transatlantic incarnations in the *Pall Mall Magazine* and *Forum*.

As Conrad saw it, magazine publication might entail any of a number of painful artistic concessions: relinquishing editorial control over language, punctuation and choice of copy-text; accepting house style in matters of length, chapter division and layout; and deferring (at least tacitly) to considerations of genre and readers' sensibilities in his choice of themes and plots. He locked horns with the editors of *London Magazine* over suggested changes to 'A Smile of Fortune', as he had with their counterparts at *Harper's*, the *Standard* and the *Daily Mail*, and he begged the literary collector John Quinn not to read *Victory* in *Munsey's Magazine*: 'I don't want you to see it in double columns and crowded type. . . . A book is written for the eye' (*CL* 5: 403). Moreover, Conrad differentiated carefully among popular magazines, as can be seen from the composition and publishing history of 'Freya of the Seven Isles', a novella about star-crossed lovers in the Malay Archipelago that he variously described as 'quite suitable for serialising' (4: 417) and 'Perfectly safe' (4: 413). In trying to persuade the *Pall Mall's* editor Charles Morley of the story's suitability 'as to subject and treatment', he hoped to rekindle an association with a periodical that, as he noted to Pinker, 'had published some of my best short writings (Typhoon. Gaspar. Mirror. Duel)' (4: 418). (Conrad's inventory of his 'best short writings' is revealingly eclectic.) He was disappointed at its finding a home in *London Magazine* and his sarcastic comment, 'I am to tinker at it to fit it quite for that exalted destiny' (4: 390), must have seemed amply justified when 'Freya of the Seven Isles' appeared in its July 1912 number as a 'Complete Novel' (*sic*) on paper of inferior quality with a mawkish illustration by

Gilbert Holiday. Still more offensive to him was the novella's progress in the United States, where the editor of either *Scribner's* or *Century Magazine* dared to ask for substantial revisions on the grounds that ' "its overpowering gloom makes it impossible for serialisation" ' (4: 464). Conrad was incandescent: 'As to faking a "sunny" ending to my story I would see all the American Magazines and all the American Editors damned in heaps before lifting my pen for that task. I have never been particularly anxious to rub shoulders with the piffle they print with touching consistency from year's end to year's end' (4: 469).[10]

By Conrad's own account, only the demands of placating his creditors forced him to endure such indignities; a cheque for one hundred pounds, he told Quinn gratefully in February 1913, had relieved him of the obligation 'to write a couple of silly stories for the magazines' (*CL* 5: 175). Thus, too, he promised Pinker that a short story about adventure set in South America would be 'silly and saleable' (3: 4), an attitude of casual indifference he may also have been assuming when he later misidentified the magazine that serialized *Nostromo* as 'M. A. P.' (5: 16), that is, *Mainly About People* – another of T. P. O'Connor's journals, which advertised its special province as 'pleasant gossip, personal portraits, and social news'. Indeed, Conrad at times gave the impression of regarding magazine publication as synonymous with the words 'silly' and 'saleable', invoking the latter term only half-ironically when arranging for the serialization of *Chance, Under Western Eyes* and 'Dollars', the short story that would become *Victory* (3: 460; 4: 9; 5: 73). Such epithets, needless to say, deserve to be treated with the utmost suspicion. Whatever merit there may be in Conrad's estimation of the magazine stories 'Gaspar Ruiz', 'An Anarchist', 'The Black Mate' and 'Freya of the Seven Isles' as 'silly' (3: 297, 3: 410, 4: 407), few today would recognize his description of *The Shadow-Line* as 'a silly sort of story' (5: 495) or his inclusion of 'Verloc', the short-story precursor of *The Secret Agent*, under the rubric 'silly fiction' (3: 350).

As much a boast as a confession, Conrad once stated that he had created 'Youth', perhaps the most anthologized of his early works, out of 'the material of a boys' story' (*CL* 2: 417). The remark lends itself to two slightly different interpretations: that Marlow's luminous memoir of being cast adrift on the high seas in an open boat is a topic normally confined to works of juvenile adventure; or that 'Youth' represents a conscious attempt to translate, rework, or write back to the plot components of popular literature in a sophisticated Modernist narrative mode. But however one chooses to read it, the statement foregrounds the role of popular magazine themes as an inspiration or catalyst for Conrad's writing.

In an article that deserves to be read far more widely, Peter Winnington has argued convincingly that Conrad's decision to abandon *The Rescue* in favour of a novella set in the Congo was triggered by his reading of C. J. Cutcliffe Hyne's adventure stories about Captain Kettle, which began serialization in *Pearson's Magazine* in July 1898 and grew into a popular phenomenon that eventually spawned a dozen books and several feature films. Winnington shows in detail how the Kettle stories provided numerous motifs and phrases for *Heart of Darkness*, ranging from Marlow's cross-legged posture like an 'idol' (*Y* 46) to his contemptuous reference to a 'two-penny-half-penny river-steamboat' (59), as well as plot elements such as the attack on the steamer (an event Conrad did not witness himself) in which a Congolese member of crew falls dead at Marlow's feet (Winnington, 1984). Cutcliffe Hyne's text even anticipates *Heart of Darkness*'s most famous use of delayed decoding:

> Another bullet came silently up out of the distance, and the nigger second engineer of the launch gave a queer little whimper and fell down *flop*, and lay with his flat nose nuzzling the still warm boiler. A hole, which showed up red and angry against the black wool underneath his grass cap, made the diagnosis of his injury an easy matter.
>
> (Cutcliffe Hyne, 1899: 23)

> The man had rolled on his back and stared straight up at me; both his hands clutched that cane. It was the shaft of a spear that, either thrown or lunged through the opening, had caught him in the side just below the ribs; the blade had gone in out of sight, after making a frightful gash; my shoes were full; a pool of blood lay very still, gleaming dark-red under the wheel; his eyes shone with an amazing lustre.
>
> (*Y* 111–12)

Winnington's discovery that *Heart of Darkness* is indebted to the Captain Kettle stories and, indeed, that Conrad's novella is in places closer to this popular cultural source than to his own experiences, has been supplemented by two similarly under-appreciated essays by Richard Ruppel. By examining 'The Lagoon' and *Heart of Darkness* in the context of short stories with 'exotic' and colonial themes in *fin de siècle* British magazines, Ruppel has managed to identify substantial parallels between, on the one hand, *Heart of Darkness* and Cutcliffe Hyne's 'The Transfer', a Congo adventure story that appeared in *Pall Mall Magazine* in December 1897, and, on the other, Conrad's early tale 'The Lagoon' and 'Chandni Bhai, the Dancing Girl', a short romance by Minnie

Anderson and Louis Tracy that appeared in the same magazine in August 1896 (Ruppel, 1989 and 1993). Without in any way diminishing Conrad's achievement, Ruppel's findings reconfirm the importance of popular magazines as an historical context for his writing. Far from being Conradian innovations, details such as the inscrutability of the European who has gone 'Fantee', the dangerous sexual allure of the native woman and the jungle atmosphere of brooding hostility are shown to be standard tropes of this period, just as Conrad's creation of a fictional mouth-piece in Marlow owes at least as much to the runaway success of popular narrators such as Captain Kettle and Arthur Conan Doyle's Dr Watson as it does to any Modernist desire to represent the epistemological instability of narrative. Even Conrad's deliberate use of the racist epithet 'nigger' follows Cutcliffe Hyne's presentation of Captain Kettle as both offensive and sincere, a half-ironic portrait of a violent yet complex protagonist that, according to Gary Hoppenstand, 'anticipated the efforts of the 1920s American school of "hard-boiled" realism which included the works of authors such as Ernest Hemingway and Dashiell Hammett' (Hoppenstand, 2002: 245). In sum, as Daphna Erdinast-Vulcan has observed: 'It may well be that [Conrad's] conscious attention to address his short fiction to the popular market had a liberating effect on his writing process and that the relative relaxation of critical self-reflection may have paradoxically enabled the radical narrative experimentation that characterizes a number of the short stories' (Erdinast-Vulcan et al., 2004: v).

No less significant than Ruppel's and Winnington's confirmation of Conrad's use of popular literary sources is the relevance of their findings for our understanding of the representation of empire in his magazine fiction. Like Anthony Easthope, who has argued in a provocative comparison of *Heart of Darkness* with Edgar Rice Burroughs' *Tarzan of the Apes* (1912) that 'It is not so much ideology as textuality which differentiates Conrad's high cultural realist novel trembling on the edge of modernism from this popular adventure story' (Easthope, 1991: 86), both authors see an underlying congruence between the politics of Conrad's stories and those of contemporary magazine fiction. Posing an implicit challenge to the notion that Conrad's works subvert the ideology of imperialism, Ruppel notes that his patronizing depiction of Arsat as a dependable 'comrade' of the anonymous white narrator in 'The Lagoon' followed contemporary convention (Ruppel, 1993: 182–3). In a similar vein, Winnington contrasts Conrad's removal of an allusion to King Leopold II from the manuscript of *Heart of Darkness* with Cutcliffe Hyne's open identification of the Congo Free State as being administered by 'Belgian swine' (Winnington, 1984: 168).[11] Conrad himself saw the novella as a tale of 'the Belgian Congo' (*CL* 2: 407) – an opinion echoed by the *Athenaeum*'s reviewer, who described its subject as 'life on the Congo and the Belgian ivory-hunt' (*CH* 139) – and he repeatedly reminds readers of the strictly national perspective from which *Heart of Darkness* is narrated:

> 'Pardon my questions, but you are the first Englishman coming under my observation . . .' I hastened to assure him I was not in the least typical. 'If I were,' said I, 'I wouldn't be talking like this with you.'
> (*Y* 58)

> 'It must be this miserable trader – this intruder,' exclaimed the manager, looking back malevolently at the place we had left. 'He must be English,' I said. 'It will not save him from getting into trouble if he is not careful,' muttered the manager darkly.
> (*Y* 100)

> The harlequin on the bank turned his little pug-nose up to me. 'You English?' he asked, all smiles. 'Are you?' I shouted from the wheel. The smiles vanished, and he shook his head as if sorry for my disappointment.
> (*Y* 122)

Indeed, the evidence of other popular fiction of this period, including much magazine fiction, suggests that *Heart of Darkness* ought perhaps to be reclassified within the sub-genre of tales about lone Englishmen struggling to retain their integrity in colonies run by brutal Belgians or Portuguese.[12]

A survey of Conrad's work for magazines throws up several other significant patterns. With the notable exception of *Blackwood's*, relatively few of the periodicals that published his writing had been established prior to 1885: in Britain, the *Fortnightly Review* ('Autocracy and War'), the *Cornhill Magazine* ('The Lagoon'), *Cassell's Magazine* ('Il Conde'), the *Illustrated London News* ('Amy Foster' and 'The Lesson of the Collision'), *Land and Water* ('The Warrior's Soul' and *The Rescue*) and *Lloyd's Magazine* (*The Arrow of Gold*); and in the United States, *Critic* ('Typhoon'), *Delineator* ('Christmas Day at Sea'), *Littell's Living Age* ('Karain') and the *North American Review* ('Autocracy and War', *Under Western Eyes*). Most appeared instead in magazines that had been founded during the boom in serial publishing between approximately 1890 and 1905. Conrad's contributions to British magazines of this vintage included: *Nostromo* in *T. P.'s Weekly* (est. 1902); 'The Tale' in *Strand*

Magazine (est. 1891); 'Books' and 'Anatole France' in *The Speaker* (est. 1890); 'Alphonse Daudet' in *The Outlook* (est. 1898); and 'To-morrow', 'Typhoon', 'The Duel', 'Gaspar Ruiz', 'The Inn of Two Witches' and portions of *The Mirror of the Sea* in *Pall Mall Magazine* (est. 1893). In the United States they included: 'The Duel' in *Forum* (est. 1886); 'The Brute' in *McClure's Magazine* (est. 1893); 'The Crime of Partition' and '*The Torrens*: A Personal Tribute' in *Collier's Weekly* (est. 1895); *Victory* in *Munsey's Magazine* (est. 1889); 'Prince Roman', 'Freya of the Seven Isles', 'The Inn of Two Witches', 'The Planter of Malata', 'The Tale', *The Shadow-Line* and part of *The Mirror of the Sea* in *Metropolitan Magazine* (est. 1895); other portions of *The Mirror of the Sea* in *Reader Magazine* (est. 1902), *Putnam's Magazine* (est. 1906) and *World Today* (est. 1901, later renamed *Hearst's Magazine*); and, posthumously, *Suspense* in *Saturday Review of Literature* (est. 1896) and 'Geography and Some Explorers' in *National Geographic Magazine* (est. 1888). To this can be added the publication of 'An Anarchist', 'The Informer', 'The Secret Sharer' and 'The Partner' in *Harper's Magazine*, which, whilst having been in existence since 1850, reinvented itself economically in the late 1880s by massively bulking out its advertising section. Only *Under Western Eyes*, *The Shadow-Line*, *One Day More*, two essays on the *Titanic* and part of *A Personal Record* were published in one of the 'little' magazines, Ford Madox Ford's *English Review*, with which literary Modernism is now so closely identified.

The fierce competition for readers and the bullish nature of the publishing market during these years evidently worked to Conrad's advantage. At the start of his career magazines provided him with a vital outlet that he would likely not have found elsewhere, thereby vindicating the claim of one contemporary commentator that 'the capable unknown is going to have his or her chance in magazinedom' ('An Editor', 1904: 4). Indeed, it is hardly coincidental that four of his more important and 'difficult' works were accepted by organs that had been recently launched for a niche audience and that folded (for other reasons, one hopes) within a year of printing his own contribution: 'The Idiots' in *The Savoy* (est. 1896), 'An Outpost of Progress' in *Cosmopolis* (est. 1896), *The Nigger of the 'Narcissus'* in the *New Review* (est. 1889) and *The Secret Agent* in *Ridgway's Magazine* (est. 1906). As Conrad understood, publication in a well-regarded magazine could be valuable advertising, albeit advertising less to the general public than to the editors and publishers to whom he wished to sell his novels and short stories. At the same time, this issue is rather more complicated than at first appears. Conrad's comments to T. Fisher Unwin that 'The Return' was 'much too good for any blamed magazine' and 'much too good to be thrown away where the right people won't see it' (*CL* 1: 405) are often cited by critics as evidence of his willingness to sacrifice badly-needed income in order to win the approval of literary reputation-makers such as W. E. Henley, a perspective that seemingly finds confirmation in his emphatic rebuffing of *Pearson's Magazine*, whose serial of H. G. Wells's *The War of the Worlds* he had presumably been reading: 'I do *not* wish the story to be offered to Pearson' (1: 413).[13] But why, then, did Conrad go on to submit 'The Return' to the hardly more prestigious *Chapman's Magazine*, a periodical of similarly recent provenance whose usual bill of fare included detective mysteries and ghost stories by popular writers such as Bret Harte and Eden Phillpotts?

As his literary reputation grew, Conrad found himself in the enviable position of being wooed by publishers of mediocre but profitable magazines who wanted to use his name to bolster their undistinguished contributor lists. Thus he allowed 'Il Conde' to be sold to *Hampton's Magazine* (est. 1905), a periodical previously known for specializing in 'naughty pictures' (Mott, 1957: 47), and he consented to *The Rover's* serialization in the *Pictorial Review* (est. 1899), an organ that is still catalogued by the New York Public Library under the heading 'Dressmaking'.[14] 'The Black Mate', 'A Smile of Fortune' and 'Freya of the Seven Isles' all appeared in *London Magazine* (est. 1898), a distinctly second-tier journal that, like *Hutchinson's Magazine* and the *Daily Mail* (for which Conrad wrote ten articles), belonged to the Harmsworth brothers' quasi-monopolistic holding company Associated Newspapers. What is more, despite Conrad's repeated protests that he would never write for boys or women, a pose of intransigence that won him plaudits from H. G. Wells and possibly the mockery of *The Waitress Bold's* would-be recipient, it is hard to gainsay either Clive Bloom's claim that his fiction 'hovered between juvenile adventure and symbolist art' (Bloom, 2002: 12) or Susan Jones's argument that his late works represent an accommodation to the interests of women readers (Jones 1999: 161–76).[15] And even if one accepts at face value Conrad's stated hostility towards the tastes of these large readerships, it does not follow that he remained uninfluenced by the writing of those who did cater for this demographic. His unflattering comments about Grant Allen, Marie Corelli, Hall Caine, Rudyard Kipling and John Buchan not only betray a more than passing acquaintance with the work and public personae of popular authors, they attest to a preoccupation with literary competitors who had succeeded in taming what he called 'the public, that mysterious beast' (*CL* 3: 488).[16] Coming as it does in the context of a letter to William Blackwood setting out his own literary strategy, Conrad's description of the present day as 'a time when Sherlock Holmes looms so big' (2: 418) reveals something that, were it in the realm of high culture, would long ago have been identified as a symptom of creative anxiety.

The arts of the magazine writer: 'Typhoon' (1902)

'We are the creatures of our light literature much more than is generally suspected' (*C* 215), observes Marlow sagely in *Chance*. In addition to recalling the youthful bovaryism of *Lord Jim*'s eponymous hero, who 'live[s] in his mind the sea-life of light literature' (*LJ* 6), Marlow's remark anticipates F. R. Leavis's famous verdict on the author of *Heart of Darkness* as standing 'convicted of borrowing the arts of the magazine writer' (Leavis, 1974: 207). For Leavis, a staunch advocate of what he styled 'minority culture', popular magazine fiction presented a dismal mirror-image of legitimate literary art and he recommended the collection *Within the Tides* to anyone who doubted Conrad's capacity to write 'shockingly bad magazine stuff' (Leavis, 1974: 217). Although Leavis's sarcastic allusion to 'the arts of the magazine writer' owes much of its wider currency to Fredric Jameson's *The Political Unconscious* (1981), where it prefaces a reading of *Lord Jim* as expressive of an historical fault-line between nineteenth-century Realism and a twentieth-century dialectic of Modernist 'high' culture and 'degraded' mass culture (Jameson, 1981: 206–7), his strangely contrary valuation – after all, Conrad was repeatedly criticized in his own lifetime for despising 'every popular and accepted method' (*CH* 118) and obscuring 'the "story" elements as these are popularly conceived' (*CH* 314) – rightly underscores the centrality of Conrad's fraught relation to magazine fiction for the works of his major phase. By 1900, having won his artistic credentials by serializing *The Nigger of the 'Narcissus'* in the *New Review* and 'Karain', 'Youth', *Heart of Darkness* and *Lord Jim* in *Blackwood's*, Conrad faced the task of finding a mode of writing that would also enable him to live. His struggle to reconcile purist principles with the formal and thematic criteria of magazine fiction is evident from his difficulties in placing 'The Idiots', which only appeared in *The Savoy* in 1896 after being rejected by *Cosmopolis* and the *Cornhill Magazine* and his outright failure to serialize 'The Return' in 1897 and 'Falk' in 1901. Stripped of its moral and aesthetic polemic, therefore, Leavis's reprimand might be rephrased as the claim that sometime around the turn of the century Conrad successfully internalized the arts of the magazine writer and, in the process, learned how to write his own style of popular (in varying degrees) magazine fiction.

The notion that writing popular stories might be an art has long been the butt of satirists. As the author of an article entitled 'How to Write a Novel for the Masses' confided facetiously to the *Atlantic Monthly*'s readers in March 1901: '[Y]ou must admit that the vast majority of the reading public is made up of dull, unthinking people, so why should writers spend so much time substantiating facts, studying costumes and scenery and other details . . . ?' (Loomis, 1901: 421). On this view, anyone wishing to acquire – or avoid – the paltry lexicon of modern magazine writing need do no more than read a few samples of such hack work. Typical of this attitude was the reviewer for the *Academy* who contrasted Conrad's maritime characters with Cutcliffe Hyne's Captain Kettle, the latter being merely a 'convention' that 'appeals to the suffrages of a popular audience', before going on to declare approvingly: 'Mr. Conrad, on the other hand, has no idea of popular appeal . . .[and] his psychology has the accuracy of brilliant diagnosis' (*CH* 151–2). Yet the *Academy*'s equating of popularity with conventionality and obliviousness to popularity with ignorance of conventionality is unconvincing. Like his quip about cliff-hangers that 'would have made the newspaper boys sit up' (*CL* 2: 27) and his mention of 'the old formulas of expression' (2: 463), Conrad's description of 'Amy Foster' as 'a story of adventure but written not exactly according to the usual formula for work of that kind' (2: 357) suggests that his own eclectic reading habits had given him a thorough understanding of the conventions and idioms of popular genre writing. As he confided ironically to Pinker about *The Rescue*: 'You may however assure the representative of the *Cosmopolitan Magazine* that the story will end as romantically as it began, and that no one of any particular consequence will have to die' (*CL* 6: 339). Why, then, should we not take seriously the possibility that a writer who scandalized his son's schoolmaster by admitting to having learned English from the *Morning Standard* might also have honed his literary skills through close study of magazine fiction? And, if so, how might we set about recovering this creative interaction that falls somewhere between osmosis and autodidacticism?

Few texts are better suited to an investigation of this kind than 'Typhoon', a novella about the life-and-death struggle that ensues when an obstinate captain insists on sailing his 'cargo' of Chinese labourers through a tropical hurricane in the South China Seas. Although Conrad first planned the tale in 1899–1900 in hopes that it might 'find hospitality' (*CL* 2: 169) in *Blackwood's Magazine*, at some point near the end of that periodical's serialization of *Lord Jim* he seems to have had a change of heart. Instead, 'Typhoon' appeared in *Pall Mall Magazine* in three instalments from January to March 1902, where it was accompanied by six fine illustrations by Maurice Greiffenhagen.[17] That Conrad wrote it expressly for this very different publishing venue of a large-circulation, colour-illustrated sixpenny magazine is evident from his statement to Pinker upon completing the story: 'I wish to reach another public than Maga's [*Blackwood's*]' (2: 321). Like his later identification of the novella as 'a turning point in my career as a writer' (5: 89–90), the remark gestures towards an ambition whose implications involve more than just money.[18] In the same way as 'Typhoon' signals a radical departure in mood, subject matter and style from the existential gloom and narrative aporias of *Heart of Darkness*, so, too, does Conrad's choice of what he later called 'a popular sixpenny' (5: 257) attest to his determination to 'reach' a middle-brow literary mainstream to which *Cosmopolis*, *Savoy* and *Blackwood's*, with their smaller circulations and niche audiences, could not give him entry.

Conrad's customary ambivalence about the aesthetic value of his magazine fiction was especially pronounced in the case of 'Typhoon', which he called 'too silly for words' (*CL* 2: 321) shortly after its completion in 1901 yet described as '*art*' (3: 320, Conrad's emphasis) to the painter William Rothenstein only a few years later. Such schizophrenia can be traced, at least in part, to the two antithetical modes of writing – Modernist abstraction and Dickensian pastiche – that run through the novella:

> It was enough, when you thought it over, to give you the idea of an immense, potent, and invisible hand thrust into the ant-heap of the earth, laying hold of shoulders, knocking heads together, and setting the unconscious faces of the multitude towards inconceivable goals and in undreamt-of directions.   (*T* 56)

> Mrs. Rout, a big, high-bosomed, jolly woman of forty, shared with Mr. Rout's toothless and venerable mother a little cottage near Teddington. She would run over her correspondence, at breakfast, with lively eyes, and scream out interesting passages in a joyous voice at the deaf old lady, prefacing each extract by the warning shout, 'Solomon says!'   (*T* 64)

Here, Conrad's inclusion of a stock comic working-class figure such as Mrs Rout in a novella otherwise distinguished by formal sophistication – unreliable narrators, Modernist 'quotation' of the sailors' correspondence, and a storm sequence that Fredric Jameson has enthusiastically described as 'a sensorium, which, like some new planet in the night sky, suggests senses and forms of libidinal gratification as unimaginable to us as the possession of additional senses, or the presence of additional colors in the spectrum' (Jameson, 1981: 231) – might be dismissed as an incidental concession to popular magazine taste. But the *Pall Mall's* transitional identity at the moment at which it serialized 'Typhoon' offers a more cogent explanation. After gathering a distinguished contributor list in 1893–94 that included Thomas Hardy, Paul Verlaine and George Meredith, the magazine had become overly reliant upon popular 'names' such as H. Rider Haggard, Ouida and Grant Allen, prompting George R. Halkett, who joined the staff as editor in 1901, to set himself the task of recruiting writers on the cusp of fame – Jack London, Ford Madox Ford, John Masefield and Conrad – whose contributions would need to display a greater degree of hybridity than their immediate predecessors, that is to say, would need to expand the horizons of the short story in ways that appealed to the magazine's highbrow readers but that did not alienate its general audience by deviating from the codes of genre fiction.[19] Far from merely offering a sop to the *Pall Mall's* popular readers or providing a cover for smuggling in a properly Modernist narrative, the 'low' elements of comedy and physical violence in 'Typhoon' ought therefore to be understood as part of a more ambitious attempt to meet the conflicting demands now being placed upon fiction magazines.[20] Where readers of the *Daily Mail*, whose reviewer had welcomed the novella as a Stevensonian 'sonata of ships and storms and breaking waves' (*CH* 146), would likely have seen in Mrs Rout an affectionate portrait of the faithful wife, masculine avantgardists of the Henleyite circle would have seen in her an embodiment of the worst vices of a feminized magazine readership, her garrulous reading aloud making a pitiable contrast to their own proletarian ideal: the tattooed 'savage' Singleton in *The Nigger of the 'Narcissus'* who reads Bulwer Lytton in silence amidst the filth and profanity of the forecastle.

To appreciate just how closely the novella's dramatic subject-matter, wealth of technical and meteorological detail, and what Conrad called 'my first attempt to treat a subject jocularly' (2: 304) would have chimed with the interests of *Pall Mall Magazine's* audience, we need look no further than the magazine's contents lists for Spring 1902: comic sketches and caricatures; poems about shipwrecks and the sea; articles on exotic foreign locales such as alpine tunnels, African pygmies and photographs of Siberia; and news reports on maritime topics such as the Panama canal and Japanese shipbuilding. Conrad's descriptions of 'breakers flung out of the night with a ghostly light on their crests' (*T* 93) and 'a white line

Plate 1 Joseph Conrad, pen-and-ink sketch, mid-1890s. Reproduced for the first time by permission of the Trustees of the Joseph Conrad Estate and the Henry W. and Albert A. Berg Collection of English and American Literature, The New York Public Library, Astor, Lenox and Tilden Foundations.

Plate 2 Advertising handbill, *c.*1900. Reproduced by permission of Bodleian Library, John Johnson Collection, Oxford.

of foam coming on at such a height that [MacWhirr] couldn't believe his eyes' (109) would have held the attention of the same readers who turned to the *Pall Mall*'s special features on adventurous travel (climbing in the Himalayas; hunting in Norway) and essays on curious natural phenomena ('Plants That Walk'; 'Change on the Moon'). An essay in literary criticism titled 'Ideal Characters in Fiction' indicates the existence of a readership who would have recognized the Dickensian echoes in Conrad's portrait of Captain MacWhirr and enjoyed the inherent paradox of the mariner's repeated assertion: ' "You don't find everything in books" ' (*T* 78, 115, 131).

Then there is the statement that 'between 4 and 6 A.M. on December 25th, Captain MacWhirr did actually think that his ship could not possibly live another hour in such a sea, and that he would never see his wife and children again' (*T* 125). At first glance, the inclusion of this minor detail in an unread letter from MacWhirr to his wife would appear simply to express Conrad's disdain for what he called 'Xmas platitudes' (*CL* 2: 228) and his corresponding animus towards those magazine readerships for whom the season figured so prominently – people like the sale-loving Mrs MacWhirr, perhaps, for whom personal relations are less important than shopping. Such a perspective is, in turn, confirmed by Conrad's late essay 'Christmas Day at Sea' (1923) in which he declares with palpable satisfaction of his twenty-year sea career: 'I can only remember one Christmas Day celebrated by a present given and received' (*LE* 31).[21]

Closer scrutiny, however, reveals the presence of Christmas in 'Typhoon' to be less a matter of serendipity than of deliberate calculation on Conrad's part. Crucially, the novella makes another, entirely unrelated allusion to the holiday in its opening pages where the sentence ' "On Christmas day at 4 P.M. we fell in with some icebergs" ' (*T* 57) is given as an example of MacWhirr's vastly understated epistolary style. Exactly why Conrad's only fictional work to mention Christmas should do so twice becomes clear in his disingenuous comment to Pinker in October 1900: 'Why however I mention ["Typhoon"] now is because it struck me casually that it is quite the thing that finds room in Xmas numbers' (2: 295). No afterthought, surely, the remark shows Conrad as coming to realize the special value of Christmas as both a fictional theme and a season for magazine publishing.[22] Indeed, the initial attitude of resentment that lay behind his angry complaint in December 1902 that 'the Bethle[h]em legend' would 'kill' magazine sales of 'The End of the Tether' (2: 468), quickly gave way to pragmatism: within a few years he would be considering in matter-of-fact fashion whether

'The Brute' might do for the 'D[ai]ly Chronicle Xmas No' (4: 31), asking whether a magazine editor would like 'a long short story to fill a whole Xmas No' (4: 282), and telling his agent: 'Harpers ask for a short story to go into the Xmas No . . . I have a subject that would do I think' (4: 81).

In Conrad's portrait of sailors fighting for their lives on Christmas Day, a coincidence that is as irrelevant to the plot of 'Typhoon' as it is devoid of irony for the tale's author, we see a threshold moment in his accommodation to the sensibilities of a popular magazine audience.[23]

Just how closely 'Typhoon' adheres to professional guidelines on publishing magazine fiction can be seen from a brief survey of the many handbooks on writing by contemporary authors and editors. Most immediately, Conrad's theme falls squarely under the category heading 'sea stories of very strong dramatic interest' on the list of 'Most Saleable Stories' in George Magnus's 1910 handbook *How to Write Saleable Fiction* (Magnus, 1910: 25). The spoken English in the novella is also far closer to what R. A. H. Goodyear, a writer of popular magazine stories and author of *Tale-Writing for Money* (1908), urged as 'bright and natural dialogue, such as bright and natural people use' (Goodyear, 1908, 21). In place of *Heart of Darkness*'s ponderous melodrama,

> 'Do you understand this?' I asked. . . .
> 'Do I not?' he said slowly, gasping, as if the words had been torn out of him by a supernatural power.   (*Y* 146)

> 'His last word – to live with,' she insisted. 'Don't you understand I loved him – I loved him – I loved him!'
> I pulled myself together and spoke slowly.
> 'The last word he pronounced was – your name.'   (*Y* 161)

'Typhoon' offers us the robust, if euphemized, banter of the sailors:

> 'Oh, go to Jericho!' said Jukes frankly; and the other emitted a triumphant little chuckle.
> 'You've said it,' he repeated.
> 'And what of that?'
> 'I've known some real good men get into trouble with their skippers for saying a dam' sight less,' answered the second mate feverishly. 'Oh no! You don't catch me.'

'You seem deucedly anxious not to give yourself away,' said Jukes, completely soured by such absurdity. 'I wouldn't be afraid to say what I think.'

'Aye, to me! That's no great trick. I am nobody and well I know it.'

(*T* 75)

Moreover, despite having chosen what many readers of *Pall Mall Magazine* would have viewed as an exotic setting, Conrad takes care to connect the action of 'Typhoon' to Britain in a way that would have gratified Goodyear, who advised those trying to place longer manuscripts that the Northern Newspaper Syndicate preferred stories 'with scenes laid mainly in the British Isles' (Goodyear, 1908: 31).[24] Unlike the labourers who are vaguely described as being en route from 'various tropical colonies' (*T* 57) to their homes in 'Fo-kien' – that is, Fujian, a southeastern province of China roughly the size of the British Isles – the novella's British protagonists have very precise geographical origins: MacWhirr is the prodigal son of a Belfast grocer; his wife lives in a north London suburb; Solomon Rout has family in Teddington, a village on the capital's western outskirts, and a mother who remembers his apprenticeship in 'some great engineering works in the North' (127); the boatswain alludes frequently to his wife's 'greengrocer's shop in the Eastend of London' (99); and the misanthropic second mate seems to have spent more time than he would have wished in West Hartlepool. Even the *Nan-Shan* herself is from Dumbarton, a Scottish town that MacWhirr is shown reaching from London in just a few hours by the midnight express. An example of what Franco Moretti has called the 'geography of ideas' (Moretti, 1998: 29), the novella's narrative universe of British locality and colonial globality corresponds neatly to the spatial imaginary of his largely domestic and metropolitan magazine readership. Thus Conrad explains MacWhirr's unfamiliarity with truly severe weather:

He knew it existed, as we know that crime and abominations exist; he had heard of it as a peaceable citizen in a town hears of battles, famines, and floods, and yet knows nothing of what these things mean – though, indeed, he may have been mixed up in a street row, have gone without his dinner once, or been soaked to the skin in a shower.

(*T* 66–7)

Even the more formally ambitious elements of 'Typhoon' could be said to remain within the parameters for magazine fiction set forth in contemporary guidebooks. The extreme simplicity of its plot – a captain sails his ship into hurricane, the Chinese passengers riot, the crew restores order, the ship emerges intact, the passengers' jumbled possessions are divided equally – illustrates Albert Bull's precept about short-story writing: 'Experienced writers can afford to make this plot very simple, for they have powers of creating atmosphere and of portraying character and maintaining dialogue that can charge the most threadbare themes with life and interest' (Bull, 1912: 44). In turn, the central events of the *Nan-Shan's* progression into the eye of the storm and its key incident, the struggle to restore order below deck, bear comparison with J. Berg Esenwein's definition of the short story as narrative that presents '*a single predominating incident and a single chief character . . . the whole treatment so organized as to produce a single impression*' (Esenwein, 1912: 40, emphasis in original). Indeed, Conrad, who had earlier complained of being unable to organize *The Rescue* around a single 'illuminating episode' (*CL* 1: 296), would later offer his own definition of the 'master quality' of a serial in a letter to his American publisher, Frank Doubleday:

> The question of what is or is not fit for serial publication reduces itself, when all is said and done, to the single point of 'suspended interest'. . . . One single episode out of a life, one single feeling combined with a certain form of action (you'll notice I say *action* not analysis) may give the quality of 'suspended interest' to the tale of one single adventure in which the deepest sensations (and not only the bodies) of the actors are involved.   (*CL* 6: 333)

Similarly, the *Pall Mall's* division of 'Typhoon' into five chapters published in three instalments was able to exploit existing points of suspense; the narrator's oft-quoted declaration with regard to MacWhirr's fear of losing the ship, 'He was spared that annoyance' (*T* 122), only functions as a 'spoiler' for chapter six in the book version. Even Conrad's preference for 'Typhoon' over 'Equitable Division' and 'A Skittish Cargo' as a title may be less a reaction against the lightness of tone suggested by the latter than an acknowledgment of Esenwein's definition of a title's primary task as being 'to attract the reader's attention by the promise of an interesting story' (Esenwein, 1912: 147).[25]

Workmanship in the easier style: 'The Brute' (1906)

In his landmark study, *Selling Culture: Magazines, Markets and Class at the Turn of the Century* (1996), Richard Ohmann has shown that mass-circulation American magazines took on an historic role at the end of the nineteenth century: to manage an acute crisis of monopoly capitalism. In so doing, he concludes, they served as midwife to a new cultural order organized around the consumption of manufactured commodities and mediated by display advertising. Ohmann has elsewhere teased out the implications of these findings for our understanding of popular, generic magazine fiction in an ingenious comparison of an advertisement for Quaker Oats and a forgotten short story titled 'On the Way North', both of which appeared in *Munsey's Magazine* in October 1895 (Ohmann, 1991).[26] Their superficial dissimilarity notwithstanding, he reveals how an image of a man in eighteenth-century Quaker costume holding a tin of oats and a tale of romance aboard a runaway train are both predicated upon a shared and thoroughly modern worldview. Just as the story's colloquial style mirrors what he calls the 'generalized neighborliness and affability' projected by the American Cereal Company's advertisement, so, too, does the romantic adventure about a promising young professional and an independent young woman celebrate the social skills and communicative codes prized by the firm's target audience (Ohmann, 1991: 34). By recasting and resolving societal conflicts in individual terms and, above all, by adopting a narratorial voice that, as Ohmann notes, 'takes its values as unproblematic and uncontested', the story's author effectively naturalizes the ideology of a particular fraction of the middle class. This reading of an otherwise undistinguished story, he stresses, 'does not look *behind* or *through* the text to "background" conditions but reconstructs meanings that were "there" in the text for properly schooled contemporaries. . . . An interpretative strategy not grounded in such knowledge and in such habits of decoding would have given the reader an experience of the story almost drained of tension, affect, and satisfaction' (Ohmann, 1991: 38–9, emphases in original).

The relevance of Ohmann's argument for Conrad can be seen from a consideration of 'The Brute', a short story about a ship named *The Apse Family* that, despite having been constructed to the highest standards of safety and comfort, has acquired a fearsome reputation among sailors. The tale is presented in the form of two anecdotes, both of which are told to the frame narrator in a pub by a seaman called Ned. The first of these is a tragic account of how Ned's brother, Charles, saw his sweetheart, the captain's niece, drowned before his eyes in a freak accident with an anchor. The second relates how the ship's bad name forced her owners to employ substandard officers, among them a womanizing second mate named Wilmot whose distraction by a female passenger results in the murderous vessel being smashed on rocks outside Port Adelaide.

'The Brute' was first published in December 1906 in the *Daily Chronicle* and appeared the following November on the other side of the Atlantic in *McClure's Magazine*, a journal that had occupied the vanguard of the periodical revolution and whose prodigious advertising section announced itself as 'The Marketplace of the World'. It has been suggested that the subtitles 'A Tale of a Bloodthirsty Brig' and 'A Piece of Invective' that Conrad added to the versions printed in the *Daily Chronicle* and *McClure's*, respectively, are indicative of his growing confidence in addressing the diversity of a periodical readership; and there is, to be sure, a curious mixture of pride and embarrassment in the way that he described the story to Ted Sanderson as 'not so bad in workmanship . . . though otherwise a trifle' before instructing his friend to read it and then throw the magazine 'out of the window' (*CL* 3: 508). Today, however, 'The Brute' is almost universally regarded as one of Conrad's slightest works, prompting even its defenders to adopt a faintly apologetic tone.[27] The *Oxford Reader's Companion to Conrad*, for example, states that it was written in haste, despite the fact that its author spent far more time on the tale, relative to its length, than he did on *Heart of Darkness*.[28] Moreover, Conrad apparently wrote the story for *Blackwood's*, with whom he wished to re-establish a valuable professional connection (a stratagem he would later try with the *Pall Mall Magazine*). Only after William Blackwood refused it on the grounds that its subject was too similar to Edward Noble's novel *The Edge of Circumstance* (1904) did 'The Brute' assume its definitive identity as a magazine potboiler self-evidently bound for what its author scornfully dubbed a 'Yankee Mag[azi]ne' (*CL* 5: 308).

The imputation of plagiarism by a connoisseur of his work must have been deeply galling to Conrad. At the same time, whether or not the charge was justified, it is significant that Blackwood should have found 'The Brute' unacceptably close to the work of another writer of magazine stories. At one level, it reminds us that thematic overlap, independent use of the same source and unconscious borrowing were professional hazards for writers of genre fiction; even H. Rider Haggard had been accused in print of having plundered material from E. F. Knight's *The Cruise of the Falcon* (1884) for his bestseller *Allan Quartermain* (1887) (Runciman, 1890). Perhaps it was his own latent anxieties on this score that provoked Conrad to denounce John Buchan, another *Blackwood's* author, as an 'unspeakable imposter' who had 'stolen from Kipling as to matter and imitated from [Neil] Munro as to style' (*CL* 2: 218).

(The vehemence of Conrad's indignation can hardly be attributed to his ambivalent opinion of Kipling.) But Blackwood's indifference towards 'The Brute' also contrasts tellingly with the esteem in which the story was held by publishers of popular magazines such as Carl Hovey, editor of *Metropolitan Magazine*, who appealed to Pinker several years later: 'If we could have from Mr. Conrad another short story like "The Brute" we would reach our public with all the certainty in the world' (5: 322n). In other words, the qualities of conventionality and reproducibility that define artistic failure in Blackwood's eyes are, for Hovey, prerequisites of the kind of effective magazine fiction needed to 'reach' the *Metropolitan's* one million readers.[29]

The plot of 'The Brute' contains two stock components of magazine fiction: an ordinary situation that has become strangely unfamiliar (here, travel aboard a ship that has a malevolent will of its own); and the erotic adventures of youth (here, the blighted romance between the stranger's brother and his sweetheart, and the ill-timed dalliance between the second mate and the passenger). Both these tropes, it will be recalled, also define the short story 'On the Way North' that Ohmann cites as evidence of magazine fiction's new ideological role. What is more, 'The Brute' shares several features with two other Conrad stories that have been widely condemned as derivative magazine fodder: 'The Black Mate', a semi-comic tale of superstitious sailors; and 'The Inn of the Two Witches', a horror story about confronting evil in an isolated setting. Nevertheless, a mere summary of its plot, which is admirably in accordance with Hovey's rule of 'mov[ing] from point to point in a simple and orderly manner' (*CL* 5: 322n), cannot fully explain why 'The Brute' proved so successful as a magazine story. Cedric Watts points out that many of Conrad's works 'in brief and superficial summary . . . seem to belong to the realm of popular commercial fiction' and that '[t]he plot-elements of most Conradian fiction can be found in a wide range of second- and third-rate texts' (Watts, 1989: 57); even the author himself had to confess that his plot outline of *Heart of Darkness* sounded distinctly funny: 'A wild story of a journalist who becomes manager of a station in the interior and makes himself worshipped by a tribe of savages' (*CL* 2: 407).[30] Indeed, given Conrad's method of starting his novels as short stories, not to mention the tale's use of delayed decoding, his personal contribution to the Modernist narrative repertoire, it would be interesting to speculate about the kind of 'serious' novel into which 'The Brute' might conceivably have evolved: a hybrid of psychological drama and youthful romance along the lines of *Lord Jim* or *Chance*, perhaps, works whose plots also feature life-and-death moments at sea and whose narratives are similarly organized around two geographically and thematically separate climaxes.

The real affinities between the 'workmanship' of 'The Brute' and magazine fiction are, however, to be found in the story's reliance upon contrived suspense, sudden reversals of fortune and the laboured trope of ship-as-woman. Cracks in the plot are papered over by clichés such as 'Strange are the instruments of Providence' (*SS* 130) and drama is replaced with melodrama when the narrator, biting his lip in concentration, announces to his listeners, 'If she wasn't mad, then she was the most evil-minded, underhand, savage brute that ever went afloat' (112), or when Conrad, with heavy-handed irony, has Charley declare, '"We've baffled her, Ned"' (121), as the brothers approach the end of their voyage apparently unscathed. Adjectival shorthand is likewise made to do the work of characterization: Maggie's virginal innocence requires her to be 'blue-eyed' (119) for the same reasons as the sexual license of the governess, whose flirting while wearing a red dressing-gown causes the shipwreck, requires her to be 'green-eyed' (127, 128). In the traditions of magazine fiction to which 'The Brute' is heir, every old family has a wayward son or 'bad egg' (127), just as every 'fine, strong, upstanding, sun-tanned, young fellow, with his brown hair curling a little' (118) can be counted on to fall in love with a 'jolly girl of the very best sort' with 'beautiful colour, and a deuce of a lot of fair hair' (119). In this rigidly Newtonian universe every action has an equal reaction – a law known to magazine readers as 'poetical justice' (130) – and every thought finds an appropriate expression in deed. Shock turns hair 'snow-white in a fortnight' (127) (a phenomenon that recurs in 'The Black Mate') and the stolid patriotism of a harbour pilot can be read off from the bare statement: 'He had been many times in charge of royal yachts' (106).

In *The Edge of Circumstance*, to which 'The Brute' does indeed exhibit some striking similarities, Edward Noble had underscored the ship's status as a workplace. The shipowner's enthusiasm for the 'novel principle . . . of Cooperation' (Noble, 1904: 9), a scheme of profit-sharing in place of wages, leaves the *Titan*'s crew not only physically but financially vulnerable to her deadly capriciousness. Conrad's story takes this dimension of social allegory even further in interpellating what Ohmann identifies as the new middle-class readership of popular magazines such as *McClure's*. Though a landlubber, the frame narrator of 'The Brute' is no fool (unlike the jejune magazine-story writer in 'The Partner') and the social superiority of the friends whom he meets in a tavern is evinced by their preference for sitting in the parlour instead of standing at the public bar. As befits 'gentlemen' (*SS* 105, 106, 109, 131), they take care to refer to barmaids and absent superiors by title, and the company shows due deference to the senior pilot who makes a whopping 'eight hundred a year' (109). For their part, Ned and Charley are exemplary juniors, conscientious and respectful of the shipboard hierarchy in which they occupy a middling position, whereas the criminally negligent second mate Wilmot who abandons his post is both a coward and an habitué of brothels. Like the frame narrator, who addresses the barmaid of The Three Crows with 'extreme propriety' (105) and suppresses a 'damn' (109), Ned is hyper-attentive to the rituals of decorum, translating a common sailor's profanity as 'sanguinary female dog' (114) and recalling how Wilmot, now reduced to working as a waggoner, 'would break off to swear something awful at every second word' (129). This is, metaphorically speaking, a view of the world from the bridge.

This somewhat bald account of the operations of social coding in 'The Brute' is complicated by the story's clubbish, almost misogynistic tone. Violence against women and cheating on one's wife are presented as the subjects of a humorous misunderstanding, and the ship's disastrous design is indirectly attributed to the captain's wife, a 'silly, hard-bitten old woman' (*SS* 121) with 'ugly false teeth' (108) who has the 'nerve' (111) to insist upon being accommodated in comfort.[31] Ned tells his listeners confidentially, 'But with women, you never know how they will take a thing' (107), and explains that *The Apse Family*'s fate was sealed by the fortuitous arrival of 'the right woman to put an end to her' (130). Even as they give voice to Conrad's scorn for the saccharine codes of gallantry prescribed by magazine romances, these comments address a set of readerly concerns whose outlines can be discerned in two otherwise unremarkable asides. The first relates to work. Ned's praise for traditional ship design – 'Good, solid, old-fashioned craft they were, too, built to carry and to last. None of your new-fangled, labour-saving appliances in them, but plenty of men and plenty of good salt beef and hard tack put aboard – and off you go to fight your way out and home again' (110) – receives the voluble assent of a North Sea pilot: 'He pointed out in doleful tones that you couldn't say to labour-saving appliances: "Jump lively now, my hearties." No labour-saving appliances would go aloft on a dirty night with the sands under your lee' (110). The second relates to working conditions. The owners of *The Apse Family*, we are told, 'treated their people well – as people don't get treated nowadays' (110). In each case, apparent nostalgia for a paternalistic past reveals itself, like Ohmann's eighteenth-century Quaker holding a tin of breakfast cereal, as the symptom of a very modern cultural crisis.

In 1907, let us recall, the advertising section of *McClure's* was a seventy-page paean to labour-saving: machines for sifting ash that even children could operate; Swan pens that wrote 'without any of the shaking and "coaxing" so often necessary to make some fountain pens work'; and Pianolas that proclaimed themselves to be thoroughly 'Twentieth Century' in having overcome the piano's 'old-time limitations of manual dexterity'.[32] In such magazines, explains Ohmann, 'No one fretted about antagonisms between the machine and the individual' (Ohmann, 1998: 246). Why, then, would the editor of the *Metropolitan*, also a magazine packed with advertisements for such appliances, describe a tale that reviled both the ethos and the technology of labour-saving as certain to help him 'reach' his subscribers? The answer lies in the differentiation of the readership of popular periodicals. As their contents lists confirm, the very largest mass-circulation magazines such as *McClure's*, *Metropolitan Magazine*, or *London Magazine* sought to present themselves as a literary smorgasbord with something for every taste. Like a good many of Conrad's tales, 'The Brute' would therefore have constituted a welcome inducement to men like Mr Johnson, the hypothetical paterfamilias whom Ohmann imagines as having to flip past the romantic stories and as reading with scepticism the articles about upper-class yachtsmen in his family's subscription copy of *Munsey's Magazine* of October 1895. No sailor, this reader would nonetheless have approved of Conrad's representation of work in terms of integrity and perhaps even have heard in Ned's 'off you go to fight your way out and home again' an echo of his own daily exertions to provide for his dependents. As a white-collar professional, he would have connected the pilot's complaint about labour-saving appliances being unable to go aloft in a storm to his colleagues' complaints about the reluctance of modern workmen to perform similarly arduous tasks, even as the pressures of his own job would have led him to sympathize with Ned's observation that workers in this era of technology and comfort are no longer treated as well as they used to be. In turn, the claim that Wilmot's loss of certificate 'was worse than drowning for a man' (*SS* 131) would have struck him less as hyperbole than as an unadorned statement of fact. And, despite his admiration for Ned's use of a bicycle to get to The Three Crows, albeit not from any Conradian animus towards leisure walking per se, he would have shared the mariner's residual unease about the spread of labour-saving devices in general.

Ohmann's hypothetical reader could probably not have explained why, but this cluster of concerns had an intimate connection with another central theme of 'The Brute': the changing role of women.

He would have grasped at once that the presence of 'petticoats' on board a ship necessarily represents a threat to the safety and efficiency of her crew (Ned presents his own retirement from the sea as the logical consequence of getting married) just as he would have recognized that Charley bears some responsibility for his sweetheart's death because he let Maggie 'have too much of her own way' (*SS* 121). As Mr Johnson and his magazine-reading contemporaries understood, the growing importance of shopping, fashion, novelty and advertising for the economy and social intercourse in general was bringing about a recalibration of traditional gender roles. In 'The Brute' – as in 'Typhoon' and 'The Partner', also stories that contrast masculine idealism with feminine materialism – they would have been reassured about their professional and gender status at the same time as receiving discreet guidance on how to find their way in this brave new world of magazine-regulated consumption.[33] Like 'The Inn of Two Witches', another magazine story in which a junior officer burdened with new responsibilities laments the nature of the so-called 'progress' by which 'any blear-eyed witch' with a machine-gun can 'lay low a hundred young men of twenty in the twinkling of an eye' (*WT* 133), 'The Brute' tells a compact fable about the challenges posed by modern women and technology even as its ostensibly extraneous descriptions of 'black waterproof . . . made of three-fold oiled silk, double-stitched throughout' (*SS* 106), 'extra superfine blue cloth' (106) and 'a man's hand-bag of the usual size' (106) direct men like Mr Johnson to appraise everyday commodities in terms of familiar 'masculine' qualities of durability, added-value and 'workmanship'.[34] In sharp contrast to the gender privileges enjoyed in this era of conspicuous consumption by women such as the odious Mrs Colchester, who 'walk[s] about in a brown silk dress, with a great gold cable flopping about her bosom' (108), Conrad has an old sailor complain feelingly: 'Men are cheap, God knows' (114).

Several conclusions can be drawn from this outline of how 'The Brute' would have resonated with the male readership of *McClure's* and (with some important differences) of *Blackwood's*. In the first place, the meaning of such works, here, a representative example of what Conrad in another context called 'a man's story' (*CL* 4: 298), cannot be reduced to any simple notion of escapism or diversion but must be understood, rather, as situated at an historically precise intersection of aesthetics, economics and the politics of gender and class. What is more, only a thorough knowledge of the conventions and idioms of popular magazines, a hitherto largely unexamined repertoire of narrative devices that parallels his acknowledged mastery of 'high' literary form, could have enabled Conrad to 'reach' the audiences of *McClure's* and its rivals with such manifest success. That these magazines, in turn, retailed to their readers a rather different cultural construction to the 'Conrad' enshrined by literary posterity is evident from his by-line in *McClure's*, 'Joseph Conrad. Author of "Romance," "Falk," "Youth," etc.', which juxtaposes a collaboration modelled on R. L. Stevenson's popular adventures, a tale of cannibalism that Conrad claimed 'stank in the nostrils of all magazine editors' (*CL* 3: 338) and a *Blackwood's* piece that to this day remains a cornerstone of his artistic reputation.[35] Above all, in place of the conventional view of magazine fiction as a threat to Conrad's artistic integrity, the case of 'The Brute' forces us to take seriously the activities of an author who believed that he could find a public of his own *within* the mass readership of popular magazines by writing 'magazineish thing[s] with some decency' (4: 464) in a mode that he memorably described as 'Conradesque (in the easier style)' (4: 413).

Conclusion

[A] motor car and Joseph Conrad couldn't be made to modulate in my mind, all of which proves the folly of preconceived portraits.

James Huneker, 'A Visit to Joseph Conrad',
New York Times Magazine, 17 November 1912 (JCIR 22)

Homo duplex has in my case more than one meaning.

Conrad to Kazimierz Waliszewski,
5 December 1903 (CL 3: 89)

An invitation to write a preface to Edward Garnett's *Turgenev: A Study* in April 1917 gave Conrad a welcome opportunity to put on record both his love of the great novelist and his gratitude to a critic who had been a faithful supporter of his own work. In the essay, which takes the form of a personal letter to his old friend, Conrad celebrates *A Sportsman's Sketches* as a chronicle of the first moral and intellectual stirrings of a country that now found itself on the brink of an historic transformation. With their 'marvellous landscapes peopled by unforgettable figures' (*NLL* 40), these acutely observed tales of rural Russian life, he declared, held the same universal appeal as 'the Italians of Shakespeare' (41). In illuminating Turgenev's particular genius, Garnett's study promised to contribute to the international recognition of a writer whose own compatriots, reactionary and revolutionary alike, had denied him the laurels to which he was entitled.

The autobiographical resonances of Conrad's eulogy are hard to miss. In introducing his wife Constance's translations of Turgenev, Garnett had played the part of intermediary between the Russian writer and the British public in much the same way as he had with Conrad, whose place in English letters he helped to secure by providing connections to the publishing firms of Blackwood and Heinemann. The final volume of Heinemann's complete edition of Turgenev, one of which was dedicated to Conrad, entered 'the twilight of public indifference in the ninety-ninth year of the nineteenth century' (*NLL* 40) at almost exactly the moment when Conrad's first works made their own inauspicious début. What is more, Conrad's description of Turgenev's tales as documents of spiritual 'unrest' (40) echoes the title of his own first short story collection, *Tales of Unrest*, just as his identification of women and love as Turgenev's recurrent themes also describes those of his most recent novels, *Chance* and *Victory*, as well as his next novel, *The Arrow of Gold*. Indeed, he had approached the publisher George Harvey in 1904 with a proposal for a volume 'in the spirit of Turgeniev's Sportsman's Sketches' (*CL* 3: 132) to be titled either *A Seaman's Sketches* or *The Mirror of the Sea*. Lastly, Conrad's stress upon Turgenev as writing for posterity independently of 'the transitory formulas and theories of art' (*NLL* 40), a pairing that suggestively lumps together conventionality and avantgardism, champions the same quality of unbending individualism that he had made central to his own literary project. After a generous reviewer compared 'Gaspar Ruiz' to 'A Lear of the Steppes', Conrad declared himself aghast at the very idea of mentioning 'that infernal magazine fake' (*CL* 4: 108) in the same breath as Turgenev's masterpiece.

Conrad's preoccupation in 'Turgenev' with the problem of popularity, a motif that we have encountered time and again in this study, is clearly visible beneath his scorn for the public's churlish treatment of an 'incomparable artist of humanity' (*NLL* 41). He notes sardonically that the achievement of greatness without ostentation 'must be fatal to any man's influence with his contemporaries' (41) and concludes his inventory of Turgenev's many virtues: 'There's enough there to ruin the prospects of any writer' (42). Conrad's diagnosis seems at once familiar and banal: a debased popular taste to whose indifference and faddishness literary production is now held hostage all but guarantees the obscurity of any writer of talent. And who would wish for popularity with such a public? As he explained to Frank Doubleday shortly before his death: 'I have this morning received a two-pages-and-a-half criticism from the editor of the *Dial* under the ominous caption, "A Popular Novel". . . I never dreamed that such a thing would happen to me' (*LL* 2: 344). 'Popular' has here become a suspect, even sinister label denoting either the absence of literary value or, what is perhaps worse, a crass attempt to advertise a work with aesthetic merit to an undiscriminating readership. Certainly, Conrad's fears must have been confirmed by the critical reception of the novel in question. Even as his well-wishers exerted themselves to underline *The Rover*'s distance from the 'superfluities' (*CH* 350) of popular writers such as G. A. Henty and Herbert Strang, reviewers normally hostile to Conrad ironically praised the novel as 'the worst he ever wrote' (*CH* 351), that is, as a concession to the common reader's desire for gripping stories. In the closing words of his preface to Garnett's book, Conrad spelled out the dire prospects for any writer forced to seek favour with a public now hopelessly distracted by what he called 'Fashions in monsters' (*NLL* 40):

> For you know very well my dear Edward that if you had Antinous himself in a booth of the world's-fair, and killed yourself in protesting that his soul was as perfect as his body you wouldn't get one per cent of the crowds struggling next door for a sight of the Double-headed Nightingale or of some weak-kneed giant grinning through a horse collar. (*NLL* 42)

This image of the aesthetic as trapped in hopeless competition with a popular freak show returns us to the received perception of Conrad as simply dismissive of or oblivious to contemporary popular culture. As we have seen in an array of contexts, Conrad energetically denounced the general public as irredeemably undiscerning from a discursive position with obvious roots in his class background in the Polish landed gentry, his movement in elite social circles in his adopted country and (to use the terminology of Pierre Bourdieu) the rules of the game that require would-be entrants to the restricted field of literary production to maintain an attitude of superiority to the masses. Like his professions of contempt for 'silly' optical entertainments, tourist 'animals', 'lying' advertisements and 'rubbishy' magazine stories, Conrad's hypothetical juxtaposition of two grotesques and the fabulously handsome companion of Emperor Hadrian appears to offer an archetypal and unambiguous rejection of popular culture's artefacts, experiences and intended audience. The reference to a 'weak-kneed giant' seems to mirror the 'knock-kneed giant' of W. S. Gilbert's humorous song about the dangers of trying to please the public in *Princess Toto* (1876), just as the reference to an unnatural bird seems to echo what John Conrad remembered as his father's solemn explanation that, whilst it was quite permissible to force dogs to dance on their hind legs, it was 'beneath their dignity' for lions, tigers, or bears to do the same (Conrad, 1981: 110).

And yet the present study has sought to present a challenge to this view by showing that Conrad, for all his protestations to the contrary, in fact had direct and substantial knowledge of popular cultural texts and practices, and that these latter exerted a significant influence on his fiction and prose writing. In support of these claims, it has submitted a series of examples drawn from both canonical and non-canonical works that reveal his engagement with a range of popular cultural arte-facts, including magic lantern dissolving views, the new sport of pedestrianism and Bovril advertising. It is therefore highly fitting that a similar pattern should characterize his disavowal of the gawping public in 'Turgenev'. Conrad's earlier mention of 'strange beasts in a menagerie' (*NLL* 41) has led readers to assume that the 'Double-headed Nightingale' is a reference to an avian freak. However, the capitalization of the phrase in both the manuscript and the typescript confirms that he is in fact alluding to Millie-Christine McCoy, conjoined twins from North Carolina who toured extensively under the stage name 'the Two-Headed Nightingale' (Figure 13). The singing duo drew large crowds at vaudeville shows across the United States and on three long tours of Britain (1855, 1871 and 1884–85), during which time they were pre-sented to Queen Victoria (Martell, 1999: 240–3). Conrad could easily have read about or seen the sisters and possibly also the giant Captain Bates with whom they shared the billing on at least one occasion; there is, to be sure, a faint suggestion of personal experience in his manuscript reference to the unnamed stage giant as 'grinning with a face of meaningless pathos, maybe; that hint of aimless, mysterious suffering exhibited for its own sake as it were. Ugh!' (*NLL* 317n). Needless to say, the twins could not have performed at a World's Fair – the international showcases for industry and design hosted by Chicago in 1893, Paris in 1900, St Louis in 1904 and Brussels in 1910 – but they may have appeared at the World's Fair Palace of Variety in Islington, London, an entertainment venue specializing in circus shows and novelty spectacles that, as one contemporary drily put it, 'in a common way meets the propensities of large masses of people' (Robertson, 1897: 218).[1]

The unlikely presence of 'the Double-headed Nightingale' in an essay on Turgenev dramatizes in striking fashion several key aspects of Conrad's relation towards popular culture. First, it exemplifies the grounding of his attitudes in particular events and artefacts rather than, as has often been assumed, abstract generalizations; it is entirely possible that Conrad knew the size of the crowds struggling to see Millie-Christine because he had once been in their number. Second, it illustrates the way in which such factors can bring new light to bear on the central themes of his fiction. Whether or not he had the twins in mind when describing the brothers Montero in *Nostromo* as 'acting

Figure 13 Millie-Christine McCoy, 'The Two-Headed Nightingale', *c*.1885. Reproduced with permission from the collection of the Spartanburg County Regional Museum of History.

together as if they were Siamese twins' (*N* 227), it is nothing less than extraordinary that one of his very few references to a person of colour who can be identified by name should have been to two former slaves who became successful international performers. Third, it shows that even so fundamental an organizing principle of his narratives as doubleness or secret sharing can repay examination in terms of a specific popular cultural context. Conrad's famous claim, 'In my case homo duplex has more than one meaning' (*CL* 3: 89), has often been taken as an adaptation of Georges-Louis Buffon's classification of the mind-body duality to his own peculiar family, national and professional backgrounds; but in a letter to Garnett written just a few days before drafting 'Turgenev' Conrad again mentions 'the double-headed Nightingale' before going on to describe himself as feeling 'broken up – or broken in two' (*CL* 6: 78). Lastly, the fact that Conrad should have chosen as the epitome of popular culture's ephemerality the name of vaudeville performers whose last visit to Britain had taken place fully twenty-five years earlier casts a long shadow over his meditation on the nature of literary posterity, not to mention his unfavourable contrasting of mere 'Fashions in monsters' (*NLL* 40) with Turgenev's women, who would endure, he declared, 'certainly for all time' (41).

During the final stages of this project, I happened to describe its subject to a delegate at an academic conference, who replied disarmingly: 'Oh, is there anything left to say about Conrad?' It is a question that been voiced with growing frequency in recent years as scholars of Conrad's work find themselves confronted by a law of diminishing returns, most acutely in the case of *Heart of Darkness*, whose power to attract at times painfully abstruse interpretations has led to more than one call for a critical moratorium. Far from seeking to give the final word on Conrad and popular culture, this study is therefore offered in hopes of encouraging or provoking others to investigate further the potential relevance of this vast field to his writing. Its synoptic accounts of the biographical and textual intersections between his *œuvre* as a whole and visual entertainment, tourism, advertising and magazine fiction are intended to illustrate how a critical methodology anchored in cultural history can reveal new dimensions to texts that have hitherto been considered in isolation or within more traditional models of literary influence. Conrad told Cunninghame Graham that he had written *The Secret Agent* as 'a sustained effort in ironical treatment of a melodramatical subject' (*CL* 3: 491). But which melodramas or genres of melodramas was he referring to? Similarly, he told Garnett that as a boy in Poland he had read *Smoke* (1867), Turgenev's satire on the Russian upper classes, in 'a feuilleton of some newspaper' (*CL* 6: 77); but the only book-length studies of Conrad and contemporary politics are now almost forty years old, Anglophone readers lack a comprehensive account of the formative influence of Polish literature and culture on his writing, and the newspapers that Conrad read, contributed to and described on numerous occasions in his fiction have hitherto received only scant attention.[2] Like the copy of Max Adeler's bestselling collection of comic sketches *Out of the Hurly-Burly* (1874) whose presence in his father's bedside library so mystified John Conrad (Conrad, 1981: 149), or St-John Perse's description of the author reciting Edward Lear's nonsense poem 'The Jumblies' (1900) from memory and 'assuring me that you found "the spirit of great adventures" there more than in the best sea writers, such as Melville' (Stape and Knowles, 1996: 173), the anomalies and inconsistencies in Conrad's astonishingly rich life – from South African stock-jobbing to video gaming in Vienna – direct us to ask genuinely new questions about his diverse body of work, the answers to which will surely open onto rather more interesting avenues than a routine application of the latest literary theory. If the present study has succeeded in showing that a very great deal remains to be said about this least classifiable of Modernists, it will have achieved at least one of its goals.

Notes

Introduction

1 Keith Summers Collection C1002/71.
2 An example of this very different performance style can be heard in the Roger Wagner Chorale's version of 'Rio Grande', with its key shifts and final Broadway-style flourish on the word 'Rio!' (pronounced 'Ree-oh').
3 As Frederick R. Karl and Laurence Davies note, Conrad is conflating two songs: 'The Banks of Sacramento' and the capstan shanty 'Santa Anna' or 'The Plains of Mexico' (*CL* 4: 352n). In 1915, Conrad declined an invitation to collaborate with the British composer Granville Bantock, pleading damaged vocal chords. The details of Bantock's proposal are not known but since he had recently begun collecting and scoring folk songs from around the world, he could well have approached Conrad about using sea-shanties in an opera or song-cycle. I am grateful to Mr Ronald Bleach for supplying biographical information about Bantock.
4 See Hawthorn, 2003.
5 I am indebted to Mr Gavin Sprott for this information.
6 *Times Literary Supplement*, 3565 (25 June 1970): 673. See Purdy, 1984; Hunter, 1983; Griffith, 1995; Hampson, 2000; Youngs, 1994; Roberts, 1993; and Parry, 1983.
7 Watts, 1989, 97–103; Morf, 1976, 80–1; Tanner, 19. See also Dryden, 2002; Collits, 2004; Mallios, 2003.
8 Morf, 1976, 292.
9 Conrad, 1981, 155; Sherry, 1966 and 1971.
10 On Conrad's enthusiasm for each of these activities, see Conrad, 1981: 20, 103, 110, and 32.
11 See Hobsbawm, 1989, and Perkin, 1989. For a detailed case study of these changes in the context of Bristol see Meller, 1976. It is a nice irony that Conrad, by inclination a Conservative, should have been offered a knighthood by the Labour Prime Minister Ramsay MacDonald.
12 See, for example, Leonard, 1998, and Varnedoe and Gopnik, 1991.
13 For a fuller account of the history of this debate in relation to the theorists of the Frankfurt School, the Centre for Contemporary Cultural Studies in Birmingham, the theories of Antonio Gramsci, and the development of Cultural Studies as a discipline in the Anglo-American academy see Strinati, 1995, and Storey, 2003: 1–62. See also Brantlinger, 1983, 222–48.
14 See Williams, 1987.
15 Possibly in hopes of resolving such 'institutions', Italy's Agricultural Ministry launched a scheme in October 2002 that would give credentials to restaurants serving 'genuine' Italian cuisine.
16 The subjects of another ink sketch that Conrad made in the mid-1890s (Knowles and Moore, 2000: 294) are not, as Jessie's pencilled caption optimistically suggests, 'ballet dancers' but, rather, chorus girls lifting their skirts.

1 Visual Entertainment

1   *Oesterreichischer Komet* 220 (July 1914): 4. Reference kindly supplied by Mr Günter Krenn.
2   *Brixener Chronik*, 9 January 1915: 3.
3   See Moore, 1997.
4   Conrad's residual unease about the medium should not be confused with the myth that early film spectators were unable to differentiate between illusion and fact. See Gunning, 1995a.
5   *Times*, 27 May 1914: 2. Marie Lloyd was appearing at the Gaiety Music Hall in Chatham when Conrad literally crashed through the village in late August 1904.
6   See Reed, 1997: 27–49.
7   See MacKenzie, 1986; Price, 1972, especially 132–77; Schivelbusch, 1988: 115–20. Conrad recalled having suppressed giggles during a visit to Sydney Pawling, his and Caine's publisher, 'with the photo of the Great Callan, on the mantelpiece, looking at me' (*CL* 3: 340).
8   See, for example, Suárez, 2001; Fraser, 1994, 1–13; Tiessen, 1997; and Cohen, 2004.
9   'There are millions of perfectly healthy people who are stupid, for whom all art other than oleograph reproduction is morbid' (*CL* 5: 238–9).
10 Shipwrecks were a favourite theme among audiences during the magic lantern's heyday in the 1880s and 1890s. A regular feature of disaster photograph-slides such as *The Bay of Panama*, a ship wrecked off Cornwall in 1891, they also appeared in painted dissolving views such as the popular melodrama *Jane Conquest* in which a captain's wife, like Jane Dunbar in Conrad's 'The Partner' (1911), watches despairingly from the shore as her husband's ship founders. See Humphries, 1989: 60–2 and 150–3.
11 Hawthorn, 2002: xxv. See also Peacock, 1996: 113–33.
12 See Hepworth, 1894: 281–2.
13 See Powell, 2002: 126–37, and Schwartz, 1998: 157–76.
14 *CL* 1: 56; *CL* 5: 452, 686; *LL* 2: 335. See Jean-Aubry, 1924.
15 Ryf, 1972; Houston, 1998; Joy, 2003.
16 See Pugliatti, 1988; Bufkin, 1975; and Baldanza, 1980.
17 See *CL* 4: 210, 4: 218, 5.696; *LL* 2: 270.
18 See also Hand, 2003; Hand and Wilson, 2002: 1–78; and Wheatley, 2002.
19 The aphorism quoted by Callan in Conrad and Ford's *The Inheritors*, 'Photography – is not – Art' (*I* 15), is pure Baudelaire.
20 On the theory of retinal retention in Victorian fiction and scientific literature see Gunning, 1995b: 37–9.
21 For humorous treatments of the subject in fiction see Lang, 1895; and Griffith, 1896. The fabrication of spirit photographs was also mocked in numerous early films, including J. Stuart Blackton's *A Visit to a Spiritualist* (1897), G. A. Williamson's *Photographing a Ghost* (1898), George Méliès' *The Spiritualist Photographer* (1903), J. H. Martin's *The Medium Exposed* (1906) and Arthur Cooper's *A Visit to a Spiritualist* (1906).
22 Conrad again associates Stead and Crookes with spirit photography in 'The Planter of Malata' (1914), where they are alluded to as 'a very famous author [whose] ghost is a girl' and 'a very great man of science' (*WT* 67).

23 On Stead and Conrad, see Donovan, 2000.

24 In 'The Return' (1898), Alvan Hervey is granted a similarly 'ghastly kind of clairvoyance' by the news of his wife's infidelity: '[H]e could see the towns and fields of the earth, its sacred places, its temples and its houses, peopled by monsters – by monsters of duplicity, lust, and murder. . . . How many men and women at this very moment were plunged in abominations – meditated crimes' (*TU* 135).

25 In *The Shadow-Line*, a photograph of the deceased captain's sweetheart reminds Conrad's narrator of 'a low-class medium' (*SL* 59).

26 See the essays by Cedric Watts, Robert Hampson and Hugh Epstein in Moore, 1992.

27 Anarchists and music-hall artists could be neighbours in other ways, too. When Conrad wrote the story in late 1905, the Variety Artists' Federation was being radicalized by an influx of anarchist militants, precipitating an acrimonious and highly public strike in Spring 1906 that was dubbed 'The Music Hall War' in the press. In a deleted manuscript passage of 'The Partner', Conrad describes a stevedore's management of two music halls in 'the "Variety"' world' as bringing him into contact with 'certain audacious unsuspected adventures which brush [past] our doors, our respectable uncontaminated doors' (Dalgarno, 1975, 42).

28 The theoretical and methodological problems raised by this 'modernity thesis' are usefully examined in Singer, 2001: 101–30.

29 Compare *The Arrow of Gold*: '. . . that odd air wax figures have of being aware of their existence being but a sham' (*AG* 69).

30 For detail of the Aquarium's entertainments see Robertson, 1897: 216.

31 A consideration which perhaps led Conrad to depart from his source: an off-hand remark that the original bomb victim's sister 'committed suicide afterwards' (*SA* 5).

32 See Hockenjos, forthcoming 2005. I am greatly indebted to Vreni Hockenjos for allowing me to read work-in-progress from her doctoral dissertation, 'Picturing Dissolving Views: August Strindberg as Media History' (Department of Film Studies, Stockholm University). For an example of immediate precursors to the cinematic life review see the description of *Dan Dabberton's Dream* (1892), a combination-photograph slide-show that featured a reformed drunkard's pictorial review of his life, in Cook, 1963, 111–13.

33 For a photograph of the life review in *Histoire d'un crime* see Olsson, 1996: 37.

34 On the prominence of tableaux in contemporary dramaturgy, see Brewster, 1997.

35 For photographs of the Musée Grévin's tableau series 'Histoire d'un Crime', see Schwartz, 1998: 124–6.

36 Curiously, Andrew Michael Roberts passes over this image without comment in his acute discussion of the novel's gendered visual politics in Roberts, 1992.

37 All are included on the 'Opinions of the Press' page of the 1898 Heinemann edition.

38 The statement also appeared in several subsequent American editions of the novel. See Najder, 1984: 205.

39 See Barnes, 1996–98, 2: 143–5, 1: 194; and Moore, 1997: 40–1. In September 1898, London newspapers such as the *Daily Mail* advertised the Palace as showing 'all the newest pictures of the Spanish-American War series'. On the

cinematic dimensions of what Conrad called Crane's 'imaged style' (*LE* 121), see Brown, 1996: 125–66.

40 Several hand-colouring processes were in existence by 1900, Kinemacolour films were shown regularly in London from 1909, and there were several attempts at synchronizing sound and projected images in the early 1910s.

41 See Cartwright, 1995: 106–7.

42 Early examples of this trope include the anonymous magazine story 'In the Dark' (*Pick-Me-Up*, 16 May 1896) and Rudyard Kipling's short story 'Mrs Bathurst' (1904).

43 See Dutheil de la Rochère, 2005.

44 Unpublished in his lifetime, Conrad's text is reprinted in Schwab, 1965.

45 In *The Man Who Was Thursday* (1908), G. K. Chesterton likens the shimmer of sunlight and shadows as 'almost recalling the dizziness of a cinematograph' before recounting a protracted chase by horse, car, and fire-engine (Chesterton, 1908: 223).

46 For illustrations of the set of *The Price of Peace* see Booth, 1981, Plates 4 and 5. See also Stottlar, 1989.

47 From Impressionist painting to computer animation, waves have traditionally served as the litmus test of representational verisimilitude.

48 See Fielding, 1968–9.

49 In *Heart of Darkness*, Marlow's fantastic vision of Kurtz 'opening his mouth voraciously, as if to devour all the earth with all its mankind' (*Y* 155) anticipates James Williamson's trick film *The Big Swallow* (1901) in which the camera lens is brought so close to a man's open mouth that the viewer has the illusion of being swallowed entirely.

50 The helmsman's memories of his old colleagues, 'bowed and enduring, like stone caryatides that hold up in the night the lighted halls of a resplendent and glorious edifice' (*NN* 26), recall the real-life illuminated façade of the Alhambra music hall and the figures adorning the Egyptian Hall in Piccadilly. See Barnes, 1996–98, 1: 117, 1: 135.

51 See Barnes, 1996–98, 1: 195; Chanan, 1980: 286.

52 Conrad's description of Donkin's loquacity as 'picturesque and filthy' (*NN* 101) anticipates his later suggestion that the 'picturesque possibilities' (*CL* 5: 461) of 'Gaspar Ruiz' made the story eminently suitable for cinematic adaptation. On the cinematographic qualities of 'Gaspar Ruiz' see Postacioglu-Banon, 2003.

53 Reviewing *Dubliners* in 1917, H. G. Wells remarked upon Joyce's preference for dashes over inverted commas: 'most of the talk flickers blindingly with these dashes, one has the same wincing feeling of being flicked at that one used to have in the early cinema shows' (Deming, 1970: 87).

2 Tourism

1 'Quelle charmante plage! On se fait l'illusion qu'ici on pourrait être toujours presque gai!' (Beerbohm, 1921, frontispiece). Conrad reportedly described the Sumatran island of Muntock, his first encounter with 'the East', as 'a damned hole without any beach and without any glamour' (Sherry, 1972: 35).

2 For example, White, 1993: 100–15.

3 On Conrad's visits to Champel see Bock, 2002: 26–40 and 65–73.

4   On English walkers in Switzerland see Withey, 1997: 202–5.

5   Also past his own house, as he explained to Ted Sanderson: '[T]he trains for Pent Farm are the trains for Paris – exactly. Also the Vienna express stops to set down and take up my guests' (*CL* 1: 234).

6   Fahlbeck, 1998: 9, my translation. For contemporary photographs see *Capri c'era una volta: Un secolo di immagini* (Napoli: Electa, 1988) and for German guidebooks see *Neapel und Capri* (Berlin: Griebens Reiseführer, 1911).

7   In *Heart of Darkness*, German East Africa is the 'purple patch . . . where the jolly pioneers of progress drink the jolly lager-beer' (*Y* 55).

8   The story reminded Arthur Symons of an encounter in Naples with 'the same kind of villain, who threatened me, and who murmured into my ears the most shameful things' (Keating, 1929: 180).

9   For details of both scandals, see Andrén, 1975: 141–3.

10   Compare *The Inheritors*: 'I felt like a man at the beginning of a long holiday – an indefinite space of idleness . . .' (*I* 151).

11   According to one of Conrad's former shipmates, the *Torrens* was advertised, somewhat inaccurately, as a 'health and pleasure voyage' in the London newspapers: 'We had many a passenger's funeral and Conrad always looked happy' (*JCIR* 61).

12   On Modernist criticism of contemporary tourists, see Carr, 2002.

13   Possibly inspired by the name of a real hotel on Gillingham Street (*SA* 424n), where Conrad had written part of *Almayer's Folly*.

14   In a draft for the stage version of *Victory*, Conrad depicts Schomberg attempting to induce Zangiacomo to part with Lena while declaring: '1st Class Hotels etc. etc. and with a girl like that I could etc. etc.' (*CL* 5: 643).

15   A cancelled passage in the MS of 'Falk' describes 'the swift rush of evolution hurrying towards these monsters of form or size that are either inhuman or gigantic aping the ways of hotels or else of warehouses' (*T* 26).

16   On the growth of tourist boating parties at the start of the twentieth century see Walton, 2000, 134–7. Like Sidmouth, Westport has an old pier, a water-front hotel and a small railway station, and overlooks a bay in the English Channel in which a cluster of half-submerged rocks poses a danger to shipping.

17   This arrival of tourist modernity to the South China Seas had a real-life counterpart in Thomas Cook's addition of British North Borneo, a close neighbour of the islands on which Conrad based Samburan, to the itinerary of its Far Eastern Tour in 1892.

18   A fact possibly reflected in Conrad's choice of the name Travers: 'The younger sons and relations of many a native ruler *traversed* the seas of the Archipelago, visited the innumerable and little-known islands, and the then practically unknown shores of New Guinea' (*Res* 68, my emphasis). Significantly, Travers plans to return via Egypt 'overland through Egypt' (34); the Suez Canal has not yet been built.

19   On the long history of this 'anti-tourist' attitude in British culture, see Buzard, 1993: 81–107.

20   Cook's tour brochure for 1918 voiced a consensus opinion on the matter: 'It is impossible to over-estimate the value of sea travel for the maintenance or the restoration of good health' (Williamson, 1998: 110). Conrad may have

had in mind Baron von Hübner's tedious memoir *A Ramble Round the World* (1871), which he also mentions in his essay 'Travel' (*LE* 86).

21 On world touring see Withey, 1997: 263–93, especially 292–3.

22 *Cook's Travellers Handbook to Florence for 1934* describes Vallombrosa as 'a fashionable summer resort (visited also for winter sports) [which] may be reached by S.I.T.A. motor bus service in 2 hours.' Conrad may have known of the convent's forcible dissolution in the late nineteenth century.

23 Conrad's library included Owen Letcher's photo-illustrated *Big-Game Hunting in North-Eastern Rhodesia* (1911), presumably a review copy sent by the *Daily Mail*. Letcher made no secret that his racist views on 'the dangerous doctrine that all men are equal' (Letcher, 1911: 230) were likely to cause offence.

24 In *The Arrow of Gold*, Henry Allegre and Doña Rita's annual holiday in Corsica is described as 'A yearly pilgrimage. Sentimental perhaps' (*AG* 33).

25 In his 1904 essay 'Anatole France', Conrad suggests that 'globe-trotting' would make a worthy target for the Frenchman's 'gentle wit' (*NLL* 37).

26 *The Excursionist* 38/5 (1 June 1888): 3.

27 *The Excursionist* 48/4 (16 April 1898): 7. The following advertisement appeared in the *Times* on 29 April 1898 and on five other occasions in the following fortnight: 'WEST AFRICA and the CONGO. INAUGURATION of the CONGO RAILWAY, MATADI (Congo River) to STANLEY POOL. Unique PERSONALLY-CONDUCTED TOUR, leaving London for Antwerp about 12th June, thence visiting Lisbon, Teneriffe, Canary Islands, Dakar, Gabon, Sierre Leone, St. Thomas, The Congo River, and Stanley Pool, returning by St. Helena, Ascension Island, Cape Verd, and Madeira to Antwerp, thence to London. Programme post-free from any office of THOS. COOK and SON. Chief office, Ludgate-circus, London.'

28 As in Conrad and Ford's *The Inheritors*: '... a little cosmopolitan Jew whose eyebrows began their growth on the bridge of his nose ... effusive and familiar, as the rest of his kind' (*I* 79).

29 Compare Conrad's description of *A Set of Six* in his typescript preface to *The Shorter Stories of Joseph Conrad*, now held at the Beinecke Rare Book & Manuscript Library, Yale University, as 'in Space [moving] from South America through England and Russia to end in the South of Italy.'

30 On Conrad's treatment of the anthropologist Alfred Wallace, his model for Stein, see Hampson, 2000: 73–8.

31 According to one historian of the Hajj, dying on pilgrimage 'was, at least in India, considered to be one of the 21 ways by which a Muslim could become a martyr, or *shahid*' (Pearson, 1994: 41).

32 This was unquestionably the same ship. *Lloyd's Register of Shipping Register of Ships* for 1886 lists the *Adowa* as a 1,538-ton, 150-horsepower iron steamer owned by Fenwick & Co, London, and currently operating out of Bombay; Conrad's certificate of discharge, dated 18 January 1894 and reprinted in Najder, 1984, describes the *Adowa* as a 150-horsepower steamer of 1,547 tons. In *Lord Jim*, the *Patna* is a 'fourteen-hundred-ton steamer' (*LJ* 30).

33 *Journal of Jaffir Ali Najuf Ali's Pilgrimage, Bombay to Mecca and back* (Appendix, No. 4), n.p.

34 'Conrad; By His Son', *Times* (7 October 1968): 8.

35 The *Times* of 16 February 1905 contains an illustrated advertisement for this latter.

36 Conrad remembered Corsica as 'a lovely island, but dangerous, – because of its drivers who are a public terror' (*LL* 2: 300).

37 In a letter of October 1918 Conrad refers to a 'motor-bandit' (*CL* 6: 287).

38 The film can be viewed online at <http://www.screenonline.org.uk/film/id/444674/#>.

39 *Chatham, Rochester, and Gillingham News* (27 August 1904): 8; (3 September 1904): 5. The national speed limit had been set at 20 m.p.h. because it was a key threshold for pedestrian fatality; by Conrad's own admission, their car had been doing 24 m.p.h. just minutes before. Whether the driver had joined Conrad in a 'brandy and soda' (*CL* 3: 159) is unknown. On Edwardian motorists' provocation of country-dwellers, see O'Connell, 1998: 166–7.

40 Conrad's familiarity with the General's predicament is suggested by his detailed road directions to visitors (*CL* 3: 353, 4: 209).

41 The cultural and philosophical dimensions of acceleration are discussed in Kern, 1983: 109–30.

42 'The Guide book is simply *magnificent*' (*CL* 2: 43), Conrad enthused to R. B. Cunninghame Graham after receiving a copy of his *Notes on the District of Menteith for Tourists and Others* (1895).

43 In *The Simple Life Limited*, Ford portrays Brandetski as visiting Brighton with 'a female companion' (Ford, 1911: 75). On the city's morally dubious reputation during this period, see Musgrave, 1970: 330–43.

44 On the politics of in early-twentieth-century pedestrianism see Solnit, 2001: 160–5, and Prynn, 1976. Speed and endurance walking received regular coverage in local and national newspapers at this time; the *Daily Mail*, for example, was running a column titled 'Country Walks Around London' in July 1910.

45 Compare *Nostromo*: 'Riding for [Charles Gould] was not a special form of exercise; it was a natural faculty, as walking straight is to all men sound of mind and limb' (*N* 48).

46 J. Charles Cox, the author of the Little Guides Series, notes that the years 1895–1906 saw the publication of an array of walking guides to Surrey (Cox, 1911: 4).

47 In 'The Duel' Conrad describes 'officers of infantry of the line' as having an imagination 'tamed by much walking exercise' and their valour as therefore being 'of a more plodding kind' (*SS* 165). There are also several references to tramping and pedestrian travelogues in *Suspense*.

48 Zoe Fyne's name recalls Zoe Pyne, who divorced Ford's brother Oliver Madox Hueffer (also an avid walker) in 1911.

49 As Conrad well knew, having himself fired a housemaid for being 'too unconventional': 'She would wander off and disappear for hours at a time. What she found to dream about on country roads in the mud and after dark I can't imagine' (*CL* 2: 120). Holidaying in 1921, he told Eric Pinker that the hotel guest-list included 'a few mature wandering women and a small proportion of (rather better class) frumps' (*LL* 255).

50 See Shaulis, 1999.

51 The setting may have been suggested by a quarry that Conrad mentions in a letter to William Rothenstein in 1906 (*CL* 3: 337).

3 Advertising

1 The Ludgate Hill incident led to the passing of a by-law prohibiting large sky-signs; a cartoon in the 1898 edition of *Successful Advertising* depicts an advertiser dreaming of swathing the dome of St Paul's with the legend 'Smith's Agency Is The Best.'

2 See Wicke, 1988; Garvey, 1996; Leonard, 1998. In *The Inheritors*, the accountant's admission to ' "teaching one of the native women" ' (*I* 68) to starch his linen is paralleled by the narratorial aside: 'They had taught the natives to use and to value sewing-machines and European costumes' (77). For illustrations of Huntley and Palmer's ornate tins, which Conrad called 'almost a national institution . . . probably known to all my readers' (*NLL* 182), see Opie, 1999: 17–21.

3 This and the following paragraphs rely heavily on Nevett, 1982. See also Benson, 1994, and Fitzgerald, 1995: 19–30.

4 *Tit-Bits*, 15 February 1890: 300.

5 Similar sentiments were voiced by J. Ashby-Sterry in *The Graphic* in December 1892. On Aestheticism's love-affair with advertising see Gagnier, 1986, and Freedman, 1990.

6 The boards in 'Karain' could have been advertising the *Daily Mail*, whose hoardings used this eye-catching colour combination on the express wishes of Alfred Harmsworth. See Fraser, 1981: 142–3. In *The Mirror of the Sea*, Conrad recalled staring in fascination at the 'letters, blue on white ground, on the advertisement-boards' (*MS* 131) that announced the names of ships in dock.

7 Hagberd's psychosis is even more pronounced in the stage version, *One Day More*: 'HAGBERD. But it's the right thing to do. Look at the Sunday papers. Missing relatives on top page – *all proper*' (Joseph Conrad, 1924: 87–8, emphasis added).

8 Paul Kirschner notes that in the MS version Hagberd's derangement is paralleled by the villagers' unfounded belief that an economic recovery is on the way (*T* 23).

9 A cottage piano, the model owned by Charles Pooter in George and Weedon Grossmith's *Diary of a Nobody* (1892), is also mentioned in *The Mirror of the Sea* and *Chance*. A contemporary historian noted that the ten-fold increase in piano production between 1869 and 1910 'was only made possible through the educational, artistic and advertising propaganda by the makers of high-grade pianos on the one hand, and the aggressive selling methods of the makers of commercial pianos on the other' (Dodge, 1911: 181).

10 'Waterbury, where the dollar watches come from,' remarks a character in Rudyard Kipling's 'The Captive' (Kipling, 1902: 49). On Waterbury advertising and the company's history, see McDermott, 1998. In *Lord Jim*, sheer boredom drives Jim to repair 'a nickel clock of New England make' (*LJ* 252).

11 See Waterbury Clock Company, 1983: 68–9.

12 This island of half a million square kilometres lies approximately 500 kilometres from Ile St Joseph; Paul remembers rowing for two days and sailing for several more. The narrator's description of a neighbouring city 'whose name, *let us say*, is Horta' (*SS* 137, emphasis added) actively invites

speculation as to its real identity. Marañon is the name of a tributary of the Amazon that runs through Peru.

13 Fitzgerald, *Rowntree*, 516.

14 Conrad may have been thinking of Carnegie's entrepreneurial manifesto *The Gospel of Wealth* (1889) when he referred dismissively to 'the gospel of the beastly bourgeois' (*CL* 1: 393).

15 In *The Arrow of Gold*, Henry Allègre is patronizingly described as 'the son of a confounded millionaire soap-boiler' (*AG* 47).

16 See *General Catalogue of 'Urban,' 'Eclipse,' 'Radios,' and 'Urbanora' Film Subjects* (1909).

17 For a contemporary advertisement for tinned food aimed at yachting parties, see Opie, 1985: 154.

18 Conrad's fictional preoccupation with eating is acutely examined in Tanner, 1976.

19 Quoted by permission of the Berg Collection of English and American Literature, The New York Public Library, Astor, Lenox and Tilden Foundations.

20 Shaddock notes that anarchists had been castigated by *Blackwood's Magazine* in 1901 as 'indolent monster[s], diseased with vanity, whose first and last desire is advertisement' (Shaddock, 1994: 56).

21 The following paragraphs are indebted to Hadley, 1972, in which many of the advertisements cited here are reproduced.

22 Bulwer Lytton is the favourite author of old Singleton in *The Nigger of the 'Narcissus'*; several of *The Coming Race*'s themes find echoes in Conrad and Ford's *The Inheritors*. Coincidentally, a Bos Whisky was being advertised in the 1900s, appearing alongside serial instalments of H. G. Wells's *War of the Worlds* in *Pearson's Magazine* in 1897. There was also a beef concentrate called Vimbos, 'The Prince of Fluid Beef'.

23 Conrad could have read about Barton's performance in nearby Maidstone on 27 April 1904 in local newspapers.

24 In *The Mirror of the Sea*, Conrad laments the disappearance of its maritime counterpart, the ornately carved figureheads that once made an 'open-air gallery of the New South Dock' (*MS* 130).

25 An advertisement in the *Daily Mail* on 24 September 1900 included praise for Bovril by Robert Baden-Powell and Rudyard Kipling as well as a lengthy testimonial by Henrietta Stannard. Edwin Arnold's endorsement of Bovril is mentioned in the *Saturday Review* of 3 October 1896.

26 The Caligraph Company, which employed Jessie Conrad until 1894 (*CL* 1: 265), seems to be the origin of Conrad's neologism in *An Outcast of the Islands*: 'a communication from Abdulla caligraphed carefully on a large sheet of flimsy paper' (*OI* 203).

27 On the marketing of Brazilian 'Fazenda' coffee in Britain in the early 1900s, see Turner, 1952: 149.

28 A double impossibility since James had long since been forced to rely on dictation as a result of what would today be diagnosed as Repetitive Strain Injury.

29 The heraldic insignia of the Korzeniowski family is reproduced in Knowles and Moore, 2000: 285.

30 Cocoa was often promoted in quasi-medical terms as 'healthful and sustaining'. See Fitzgerald, 1995: 93. When Doña Rita collapses in hysterics in

The Arrow of Gold, her servant asks Therese to 'go down and make a cup of chocolate for her Madame' (*AG* 235).

31 Discussing Edward Garnett's *The Breaking Point* in 1906, Conrad remarked: 'If the phrase weren't idiotic I would say that the play is too concentrated' (*CL* 3: 375).

32 Cloete expects the *Sagamore* to break from her moorings in Port Elizabeth harbour in Australia while the crew are safely ashore but in the event she runs aground in the English Channel during a freak storm. There are, it would seem, no sure things in marine insurance.

33 After Lord Northcliffe's death in 1922, Conrad noted approvingly that the baron's fortune 'was not made by sweating the worker or robbing the widow and the orphan' (Joseph Conrad, 1969: 194).

34 In 'The Black Mate', Captain Johns describes his first officer as 'the sort of man that was ready for anything; from pitch-and-toss to wilful murder, as the saying goes' (*TH* 108). Similarly, in *Victory*, Martin Ricardo boasts of being 'game for anything, from pitch and toss to wilful murder' (*V* 130).

35 On the growing demands for the pharmaceutical industry to be regulated, see Fraser, 1981: 139–41. On public perceptions of patent medicines and the industry's use of advertising see Richards, 1990: 168–204.

36 As the two-page entry for 'health' in *The Oxford Reader's Companion to Conrad* indicates, illness and medication were constant themes for the ailing Conrads, for whom the difference between scientific remedies and quack nostrums was often slight. See Bock, 2002.

37 Cloete's proposal to George is said to have 'struck in his mind' (*SS* 101) just as the *Sagamore* is twice described as having 'struck' the rocks (114, 117). Conrad presumably meant to write 'stuck in his mind' but the word is uncorrected in the typescript now held in the Polish Library, London.

38 After being fatally wounded by her father, Nostromo tells Giselle that 'the price of a charge of powder might have been saved' (*N* 558).

39 In a *Personal Record* Conrad recalled the 'house flag, all white with the letters F.C.T.C. artfully tangled up in a complicated monogram' of an 'ephemeral' Franco-Canadian Transport Company whose 'tricolour posters' had deceived employees into thinking themselves part of 'a large fleet with fortnightly departures for Montreal and Quebec as advertised in pamphlets and prospectuses which came aboard in a large package' (*PR* 6).

40 A suburb where Sherlock Holmes outwits a murderous swindler in 'The Adventure of the Norwood Builder' (1903). Conrad's portraits of 'far away' Leytonstone in 'The Black Mate', 'the distant desolation of Barking-town' in the manuscript of *The Rescue* (British Library, Ashley 4787 f. 18), and 'beyond Dalston, away to the devil' (*C* 18) in *Chance* reflect the wider antipathy towards suburbia among contemporary writers. See Keating, 1989: 320–6.

41 The Alhambra's Promenade was the scene of a 'riot' in November 1894 when Winston Churchill and other society 'bloods' tore down a screen intended to shield the prostitutes from public view. In the MS, Conrad's stevedore is also the manager of two music-halls. See Dalgarno, 1975: 41–4.

42 *Harper's* had made unauthorized cuts in 'The Partner'. As Dalgarno notes, this final section was added sometime between January 1912 and 1915 when Conrad had had time to reflect on the treatment of his text.

43 As Lawrence Graver notes, the tale is 'the only one of Conrad's forty-two works of fiction in which money allows a man and a woman to live happily ever after' (Graver, 1964–65: 165).

44 Since bank-savings accounts were uncommon among the lower-middle and working classes at this time, de Barral's swindle is itself distinctly *popular* in character. See Villa, 2000: 67–98.

45 Conrad here plays on the financial term *trust*. As Captain Anthony reflects, 'Trusted! A terrible word to any man somewhat exceptional in a world in which success has never been found in renunciation and good faith' (*C* 292–3).

46 In blaming this failure on landlubbers' knowledge that 'no matter what they do this tight little island won't turn turtle' (*C* 7), Powell echoes Conrad's observation in *Mirror of the Sea*: 'The risk of advertising [a ship] as able to sail without ballast is not great, since . . . . most ships will sail without ballast for some time before they turn turtle' (*MS* 46).

47 Conrad's meditation in 'Confidence' on the Red Ensign's status as a 'trade emblem, nationally expressive' (*NLL* 160) also echoes *Successful Advertising*'s description of the 'advertisement of British naval or mercantile power . . . by the flag itself flying at the mizen-mast head' (Smith, 1902: 151). Is it coincidence that de Barral chooses the common name 'Smith' as an alias? Marlow notes: 'I don't think that a mere Jones or Brown could have fished out from the depths of the Incredible such a colossal manifestation of human folly as that man did' (*C* 55). Thomas Smith was also the publisher of *The Travelling Partner*, a trade journal for salesmen.

4   Magazine Fiction

1 See Carter and Weston, 1903.

2 See Kirschner, 1968: 206–28; Hervouet, 1990; Carabine, 1992, 4: 98–143; Dryden, 2000; and White, 1993.

3 See, however, the chapter on Conrad in Peck, 2001: 165–85.

4 'They [*A Set of Six*] are just stories in which I've tried my best to be simply entertaining' (*CL* 4: 30), Conrad explained to Algernon Methuen. On W. W. Jacobs see Cloy, 1996. John Conrad recalled that his father's bedside library contained a volume of Jacobs's stories (Conrad, 1981: 149).

5 On the publication of Filippo Marinetti's manifesto 'The Variety Hall' in the *Daily Mail* and the coverage of his activities in mass-circulation magazines such as the *Sketch* and the *Graphic* see Rainey, 1998: 32–7. See also Morrisson, 2001: 3–16 and 84–132.

6 See also Cawelti, 1976.

7 The term 'penny blood' refers to the violent horror serials published by Edward Lloyd and George Reynolds at mid-century as a sensational alternative to the 'morally improving' literature sponsored by middle-class reformers. See James, 1963: 28–44.

8 For examples of the growing interest in Conrad's magazine fiction, see Erdinast-Vulcan, 1999; Billy, 2003; and the 'Conrad and Serialization' double-issue of *Conradiana* forthcoming in Spring–Summer 2006.

9 A definition of 'living' that greatly exceeded the expectations of most contemporaries. On Conrad's bohemian spending habits see Carabine, 1996: 4–6.

10 Such bluster did not prevent Conrad from writing what he called a '"nicer" ending' (*CL* 5: 49) for *Chance*'s readers in the *New York Herald* in 1912. See Jones, 1999: 154–60; and Reid, 2003: 73.

11 See in this connection Donovan, 1999.

12 Stories and popular novels in this category include: Anon, 1882; Landers, 1883; Anon, 1892; Cutcliffe Hyne, 1897; Strang, 1904 and 1906; Graydon, 1907; and 'A Congo Resident', 1910.

13 See McDonald, 1997: 24–5.

14 On the *Pictorial Review*'s serialization and illustration of *The Rover*, see Jones, 1999: 165–9.

15 In 1896, H. G. Wells wrote to the unknown author of *An Outcast of the Islands*: 'Since you don't make the slightest concessions to the reading young woman who makes or mars the fortunes of authors, it is the manifest duty of a reviewer to differentiate between you and the kind of people we thrust into the "Fiction" at the end, the Marples and Schoolbreds of literature' (Stape and Knowles, 1996: 21).

16 See *CL* 2: 137–8, 2: 216, 2: 298, 3: 3–4, 3: 488, 4: 458; and Jones, 2002.

17 *Lord Jim*'s massive over-run in *Blackwood's* may have exacerbated Conrad's fears that he was trespassing upon the patience of William Blackwood, whom he had also asked to be the guarantor for a life insurance policy.

18 Pinker's £100 advance on the serial sale dwarfed the £40 Conrad had received from *Blackwood's* for *Heart of Darkness*, his only other novella to date. Conrad later claimed that his agent 'had the greatest difficulty in placing that story and ultimately had to let it go for a few pence so to speak' (*CL* 3: 320).

19 See Rutenburg, 1984.

20 On the special status of such 'popular middle-class fiction' as a cultural dominant around 1900, see Daly, 1999: 4–9.

21 In Max Beerbohm's witty parody of a Conrad short story, a colonial official awakens on Christmas morning to find himself the principal item on a cannibal menu (Beerbohm, 1950).

22 W. Clark Russell had recently published 'Christmas Day at Sea' in *Temple Magazine* in October 1899. For a typical example of this genre of article, see Raife, 1914–15.

23 For a detailed analysis of Conrad's stylistic revisions to 'Typhoon', see Purdy, 1987: 104–10.

24 In 1902, Conrad briefly considered submitting the novella that became *Nostromo* to the Northern Newspaper Syndicate (*CL* 2: 455; 3: 22) and in 1911 he complained to Pinker: 'The N[orther]n Newspaper Synd[ica]te Kendal are everlastingly writing to me' (4: 462). The Syndicate's origins are discussed in Law, 2000: 99–100.

25 See also Birrell, 1980.

26 See also Ohmann, 1998: 297–312.

27 See Lucas, 2003.

28 Begun sometime after 4 January 1906, 'The Brute' (8000 words) had been completed by 21 February; *Heart of Darkness* (38,000 words) was begun in

mid-December 1898 and finished by 6 February 1899. In this context it is worth recalling that *New Grub Street*, George Gissing's classic satire on magazine writing, was written at the rate of nine pages a day.

29 'The Brute' is the only Conrad work on the list of 'One Hundred Representative Short Stories' appended by J. Berg Esenwein, editor of *Lippincott's Magazine*, to his handbook *Writing the Short-Story*. See also Dalgarno, 1977.

30 Compare also Conrad's plot summaries of 'Amy Foster', 'Falk', and 'To-morrow' in *CL* 2: 401–3.

31 In *The Edge of Circumstance*, the flawed design of the ship is motivated by considerations of safety alone.

32 *McClure's Magazine* 30/1 (November 1907): 24 (i–iii) and 36. The instalment of *The Secret Agent* that appeared in *Ridgway's* for 17 November 1906 was set alongside an advertisement for a 'Self-Working Washer' (Reid, 2003: 86).

33 On women's role in the cultural imaginary of modern magazines and the promotion of 'the class project of modernity', see Ohmann, 1998: 270–2 and 312–29.

34 In her examination of the similarities between 'The Brute' and Wilkie Collins's 'A Very Strange Bed' (1856), Barbara H. Solomon does not mention the appearance of Conrad's tale in a magazine (Solomon, 1975).

35 Conrad believed that *Romance*, a tale of Caribbean piracy, might be successfully marketed on the basis of its popular romance 'formula' (*CL* 2: 357), which included 'easy style, plenty of action, a romantic atmosphere and a happy ending after no end of hair's breadth escapes' (2: 366).

Conclusion

1 Blondin performed his celebrated high-wire act at the World's Fair in December 1898 and an advertisement for the venue in the *Times* on 26 December 1898 listed 'giant women . . . midgets, freaks, and other odd persons and strange things' among the treats in store for the curious.

2 See Hay, 1963; Fleishman, 1967; Van Domelen, 1970; Donovan, 2002; Nohrnberg, 2003; Rubery, 2004.

Works Cited

'A Congo Resident.' *Bokwala: The Story of a Congo Victim*. London: Religious Tract Society, 1910.

Adorno, Theodore. *Theodore Adorno: The Stars Down to Earth and Other Essays on the Irrational in Culture*. Ed. Stephen Crook. London: Routledge, 1994.

Allen, Grant. 'Miss Cayley's Adventures. II. The Adventure of the Supercilious Attaché.' *Strand Magazine* XV/88 (April 1898): 424–35.

Allen, Vio. 'Memories of Joseph Conrad.' *Review of English Literature* 8/2 (April 1967): 77–90.

'An Editor.' *How to Write for the Press: A Practical Handbook for Beginners in Journalism*. London: Horace Cox, 1904.

Andrén, Arvid. *Capri: Från stenaldern till turiståldern*. Lund: Svenska Humanistiska Förbundet, 1975.

Anon (J. Landers). 'The Story of James Barker: A Tale of the Congo Coast.' *Blackwood's Magazine* 132/804 (October 1882): 495–523.

Anon. 'Picturesque London; or Sky-Signs of the Times.' *Punch* (6 September 1890): 119.

Anon. 'Fida: A Congo Story.' *Belgravia Magazine* 78 (1892): 183–9.

Anon. 'The Romance of Commerce: The Story of the Great Businesses. III. – The Business of Travel.' *The Young Man* (December 1900): 159–61.

Anon. *How To Walk: The Whole Art of Training Without a Trainer*. London: Evening News, 1904.

Anon. 'The March of Events.' *The World's Work* XII/1 (May 1906): 7469–87.

Anon. 'Rambling.' *Punch* 136 (17 February 1909a): 114–15.

Anon. 'Scented Corsica.' *Cook's Traveller's Gazette* 59/2 (March 1909b): 15.

Anthony, Barry. *The Kinora*. London: The Projection Box, 1996.

'A.W.' 'First Attempts at Photography. No. I.' *Pearson's Magazine* 1/1 (June 1896): 43–4.

Baldanza, Frank. 'Opera in Conrad: "More Real than Anything in Life."' *Studies in the Literary Imagination* 13 (1980): 1–16.

Barnard, Charles. 'The New Photography.' *Chautauquan* 20/1 (April 1896): 75–79.

Barnes, John. *The Beginnings of Cinema in England: 1894–1901*. 5 vols. Exeter: University of Exeter Press, 1996–98.

Batchelor, John. *The Life of Joseph Conrad: A Critical Biography*. Oxford: Blackwell, 1994.

Baudelaire, Charles. 'The Modern Public and Photography.' *Classic Essays on Photography*. Ed. Alan Trachtenberg. New Haven, CT: Leete's Island Books, 1980. 83–9.

Beardsley, Aubrey, with Jules Cheret and Dudley Hardy. 'The Art of the Hoarding', *New Review* (July 1894): 47–55.

Beerbohm, Max. *A Survey*. London: Heinemann, 1921.

Beerbohm, Max. 'The Feast.' *A Christmas Garland*. London: Heinemann, 1950. 129–34.

Beerbohm, Max. *Around Theatres*. London: Rupert Hart-Davis, 1953.

Beetham, Margaret. 'Towards a Theory of the Periodical as a Publishing Genre.' *Investigating Victorian Journalism*. Ed. Laurel Brake, Aled Jones and Lionel Madden. Basingstoke: Macmillan, 1990. 19–32.

Benson, John. *The Rise of Consumer Society in Britain, 1880–1980*. London: Longman, 1994.

Berthoud, Jacques. 'Narrative and Ideology: A Critique of Fredric Jameson's *The Political Unconscious*.' *Narrative: From Malory to Motion Pictures*. Ed. Jeremy Hawthorn. London: Stratford-upon-Avon Studies, 1985. 100–15.

Billy, Ted. *A Wilderness of Words: Closure and Disclosure in Conrad's Short Fiction*. Lubbock: Texas Tech University Press, 2003.

Birrell, T. A. 'The Simplicity of *Typhoon*: Conrad, Flaubert and Others.' *Dutch Quarterly Review of Anglo-American Letters* 10 (1980): 272–95.

Blackburn, William, ed. *Joseph Conrad: Letters to William Blackwood and David S. Meldrum*. Durham, NC: Duke University Press, 1958.

Bloom, Clive. *Bestsellers: Popular Fiction Since 1900*. Basingstoke: Palgrave Macmillan, 2002.

Bock, Martin. *Joseph Conrad and Psychological Medicine*. Lubbock: Texas Tech University Press, 2002.

Bojarski, Edmund A. 'Conrad at the Crossroads: From Navigator to Novelist with Some New Biographical Mysteries.' *Texas Quarterly* XI/4 (Winter 1968): 15–29.

Booth, Michael R. *Victorian Spectacular Theatre 1850–1910*. London: Routledge, 1981.

Bourdieu, Pierre. *Distinction: A Social Critique of the Judgement of Taste*. Trans. Richard Nice. Cambridge, MA: Harvard University Press, 1984.

Brantlinger, Patrick. *Bread & Circuses: Theories of Mass Culture and Social Decay*. Ithaca, NY: Cornell University Press, 1983.

Brantlinger, Patrick. *Rule of Darkness: British Literature and Imperialism, 1830–1914*. Ithaca, NY: Cornell University Press, 1988.

Brewster, Ben. *Theatre to Cinema: Stage Pictorialism and the Early Feature Film*. Oxford: Oxford University Press, 1997.

Bridgewater, Howard. *Advertising, or the Art of Making Known*. London: Pitman, 1910.

Brown, Bill. *The Material Unconscious: American Amusement, Stephen Crane, and the Economies of Play*. Cambridge, MA: Harvard University Press, 1996.

Buchanan, Robert W. 'The Voice of "the Hooligan."' *Contemporary Review* 76 (December 1899): 774–89.

Bufkin, E. C. 'Conrad, Grand Opera, and *Nostromo*.' *Nineteenth Century Fiction* 30 (1975): 206–14.

Bull, Albert E. *How to Write for the Papers: A Guide for the Young Author*. London: Arthur Pearson, 1912.

Buzard, James. *The Beaten Track: European Tourism, Literature, and the Ways to Culture, 1800–1918*. Oxford: Clarendon Press, 1993.

Cain, P. J., and A. G. Hopkins. *British Imperialism: Innovation and Expansion, 1688–1914*. London: Longman, 1993.

Calkins, Ernest, and Ralph Holden. *The Art of Modern Advertising*. London: Appleton, 1905.

Carabine, Keith. '"The Black Mate": June–July 1886; January 1908.' *The Conradian* 13 (1988): 128–48.

Carabine, Keith, ed. *Joseph Conrad: Critical Assessments*. 4 vols. Mountfield: Helm Information, 1992.

Carabine, Keith. *The Life and The Art: A Study of Conrad's 'Under Western Eyes'*. Amsterdam: Rodopi, 1996.

Carey, John. *The Intellectuals and the Masses: Pride and Prejudice Among the Literary Intelligentsia, 1880–1939*. London: Faber, 1992.

Carr, Helen. 'Modernism and Travel, 1880–1940.' *The Cambridge Companion to Travel Writing*. Ed. Peter Hulme and Tim Youngs. Cambridge: Cambridge University Press, 2002. 70–86.

Carter, Frank W., and Robert P. Weston. *The Bald-Headed Man*. London: Francis, Day & Hunter, 1903.

Cartwright, Lisa. *Screening the Body: Tracing Medicine's Visual Culture*. Minneapolis: University of Minnesota Press, 1995.

Cawelti, John G. *Adventure, Mystery, and Romance: Formula Stories as Art and Popular Culture*. Chicago: University of Chicago Press, 1976.

Ceram, C. W. *Archaeology of the Cinema*. Trans. Richard Winston. London: Thames and Hudson, 1965.

Chanan, Michael. *The Dream That Kicks: The Prehistory and Early Years of Cinema in Britain*. London: Routledge, 1980.

Chapman, Pauline. *Madame Tussaud's Chamber of Horrors: Two Hundred Years of Gruesome Murder*. London: Grafton Books, 1984.

Chesterton, G. K. *The Man Who Was Thursday*. Bristol: Arrowsmith, 1908.

Cholmondeley, Mary. 'An Art in its Infancy.' *Monthly Review* 3 (June 1901): 79–90.

Christie, Ian. *The Last Machine: Early Cinema and the Birth of the Modern World*. London: British Film Institute, 1994.

Church, Roy. 'Advertising Consumer Goods in Nineteenth-Century Britain: Reinterpretations.' *Economic History Review* 53/4 (2000): 621–45.

Cloy, John D. *Pensive Jester: The Literary Career of W. W. Jacobs*. Lanham, MD: University Press of America, 1996.

Cohen, Scott. 'The Empire from the Street: Virginia Woolf, Wembley, and Imperial Monuments.' *Modern Fiction Studies* 50/1 (Spring 2004): 85–109.

Collits, Terry. 'Jewel in the Crown: Desire, Popular Culture and *Lord Jim*'. *Epoque Conradienne* 30 (2004): 19–28.

Conrad, Borys. *My Father: Joseph Conrad*. London: Calder & Boyars, 1970.

Conrad, Jessie. *A Handbook of Cookery for a Small House*. London: Heinemann, 1923.

Conrad, John. *Joseph Conrad: Times Remembered*. Cambridge: Cambridge University Press, 1981.

Conrad, Joseph. *Laughing Anne & One Day More*. Introduction by John Galsworthy. London: John Castle, 1924.

Conrad, Joseph. *Letters to R. B. Cunninghame Graham*. Ed. C. T. Watts. Cambridge: Cambridge University Press, 1969.

Cook, John. *The Mecca Pilgrimage*. Privately printed. London: Thomas Cook and Sons, 1886.

Cook, Olive. *Movement in Two Dimensions: A Study of the Animated and Projected Pictures which Preceded the Invention of Cinematography*. London: Hutchinson, 1963.

Cook, Thomas. *Cook's Tourist's Handbook for Southern Italy*. London: Thomas Cook, 1905.

Cook, Victor W. 'The Humours of "Living Picture" Making.' *Chambers's Journal* 6s 3/135. 30 June 1900.

Cooper, Frederic Taber. *Some English Story Tellers*. London: Grant Richards, 1912.

Coroneos, Con. *Space, Conrad, and Modernity*. Cambridge: Cambridge University Press, 2002.

Cox, J. Charles. *Rambles in Surrey*. London: Methuen, 1911.

Crane, Stephen. *The Work of Stephen Crane. Volume IV. Active Service*. Ed. Wilson Follett. New York: Knopf, 1926.

Crangle, Richard. 'Saturday Night at the X-Rays: The Moving Picture and "The New Photography" in Britain, 1896.' *Celebrating Cinema: The Centenary of Cinema*. Ed. John Fullerton. Sydney: John Libbey, 1998. 138–44.

Crary, Jonathan. *Suspensions of Perception: Attention, Spectacle, and Modern Culture*. Cambridge, MA: The MIT Press, 1999.

Cunninghame Graham, R. B. ' "Bloody Niggers." ' *Social-Democrat* 3 (March 1897): 104–9.

Cunninghame Graham, R. B. 'Bovril.' *Justice* (22 July 1911): 8.

Curle, Richard. *The Last Twelve Years of Joseph Conrad*. London: Sampson Low, 1928a.

Curle, Richard, ed. *Conrad to a Friend: 150 Selected Letters from Joseph Conrad to Richard Curle*. London: Sampson Low, Marston, 1928b.

Cutcliffe Hyne, C. J. 'The Transfer.' *Pall Mall Magazine* 13 (December 1897): 495–507.

Cutcliffe Hyne, C. J. *The Adventures of Captain Kettle*. Preston: James Askew, 1899.

Dalgarno, Emily K. 'The Textual History of Conrad's "The Partner." ' *The Library* 5th series xxx (1975): 41–4.

Dalgarno, Emily K. 'Conrad, Pinker, and the Writing of *The Secret Agent*.' *Conradiana* 9/1 (1977): 47–58.

Daly, Nicholas. *Modernism, Romance and the* Fin de Siècle: *Popular Fiction and British Culture, 1880–1914*. Cambridge: Cambridge University Press, 1999.

Danius, Sara. *The Senses of Modernism: Technology, Perception, and Aesthetics*. Ithaca, NY: Cornell University Press, 2002.

Day, Lewis F. 'Art in Advertising.' *Art Journal* 13 (February 1897): 49–53.

Deming, Robert H. *James Joyce: The Critical Heritage: Volume One*. London: Routledge, 1970.

Dodge, Alfred. *Pianos and Their Makers*. Covina, CA: Covina Publishing, 1911.

Donovan, Stephen. 'Figures, Facts, Theories: Conrad and Chartered Company Imperialism.' *The Conradian* 24/2 (Autumn 1999): 31–60.

Donovan, Stephen. 'That Newspaper Fellow – What's His Name: Joseph Conrad on W. T. Stead.' *NewsStead: A Journal of History and Literature* 17 (Fall 2000): 3–10.

Donovan, Stephen. 'Prosaic Newspaper Stunts: Conrad, Modernity and the Press.' *Conrad at the Millennium: Modernism, Postmodernism, Postcolonialism*. Ed. Gail Fincham. Boulder, CO: Social Science Monographs, 2002. 53–72.

Driver, Felix. *Geography Militant: Cultures of Exploration and Empire*. Oxford: Blackwell, 2001.

Dryden, Linda. *Joseph Conrad and the Imperial Romance*. Basingstoke: Macmillan, 2000.

Dryden, Linda. ' "To Boldly Go": Conrad's *Heart of Darkness* and Popular Culture.' *Conradiana* 34/3 (Fall 2002): 149–70.

Dutheil de la Rochère, Martine Hennard. 'Conrad's Anatomy of Empire in *Heart of Darkness:* Body Politics and The Hollow Men of Empire.' *Conrad In The Twenty-first Century: Contemporary Approaches And Perspectives.* Ed. Carola Kaplan, Peter Mallios, and Andrea White. London: Routledge, forthcoming 2005.

Easthope, Anthony. *Literary into Cultural Studies.* London: Routledge, 1991.

Eliot, T. S. *Complete Poems and Plays.* London: Faber, 1989.

England, George Allan. 'A Message from the Moon: The Story of a Great Coup.' *Pearson's Magazine* 23/136 (April 1907): 376–81.

Erdinast-Vulcan, Daphna. *The Strange Short Fiction of Joseph Conrad: Writing, Culture, and Subjectivity.* Oxford: Oxford University Press, 1999.

Erdinast-Vulcan, Daphna, Allan H. Simmons, and J. H. Stape, eds. *Joseph Conrad: The Short Fiction.* Rodopi: Amsterdam, 2004.

Esenwein, J. Berg. *Writing the Short-Story: A Practical Handbook on the Rise, Structure, Writing, and Sale of the Modern Short-Story.* London: Melrose, 1912.

Evans, Richardson. 'The Age of Disfigurement.' *National Review* XVI/92 (October 1890): 166–82.

Fahlbeck, Anders. *Ellen Key – Strand, Axel Munthe – Villa San Michele.* Linköping: Nova Print, 1998.

Fielding, Raymond. 'Hale's Tours: Ultra-Realism in the pre-1910 Motion Picture.' *Smithsonian Journal* 3/4 (Winter 1968–9): 101–24.

Fitzgerald, Robert. *Rowntree and the Marketing Revolution.* Cambridge: Cambridge University Press, 1995.

Fleishman, Aaron. *Conrad's Politics: Community and Anarchy in the Fiction of Joseph Conrad.* Baltimore: Johns Hopkins University Press, 1967.

Ford, Ford Madox (pseud. Daniel Chaucer). *The Simple Life Limited.* London: John Lane, 1911.

Fowler, Nathaniel C. *About Advertising and Printing.* Boston: Thyer and Co, 1889.

Fraser, Gail. 'The Short Fiction.' *The Cambridge Companion to Joseph Conrad.* Ed. J. H. Stape. Cambridge: Cambridge University Press, 1996. 25–44.

Fraser, Robert. *Proust and the Victorians.* Basingstoke: Macmillan, 1994.

Fraser, W. Hamish. *The Coming of the Mass Market, 1850–1914.* London: Macmillan, 1981.

Freedman, Jonathan. *Professions of Taste: Henry James, British Aestheticism, and Commodity Culture.* Stanford, CA: Stanford University Press, 1990.

Fritz, Walter. *Dokumentarfilme aus Österreich 1909–1914.* Wien: Schriftenreihe des Österreichischen Filmarchiv, 1980.

'G.' *The Perfect Holiday: A Talk About Walking Tours.* London: Hodge and Co, n.d. [1908].

Gagnier, Reginia. *Idylls of the Marketplace: Oscar Wilde and the Victorian Reading Public.* Palo Alto, CA: Stanford University Press, 1986.

Garvey, Ellen Gruber. *The Adman in the Parlor: Magazines and the Gendering of Consumer Culture, 1880s to 1910s.* New York: Oxford University Press, 1996.

Gatrell, V. A. C. *The Hanging Tree: Execution and the English People, 1770–1868.* Oxford: Oxford University Press, 1994.

Gissing, George. *In The Year of Jubilee.* London: Everyman, 1994.

Goodyear, R. A. H. *Tale-Writing for Money.* Southport: Magazine Syndicate, n.d. [1908].

Graver, Lawrence. 'Conrad's First Story.' *Studies in Short Fiction* 2/2 (1964–65): 164–9.

Graydon, W. Murray. 'Sexton Blake in the Congo.' *The Boys' Friend.* 22 parts. 26 January–22 June 1907.

Griffith, George. 'A Photograph of the Invisible.' *Pearson's Magazine* 1/25 (December 1896): 376–80.

Griffith, John W. *Joseph Conrad and the Anthropological Dilemma: 'Bewildered Traveller'.* Oxford: Clarendon Press, 1995.

Gunning, Tom. 'The Cinema of Attractions: Early Film, Its Spectators and the Avant-Garde.' *Early Cinema: Space, Frame, Narrative.* Ed. Thomas Elsaesser and Adam Barker. London: BFI, 1990. 56–62.

Gunning, Tom. 'An Aesthetic of Astonishment: Early Film and the (In) Credulous Spectator.' *Viewing Positions: Ways of Seeing.* Ed. Linda Williams. New Brunswick, NJ: Rutgers University Press, 1995a. 114–33.

Gunning, Tom. 'Tracing the Individual Body: Photography, Detectives, and Early Cinema.' *Cinema and the Invention of Modern Life.* Ed. Leo Charney and Vanessa R. Schwartz. Berkeley: University of California Press, 1995b. 15–45.

Gunning, Tom. 'Phantom Images and Modern Manifestations: Spirit Photography, Magic Theater, Trick Films, and Photography's Uncanny.' *Fugitive Images: From Photography to Video.* Ed. Patrice Petro. Bloomington: Indiana University Press, 1995c. 42–71.

Gutsche, Thelma. *The History and Social Significance of Motion Pictures in South Africa 1895–1940.* Cape Town: Howard Timmins, 1972.

Hadley, Peter. *History of Bovril Advertising.* London: Bovril, 1972.

Hamilton, Carol Vanderveer. 'Revolution From Within: Conrad's Natural Anarchists.' *The Conradian* 18/2 (Summer 1994): 31–48.

Hampson, Robert. '"Topographical Mysteries": Conrad and London.' *Conrad's Cities: Essays for Hans van Marle.* Ed. Gene M. Moore. Amsterdam: Rodopi, 1992. 159–74.

Hampson, Robert. 'Storytellers and Storytelling in "The Partner," "The Informer," "The Lesson of the Master" and *The Sacred Fount*.' *Conrad, James and Other Relations.* Ed. Keith Carabine and Owen Knowles. Boulder, CO: Social Science Monographs, 1998. 123–46.

Hampson, Robert. *Cross-Cultural Encounters in Joseph Conrad's Malay Fiction.* Basingstoke: Palgrave, 2000.

Hand, Richard J. 'Staging an "Unbearable Spectacle": Joseph Conrad's *Laughing Anne*.' *Studies in Theatre and Performance* 21/2 (2001): 109–17.

Hand, Richard J. 'Producing *Laughing Anne*.' *Conradiana* 34/1–2 (Spring–Summer 2002): 43–62.

Hand, Richard J. '"Loving and Killing: the Two Great Adventures in Life": Maurice Tourneur's 1919 Screen Version of Joseph Conrad's *Victory*.' *Conradiana* 35/3 (Fall 2003): 226–36.

Hand, Richard J. and Michael Wilson. *Grand-Guignol: The French Theatre of Horror.* Exeter: University of Exeter Press, 2002.

Harding, Colin and Simon Popple, eds. *In the Kingdom of the Shadows: A Companion to Early Cinema.* London: Cygnus Arts, 1996.

Hawthorn, Jeremy. 'Introduction.' *Under Western Eyes.* Oxford: Oxford University Press, 2002.

Hawthorn, Jeremy. 'The Richness of Meanness: Joseph Conrad's "To-morrow" and James Joyce's "Eveline." ' *Literary Sinews: Essays in Honour of Bjørn Tysdahl.*

Ed. Jakob Lothe, Juan Christian Pellicer, and Tore Rem. Oslo: Novus Press, 2003. 107–20.

Hay, Eloise Knapp. *The Political Novels of Joseph Conrad: A Critical Study*. Chicago: University of Chicago Press, 1963.

Hayes, Michael. 'Popular Fiction and Middle-Brow Taste.' *Literature and Culture in Modern Britain, Volume One: 1900–1929*. Ed. Clive Bloom. London: Longman, 1993. 76–99.

Hepworth, T. C. *The Book of the Lantern, Being a Practical Guide to the Working of the Optical (or Magic) Lantern*. London: Hazell, Watson, and Viney, 1894.

Hervouet, Yves. *The French Face of Joseph Conrad*. Cambridge: Cambridge University Press, 1990.

Hichens, Robert Smythe. *The Green Carnation*. New York: Appleton and Co, 1895.

Hiley, Nicholas. '"At the Picture Palace": The British Cinema Audience, 1895–1920.' *Celebrating Cinema: The Centenary of Cinema*. Ed. John Fullerton. Sydney: John Libbey, 1998. 96–103.

Hill, Howard. *Freedom to Roam: The Struggle for Access to Britain's Moors and Mountains*. Ashbourne, Derbyshire: Moorland Publishing, 1980.

Hobsbawm, Eric. *The Age of Empire, 1875–1914*. New York: Vintage Books, 1989.

Hobsbawm, Eric and Terence Ranger, eds. *The Invention of Tradition*. Cambridge: Cambridge University Press, 1983.

Hockenjos, Vreni. 'Facing Death with Moving Images: Strindberg's Protocinematic Figurations of a Life Passed By.' *Allegories of Communication: Intermedial Concerns from Cinema to the Digital*. Ed. Jan Olsson. Berkeley: University of California Press, 2005.

Hoppenstand, Gary. 'Afterword.' *The Lost Continent: The Story of Atlantis by C. J. Cutcliffe Hyne*. Lincoln, NE: University of Nebraska Press, 2002. 241–57.

Houston, Amy. 'Joseph Conrad Takes the Stage: Dramatic Irony in *The Secret Agent*.' *Conradian* 23/2 (Autumn 1998): 55–69.

Howard, Merriden. 'Wonders of the Waxwork World.' *Pearson's Magazine* 4/22 (October 1897): 388–392.

Hughes, Douglas A. 'Conrad's "Il Conde": "A Deucedly Queer Story."' *Conradiana* 7/19 (Fall 1975): 17–25.

Hugill, Stan. *Shanties from the Seven Seas*. London: Routledge, 1961.

Humphries, Steve. *Victorian Britain Through the Magic Lantern*. London: Sidgwick & Jackson, 1989.

Hunter, Allan. *Joseph Conrad and the Ethics of Darwinism: The Challenges of Science*. London: Croom Helm, 1983.

Jackson, Kate. *George Newnes and the New Journalism in Britain, 1880–1910: Culture and Profit*. Aldershot: Ashgate, 2001.

James, Louis. *Fiction for the Working Man, 1830–1850*. London: Oxford University Press, 1963.

Jameson, Fredric. *The Political Unconscious: Narrative as a Socially Symbolic Act*. London: Methuen, 1981.

Jean-Aubry, G. 'Joseph Conrad and Music.' *The Chesterian* 6 (November 1924): 37–42.

Jones, Susan. 'The Three Texts of *Chance*.' *The Conradian* 21/1 (Spring 1996): 57–78.

Jones, Susan. *Conrad and Women*. Oxford: Oxford University Press, 1999.

Jones, Susan. ' "Creatures of Our Light Literature": The Problem of Genre in *The Inheritors* and Marie Corelli's *A Romance of Two Worlds.*' *Conradiana* 34/1–2 (Spring–Summer 2002): 107–21.

Joy, Neill R. 'The Conrad–Hastings Correspondence and the Staging of *Victory.*' *Conradiana* 35/3 (Fall 2003): 184–225.

Joyce, James. *Letters.* Ed. Stuart Gilbert and Richard Ellmann. 3 vols. New York: Viking Press, 1966.

Joyce, James. *Ulysses: The Corrected Text.* Ed. Hans Walter Gabler with Wolfhard Steppe and Claus Melchior. Harmondsworth: Penguin, 1986.

Karl, Frederick. *Joseph Conrad: The Three Lives.* New York: Farrar, Straus & Giroux, 1979.

Keating, George T. *A Conrad Memorial Library.* Garden City, NY: Doubleday, 1929.

Keating, Peter. *The Haunted Study: A Social History of the English Novel: 1875–1914.* London: Secker & Warburg, 1989.

Keith Summers Collection C1002/71, National Sound Archive, British Library.

Kern, Stephen. *The Culture of Time and Space, 1880–1930.* Cambridge, MA: Harvard University Press, 1983.

Kipling, Rudyard. *Traffics and Discoveries.* Harmondsworth: Penguin, 1987.

Kirschner, Paul. *Conrad: The Psychologist as Artist.* Edinburgh: Oliver and Boyd, 1968.

Kittler, Friedrich A. *Gramophone, Film, Typewriter.* Trans. Geoffrey Winthrop-Young and Michael Wutz. Stanford, CA: Stanford University Press, 1999.

Klein, Naomi. *No Logo.* London: Flamingo, 2001.

Knelman, Judith. *Twisting in the Wind: The Murderess and the English Press.* Toronto: University of Toronto Press, 1988.

Knowles, Owen and Gene M. Moore. *Oxford Reader's Companion to Conrad.* Oxford: Oxford University Press, 2000.

Landers, J. 'On the Congo: A Sketch.' *Tinsley's Magazine* 33 (1883): 334–49.

Lang, Andrew. 'The Spectre and the Camera.' *Illustrated London News* CVII/2933 (6 July 1895): 14.

Law, Graham. *Serializing Fiction in the Victorian Press.* Basingstoke: Palgrave, 2000.

Leavis, F. R. *The Great Tradition: George Eliot, Henry James, Joseph Conrad.* Harmondsworth: Penguin, 1974.

Leonard, Gary. *Advertising and Commodity Culture in Joyce.* Gainesville, FL: University of Florida Press, 1998.

Letcher, Owen. *Big-Game Hunting in North-Eastern Rhodesia.* London: Long, 1911.

London, Jack. *The People of the Abyss.* London: Journeyman Press, 1978.

Loomis, Charles Battell. 'How to Write a Novel for the Masses.' *Atlantic Monthly* 521 (March 1901): 421–4.

Low, Rachael, and Roger Manvell. *The History of the British Film 1896–1906.* London: Allen & Unwin, 1948.

Lucas, Michael. 'Rehabilitating "The Brute." ' *The Conradian* 28/2 (Autumn 2003): 61–71.

Luckhurst, Roger. 'W. T. Stead's Occult Economies.' *Culture and Science in the Nineteenth-Century Media.* Ed. Louise Henson et al. Aldershot: Ashgate, 2004. 125–35.

MacKenzie, John M., ed. *Imperialism and Popular Culture.* Manchester: Manchester University Press, 1986.

Magnus, George. *How to Write Saleable Fiction*. London: Cambridge Literary Agency, n.d. [1910].

Mallios, Peter Lancelot. 'Declaring *Victory*: Toward Conrad's Poetics of Democracy.' *Conradiana* 35/3 (Fall 2003): 145–83.

Martell, Joanne. *Millie-Christine: Fearfully and Wonderfully Made*. Winston-Salem, NC: John F. Blair Publishing, 1999.

Marx, Karl. *Capital: A Critique of Political Economy: Volume One*. Trans. Ben Fowkes. Harmondsworth: Penguin, 1976.

McCracken, Scott. 'Postmodernism, a *Chance* to Reread?' *Cultural Politics at the Fin de Siècle*. Ed. Sally Ledger and Scott McCracken. Cambridge: Cambridge University Press, 1995. 267–89.

McDermott, Kathleen. *Timex, A Company and Its Community 1854–1998*. New York: Timex, 1998.

McDonald, Peter D. *British Literary Culture and Publishing Practice, 1880–1914*. Cambridge: Cambridge University Press, 1997.

McLaughlan, Juliet. 'Conrad's "Decivilized" Cities.' *Conrad's Cities: Essays for Hans van Marle*. Ed. Gene M. Moore. Amsterdam: Rodopi, 1992. 57–84.

Meller, H. E. *Leisure and the Changing City, 1870–1914*. London: Boston, 1976.

Metz, Christian. *Film Language: A Semiotics of the Cinema*. Trans. Michael Taylor. New York: Oxford University Press, 1974.

Moore, Gene M., ed. *Conrad's Cities: Essays for Hans van Marle*. Amsterdam: Rodopi, 1992.

Moore, Gene M. 'Conrad's "Film-play" *Gaspar the Strong Man*.' *Conrad on Film*. Ed. Gene M. Moore. Cambridge: Cambridge University Press, 1997. 31–47.

Moretti, Franco. *Atlas of the European Novel 1800–1900*. London: Verso, 1998.

Morf, Gustav. *The Polish Shades and Ghosts of Joseph Conrad*. New York: Astra Books, 1976.

Morris, William. *Three Works: News from Nowhere, The Pilgrims of Hope, A Dream of John Ball*. London: Lawrence & Wishart, 1986.

Morrisson, Mark S. *The Public Face of Modernism: Little Magazines, Audiences, and Reception*. Madison, WI: University of Wisconsin Press, 2001.

Moser, Thomas. *Joseph Conrad: Achievement and Decline*. Cambridge, MA: Harvard University Press, 1957.

Moser, Thomas C. 'Conrad, Ford, and the Sources of *Chance*.' *Conradiana* 7/3 (Fall 1975): 207–24.

Moser, Thomas, ed. *Lord Jim by Joseph Conrad*. New York: Norton, 1996.

Mott, Frank. *A History of American Magazines: Volume 4, 1885–1905*. Cambridge, MA: Harvard University Press, 1957.

Munro, Neil. *The Brave Days: A Chronicle from the North*. Edinburgh: Porpoise Press, 1931.

Musgrave, Clifford. *Life in Brighton from the Earliest Times to the Present*. London: Faber, 1970.

Musser, Charles. *Before the Nickelodeon: Edwin S. Porter and the Edison Manufacturing Company*. Berkeley: University of California Press, 1991.

Najder, Zdzisław, ed. *Congo Diary and Other Uncollected Pieces*. Garden City, NY: Doubleday, 1978.

Najder, Zdzisław, ed. *Conrad Under Familial Eyes*. Trans. Halina Carroll-Najder. Cambridge: Cambridge University Press, 1983.

Najder, Zdzisław. *Joseph Conrad: A Chronicle*. New Brunswick, NJ: Rutgers University Press, 1984.

Neil, C. Lang. *Walking: A Practical Guide to Pedestrianism for Athletes and Others*. London: Arthur Pearson, 1903.

Nevett, T. R. *Advertising in Britain: A History*. London: Heinemann, 1982.

Noble, Edward. *The Edge of Circumstance*. New York: Dodd, Mead, & Co, 1905.

Nohrnberg, Peter. '"I wish he'd never been to school": Stevie, Newspapers and the Reader in *The Secret Agent*.' *Conradiana* 35/1–2 (Spring–Summer 2003): 49–61.

O'Connell, Sean. *The Car and British Society*. Manchester: Manchester University Press, 1998.

Oettermann, Stephan. *The Panorama: History of a Mass Medium*. Trans. Deborah Lucas Schneider. New York: Zone Books, 1997.

Ohmann, Richard. 'History and Literary History: The Case of Mass Culture.' *Modernity and Mass Culture*. Ed. James Naremore and Patrick Brantlinger. Bloomington: Indiana University Press, 1991.

Ohmann, Richard. *Selling Culture: Markets, Magazines and Class at the Turn of the Century*. London: Verso, 1998.

Olsson, Jan. 'Förstorade attraktioner, klassiska närbilder.' *Aura* (Stockholm) 2/1–2 (1996): 34–79.

Opie, Robert. *Rule Britannia: Trading on the British Image*. London: Viking, 1985.

Opie, Robert. *Advertising Tins: A Collector's Guide*. London: Miller, 1999.

Orwell, George. *Collected Essays, Journalism and Letters. Volume III. As I Please*. London: Secker & Warburg, 1968.

Parry, Benita. *Conrad and Imperialism: Ideological Boundaries and Visionary Frontiers*. London: Macmillan, 1983.

Peacock, Noel. 'The Russian Eye: Surveillance and the Scopic Regime of Modernity.' *Conrad and Poland*. Ed. Alex S. Kurczaba. Boulder, CO: East European Monographs, 1996.

Pearson, M. N. *Pious Passengers: The Hajj in Earlier Times*. London: Hurst, 1994.

Peck, John. *Maritime Fiction: Sailors and the Sea in British and American Novels, 1719–1917*. Basingstoke: Palgrave, 2001.

Perkin, Harold. *The Rise of Professional Society: England Since 1880*. London: Routledge, 1989.

Popple, Simon. 'The Diffuse Beam: Cinema and Change.' *Cinema: The Beginnings and the Future*. Ed. Christopher Williams. London: University of Westminster Press, 1996. 97–106.

Postacioglu-Banon, Sema. '"Gaspar Ruiz": A Vitagraph of Desire.' *The Conradian* 28/2 (Autumn 2003): 29–44.

Powell, Hudson John. *Poole's Myriorama: A Story of Travelling Panorama Showmen*. Bradford on Avon, Wiltshire: ELSP, 2002.

Price, Richard. *An Imperial War and the British Working Class: Working-Class Attitudes and Reactions to the Boer War, 1899–1902*. London: Routledge, 1972.

Proust, Marcel. *Swann's Way*. Trans. C. K. Scott Montcrieff. Harmondsworth: Penguin, 2000.

Prynn, David. 'The Clarion Clubs, Rambling and the Holiday Associations in Britain since the 1890s.' *Journal of Contemporary History* 11 (July 1976): 65–77.

Pugliatti, Paola. 'From Narrative to Drama: Conrad's Plays as Adaptations.' *The Ugo Mursia Memorial Lectures*. Ed. Mario Curelli. Milan: Mursia International, 1988. 297–316.

Purdy, Dwight. *Joseph Conrad's Bible*. Norman, OK: University of Oklahoma Press, 1984.

Purdy, Dwight H. 'Conrad At Work: The Two Serial Texts of *Typhoon*.' *Conradiana* 19/2 (Summer 1987): 99–119.

Radek, Karl. 'Contemporary World Literature and the Tasks of the Proletariat.' *Soviet Writers' Congress 1934: The Debate on Socialist Realism and Modernism*. Trans. and ed. H. G. Scott. London: Lawrence and Wishart, 1977. 73–162.

Radway, Janice. 'Reading is Not Eating: Mass-Produced Literature and the Theoretical, Methodological, and Political Consequences of a Metaphor.' *Book Research Quarterly* 2/3 (Fall 1986): 7–29.

Raife, Raymond. 'Christmas Day on a Big Liner: How Festive Yule is Honoured in Mid-Ocean.' *Boy's Own Annual* 37/2 (1914–15): 98–100.

Rainey, Lawrence. *Institutions of Modernism: Literary Elites and Public Culture*. New Haven, CT: Yale University Press, 1998.

Randall, Dale. *Joseph Conrad and Warrington Dawson: The Record of a Friendship*. Durham, NC: Duke University Press, 1968.

Reed, David. *The Popular Magazine in Britain and the United States*. London: British Library, 1997.

Reid, Sid. 'American Markets, Serials, and Conrad's Career.' *The Conradian* 28/1 (Spring 2003): 57–99.

Richards, Thomas. *The Commodity Culture of Victorian England: Advertising and Spectacle, 1851–1914*. Stanford, CA: Stanford University Press, 1990.

Roberts, Andrew Michael. 'The Gaze and the Dummy: Sexual Politics in Conrad's *The Arrow of Gold*.' *Joseph Conrad: Critical Assessments*. Ed. Keith Carabine. Mountfield, East Sussex: Helm, 1992. 528–50.

Roberts, Andrew Michael, ed. *Conrad and Gender*. Amsterdam: Rodopi, 1993.

Robertson, Andrew A. 'Some Aspects of Modern Amusements.' *The Scots Magazine* 19/111 (February 1897): 214–19.

Roger Wagner Chorale. 'Rio Grande.' *Sea Shanties*. LP. Capitol Records, 1959.

Rossell, Deac. *Living Pictures: The Origins of the Movies*. Albany, NY: State University of New York Press, 1998.

Rubery, Matthew. 'Joseph Conrad's "Wild Story of a Journalist."' *ELH* 71/3 (2004): 751–74.

Rude, Donald W. 'Joseph Conrad's Advertisement for Himself.' *The Conradian* 9/1 (April 1984): 28–30.

Rude, Donald W., Kenneth W. Davis and Marlene Salome. 'The American Serial Edition of *The Nigger of the 'Narcissus'*.' *Conradiana* 9/1 (Spring 1977): 35–46.

Runciman, James. 'King Plagiarism and His Court.' *Fortnightly Review* 47ns (February 1890): 421–39.

Ruppel, Richard. '*Heart of Darkness* and the Popular Exotic Stories of the 1890s.' *Conradiana* 21/1 (Spring 1989): 3–14.

Ruppel, Richard. '*The Lagoon* and the Popular Exotic Tradition.' *Contexts for Conrad: Volume II*. Ed. Keith Carabine, Owen Knowles, and Wiesław Krajka. New York: Columbia University Press, 1993. 177–87.

Ruskin, John. *The Seven Lamps of Architecture*. London: Smith Elder, 1849.

Russell, W. Clark. 'Christmas Day at Sea.' *Temple Magazine* 4 (October 1899): 168–170.

Rutenburg, Daniel. '*Pall Mall Magazine*.' *British Literary Magazines: The Victorian and Edwardian Age, 1837–1913*. Ed. Alvin Sullivan. Westport, CT: Greenwood Press, 1984. 306–10.

Ryf, Robert S. '*The Secret Agent* on Stage.' *Modern Drama* 15 (1972): 54–67.

Sandberg, Mark. 'Effigy and Narrative: Looking into the Nineteenth-Century Folk Museum.' *Cinema and the Invention of Modern Life*. Ed. Leo Charney and Vanessa R. Schwartz. Berkeley: University of California Press, 1995. 320–61.

Schivelbusch, Wolfgang. *The Railway Journey: The Industrialization of Time and Space in the Nineteenth century*. Trans. Angela Davies. Berkeley, CA: University of California Press, 1986.

Schivelbusch, Wolfgang. *Disenchanted Night: The Industrialisation of Light in the Nineteenth Century*. Trans. Angela Davies. Oxford: Berg, 1988.

Schudson, Michael. *Advertising, the Uneasy Persuasion: Its Dubious Impact on American Society*. London: Routledge, 1993.

Schwab, Arnold T. 'Conrad's American Speeches and His Reading from *Victory*.' *Modern Philology* 62 (May 1965): 342–7.

Schwartz, Vanessa R. 'Cinematic Spectatorship Before the Apparatus: The Public Taste for Reality in *Fin-de-Siècle* Paris.' *Cinema and the Invention of Modern Life*. Ed. Leo Charney and Vanessa R. Schwartz. Berkeley: University of California Press, 1995. 297–319.

Schwartz, Vanessa R. *Spectacular Realities: Early Mass Culture in Fin-de-Siècle Paris*. Berkeley: University of California Press, 1998.

Schwarz, Daniel R. 'The Lepidopterist's Revenge: Theme and Structure in Conrad's "An Anarchist."' *Studies in Short Fiction* VIII/2 (Spring 1971): 330–4.

Schwarz, Daniel R. 'Abroad as Metaphor: Conrad's Imaginative Transformation of Place.' *The Ends of the Earth, 1876–1918*. Ed. Simon Gatrell. London: Ashfield, 1992. 173–86.

Shaddock, Jennifer. 'Hanging a Dog: The Politics of Naming in "An Anarchist."' *Conradiana* 26/1 (Spring 1994): 56–69.

Shaulis, Dahn. 'Pedestriennes: Newsworthy but Controversial Women in Sporting Entertainment.' *Journal of Sports History* 26/1 (Spring 1999): 29–50.

Sherry, Norman. *Conrad's Eastern World*. Cambridge: Cambridge University Press, 1966.

Sherry, Norman. *Conrad's Western World*. Cambridge: Cambridge University Press, 1971.

Sherry, Norman. *Conrad and His World*. London: Thames and Hudson, 1972.

Shore, W. Teignmouth. 'The Craft of the Advertiser.' *Fortnightly Review* (February 1907): 301–10.

Singer, Ben. 'Modernity, Hyperstimulus, and the Rise of Popular Sensationalism.' *Cinema and the Invention of Modern Life*. Ed. Leo Charney and Vanessa R. Schwartz. Berkeley: University of California Press, 1995. 72–99.

Singer, Ben. *Melodrama and Modernity: Early Sensational Cinema and Its Contexts*. New York: Columbia University Press, 2001.

Smith, David R. *Conrad's Manifesto: The History of the Preface to the 'Nigger of the 'Narcissus' with Facsimiles of the Manuscripts*. Northampton, MA: Gehenna Press, 1966.

Smith, Thomas. *Successful Advertising: Its Secrets Explained by Smiths' Advertising Agency*. 21st edition. London: Smiths' Printing and Publishing Agency, 1902.

Solnit, Rebecca. *Wanderlust: A History of Walking*. Harmondsworth: Penguin, 2001.

Solomon, Barbara H. 'Conrad's Narrative Material in "The Inn of the Two Witches."' *Conradiana* 7/1 (1975): 75–82.

Stape, J. H. and Owen Knowles, eds. *A Portrait in Letters: Correspondence to and About Conrad.* Amsterdam: Rodopi, 1996.

Stape, J. H. and Hans van Marle, '"Pleasant Memories" and "Precious Friendships": Conrad's *Torrens* Connection and Unpublished Letters from the 1890s.' *Conradiana* 27/1 (1995): 21–44.

Stead, W. T. *The Magic Lantern Mission.* London: Review of Reviews, 1891.

Stead, W. T. 'Halt! For the Present.' *Borderland* 4/4 (October 1897): 339–42.

Stead, W. T. 'Russia: "Ghost, Ghoul, Djinn, Etc.": The Fantastic Rhetoric of Mr. Conrad.' *Review of Reviews* 33/187 (July 1905): 51–2.

Stead, William, Jr. *The Art of Advertising.* London: Browne, 1899.

Steuart, John A. 'Authors, Publisher, Booksellers.' *Fortnightly Review* 69 os 63 ns (February 1898): 255–63.

Stevenson, R. L. *Kidnapped.* New York: Charles Scribner's Sons, 1925.

Storey, John. *Inventing Popular Culture: From Folklore to Globalization.* Oxford: Blackwell, 2003.

Stottlar, James. '"A House Choked with Gunpowder and Wild with Excitement": Augustus Harris and Drury Lane's Spectacular Melodrama.' *When They Weren't Doing Shakespeare: Essays on Nineteenth-Century British and American Theatre.* Ed. Judith L. Fisher and Stephen Watt. Athens, GA: University of Georgia Press, 1989.

Strang, Herbert. *Tom Burnaby: A Story of the Great Congo Forest.* London: Blackie, 1904.

Strange, Herbert. *Samba: A Story of the Congo.* London: Oxford University Press, 1906.

Strinati, Dominic. *An Introduction to Theories of Popular Culture.* London: Routledge, 1995.

Suárez, Juan A. 'T. S. Eliot's *The Waste Land*, the Gramophone, and the Modernist Discourse Network.' *New Literary History* 32/3 (Fall 2001): 747–68.

Tanner, Tony. '"Gnawed Bones" and "Artless Tales" – Eating and Narrative in Conrad.' *Joseph Conrad: A Commemoration.* Ed. Norman Sherry. London: Macmillan, 1976. 17–36.

Thompson, Sylvanus. *Light Visible and Invisible.* London: Macmillan, 1897.

Tiessen, Paul. 'Literary Modernism and Cinema: Two Approaches.' *Joyce/Lowry: Critical Perspectives.* Ed. Patrick McCarthy and Paul Tiessen. Lexington, KY: University Press of Kentucky, 1997. 159–76.

Turner, E. S. *The Shocking History of Advertising!* London: Michael Joseph, 1952.

Urbain, Jean-Didier. *On The Beach.* Trans. Catherine Porter. Minneapolis, MN: University of Minnesota Press, 2003.

Urry, John. *The Tourist Gaze: Leisure and Travel in Contemporary Societies.* London: Sage, 1990.

Van Domelen, John E. 'Conrad and Journalism.' *Journalism Quarterly* 47/1 (Spring 1970): 153–6.

van Marle, Hans. 'A Novelist's Dukedom: From Joseph Conrad's Library.' *The Conradian*, 16/2 (1991): 55–78.

Varnedoe, Kirk, and Adam Gopnik. *High & Low: Modern Art and Popular Culture.* New York: Museum of Modern Art, 1991.

Verne, Jules. 'Au XXIXme Siècle: La Journée d'un Journaliste Américain en 2889.' *Le Secret de Wilhelm Storitz, Hier et Demain: Contes et Nouvelles.* Paris: Collection Hetzel, 1910.

Villa, Luisa. 'Ethos professionale, speculazione e affetti domestici: *Chance* di Joseph Conrad.' *Moderna* (Pisa) II/1 (2000): 67–98.

Walton, J. K. 'Working Class Seaside Holidays.' *Economic History Review* 34/2 (1981): 249–65.

Walton, John. 'Fishing communities 1850–1950.' *England's Sea Fisheries: The Commercial Sea Fisheries of England and Wales Since 1300.* Ed. David J. Starkey, Chris Reid, and Neil Ashcroft. London: Ashcroft, 2000. 127–37.

Waterbury Clock Company. *Waterbury Clocks: The Complete Illustrated Catalog of 1893.* New York: Dover, 1983.

Watts, Cedric. *Joseph Conrad: A Literary Life.* Basingstoke: Macmillan, 1989.

Watts, Cedric. *A Preface to Conrad.* Harlow, Essex: Longman, 1993.

Wells, H. G. *The Time Machine.* London: Heinemann, 1977.

Wheatley, Alison E. '*Laughing Anne*: "An Almost Unbearable Spectacle."' *Conradiana* 34/1–2 (2002): 63–76.

White, Andrea. *Joseph Conrad and the Adventure Tradition: Constructing and Deconstructing the Imperial Subject.* Cambridge: Cambridge University Press, 1993.

Wicke, Jennifer. *Advertising Fictions: Literature, Advertisement & Social Reading.* New York: Columbia University Press, 1988.

Williams, Raymond. 'Advertising: The Magic System.' *Problems in Materialism and Culture.* London: New Left Books, 1980. 170–95.

Williams, Raymond. *Culture and Society: Coleridge to Orwell.* London: Hogarth, 1987.

Williamson, Andrew. *The Golden Age of Travel: The Romantic Years of Tourism in Images from the Thomas Cook Archives.* Peterborough: Thomas Cook, 1998.

Winnington, Peter. 'Conrad and Cutcliffe Hyne: A New Source.' *Conradiana* 16/3 (Fall 1984): 163–82.

Winter, J. E. 'The Future of the Cinematograph.' *Chambers's Journal* 6s 3/129 (19 May 1900): 391–2.

Withey, Lynne. *Grand Tours and Cook's Tours: A History of Leisure Travel, 1750–1915.* London: Aurum, 1997.

Woolf, Virginia. *A Passionate Apprentice: The Early Journals, 1897–1909.* Ed. Mitchell A. Leaska. London: Hogarth Press, 1990.

Young, A. B. Filson. *The Complete Motorist: Being an Account of the Evolution and Construction of the Modern Motor-Car.* London: Methuen, 1904.

Youngs, Tim. *Travellers in Africa: British Travelogues, 1850–1900.* Manchester: Manchester University Press, 1994.

Index

References to illustrations are given in bold.